NEVER
LOOK BACK

OTHER BOOKS AND BOOKS ON CASSETTE
BY BETSY BRANNON GREEN:

Hearts in Hiding

Don't Close Your Eyes

NEVER
LOOK BACK

a novel

BETSY BRANNON GREEN

Covenant Communications, Inc.

Cover photograph by Maren Ogden

Cover design copyrighted 2002 by Covenant Communications, Inc.

Published by Covenant Communications, Inc.
American Fork, Utah

This is a work of fiction. The characters, names, incidents, places, and dialogue are products of the
author's imagination, and are not to be construed as real.

Printed in Canada
First Printing: January 2002

08 07 06 05 04   10 9 8 7 6 5 4 3

ISBN 1-57734-982-2

For my grandmother, Grace Vann Brannon,
who has always had room in her
home and heart for me.

ACKNOWLEDGEMENTS

A special thanks to Julie B. Brown, BS, RN for sharing her medical expertise. She is a dedicated nurse, a wonderful friend and just happens to be my sister. Thanks also to Julian A. Brannon, former Henry County Commissioner, experienced cow farmer and my grandfather. I'm grateful to my husband and children for making the sacrifices necessary to give me the time I need at the computer. I express deep appreciation to all my readers, especially family and friends who belong to other faiths, but buy my books, then wade through the LDS terminology to actually read them! And finally, many thanks to all the people at Covenant for taking a chance on me.

PROLOGUE

Sydney stared resentfully at the legal pad that the bishop had put in front of her. Bishop Middleton continued to distribute the tablets, then addressed the group. "I'm going outside to take care of the livestock. While I'm gone there will be no talking." This comment he directed specifically toward Sydney. "When I'm done I expect to see those pads filled." He moved to the door and put his coat on, then stuck his head back into the living room. "And don't worry about anyone seeing what you write. I'll keep what you tell me strictly confidential." With those words, he opened the front door and walked out into the snow.

Sydney resisted for a few seconds, but as everyone else picked up their legal pads, she scowled and grabbed hers too.

<u>Legal Pad #1</u>

My name is Sydney Cochran, and I am being forced to write this. It is a complete waste of time since I know that putting my miserable life into words can't possibly make any difference. We should be concentrating on the crimes that have been committed and the obviously guilty party, but since I'm outnumbered, I'll play along.

I was born and raised in Eureka, Georgia, a town of about 30,000 people right on the Alabama state line, situated between a U.S. Army base and one of the most popular bass fishing lakes in the southeastern United States. I am thirty-one years old and the only messed-up member of my otherwise perfect family. My father teaches European history at Auburn University and is on the Columbus stake high council. My mother is an accomplished homemaker. My two older sisters graduated from college, married in the temple, and then did their parts toward multiplying and replenishing the earth.

I was different from the very start. My sisters are named Rebecca and Rachel and after having them, my parents thought their family was complete. Then, four years after Rachel's birth, my father was chosen to fill a highly coveted professorship in Auburn's history department. To celebrate, my parents took a two-week trip to Australia, where I was conceived. Still giddy from my father's professional success and the opportunity to travel, they named me Sydney and called me their little souvenir. However, the novelty of having a baby wore off quickly.

My father's new job included arduous social obligations, and while my sisters were old enough to behave like perfect little ladies, I didn't fit very well into the polite, academic world. My mother still shudders when she tells of lectures I disrupted and concerts ruined by my presence. After I broke a rare Native American artifact at the home of a colleague, I stayed with Grandma Lovell whenever my parents hosted a dinner, attended a seminar, or traveled to a convention. So, for as long as I can remember, I've had my own room at Grandma's.

The Lovells are Baptists, but Mother joined the Church shortly after her marriage to my father. I doubt Grandma was happy about her daughter embracing my father's religion, but she didn't let that affect her relationship with us. Grandma is not a hugging, snugly type of person, but I never questioned her feelings for me. At her house I could watch any television show, regardless of its educational value, my clothes didn't have to match unless we were going into town, she cooked what I liked to eat, and bedtime was negotiable.

The only obligation intrinsic with spending the night at Grandma's was that in the morning I had to pay visits to her immediate neighbors. She would pull my hair into a tight ponytail before I made my rounds and give me instructions like, "Be sure to tell Miss Mayme that her roses are looking particularly lovely this year" or "If Miss Glida Mae is wearing a new dress, say it's very becoming."

Grandma lives in a settled community, and when I was young I thought her neighbors were ancient. From my current, more mature perspective, I realize that they were just middle-aged then. Now they are ancient.

I would begin my morning with Miss Glida Mae Magnanney, who lives in a pink house to the right. Miss Glida Mae has always been partial to floor-length gowns and has large, butterscotch-colored, sausage curls that frame her pudgy face. She claims to have been in several films during the 1940s and whenever I watched an old movie I studied the credits carefully, but never saw her name. I liked to visit her first because she didn't have air-conditioning and by ten o'clock her house was stifling. She usually offered me candy, and her general kookiness was entertaining to a point, but I tried to escape before I started to sweat.

From Miss Glida Mae's I would walk across the street to spend some time with the Warrens. They are devout Auburn fans, and I felt an obligation to like them since my father worked for their favorite university. They painted their garbage cans orange and blue, and had a custom War Eagle license plate. It was even reported that Mr. Warren wore Auburn underwear, although I never witnessed this personally. His wife, Miss Thelma, made fresh cookies every day and always sent some home with me in a foil-wrapped packet.

To their immediate right was a couple from Vermont named Howart. Miss Glida Mae told me that when the Howarts moved to Eureka, the neighborhood welcomed them enthusiastically with casseroles and frequent visits. Then Mrs. Howart informed a delegation from the Baptist Church, who had stopped by to invite them to Sunday services, that they didn't socialize and would prefer to be left alone. I tried to get Grandma to confirm this, but every time I broached the subject, she would just shake her head and mutter under her breath. In spite of their rumored unfriendliness, Grandma insisted that I go by the Howarts' each morning, which only took a few minutes since they rarely answered the doorbell and never let me inside.

I saved my visit to the Camps on the left side of Grandma for last. Miss Mayme Camp was an energetic housekeeper, and if I arrived too early, I would be drafted into helping with chores. However, if I got there after the house was clean and Miss Mayme was safely on the phone, Mr. Camp would be free to take me out back for a two-man game of baseball.

Miss Mayme was concerned about my soul because of my mother's odd determination to raise her children in the Mormon faith. Therefore she often invited me to stay for dinner so she could teach me New Testament scripture verses and Protestant hymns. Every summer she arranged for me to attend Vacation Bible School with the Baptists and could usually convince Grandma to bring me to the semiannual revivals. At these meetings, traveling evangelists predicted awful fates for those who had not been saved, sinners confessed all, and an occasional devil had to be cast out. They were more exciting than anything I'd seen on television, and I looked forward to them almost as much as Christmas.

When I was ten I convinced Grandma to take me by the local YMCA during their boys' baseball registration. I assured her that my parents wouldn't mind me trying out. To their credit, my mother and father attended my games, sitting uncomfortably in the stands. I'm sure they hoped I would outgrow my roughneck ways, but I didn't. I played soccer, basketball, and softball all the way through my junior year in high school.

I always made my parents drop me off at Grandma's after a particularly painful defeat or stunning victory. The Howarts stayed safely in the walls of their quiet home, but when the other neighbors saw us arrive, they found an excuse to come over. If my team lost, Mr. Warren would call the officials names and Grandma would fix biscuits and gravy to comfort me. If we won, Mr. Camp made me describe every play, and Grandma would make a banana pudding to celebrate.

By the end of tenth grade, my GPA was adequate and my athletic ability had me within reach of several college scholarships. My parents no longer complained about attending games and even started a scrapbook for newspaper clippings. Then Craig Cochran entered my life.

There are two wards in Eureka, and right after my sixteenth birthday the boundaries were redrawn, which moved my family from the second to the first ward. Church was not my highest priority, and I didn't really care about the change until that first Sunday. From my slouched, bored position in the back of the chapel, I noticed the Cochran family before we finished the opening song.

Brother Cochran was the weatherman for Channel 8 in Columbus. Every responsible Georgian watches the weather religiously to keep informed about hurricanes blowing up from the Gulf, hot and cold air colliding to create tornadoes any month of the year, rare paralyzing snowstorms, and life-threatening heat indexes. My parents were loyal viewers of Channel 8, so Brother Cochran was like a family friend. My eyes skimmed over Sister Cochran and studied their three sons.

I never thought much about boys except in terms of how fast they could run or how far they could throw a ball, but the Cochran's oldest son was cute enough to make me forget my batting average. He was tall with black hair, bright blue eyes, and a sunburned nose. After a few discreet inquiries I learned that his name was Craig, and his parents were moving permanently into their vacation home on Lake Eureka so that Sister Cochran could have the inspiration of nature to write children's books about a family of chipmunks.

For the first time in my life, I was actually anxious to attend youth activities, and my parents attributed this change of heart to their fervent prayers. In July Craig left on his mission and I watched until his address was posted on the bulletin board. I rewrote my first letter to him at least seven times before I mailed it, and then I waited to see if he would respond. He wrote me back in less than a week and said he had enjoyed my letter and asked me to write again soon.

With that encouragement, I mailed him letters weekly for the next two years. I sent him jokes, misprints from the paper, Halloween candy at Easter, and tacky cards of every variety. I was so obsessed with Craig that I didn't have time for sports or studying. When my senior year began, the school counselor told me that with my grades, the chances of me getting a scholarship, even to a small college, were slim to none. But who cared about college, anyway?

Craig Cochran came home at the end of May, and by that point there was some question as to whether or not I would even graduate. I went to the airport the night he flew in and kept telling myself that no human being could live up to my expectations, but I was wrong. Craig was breathtakingly perfect and hugged me along with his family and friends, then asked if I would come to the stake center where he was going to be released. After the trip to Columbus he insisted that I accompany him to an open house in his honor. Throughout the evening he kept me close to his side, sometimes even taking my hand in his, clearly defining our relationship to other guests.

He attended my graduation and then for the next few weeks he called me every day. He took me hiking and fishing and out to dinner at the waterside resorts around Lake Eureka. My parents were mildly alarmed by the relationship and advised us not to get too serious. Craig's father was in Columbus most of the time, and his mother was too busy writing about chipmunks to notice that he was dating me exclusively.

Craig got a letter in July saying that he had been accepted at BYU for the fall term, and my father took us all out for dinner to celebrate. Afterward Craig and I drove to the lake. Then, as we looked out at the lights of Eureka, he asked me to marry him. I knew I was very young, but I felt so wise. I said yes and, in spite of my parents' strong objections, we were married in August in the Atlanta Temple.

For the first few months of our marriage we were both busy getting settled into our new lives in Provo. I had never been west of the Mississippi, had never seen a real mountain or streets named after four-digit numbers. By the time I learned my way around, I was pregnant.

I don't know exactly when Craig's discontentment began. Later he told me that he realized he had made a terrible mistake almost instantly. At first he tried to talk to his parents, who told him no marriage was perfect and that over the years he would learn to be content.

Our oldest son, Ryan, was born the next fall, and Trent came along less than two years later. Craig was gone a lot, either at the library studying or attending extra classes or lectures. He wasn't very romantic, but I blamed it on his schedule and fatigue. I threw myself into motherhood, and the boys kept me too busy to worry about Craig or our relationship.

Craig graduated from BYU and was accepted into the medical program at the University of Utah. When his parents came for graduation they bought us a small house near the campus in Salt Lake, and I thought I would die of happiness. I had a brilliant, handsome husband, two beautiful boys, and a home of my own. I stayed up late at night to watch *Home and Garden* on TV and used the ideas I saw to decorate our house.

Craig took a nights-and-weekends job at the hospital in addition to his classes and was rarely home. We would go for days without even seeing him and he missed church often, but since he was working hard for our future, I tried not to complain about his long hours. Sarah was born the year Ryan started kindergarten, and as Craig's residency drew to a close, he was offered several jobs but accepted a position at Lakeside Hospital in Eureka so we could go home.

During the Christmas break that year we returned to Georgia for the first time since our marriage. Both families were pleased about our plans to move and offered to help us prepare. The Cochrans took us on tours of countless neighborhoods looking for a house, but Craig's parents didn't like anything that was available and finally insisted that we build. They bought a lot for us near them, then we met with the developer and chose a floor plan. The developer said that construction would begin as soon as the weather permitted.

After the holidays we went back to Utah for Craig to complete his residency. By the time school ended for the summer there were decisions to be made about our new house on almost a daily basis. To speed things up, Craig suggested that the kids and I move in with his parents for a few weeks so I could work with the contractors while he sold our house in Salt Lake.

When the house was finished, Craig's mother helped me decorate it, insisting on all new furniture. We closed on August 15, and Craig started his job at Lakeside Hospital the next day. When he came home for dinner that first night, neither of us knew what to say. It had been months, maybe years, since we had eaten a regular family dinner together. I felt the awkwardness but was sure that after we got used to each other again things would be fine.

I also thought that once we were back home Craig would start coming to church, but he didn't. Every week he had a new excuse and finally I just stopped asking. Then shortly after Christmas I came in from the grocery store and found Craig sitting alone in the living room. He said the kids were with a neighbor and he had something important to discuss with me.

I thought maybe he didn't like his job or the new house or living in Eureka. Instead Craig told me he wanted a divorce. He said he was desperately unhappy in our marriage. It was not my fault, he assured me. We were just not right for each other. He had tried to "tough it out" but he had recently met someone else. She was a nurse at the hospital, and while their relationship could still be classified as a close friendship, he wanted to make a clean break with me so that he would be free if marriage became a consideration at some point in the future. Therefore, he had rented an apartment near the hospital and planned to move out that very night.

I cried and begged and pleaded and promised to change anything, but he was firm in his decision. I called his parents to come over and talk him out of it, and he sat in silence while they told him all the reasons he shouldn't throw our marriage away. Then the bishop arrived. After listening to my tearful narrative, he said that there was no need to rush into anything. He recommended that Craig stay at his parents' house for a few days and then we could talk again.

Finally Craig sat forward and addressed us all. "It's not a matter of trying harder. I don't love Sydney and I never did. When I could stay away from home a lot I was able to deal with it. But now . . . " He waved around the brand-new, beautifully furnished room. "Sydney can have the house. I'll agree to whatever alimony and child support she needs. I'm not trying to ruin her life; I just want a chance at happiness."

What was there left to say? His parents told me he would come to his senses. The bishop told me if I prayed and read my scriptures, things would work out. Craig told me the name of his attorney and recommended that I get one of my own. I dragged my feet for several days hoping that Craig would realize his mistake. I thought he'd miss the clothes I kept washed and folded in his drawers, the nutritious meals I put on the table, the children, and the well-ordered life we had built together. I thought he'd come back, but he didn't.

During our marriage, Craig never had much time for the children, and probably didn't even know what grade they were in. But after he left us he called them every night, bought them gifts, stopped by their schools and introduced himself to their teachers, and occasionally even suffered through lunchroom food with them. His message was clear. He loved the children. The only member of the family he wanted a divorce from was me.

The day the papers were delivered was unquestionably the worst of my life. Up until then, it had all been like a nightmare that I just had to work my way through. The words, typed neatly on fresh white paper, made it terribly real.

As promised, he was giving me the house and the van we had recently purchased. He offered a generous monthly living allowance and half of our meager savings. All he asked in return was a liberal custody agreement. I had read articles about divorce, urging that children not be used as pawns, and couldn't imagine any reasonable parent doing such a thing. But when I realized that Craig was really going to break his covenants and promises to me, I wanted revenge. And since the children were all that mattered to him, they became my only weapon.

I found myself a lawyer and told her to demand everything Craig had offered and in return give him the minimum visitation rights allowed by law. The new papers gave Craig the third Saturday each month, Christmas Day from noon until six and three weeks in the summer. His lawyer called the proposal absurd, but I held firm. If Craig got a divorce, it would be on my terms. I never expected him to accept, but finally he did.

My parents had moved to Columbus, but they visited me frequently. My sisters came, too, offering words of comfort and support. But everything they said sounded like different variations of the basic idea that I had somehow ruined my marriage. If I had been a better wife, Craig wouldn't have looked to someone else and now I had to live with the consequences.

On the day we met at my lawyer's office to sign the final papers, I knew I looked haggard and defeated. Craig, on the other hand, looked better than he had in years. He had gained a few pounds, he seemed rested, and his nose was sunburned. I could have easily killed him.

I left the lawyer's office feeling utterly worthless, so I turned toward the one place where I had always found acceptance and solace. Grandma met me on the back porch and led me to the kitchen table.

While she rolled out buttermilk biscuits, Miss Mayme and Mr. Camp came in. Miss Mayme said that she was morally opposed to divorce but would continue to pray for us anyway. Mr. Camp sat beside me and patted my hand awkwardly.

Miss Glida Mae arrived at this point and told me that after Humphrey Bogart had divorced her she thought she had no reason to live, but in time she had gotten over him just as I would with Craig. Miss Mayme told Mr. Camp to escort the actress home so she could take another dose of her medication. As they left, they passed the Warrens, dropping by to offer their support.

When Mr. Camp returned, we sat around the table and discussed my future. I was determined not to accept anything from Craig. Not the house, not alimony, not even child support. To this end, Grandma suggested I move in with her. I didn't want to be more of a burden than absolutely necessary, so I agreed on the condition that she would let me buy the groceries, pay the utilities, and handle the housework.

Mr. Warren said that even though living with Grandma would save me money, in order to buy groceries and pay the power bill I still needed a source of income. I told them that I had no special skills but wanted flexible hours so I could be home when the kids were. This was a tall order and everyone was quiet for a few minutes. Then Mr. Camp said the clubs on Lake Eureka were always advertising for waitresses, and he had heard that they earned good tips.

Miss Mayme was horrified at the idea of me working in an establishment that sold alcohol, but Mr. Camp pointed out that I would be *serving* the beverages, not *drinking* them. A newspaper was located and calls were made. A quick investigation determined that the best hourly wage and greatest tip potential was available at a large, new dinner club called The Lure. I could work mostly during the hours when the children were asleep, and I couldn't help but smile at the public humiliation Craig would suffer when it was known that his ex-wife was working at a club to support his children.

The Lure offered a training course to interested applicants for a fee of $120, and this amount would be refunded to anyone who was actually hired. All the neighbors thought this was a very good deal and encouraged me to sign up immediately. Since I had exactly $23 in my purse, I nodded and silently abandoned the idea.

The old folks began formulating a plan for moving our posses-
sions to Grandma's. Mr. Warren offered the use of his pickup truck
and Miss Thelma said she'd call her son to provide additional
manpower. I left my children in Grandma's care and led the way to
Craig's house with Mr. Warren and Mr. Camp following close behind
me in the pickup. Mr. Warren's son met us there and I showed them
the things that needed to be transferred. When we left with the last
load, I put my keys to the house and the van on the kitchen counter
without a note of explanation. Then I climbed into the truck and sat
between Mr. Warren and Mr. Camp on the drive back to Grandma's.
I knew Craig would hate it that his children were living in my grandmother's old neighborhood, leaving their schools and making friends
all over again.

I informed the new principals that allowing Craig access to the
children during school hours violated our custody arrangement, so he
couldn't meet with teachers or eat in the cafeteria. Even though Craig
had never been a particularly good father, I knew that the kids loved
him and I regretted the necessity of my actions. But the whole mess
was his fault and I hoped that someday they would understand. If I
redoubled my efforts and became the "perfect mother" surely I could
compensate for Craig's absence from their lives.

When Craig finally found us at Grandma's house, I made him
stand on the front porch, pointing out that he wasn't scheduled for a
visit until a week from Saturday at eight in the morning. He started
to argue, but I reminded him that this was the life he had chosen,
since he had been so unhappy married to me. His eyes held mine for
a few seconds, then he turned and walked away in defeat.

I have always been active in the Church, but after Craig left me I
found going to my meetings difficult. I felt like such a failure and was
uncomfortable around the ward members. Ironically, Craig's decision
to end our marriage was followed closely by a new interest in religion
and he started attending regularly. There was no way I was going to
sit in the same chapel with him and our children like one big happy
broken family, so I quit going to church altogether.

Our move to Grandma's house placed us in the second ward
boundaries, and although I hated to inflict more change on my children, I thought it might be easier to adjust to my divorced status in a

ward where I wouldn't have to worry about seeing Craig. So I asked that our records be transferred to the second ward. But the next Sunday as I dressed for church, I thought about going through the whole story with a new bishop and started feeling ill. Then I imagined the reunion with members of the second ward, who had known me since I was a little girl. They had been my Primary teachers and Young Women advisors. They had taught me to follow the pathway to lasting joy and to choose the right. I couldn't face them now that my life was irretrievably ruined. So each Sunday I took Grandma to the Baptist Church and dropped my children off at the second ward chapel, then went back to sit alone in the empty house until it was time to pick them up.

Shortly after our move to Grandma's, I found an envelope addressed to me in the mailbox. There was no postage or return address, so I knew that one of the neighbors had put it there. Inside I found six crisp twenty-dollar bills and an application for The Lure's waitressing course. The next day I enrolled in the class and a month later had a job at the biggest dinner club on Lake Eureka.

CHAPTER ONE

Sydney Cochran stared out across The Lure's large dining room, where fifty-four tables were distributed evenly. The tabletops were plastic, but made to look like wooden slabs cut from the center of giant trees. The laminate had age rings intricate enough to impress an experienced carbon-dater, and there was even a strip of fake bark along the edges to add authenticity.

Using the mirror over the bar, Sydney straightened her bow tie, then studied herself critically. She touched her hair and worried that her new perm might have been a mistake. Then she turned for a side-view and wondered if her tuxedo pants were a little snug. With a frown, she resolved once again to stay away from the cocktail peanuts.

Sydney leaned across the bar, which was made out of huge log halves propped on sturdy metal posts, to get her apron. The bartender's name was Vernon and he waved from behind the lumber. "Isn't it great to be alive?" he asked as he polished a glass.

"Ask me in a couple of hours," she replied with a grimace. Thursday was her day off, but it was The Lure's monthly amateur night and the manager expected a big crowd. She needed the extra money to pay for Ryan's soccer registration and so she had reluctantly agreed to come in.

After making sure that all the condiments were neatly arranged in the middle of her tables, Sydney watched the first few people start to trickle in. She then proceeded to provide her usual excellent service to those who chose to sit in her area. Everything went well until seven-thirty, when a rowdy group came in and sat at table seven. Forcing a smile onto her face, Sydney walked over to the men.

"Hey, baby!" a big, dumb-looking guy yelled as she approached.

Oh, how she hated men! "You boys seem like you're having a good time," she said neutrally, careful to stand out of reach as she wrote down their order for the bar.

"Oh yeah, we're having a blast. We're here to watch the amateurs sing," another man informed her. "It's the cheapest laugh in town!"

"Can I get you anything to eat?" Sydney asked as she flipped the pages of her order pad.

"Bring us some buffalo wings!" a man across the table hollered.

"How about some raw oysters?" the big guy asked with a lewd grin. "Maybe you and me could eat a few and then have a little date later on."

Sydney pressed her lips together. "I'm no good in the romance department. Just ask my ex-husband," she said lightly and heard them laughing as she turned away to place their order.

She liked to think she kept on top of her tables and was displeased to see that a man had managed to slip in unnoticed and was now sitting at table nine. Taking out her order pad, she started to ask if he wanted anything from the bar, then knew instinctively that he didn't. He had short blonde hair, clear blue eyes and a clean-cut, almost angelic look she had learned to spot. "What can I get for you?" She made no effort to hide her impatience.

He looked mildly surprised by her manner. "A Sprite and some cheese fries. I'm here for the amateur show, too." He glanced over at the loudmouths at table seven.

She nodded as she wrote down the order, then walked to the kitchen. Carmella Winslow, a fellow waitress and her one friend, was standing at the order window waiting for a bacon cheeseburger. "Why do I always get the holy ones?" Sydney asked, tipping her head toward her latest customer. "You can almost see his halo."

Carmella gave table nine a quick assessment with an experienced eye. "He's cute," she pronounced. Carmella was a few years older than Sydney and already a veteran of three divorces. However, all of them had been amicable and she still liked men in general. "You don't care for the All-American type?"

"I don't 'care for' men period." Sydney looked up at the bartender who was listening. "Except for Vernon, of course."

"Hey, baby. How about a date after you get off tonight?" the bartender mimicked the fat guy at table seven.

"I take that back. I hate Vernon, too." Her eyes moved back to table nine. "And I find sincere returned missionaries particularly irritating."

Carmella turned to Sydney. "You mean he's one of those Mormon boys who ride around on bicycles?"

Sydney squinted at table nine. "Not anymore, but I'd be willing to bet next week's paycheck that he used to be."

Carmella knew how serious Sydney was about money and looked at the stranger with more interest. "Maybe he'll be a good tipper," she suggested.

"They never are. They're all poor as dirt, usually students saving money to buy an engagement ring for Little Miss Right."

"He's not that young," Carmella murmured thoughtfully. "At least thirty, I'd say."

Sydney stared at the man's profile. "Well, he's still squeaky clean and he's not wearing a wedding ring."

Carmella laughed. "Imagine *you* noticing a thing like that!"

Sydney scoffed, "I'm always on the lookout for a cheating husband."

"Speaking of cheating husbands," Vernon spoke from behind the bar. "Here comes the good doctor now." Carmella gave Sydney a sympathetic look as she slid the cheeseburger out from under the heat lamp. Sydney watched her walk away, then turned to face Craig. She sucked in her stomach and tossed her new curls.

"What are you doing here on a Thursday night?" he asked when he reached her.

"Earning extra money so Ryan can play soccer," she said louder than necessary. "You know how it is with us single moms."

Craig exhaled heavily. "If you would cash my checks, you wouldn't have to work at all."

"You gave up the right to pay our bills when you walked out on us." Sydney's tone was cold. "And how did you find out I was working?"

"You know I call the kids every night. Ryan told me."

Sydney picked up the buffalo wings and the cheese fries as they slid across the counter from the kitchen. "If you want to catch the amateur show, have a seat. Just make sure you don't sit in my section." She walked back to her tables and left him standing alone. As she dropped off the fries at table nine, she could tell from her customer's uncomfortable expression that he had overheard her exchange with Craig. Then she faced the loudmouths.

"The amateur night here is the best! We came last month and I never laughed so hard!" one of them snickered as she put the wings in the middle of the table. They already had their drinks and she silently blessed Vernon for helping her out.

"You fellows let me know when you're ready to order something else. I'll be around," she assured them. Craig was still standing by the food counter when she turned in an order of onion rings for table three.

"I'm kind of busy here," she said curtly. "If you've got something to tell me, go ahead so I can get back to work."

"I just wanted to make sure you were okay."

"Too late to worry about that," she told him as Eureka's town drunk, Henry Lee Thornton, walked past them and took his regular seat at the end of the bar. A group of six claimed table five and a lovely young girl with dark blonde hair and soft brown eyes slipped into a seat beside the man at table nine. She looked so sweet and unsure of herself as she gazed up at him that Sydney just had time to think he'd better be saving double time for that engagement ring when Craig spoke again.

"Well, I guess I'll go."

She nodded and went back to work without further comment. It was a busy night and Sydney didn't have much time to think about Craig or any of her other problems. Most people came and stayed for an hour or so to see their particular person perform and then left. But the loudmouths at table seven seemed to be enjoying the evening every bit as much as they thought they would. By ten o'clock when Sydney took her break they showed no signs of leaving. They did order frequently and always told her to add a gratuity, so at least she wasn't losing money on them. The guy at table nine stayed too, but he was still working on his original plate of cheese fries.

Sydney took a seat at the bar to rest her feet for a few minutes and eyed the cocktail peanuts. Bravely she turned away from them and watched the stage where the pretty blonde with soft, hopeful eyes was walking to the microphone. Sydney glanced over at the man at table nine and saw that he was sitting ramrod straight. To her amazement, the hecklers at table seven were as quiet as if they were in Sunday School.

The blonde started singing and her voice really wasn't bad. She had wisely chosen a familiar ballad, and had a few nervous wobbles during the first verse. When she got to the chorus the drunks at table seven joined in. Soon the whole room was singing with her, and she was smiling with newfound confidence.

She made it through the second verse without a problem, and everyone sang the chorus with her again. When she was finished, table seven gave her a standing ovation complete with whistles, cheers, and calls for an encore. The Lure's manager, Pinkie Howton, came out and thanked the crowd for their enthusiastic response. He said that Miss Calhoun was not prepared to do a second number tonight but she had promised to come back and perform again soon. Table seven cheered at this news, then settled down in their seats.

Sydney made the rounds after her break and when she passed table nine, the man there motioned to her. She thought he had finally decided to get some fresh cheese fries, but instead he ordered eight draft beers. This request astounded her. She had honed her characterization skills over the past year at The Lure and couldn't believe she had been so wrong about him. When he asked her to deliver the drinks to table seven, she understood. "You bribed them," she said slowly as she wrote down the order. He nodded but didn't look ashamed. "Buying beer, even for someone else to drink, has got to be stretching the Word of Wisdom."

His eyes widened slightly at her reference to the Church. "I can't think of any scripture that specifically prohibits buying a table of drunks one beer so they won't heckle a nervous girl," he replied evenly.

She watched him as she extended the bill for him to sign. "It's standard policy to add a gratuity to any order over $20." She indicated the $3 tip she had written in. He tripled the tip, initialed the correction, and signed the charge slip.

"I know you're not making any money on this table tonight and I apologize, but it was very important to Lauren that I be here."

Surprised by his generosity, Sydney went to the bar to get the beers for table seven. As she distributed the rewards, Sydney noted their inebriated state and asked if they had a designated driver. "We always go home in cabs so everyone can enjoy the evening," one of them said. She offered to call a couple of taxis for them whenever they were ready and they laughed uproariously.

"The night's young and it'll be hours before we leave!" one declared. Sydney accepted this news with a grim nod, then went to check on her other tables.

About thirty minutes later the young singer joined the man at table nine again. His name was Coleman Brackner, according to his Visa card, and as the girl took a seat they clutched hands. Sydney was sure that only the rowdy crowd kept them from a passionate embrace. They whispered excitedly together, then Mr. Brackner looked up and caught Sydney watching them. Horrified, she tried to turn away, but he waved for her to come to their table. She made her way over, hoping the dim lighting hid the color staining her cheeks.

"Would you get me another Sprite?" he asked politely. Then he turned to the girl. "Do you want anything to eat, Lauren?"

The girl shook her head. "I'm too excited to eat! But a Sprite would be nice."

The amateurs continued to perform until midnight. When the stage was finally empty, the big man at table seven yelled across the room for Sydney to call them two cabs and get them there quick. "Horace here is about to throw up!" he added.

Sydney had two taxi drivers on standby in front of the club, so she ushered the staggering men outside and watched as they fell into the cabs. Greatly relieved, she returned to clean up her tables and count her tips.

Coleman Brackner was standing beside table nine when she walked back in. He appeared to be just under six feet tall, with a muscular build like a weight lifter. Irritated with herself for noticing his physique, she walked on to the bar. Vernon loaned her a calculator and she added up her tips. They totaled a respectable $105, which combined with her leftover grocery money, would be just enough for Ryan's soccer fees.

Stuffing the money in her pockets, Sydney went out the back door, down a dark alley, and into the poorly lighted parking lot. She opened the Crown Victoria and climbed inside, locking the doors immediately. As she pulled out of the parking lot, she didn't notice the van that followed her at a discreet distance.

The house was quiet when she got home. She let herself inside and walked straight to her room to change clothes. Sarah was asleep in one of the twin beds, curled around an old teddy bear. Sydney sat on the edge of her bed and stroked the child's dark curls for a few minutes before putting on sweat pants and a bleach-splattered T-shirt. Stooping to pick up Sarah's tennis shoes, Sydney walked down to the boys' room. Ryan opened his eyes as she tiptoed in.

"I didn't mean to wake you," she whispered although it would take a lot to disturb ten-year-old Trent on the neighboring bed.

"I always listen for you to come in," Ryan answered solemnly.

Sydney swallowed the lump in her throat and smiled. "I appreciate you looking out for me," she said. "Go on back to sleep." She allowed herself a caress along his cheek. "I'm just picking up the dirty clothes." She turned and straightened Trent's tangled bedcovers, then walked toward the laundry room to begin her nightly routine.

She put in a load of whites and checked everyone's backpack. After she made certain that all the children had completed their homework, she preheated the oven and mixed up a batch of oatmeal cookies. While the cookies baked she moved the clothes from the washer into the dryer and put in a load of dark clothes. Then she mixed up some bread dough and set it on the counter to rise.

Next, she scrubbed out the bathtub, then divided the bread dough into loaves and let them rise again while she put in the last batch of cookies. She ironed clothes straight from the dryer, and after everything was starched or folded, she took the clothes to the appropriate rooms. Then she came back to the kitchen to put the bread loaves in the oven.

When her second load of clothes was dry, ironed, folded, and distributed, she squeezed orange juice and put it in the refrigerator to chill. Since it was time to wake the children for breakfast, she made French toast for Sarah and Trent, and scrambled some eggs and fried two big pieces of sausage for Ryan. The homemade bread cooling on the counter had the whole house smelling good by the time she went to wake the children up.

She was cutting up Sarah's French toast and coaxing the sleepy child to eat when Trent bounded in wearing the T-shirt he had slept in. With a few words, Sydney sent him back to change in a hurry. Ryan entered the kitchen more sedately and sat in front of his plate. He took a sip of orange juice and asked why he couldn't have French toast like everyone else.

"You need to gain a few pounds," Sydney told him carefully. "Protein will help you build muscle, especially now that you'll be playing soccer."

"I told you I don't eat pig meat." He pushed the sausage to the far side of his plate.

Sydney had a vague memory of a conversation a few weeks before during which he had expressed his concerns about pork products, but couldn't remember his specific objections.

"Leave the sausage then, but eat all your eggs." She poured him a glass of whole milk.

Trent came back in wearing a different shirt with a rip on the right shoulder.

"Eat your breakfast," Sydney said, frowning, "but you'll have to change your shirt again before I take you to school."

"Ah, Mom!" Trent wailed. "Rips and holes are in style," he claimed, and Sydney stared at him in horror. "I mean it! All the guys wear stuff like this. I'm the only one who dresses like a baby."

"Wearing clean, ironed, untorn clothing is not babyish," Sydney assured him as she moved to the counter and began slicing home-made bread for sandwiches. She didn't notice the firm look Ryan gave Trent or the tongue the younger boy stuck out in response. "Hurry and finish eating so you won't be late," Sydney admonished as she spread peanut butter and jelly.

"I don't like peanut butter," Trent said with his mouth full. "Can I have bologna?"

She turned to open the refrigerator and caught Ryan scraping most of his eggs into the garbage can. Sydney eyed the eggs, then looked at her son. "Maybe we should try one of those liquid dietary supplements."

Ryan nodded in resignation. "I'll drink it if you want me to."

"I'll pick some up at the drug store after I drop you off at school. Trent," she addressed her other son, "go change your shirt. Sarah, get me a brush so I can fix your hair." Ryan walked back to his room while Sydney put oatmeal cookies in plastic bags. She washed and polished an apple for each child and folded their napkins before dropping them into cartoon print lunch sacks.

Sarah returned with the brush just as Grandma Lovell walked in. "Good morning," Sydney greeted as she pulled Sarah's silky hair in a perfect ponytail. "I'm going to be stopping by the drug store after I drop the kids off. Do you need anything?"

The older woman shook her head. "No, but thank you, dear," she replied, stacking the breakfast dishes.

"Don't worry about the kitchen, Grandma. I'll clean up when I get home," Sydney said as she herded her children out the back door.

On the way to school Sydney reminded Ryan about the soccer tryouts that afternoon. "It's dumb to call them tryouts," Trent commented from his seat by the back window. "Everybody that pays their money gets to be on a team." Sydney explained that the coaches evaluate each participant so that the teams would all get an equal share of experienced players and beginners. "I don't know why Ryan is playing soccer anyway. I think it's a stupid game," Trent continued. "Why don't you let him play football? That's where the real money is."

"Ryan isn't going to play soccer for a living. It's just fun and a good way to stay in shape. I played soccer for years," Sydney reminded them.

"Dad played football," Trent noted and the conversation stalled.

Finally Sarah spoke into the silence, "Can Brianna spend the night with me today?"

Sydney shook her head regretfully. "You know I have to work on Friday nights and I don't want to ask Grandma to watch an extra child."

"I'll bet she wouldn't say no," Sarah suggested.

Sydney smiled. "She probably wouldn't say no, but I'm not going to ask her anyway. We'll wait until I have a night off and then invite Brianna over." Sarah might have continued to argue, but they were pulling up to the elementary school so she slipped on her backpack and followed Trent out of the car. Sydney dropped Ryan off at the middle school and then turned back into town. She bought two cans of Bulk-Up powder at the drugstore before returning to Grandma's and didn't even allow herself a glance toward the west and Craig's house.

Grandma had straightened the kitchen and washed the breakfast dishes by the time Sydney got home, but Sydney wiped down the counters with Clorox water. Grandma was old and didn't see well anymore and might have left some germs. Sydney was resweeping when Grandma came through again. "That new bishop from your church called again last night," she said as she took a seat at the table. "He seems determined to meet with you, Sydney."

"He's only been the bishop for a month. Give him a few more weeks in the pressure cooker and he'll be glad he doesn't know me or my problems," Sydney responded.

Grandma stood and handed her the dustpan. "I don't know about that. He's called several times already and I keep telling him that you'll call him back, but you never do."

Sydney bent down to sweep a few crumbs into the dustpan and stood up with a sigh. "If he calls again, tell him that between work and sleep and the kids, his only chance of getting to meet me is to come to The Lure at ten o'clock when I take my break." Sydney put up the broom with a smile, knowing that the new bishop probably would not accept her challenge.

She had planned to take a shower, but exhaustion overwhelmed her as she walked to her room. She fell to her knees and said a quick, repetitious prayer, then pulled her scriptures off the nightstand and turned to 2 Nephi 31. After the divorce her old bishop had encouraged her to study the scriptures and apply the principles in her life. She had progressed rapidly through 1 Nephi, reading about obedience and the consequences of unrighteousness. After skimming the excerpts from Isaiah she ran into trouble at the end of 2 Nephi.

Chapter 31 verse 20 said that she not only had to press forward, but she had to do it with a perfect brightness of hope. Since she was pressing forward, but without any hope at all, she didn't feel that she could move on to the next chapter. So every day she reread 2 Nephi 31, half-expecting "there is hope for everyone except you, Sydney" to appear after the final verse.

Her alarm woke her four hours later and she forced herself into a sitting position. Almost nauseous with fatigue, she took a quick shower, then dressed in jeans and a fresh T-shirt. On her way out of the room she caught a glimpse of herself in the mirror and wondered if her pants were too tight. She was still thinking about a way to cut calories when she ran out the door, anxious to be first in the car line at the elementary school.

The second-grade classes came out precisely at 2:50, and Sydney scanned the crowd until she spotted her daughter's pink bow. One of the fifth grade crossing guards helped Sarah into the car, and Sydney checked the little girl's papers while they waited for Trent.

Sarah was in the middle of a discourse on dinosaurs when Trent threw himself into the car. "I got the fastest time in the 50-yard dash!" he announced breathlessly. "Barry Sager would have won, but he fell down." Sydney congratulated Trent and expressed concern for Barry. "Ah, he's okay. He got to sit in the nurse's office all afternoon and eat crackers." Trent fished around in his backpack and produced a note with "Community League Football" printed across the top in bold letters. "The PE coach said I should play and I told him I'd ask you."

Sydney took the form and glanced at it as they made their way toward the middle school. The registration was $155 and parents were responsible for purchasing pads, cleats, a helmet, and a mouthpiece. Practices would be daily from six to eight. There was no possible way she could do it. "Maybe next year, Trent," she said softly.

"Oh, Mom!" Trent howled. "Why does Ryan get to play soccer if I can't play football?"

"Ryan is older."

"But he doesn't even like sports. He told me if you were going to spend a hundred dollars on him, he wished you'd buy him a computer instead."

"Computers cost much more than a hundred dollars," Sydney replied, her mind already calculating how many weeks she would have to work her off night to buy one.

"Ryan says he could get a broken one for that much and fix it himself."

"Well, I'm sorry, Trent, but I can't do football this year. The practices don't get over until after I'm at work," Sydney said firmly as she turned in front of Ryan's school. They were never first in line at the middle school, so she pulled in behind the other parents trying to collect their children and kept an eye on the temperature gauge. The old car had been running hot lately, and she hoped they'd be able to get Ryan before she had to turn it off.

"Dad could pick me up after practice," Trent refused to let the subject drop.

"No he can't. He's only allowed to see you one Saturday a month," Sydney reminded him as Ryan opened the car door. He tossed his book bag into the back, narrowly missing Trent, who complained loudly. He ignored his brother and climbed into the front with Sydney. Normally a reserved child, Ryan was in a particularly cheerful mood that afternoon. "Good day?" Sydney asked with a smile.

"A bunch of other guys at school play soccer," he answered. "And some of them aren't any bigger than me!"

Sydney maneuvered the old car onto the street, encouraged by his enthusiasm. Trent re-entered the conversation by reporting that six people in Mrs. Jepson's class had chicken pox. "The principal came on the intercom and said if you have spots you can't come to school," he concluded, at which point Sarah examined two well-scratched mosquito bites on her leg and said she should probably stay home on Monday.

Grandma was waiting on the porch when they pulled up. She waved to Sydney as the younger children jumped out of the car and ran up the front steps. Sydney offered to buy Ryan a snack to eat on the way to the community baseball field that the Parks and Recreation Department used for soccer. He declined, saying, "If I run on a full stomach, I might throw up in front of everybody."

At the gate a man directed Ryan toward the field and Sydney to the administrative office. Sydney wished Ryan luck, then went in to pay his fees. Sydney didn't mind waiting. She had worked hard but had earned the extra money she needed for Ryan to play soccer, without having to ask anyone for help. And Ryan, who usually avoided all sports, had actually seemed anxious to come to the soccer tryouts.

Feeling like a good mother, she inched her way forward. When she reached the edge of the counter that separated the parents from the Parks and Recreation Department employees she happened to see a clipboard listing the names of all the coaches resting on a desk in the office area. She was casually trying to read them upside down until she saw Craig's name, second from the bottom. Then fury engulfed her.

She thought about Craig coming by The Lure, asking why she was working her off night and acting like he cared. Really, he had just been spying. As soon as he had learned that she was going to register Ryan for soccer, he had rushed over here and signed up to be a coach. An unfortunate registrar walked by at that moment.

"I need to talk to someone right now!" Sydney stepped out, blocking the woman's path.

"We're all pretty busy. Could you make an appointment and come back on Monday?" the woman suggested wearily.

"Somebody will talk to me now or to my lawyer in about thirty minutes," Sydney threatened. The woman flinched and Sydney wished momentarily that she could explain that she never used to be like this, that at one time she had been just a regular person before Craig turned her life upside down and forced her into the role of desperate shrew.

"I'll get Mr. Roosevelt," the woman said through stiff lips.

Sydney waited impatiently, careful to avoid eye contact with any of the other parents who had witnessed her tantrum. After a few minutes a small, balding man with a whistle around his neck rushed in. The park employee pointed to Sydney and the man approached her. "We are about to start the tryouts, but Mrs. Nabors said that you have an emergency."

Sydney nodded. "Is there someplace we can speak privately?"

The little man led the way into a small glass enclosure to the left of the registration desk. "Now, what can I do for you?"

"My son, Ryan Cochran, is trying out for a soccer team today," Sydney began. "His father and I are divorced, and we have a very strict visitation arrangement. I noticed that Craig has signed up to be a coach, and I just wanted to make sure that Ryan is not put on his team."

Mr. Roosevelt regarded her steadily. "It is standard policy for the coach's children to be assigned automatically to them."

"That's why I had to speak to you. If Ryan is on his father's team it will violate our custody agreement, and I know you don't want to place the Parks and Recreation Department in a precarious legal position."

The man's face flushed. "Are you threatening to sue us?"

"I am telling you that under no circumstances will I allow Ryan to be on his father's team. At the very least I won't let him try out, but legal action is not out of the question."

The director's expression was grim as he nodded. "I'll take care of it."

The crowd in the registration area had thinned when Sydney returned. She only had to wait a few minutes, then she filled out Ryan's forms, paid his fees, and walked outside. The children were lined up on the far side of the field, each with a number pinned to their backs. She located Ryan, who was number 48, then turned to the bleachers.

She took a seat several rows up and saw the coaches milling together at center field. Craig was wearing baggy cotton shorts and a BYU T-shirt that she had washed a thousand times. Then she looked down the metal bench and saw Brittni, the nurse. Brittni and Craig were still dating, but there had been no recent mention of marriage. And as long as the woman wasn't a permanent part of Craig's life, Sydney was able to tolerate her presence.

Sydney returned her attention to the field and noticed that all the coaches had clipboards. They were watching as the first group of children ran out and lined up. A park employee led them through a series of drills and had each of them kick a soccer ball.

Uninterested in the performance of other people's children, Sydney kept her eyes on Craig. Soon the little man with the whistle came up beside him and drew him away from the crowd. As the man spoke to Craig, Sydney could sense his surprise, his disappointment, and then his acceptance. Finally he nodded and looked up into the stands. Their eyes met briefly before he walked back to join the other coaches.

After the tryouts were over, Sydney collected Ryan and they started for home. She told him that someone would call later that night and let him know which team he was on. Ryan laughed. "They don't have to call me. I'm a coach's son so I'll be on Dad's team."

Sydney felt a little flutter in her stomach. "Actually, you won't," she said quietly. "Dad can't be your coach because of the divorce."

The look on Ryan's face was worse than a knife in her heart. "I didn't even try hard because the guys said if your dad's a coach you get to be on his team! Now no one will want me." His voice was full of dread.

Sydney knew that Ryan's athletic abilities were limited, so even if he had tried harder it was doubtful that his performance would have been greatly improved. "It doesn't really matter what team you're on. I'm sure all the coaches are nice, and it will be a good way for you to make friends."

Ryan had suffered the most by changing schools. Trent was gregarious and had adjusted well. Second graders were naturally kind and Sarah had made friends easily. Craig's neighborhood was zoned for the county school system, and the sixth grade was a part of the elementary school. But their move into Grandma's house had required the switch to Eureka city schools, where sixth graders went to the middle school. Ryan was shy and small for his age, so making friends and dealing with older children was proving difficult. Sydney hoped that soccer would help.

Ryan nodded, but the excitement he had exhibited earlier was gone. Feeling guilty, she offered to get him a hamburger, but he declined. Then she suggested pizza and he refused that too. "I don't even really want to play soccer," he told her finally.

"I'm sorry you can't be on your dad's team," she said gently and it was true. She wished more than anything that she and Craig were still married, that they were just a regular, happy family. Ryan didn't answer, but stared silently out the window. As soon as they pulled up to Grandma's house Ryan rushed inside. Sydney sat behind the wheel until she was sure she had her emotions in check, then got out of the car and went into the house.

Sarah was sitting at the table, working on her spelling sentences. Trent had finished his homework and was involved in a video game. Sydney warmed the soup she had made earlier, then sent Trent upstairs to get Ryan. Once the family was assembled around the table she asked Sarah to pray, then served the soup with cheese toast and steamed vegetables.

Sydney watched until they had all eaten a sufficient amount of dinner, then let Grandma give them ice cream while she went up to get ready for work. Rain was forecast for that evening and the moisture in the air made her new perm frizz. Sydney struggled with her hair for a few minutes, then scowled at her reflection. She had purchased this particular body wave at Wanda's Beauty Supply because the instructions had promised natural, effortless curls. However, she had ended up with hair that resembled a Brillo pad. Sighing, she pulled it into a bushy ponytail and walked downstairs. The kids were settled cozily in front of the television when she slipped out the back door into the drizzle and headed for The Lure.

Friday was always a big night and the Braves were in the play-offs, which increased the normal crowd. Sydney barely had time to breathe, but at 7:45 she noticed the pious All-American walk in and take a seat. Tonight he had on a dark green shirt with the edge of a white T-shirt showing at the neck. Starla was responsible for table eight, so when they met at the bar, Sydney asked her if the guy had ordered anything yet.

Starla was still young enough to believe in love. She turned dreamy eyes toward table eight. "Isn't he the cutest thing?" she breathed. "He asked me to bring him some cheese fries and a Sprite," she added in response to the original question.

Sydney laughed. "He'll stay all night and won't order anything else," she predicted. "Go back and tell him last night's waitress wants to know if you should bring his fries to him one at a time so they won't get cold."

Starla looked uncertain about this, but she was afraid of Sydney, so she walked over to table eight. Sydney watched out of the corner of her eye as the girl approached Coleman Brackner. He listened to her message, then looked toward the bar. Sydney raised a plate of mozzarella sticks in salute and he nodded back. When Starla returned she said Mr. Brackner preferred to get his cheese fries all at one time and eat them cold.

Sydney resisted a smile but caught herself humming as she worked. The regular country band came in to warm up, and the baseball fans seated at her tables complained. "The music won't interfere with your ability to see the game," she told them as steel guitars started whining. "And if any of you can't figure out what's going on without commentary, just ask me."

A little before ten o'clock, the band announced that they were taking a break, which earned them a big round of applause from the baseball fans. Then Pinkie Howton, the restaurant manager, stepped up to the microphone. "I sure am glad you're all enjoying the music," Pinkie bellowed. "I know you hate to see these boys go, but I promise you will be well entertained while the band is grabbing a bite to eat. This young lady is Miss Lauren Calhoun, and she's going to sing us a few songs. Come on out here," Pinkie encouraged, waving one of his massive arms. Pinkie had played fullback for the University of Georgia thirty years before and looked like he could still blow holes in any defense.

Sydney glanced over to see the young woman from the night before walk onto the stage. She strummed her guitar a few times, then started singing "Dixie."

"What's this?" Sydney asked Carmella when her friend walked by.

"Pinkie said she was the only amateur that didn't get booed last night, so he hired her to fill in when the band takes their breaks."

Sydney was still laughing when her relief arrived five minutes later. She took off her apron and scanned the crowd, searching for an empty table where she could sit and watch the girl sing. When her eyes passed table eight she did a double take. She had only seen the bishop of the Eureka second ward a few times from a distance, but the man now sitting with Coleman Brackner looked disturbingly like Bishop Middleton. To her horror, he waved, indicating that she should join them. Sydney looked around, but there was no obvious route of escape. So she approached the table cautiously.

"Good evening, Sister Cochran," the man greeted her as he stood and held out his hand. "I'm Bishop Middleton and I appreciate your invitation. Coming here tonight gives me the opportunity to meet you and hear Lauren sing at the same time." He pointed at the stage.

Sydney accepted the bishop's handshake reluctantly. She hadn't expected him to come and was unnerved by his presence. "There aren't any empty tables." She studied the room again. "Maybe we could arrange another time . . ."

"You're welcome to sit here with me," Coleman offered and Sydney gave him an impatient look.

"Thanks," she said without sincerity.

"Cole has to be nice to me since we're neighbors," Bishop Middleton provided. "His farm borders some of my property. He wastes his time raising cows instead of fishing." The bishop shook his head. "I don't hold it against him though." Cole smiled and Sydney stared at both of them as if they had lost their minds.

The blonde finished her final number and the country singers returned to the stage. Seconds later the girl rushed up to their table and threw her arms around Cole's neck from behind. "Well, what did you think?" she demanded as she reached over his shoulder and took a few cheese fries off his plate.

"I think you were stupendous!" the bishop told her with enthusiasm.

"You're my bishop. You have to say that." The girl blushed with pleasure in spite of her demure words.

"I think you were great," Cole added his praise.

"Yeah, but you have to be nice too." Her gaze swung to Sydney, who raised an eyebrow, daring her to ask. "Well, I guess I can believe you," the girl said as she took a seat.

"Was there some particular reason you wanted to see me?" Sydney asked the bishop, glancing at her watch.

"Your son, Ryan, turns twelve tomorrow," he said in a conversational tone.

"I'm sorry that you took time out of your busy schedule and risked your reputation by coming to a place that serves alcohol just to tell me, because I already knew," Sydney replied.

The bishop nodded good-naturedly. "I talked to Ryan last week about being ordained to the Aaronic Priesthood. I told him I would arrange things, but I've had a hard time getting in touch with you."

Sydney was mildly ashamed. She thought the bishop was trying to reach her so he could write her name down on a report as a less-active member contact. It never occurred to her that he was trying to help Ryan. "So, when will he be ordained?" She couldn't make herself apologize.

"Sunday, if possible, and he'd like his father to ordain him," the bishop added softly.

Sydney's stomach muscles clenched but she controlled her facial expression. "Who gets to decide?"

The bishop's eyes met hers. "You do, I guess."

Sydney nodded, assimilating this information. "In that case, my father will ordain him. Does it have to be done at church?"

"Not necessarily." The bishop was watching her closely.

"My work schedule prevents me from going to church, so I'd like to have the ordination at my grandmother's house on Sunday afternoon." Having guaranteed the most uncomfortable situation possible for Craig, Sydney didn't even try to keep her triumph from showing.

"About three o'clock?" the bishop suggested and Sydney agreed with a nod.

Cole stood and asked the blonde girl to walk around with him so he could stretch his legs. It was an obvious attempt to give the bishop a few minutes alone with her, and Sydney was immediately on guard. However, Bishop Middleton just told her how impressed he was with her children. When he said that they were always exceptionally well groomed, she relaxed. When he said that Ryan displayed a remarkable knowledge of the gospel during his interview, she felt a blush of pleasure rise in her cheeks. When he said that she was a good mother, tears actually sprang into her eyes.

To cover her unexpected sentimentality, Sydney jumped to her feet and said she had to get back to work. Cole and the blonde returned and the bishop stood up beside them. After shaking hands with everyone, the bishop left and Cole settled back at his table while Lauren went backstage to get ready for her next performance. Sydney moved into her routine and tried not to stare at table eight. Henry Lee Thornton got up to use the restroom and when he came back, someone had taken his regular barstool. This upset him greatly and he tried to get Sydney to make the man move.

"This isn't kindergarten, Henry Lee. We don't have assigned seats and you can't save places," she told him as she delivered grilled chicken sandwiches to table five.

"I'm one of The Lure's best customers," Henry Lee complained.

"Coming here often doesn't necessarily make you a good customer." Sydney knew she shouldn't have said it, but Henry Lee was such a weasel.

"You can't talk to me like that!" His face turned an ugly purple. "I could get you fired!"

A couple left the bar and Sydney waved toward the seats they had vacated. "Sit down and be quiet, Henry Lee."

He looked longingly toward his favorite spot, but shuffled over to the empty places. "I don't know why you have to be so mean all the time," Henry Lee sniveled.

"Because I'm a mean person," Sydney replied pleasantly as she walked down to the other end of the log bar to pick up several drinks Vernon had prepared for her.

The crowd thinned after the ball game ended, and Henry Lee was able to move to his regular chair. Sydney was grateful when the country band played its last number and said good night. Then the blonde took her position on the stage. Sydney noticed that Starla refilled Cole Brackner's Sprite frequently, and when they met by the kitchen door, she had to say something about Starla providing certain customers with better than average service. The other waitress looked surprised by the comment. "You mean Mr. Brackner at table eight?"

"Have you been giving anyone else free soft drinks all night?" Sydney asked irritably.

"A little Sprite isn't going to hurt The Lure. I mean, it's not like I'm giving him beer or something," Starla replied with more spirit than usual. "And Mr. Brackner is so nice and polite, not to mention gorgeous."

"I think gorgeous might be stretching it." Sydney stared at his profile. Nice hair, firm jaw, deep green eyes—maybe hazel—straight white teeth . . . She shook her head and looked away.

"Well, he's the best-looking man I've met lately, and if I'm extra friendly maybe he'll ask me out."

"Haven't you noticed that he comes here with the singer?" Sydney pointed at the stage where his girlfriend was into the second verse of "God Bless America."

"Until he's wearing a wedding ring, he's fair game," Starla declared as she flounced off.

By midnight The Lure was almost empty and Henry Lee was slumped in his chair, so Sydney asked Vernon to call his wife. A customer was using the phone at the bar, so Vernon had to go to Pinkie's office. While he was gone, Henry Lee regained consciousness long enough to demand a Scotch on the rocks. Sydney told him that he'd already had too much.

"I can't believe you're going to deny a thirsty man one little drink!" he whined but Sydney continued to wash off her tables, unmoved by this plea. "You are the most coldhearted woman," Henry Lee hurled the insult desperately.

Sydney glanced up at him. "Henry Lee, are you trying to hurt my feelings?" Her tone was incredulous. "Because if you are, you're wasting your time. I'm not just coldhearted, I'm completely devoid of human emotion. Now hush or the next time you pass out at the bar, I'll tell Vernon to call the police instead of your poor wife."

Henry Lee blinked his bloodshot eyes at her, working his thick lips. Sydney ignored him and out of the corner of her eye she could see Cole Brackner and the singer leaving together. A little while later Henry Lee's wife came to get him, and Sydney helped her take him outside. Henry Lee started to cry as they put him in the backseat of his wife's old car and apologized for his earlier comments. "I'm sorry I called you heartless and cold. You're the best waitress in Eureka and I don't want you to be mad at me."

Sydney was certain that most of his remorse was generated by the fear that she would find a way to limit his access to alcohol in the future, but she assured Henry Lee that she was not mad at him as they wedged his legs into the car. When she walked inside rubbing her back, she passed Carmella and the other waitress laughed.

"Tucking Henry Lee in for the night again?" Carmella asked from the table where she was counting tips and Sydney nodded. "See, Sydney, there are worse things than being divorced. You could be married to Henry Lee."

Sydney had to admit that this was food for thought as she pulled up a chair and sat down beside her friend. "I really should go." She took the change and a few crumpled bills from her pockets and piled them on the table. Then she looked at the rain beating against the glass of the lakeside windows.

"Might as well stay for a few minutes and see if the weather lets up," Carmella suggested. "How are the kids?" Wearily Sydney told her friend about the episode at the soccer field. "When are you going to stop making everything so much harder than it has to be? You're not the first woman in the world to get divorced, and there is life after Craig Cochran."

"I don't want to talk about Craig or our divorce. I'd rather walk around in the rain." Sydney scraped the uncounted money into her purse and went out to The Lure's back parking lot. As she pulled onto the street she saw a car turn onto the road behind her. Ordinarily she wouldn't even have noticed such a thing, but it was late and Eureka was deserted. She slowed down and watched the car in her rearview mirror, but a couple of blocks later it turned off to the right. Sydney signed with relief, unaware that the car had pulled back behind her.

C H A P T E R T W O

It was late and Sydney wanted nothing more than to crawl between the soft warm sheets of her bed and get some much-needed sleep, but instead she changed into her cleaning clothes and began her usual routine. When she went in to check on Ryan, he rolled over and opened his eyes. She asked if his new soccer coach had called and the boy nodded. "His name is Mr. Lydell and his son, Preston, is in my math class. I heard Preston tell some of the other guys that his dad's team always wins the league championship," the boy reported drowsily.

Sydney sat down on the edge of his bed and ran her hand across his hair. "That sounds good," she said with a smile as he curled over into his covers and closed his eyes. Sydney watched him sleep for a few minutes, then started on the laundry.

Once she had a load of clothes washing and the bathroom spotless, she made Ryan's birthday cake. Although he would probably have been happy with one of the cakes in plastic boxes at the Piggly Wiggly, she wanted it to be homemade. So she put the pans in the oven, then moved the laundry to the dryer and made her grocery list. Ryan had insisted that he didn't want a birthday party, but she was determined that he would at least have all his favorite foods for dinner. Her parents were invited to eat with them after church and before Ryan's ordination on Sunday, which would require extra groceries and she still had to buy Ryan some cleats and a new suit.

Finally she got out a calculator to estimate the total cost. Since she didn't get paid again until next Friday, she was probably going to have to charge a few things on her credit card.

By the time she had the laundry finished, the cake frosted, and the kitchen cleaned, it was starting to get light outside. She stretched out on top of her covers, fully dressed, for a short nap before the kids got up. Sarah woke her two hours later screaming because Trent wouldn't let her watch cartoons. Groggily, Sydney went into the living room to restore peace.

After setting up a television schedule, Sydney changed into blue jeans and a sweater, then took Ryan into downtown Eureka for some shopping. The heart of the city had recently been updated as part of an extensive urban renewal project. They had to park several blocks away from the stores and as they walked up the street, Sydney admired all the improvements.

Their first stop was an athletic shoe store where she bought Ryan top-of-the-line cleats. With the shoebox tucked under her arm, Sydney led the way to Burns and Banks Fine Men's Clothing Store. As they walked, Ryan looked longingly at the sloppy window displays of The Gap and Banana Republic. Sydney noticed his interest and increased her pace. Minutes later they entered the exclusive and very expensive store that smelled like leather and wool.

The salesman was about seventy years old and kept calling Ryan a "little man." After measuring him exhaustively, the elderly gentleman gathered a selection of suits for Ryan to try on. Sydney was so affected by the sight of Ryan in a grown-up suit that she allowed the man to talk her into a silk tie, two new white dress shirts, and a $15 pair of socks. These additional purchases settled the question of whether she would use her credit card. As she signed the charge slip, the salesman dug a piece of peppermint candy out of his pocket and offered it to Ryan.

They had lunch in an open food court and then made their way slowly back to the car. Suddenly, Ryan stopped. He hadn't shown much interest in any of the shops or boutiques but as they passed a computer outlet, he walked over and peered through the tinted glass. A computer was out of the question now, although one might be a possibility for Christmas if she worked regularly on her off night. She almost said they needed to hurry, but the longing in his eyes convinced her to let him go inside.

A salesman met them at the door and offered assistance. Sydney assured him that they were just looking, but he followed at their heels anyway. Sydney was amazed by Ryan's knowledge as he discussed the various models with the optimistic salesman. When Ryan pointed out the system he would buy if he could, the man laughed and said he had a good eye for hardware. Ryan blushed with pleasure, and Sydney's heart ached knowing that he wanted something so much and she was powerless to provide it.

After a stop at the grocery store, Sydney drove home and started the charcoal in Grandma's ancient barbecue grill. For dinner they roasted hot dogs and made homemade ice cream to celebrate Ryan's birthday. They sang, then Ryan blew out his candles and smiled happily when he didn't leave any flames burning.

As Sydney cut his cake, Sarah expressed concern. "If we eat some of Ryan's cake now, we might not have enough for tomorrow when everybody comes!"

"I'll make another one," Sydney promised, giving Ryan an extra-large piece. When they were through eating, all the children piled into the living room to watch a video while Sydney went to take a shower and get ready for work.

She lingered in the doorway on her way out. The boys were draped across the two well-worn chairs and Sarah was sitting beside Grandma on the couch. They looked safe and warm. Sydney allowed herself a few seconds of self-pity, wishing that she could stay and watch the movie with them. Then she hurried through the night air to her grandmother's car and drove to The Lure.

By seven o'clock a few couples were eating dinner and the country band was warming up. Sydney hated herself for checking table eight every few minutes to see if Cole Brackner had arrived, but she couldn't seem to help it. At seven-thirty she glanced over and met his gaze. Embarrassed to be caught acting interested, she gave him a half-hearted wave and he kindly smiled back.

Sydney spotted Carmella the minute her friend walked into the big room. On Saturdays all the waitresses had to wear football jerseys for one of the teams in the Southeastern Conference. Most of them chose to represent the University of Georgia, Auburn, or Georgia Tech since they were the closest schools, in hopes of getting better tips from devoted fans. Sydney had several, but usually wore an Auburn shirt. This was partly a tribute to her father, but mostly because that particular jersey fit loosely and made her feel thin. Carmella always wore an old LSU jersey she insisted had been given to her by an actual player back in the eighties.

Sydney couldn't help but smile as her friend approached. Carmella nodded her head toward table eight. "I see your boyfriend's back."

Sydney's smile turned into a frown. "He's not my boyfriend. You're the one who's always looking for a new husband. Why don't you go talk to him?"

"Unfortunately he's not sitting in my section," Carmella replied with disappointment. "Besides, my divorce from Dwayne won't be final until next month." Sydney rolled her eyes as Carmella gave Cole Brackner one more glance, then picked up her order pad and went to work.

Starla again provided Mr. Brackner with excellent service, including his own bowl of cocktail peanuts and a full pitcher of Sprite. Just before her break, Sydney glanced over to see if Starla had supplied him with a double order of buffalo wings or a twelve-ounce steak. To her utter astonishment, Sydney saw her sister, Rachel, sitting at table eight, engaged in friendly conversation with Starla's preferred customer.

Sydney was staring stupidly at her sister when Henry Lee Thornton shuffled by on his way to his favorite barstool. He apologized again for his behavior the night before and Sydney accepted absently. Pulling her gaze away from table eight, she quickly delivered two fried catfish dinners as the relief waitress walked up and said it was time for Sydney's break. With a brief nod, she took off her apron and headed for table eight.

"Hi!" Rachel greeted as Sydney took a seat beside her.

"What are you doing here?" Sydney demanded without preamble.

"I called Grandma's and she said that the best time to talk to you was at work during your break. So, here I am!"

"What was so important?"

"We're just worried about you. You work all the time and you never come to family gatherings," Rachel expressed concern.

Sydney glanced at Cole Brackner. "Why are you sitting here with him?" She pointed at the table's other occupant, and the cow farmer's eyebrows rose.

Rachel laughed. "Cole's sister, Michelle, and I were at Ricks together. You two don't know each other?" Rachel looked between them in surprise and Sydney shook her head. "We went to Eureka High School, but since you live out on the lake I guess you were zoned for Jefferson Davis High," Rachel frowned at Cole as she thought out loud.

"My grandfather died in the middle of my junior year and we moved here from Atlanta to run the farm, so I graduated from Jefferson Davis," Cole confirmed.

"But even though you went to a different high school and were in another ward, it seems like at some point back when you were teenagers, the two of you would have met at a stake activity or something," Rachel pursued the issue.

"My dad and I were so busy learning to run the farm that I didn't have much time for social activities," Cole explained simply. "We went to church on Sunday, but not much else."

Sydney acknowledged this comment with a nod. "I wasn't crazy about church myself, especially dances and youth activities."

"And once you started writing to Craig on his mission you lost interest in everything else," Rachel added helpfully. Sydney gave her a cross look and Rachel cleared her throat. "So, why don't you ever come to dinner at Mom and Dad's anymore?" Rachel asked, returning to the original topic.

"I'm too busy for that kind of thing," Sydney said with a wave of her hand. "Between work and keeping the house and taking the kids to school and checking homework and Ryan's soccer." She was pleased to be able to add this last part.

"Rebecca and I have our problems too," Rachel replied blithely. "But we manage to visit our parents every now and then."

Sydney shook her head. "Well, when your husband tells you he never loved you and wants a divorce so he can pursue a relationship with an unattractive nurse he works with, come back and we'll compare notes."

Rachel sat up straight. "I know that you've been through a bad time, but the divorce was more than a year ago and you've got to quit dwelling on it so much."

Sydney leaned forward. "I can't just forget it ever happened," she whispered.

Rachel sighed and changed the subject. "I didn't come here to fight with you. We're planning a forty-sixth anniversary party for Mom and Dad in December and want your input."

This excuse was so transparent as to be ridiculous. "You want my advice on a social function?" Sydney repeated her sister's patent falsehood just to make Rachel squirm.

"Of course we want your ideas. You're a daughter too."

Sydney smirked. "Isn't a forty-sixth year anniversary party a little unusual? I mean, most people wait until fifty." She pretended to consider. "I'm relatively certain that I've never seen hats proclaiming 'Happy Forty-Sixth Anniversary' or banners saying 'You've made it forty-six years together,'" she couldn't resist teasing her sister.

At this point Rebecca, Sydney's oldest sister, would have gotten mad, called her names like "immature" and "childish" and probably stormed out. However, Rachel's eyes were now sparkling with mischief. "Anybody can do a fiftieth anniversary party. It takes real class to pull off a forty-sixth!"

Cole Brackner made a noise in his throat, and Sydney turned her head to study him through narrowed eyes. He was staring resolutely at the stage where the band was winding down, so Sydney turned her attention back to Rachel. "Plan whatever you want and give me an assignment," she said finally.

"You'll come then?" Rachel asked.

"I'll come," Sydney agreed. "Just don't visit me at work anymore."

"Why not? This has been fun!" she exclaimed. Sydney rolled her eyes. "Oh, and I've got more good news!" Rachel enthused. "Daddy got tickets for all of us to the Alabama versus Auburn game!"

Sydney gave this a few seconds of thought. Even though her father was a teacher at Auburn, she had never known him to attend a college-sporting event of any kind. Since she was the only member of the family who really enjoyed football, she thought this announcement looked a little fishy, too. Besides, Auburn had a new coach and had lost three of their last four games. They would probably lose more before Thanksgiving weekend and would almost surely be defeated by Alabama, who was currently ranked fourth in the country.

"Why would we want to go watch Alabama beat Auburn?" she asked cautiously.

Rebecca might have bristled, but Rachel only smiled. "Auburn fans have learned through the years to enjoy the game regardless of the score. It's the Alabama fans who need to win to have fun," Rachel said firmly, and Sydney raised her eyebrows. "Anyway, we thought we might have a tailgate party." Sydney tried without success to picture her staid, dignified parents eating fried chicken and potato salad out of the trunk of their car in a crowded parking lot in Auburn.

"If they're smart, they'll sell the tickets to an Alabama fan," Sydney advised.

"Come on, Sydney. Daddy thought you'd be so pleased."

This last part made her heart quiver a little, but Sydney shook her head firmly. "Game days are always big for us. I'm sure I'll have to work." Rachel started to protest again, but Sydney stood up. "I've got to get back to work. Call me about the big forty-sixth anniversary party," she said over her shoulder as she walked to the kitchen to get her apron. She immediately started filling orders and watched for her sister to leave. But by eleven-thirty Rachel showed no signs of going home, so Sydney walked over to table eight where her sister was nibbling from a fresh plate of complimentary cheese fries.

"What are you still doing here?" Sydney demanded. The singer had just left the table and was headed backstage.

Rachel looked up in surprise. "I want to hear Lauren sing again," she answered. "Bill doesn't let me out much, so I have to take advantage of my night on the town," she added with a smile at Cole.

Sydney went to the edge of the bar and stared sullenly at the stage while Cole's girlfriend sang a few songs. When Lauren's set was over, Rachel stood to go. She waved at Sydney, then walked into the lobby. The crowd started to thin so Sydney was able to begin cleaning up, but it was still almost two o'clock when she got back to her grandmother's house.

She put in a load of towels and checked the kids' Sunday clothes. As she admired Ryan's new suit, spread out on a chair in his room, she had a momentary flash of regret that she wouldn't be at church to see him wear it for the first time. Refusing to wallow in self-pity, she turned away from the suit and went to the kitchen. There she made Ryan another birthday cake, mixed up roll dough, and dissolved Jell-O for a salad.

After she put the towels in the dryer, she sliced carrots and potatoes to cook with her large pot roast, then mixed up a green bean casserole. Once the clothes were folded and put away, she dozed in a living room chair until it was time to wake the children. She made waffles for breakfast and put a big glass of Bulk-Up beside Ryan's plate. While they ate she told him that his grandfather would ordain him at home that afternoon. She expected at least a mild argument from her son, but he just nodded and drank his protein drink.

When the children were through with breakfast, she supervised Sarah's bath while the boys got dressed. Finally they were all lined up by the front door—spotlessly clean, impeccably dressed, with scriptures in hand—and she thought her heart would burst with pride. Surely they were the most beautiful children on earth. They waited for Grandma to join them, then Ryan said a quick family prayer. Sydney dropped Grandma off first, then took the children to church. She allowed herself the pleasure of watching until they disappeared through the big glass doors before she drove back home.

She put her pot roast in the oven to cook, marinated the sliced tomatoes, set the rolls out to rise, then fell into bed for an hour. At eleven she got up and set the table, iced Ryan's second birthday cake, and deviled two dozen eggs. She was waiting in front of the meetinghouse at 11:55 and was unpleasantly surprised when Craig and his parents came out of the building with the children.

Brother Cochran's hair was white now, but he still looked distinguished. Sister Cochran was as thin as a teenager and stylishly dressed. When they reached the car door, Craig explained that they thought Ryan was being ordained at church and had arranged to attend meetings with the second ward so they could be present.

"But Ryan says that he's being ordained later this afternoon at your grandmother's house." Craig's tone was neutral, but Sydney knew he was irritated and her mood improved.

"I asked Gran and Papa if they can eat dinner with us and have some of Ryan's new birthday cake," Sarah announced as she piled into the back seat. "They said they weren't busy and neither is Daddy." Sydney didn't try to hide her displeasure. "I told them Trent and I could sit on the piano bench," Sarah added, referring to the limited seating available at Grandma's house.

"We'll eat as soon as I can get it on the table," Sydney said to Craig. "Move over so Ryan can get in," she told Trent. "Grandma will sit in front."

"I could ride with Dad to make more room," Ryan proposed.

"I don't think so. It's not the third Saturday, and I'm already making a generous exception by allowing him to come to the house this afternoon." Sydney saw Craig's parents exchange a glance as Ryan climbed in beside Trent. Starting the car, Sydney pulled away from the curb.

When they got home Sydney's parents were already there. Several presents for Ryan were stacked on the floor of the living room and Sydney was pleased to see the anticipation in her son's eyes as he examined them. When the Cochrans rang the doorbell a few minutes later, Sydney told Trent to answer it and went into the kitchen. She served the meal waitress-style, refusing to sit down and act like part of the family. She felt Craig's eyes on her regularly and knew that her point was not lost on him.

Sister Cochran complimented her several times on the food and finally Sydney was forced to respond. "Thank you. I guess cooking is one of the few things I do well," she replied with a look at her ex-husband. Craig flushed and put his fork down as Sydney walked back into the kitchen.

Once dinner was over and the table was cleared, Sydney herded everyone into the living room. It was a little while before the bishop was due to arrive, so she told Ryan he could open his presents. Brother Cochran and Craig excused themselves to get gifts out of the car while Ryan showed everyone the pajamas Sydney had bought for Sarah to give him. He opened a game from Trent and a chemistry set from Sydney's parents.

He was just tearing the wrapping paper off of the newest chipmunk book in Sister Cochran's never-ending series when Craig and his father came back in, each carrying a large box. Sydney got a sinking feeling in the pit of her stomach when they placed them on the floor in front of the boy. Ryan abandoned the half-opened book immediately and leaned forward with reverence. His hand trembled as he pulled the paper off the closest box to reveal a computer monitor. It was exactly like the one he had shown her the day before.

"Oh Dad!" Ryan breathed. "It's just what I've been wanting!" He crossed the few feet that separated them and threw his arms around his father. The sight of the new computer and Ryan wrapped in Craig's embrace was more than Sydney could bear, so she walked to the kitchen and started washing dishes. Craig found her there a little while later.

"I hope you don't mind about the computer," he began slowly. "I'll pay for an extra phone line or whatever else you need—"

"Thanks so much, but I pay the bills here," Sydney replied. "And you don't really care if I mind or you would have asked me before you bought it."

Craig sighed. "He told me he'd been wanting one."

"I had already made plans to buy him a computer for Christmas." She stretched the truth just a little. "Next time, ask me before you make a major purchase."

Craig stood up straight. "That was one of the few things you forgot to put in our divorce agreement. I can give Ryan anything I want to, and I don't have to get your permission first."

She started to reply, but when she looked up she saw Ryan standing in the doorway. The excitement was gone from his face, and he was looking anxiously from one parent to the other. "You don't want me to have the computer?" he asked Sydney.

She pulled her hands out of the soapy water and turned toward her son. "It's not that, honey," she assured him, drying her hands on a dish towel. "It's just that I had planned to buy you one for Christmas and now my surprise is ruined. I wish your father had asked me first is all."

"I thought you'd be glad. Computers cost a lot and Dad has more money than you," Ryan pointed out logically.

"I am glad for you," Sydney relented. She loved the boy so much, how could she not? "But be sure and thank your grandparents for their gifts, too. Just because they didn't spend thousands of dollars doesn't mean they don't love you." This last part was added for Craig's benefit.

Bishop Middleton arrived at this point and Sydney was grateful that they could go ahead and get the ordination over with. When Sydney's father stepped up behind Ryan, Craig and his father stood back along the wall. Bishop Middleton invited them to join the circle without asking for Sydney's approval.

Afterward all the men shook hands and Grandma told the guests to come into the kitchen for birthday cake. Sydney waited until the living room was empty and then slipped up to her room. She dropped onto her bed and buried her face in a pillow, absolutely refusing to allow herself to cry. A few minutes later she drifted off into an exhausted sleep.

Sydney awoke at three o'clock the next morning to a dark, quiet house. Surprised that she had slept so long, she got up and looked around. The kitchen was clean, Ryan's gifts were stacked neatly in the living room and the children all had clothes spread out for the next day. Sarah's cheeks were a little red, so Sydney checked the child's temperature. The thermometer registered 101 degrees. She woke Sarah to take some Tylenol, then held her until dawn.

Sydney left Sarah with Grandma while she took the boys to school, then hurried home and called the pediatrician's office. They told her to come in at 9:45, but she was there by 8:30. The doctor examined Sarah and said that it was a strep infection in the throat. Since they had caught it in the early stages, he said the discomfort would be minimal. He wrote out a prescription for an antibiotic and told Sydney that Sarah could return to school the next day.

Sydney stopped by the drive-through window at the pharmacy and got Sarah's medicine. Then she went home and spent the rest of the day catering to the child's every wish. She picked up the boys at school, dropped Ryan off for his first soccer practice, and took Trent home to start on his homework. Sarah had requested some banana split ice cream, so she ran by the Piggly Wiggly on her way back to get Ryan. Driving home, she asked Ryan what position he was going to play and he said the coach wanted him to just watch for now.

Sydney was still considering this as she dished up ice cream for Sarah. Having children watch seemed like an odd way to teach them to play soccer, but the man won every year so he must know what he was doing. She hated leaving the children when they were sick and gave Grandma the same instructions over and over until finally Trent said they all had them memorized. Sydney reminded Ryan to do his homework after dinner and rushed to the door. As she left she noticed that Ryan's new computer was still in boxes, stacked in the corner of the living room.

Sydney worried all during her drive to The Lure. Had she ruined the computer for Ryan by fighting with Craig about it? Was Ryan's coach just waiting to find the right position for him or did he dislike her son for some reason? Was Sarah really better or would her strep throat progress into scarlet fever and eventually rheumatic heart disease? By the time she walked into The Lure she was beyond irritable. Her mood didn't improve when she saw that Cole Brackner was already sitting at table eight.

She made a comment to Carmella that he seemed particularly devoted to the young singer and the waitress gave her a startled look. "Is that why he's been coming here every night?"

"Of course, why else?" Sydney was surprised by Carmella's denseness.

"I heard her talking about her husband the other night and she wears a wedding ring."

This was unexpected information and Sydney was momentarily stunned, but after a few seconds she shrugged. "Oh well, I don't know why I'm surprised. Nobody takes wedding vows seriously anymore."

Carmella glanced back at table eight. "I thought that sort of thing mattered a lot to members of your church."

"Yeah, I used to think so too," Sydney agreed grimly.

"Mr. Brackner is a member of your church?" Starla asked as she joined them and Sydney nodded. "There's something I've been wanting to ask you," the girl began slowly. "It's just, well, I'm curious . . ."

Sydney waited with resignation.

"Why can't Mormon women wear makeup or paint their fingernails?"

Sydney considered the question for longer than absolutely necessary to make sure that Starla realized it was ridiculous. "I wear makeup." She held up her hands for Starla's inspection. "And paint my nails."

Starla blushed and looked at the order pad in her hand. "Well, I know, but I thought since you didn't really go to church . . ." Starla trailed off, embarrassed.

"Even good Mormon women can wear makeup." Sydney had had enough of Starla and left the waitress staring after her while she went to check on her tables.

Monday night was usually slow, but the Braves were winning so Sydney's tables stayed full. In spite of the hectic atmosphere, she couldn't stop thinking about Cole Brackner. Even though the past year had taught her that nothing was certain and people were not always what they seemed, it disturbed her a great deal that he was involved with a married woman.

Her covert surveillance of table eight distracted Sydney so much that she didn't see the woman until she was standing just a few feet away. Like Cole Brackner, she exuded saintliness, so even if she hadn't been dressed from head to toe in Laura Ashley, Sydney would have known that she belonged in a Relief Society meeting and not a boisterous dinner club. The woman looked from side to side uncertainly until finally Sydney took pity on her. "Can I help you?" she asked, crossing the short distance that separated them.

The woman focused on her and smiled. "You must be Sydney Cochran," she said sweetly. Sydney nodded and the woman took a step closer. "You look just like Sarah."

"You know Sarah?" Sydney asked.

"I'm her Primary teacher. In fact, that's why I'm here. When I called your house, your grandmother said you would be free around ten o'clock."

Sydney gritted her teeth and promised herself a good talk with Grandma. "I'll see if I can take my break a little early," Sydney offered, noting that it was only 9:45.

"Oh, that's okay. Finish what you're doing. I'll just wait with Cole until you're ready." She pointed toward table eight. Sydney watched as the home wrecker stood and extended his hand. Unable to stand the suspense, Sydney found Pinkie and asked if her relief could come a few minutes early. He said he'd try to arrange it and Sydney hurried back to the edge of the bar.

Vernon went to the kitchen for more olives, and Henry Lee asked Sydney for another whiskey sour. "I'm going on break any minute. When Vernon gets back, ask him," she replied absently, inching forward to get a better look at Cole Brackner and her daughter's Primary teacher.

"Why can't you do it? You're not busy," Henry Lee whined, craning his neck to see where she was looking. "And who is that guy you started sitting with during your break?" he demanded when he spotted Cole.

"I guess he's the only man in Eureka who hasn't heard how mean and heartless I am," Sydney responded as she saw her relief walking through the door. She was untying her apron when Henry Lee reached out and grabbed her hand.

"I told you I was sorry for saying that." He pushed his face up close to hers.

Sydney looked down at his fingers wrapped around her wrist. "Henry Lee, don't you ever touch me again," she said, her tone cold.

The man snatched his hand back as if he had been burned. Sydney dropped her apron and walked to table eight. She had been in a hurry to get there but once she arrived, she wasn't sure what to say. Cole spoke first. "Have a seat," he offered without looking in her direction. His attention was focused on the stage where Lauren Calhoun was taking her position in front of the microphone. The Primary teacher was watching as well, so Sydney sat through two verses of the first song, then leaned forward.

"You wanted to see me?" she whispered to the woman.

"Oh, yes." She dragged her eyes away from the singer. "I never realized that Lauren was so talented!"

Sydney glanced at the stage, thinking that the members of the second ward were certainly open-minded about Cole Brackner showing such a dedicated interest in a married woman. "Are you having some kind of problem with Sarah?" she asked. It was the thing she dreaded most. Her children were now products of a "broken home" and who knew how that would eventually affect them?

"Oh, no! Sarah is never any problem at all." The woman shook her head. She was attractive in a plain, no-nonsense sort of way, with sparkling blue eyes and dark auburn hair that was cut off level with her chin and tucked behind her ears. "I don't think I even introduced myself," she said with a smile. "I'm Maralee Tucker."

"I am really enjoying this class," she continued. "The children are so genuine and eager to learn. This past Sunday our lesson was about reaching the celestial kingdom. To introduce the concept I was supposed to ask the children to write down what they would like more than anything in the world." Sister Tucker paused from her discourse to pull a few folded sheets of paper from her large purse.

"One of the children said that he would like a bicycle, another wanted a video game, and I think there were three who chose puppies." The teacher spread the pages out for Sydney to see. "But I was particularly touched by Sarah's response, and I felt that you should see it."

Sydney stared at the back of the last sheet of paper in Sister Tucker's hand, and her heart began to ache. She didn't have to see what Sarah had written to know what the child wanted most in the whole world. "You look like a nice person, Sister Tucker," Sydney began, trying to speak kindly. "And I'm sure that you have no idea the amount of pain you are causing me by coming here tonight and telling me that my child wants more than anything in the world something that I cannot possibly provide. I work long hours and almost never sleep so that I can take good care of my children. However, despite all my efforts, I cannot make their father love me. I cannot make him come home. I can't make us into a real family again."

The words hung over them like a thundercloud, and Sister Tucker's eyes were anxious as she held the paper out to Sydney. She recognized Sarah's scrawl and took the paper in spite of her reluctance. In purple crayon Sarah had written, "I want my mom to come to church." Sydney stared at the simple statement, wishing that Sarah had asked for something impossible.

"I can't come to church because of my job," she forced the words past her lips.

Sister Tucker looked around the big room. "This place is open on Sunday mornings?"

Sydney shook her head impatiently. "No, of course not, but I work very late on Saturday and I have to sleep sometime."

Sister Tucker reached out and touched Sydney's clenched fist. "I know that your life must be very difficult. I have three children myself and just the job of being a mother is enough to overwhelm me. I can't imagine having to shoulder the financial responsibility for them as well." Sydney was slightly mollified by Sister Tucker's sincerity. "I know that it would be a huge sacrifice for you, but it's what Sarah wants more than anything in the whole world."

Sydney stared at the purple words again. She was aware of Cole Brackner's presence although he was still looking at the stage. She felt Sister Tucker willing her to commit to attend church on Sunday and wasn't sure that the woman would leave without a promise. And more than anything she wanted to give Sarah what she wanted most. But the thought of church made her shudder. "I can't," she whispered finally. "I can't face them all."

"Who?" Sister Tucker leaned forward.

"I grew up in that ward. Those people were my classmates, my teachers and leaders. I can't go back now that my life is such a mess. Besides, Craig comes sometimes."

"Actually Brother Cochran never attends our ward. I saw him last week but Sarah said it was because Ryan was being ordained to the office of a deacon. And I don't see that you've made such a mess of your life. You've got three wonderful children, and all your old friends will probably just be glad to see you again!" Sister Tucker predicted. "And being divorced is not so unusual."

Sydney shook her head. "I know how that is. When you're divorced you're an outcast, a misfit. You're not part of the 'regular' Church anymore, just someone for the ward council to talk about."

Sister Tucker's eyes squinted with confusion. "I think you're wrong, Sister Cochran. A divorce doesn't prevent anyone from participating fully in the gospel." Sydney opened her mouth, but Sister Tucker spoke again before she could disagree. "The Primary sacrament meeting program is in two weeks, and Sarah has a solo in it. This Sunday we'll be rehearsing during sharing time. You could hear Sarah sing and then come straight into our class. Sarah would be thrilled, and you wouldn't have to see more than a handful of people."

For someone who looked so sweet, Sister Tucker was proving to be unpleasantly tenacious. Her break was over and Sydney knew that she had to get back to her tables. She didn't want to find Sister Tucker still waiting at table eight when it was time to go home, so she nodded slowly. "I can't promise, but I'll think about it."

Sister Tucker beamed at her. "You'll find the courage! Just imagine the look of happiness on Sarah's face when she sees you there!"

Sydney nodded and hurried back to the kitchen with the image of Sarah's ecstatic expression emblazoned on her mind. The relief waitress made a remark about her taking a long break, and Henry Lee started whining immediately that he wasn't receiving adequate service. "If Vernon keeps ignoring me like this, I'm going to have to report him to Mr. Pinkie," Henry Lee threatened as Sydney loaded several bottles of iced beer onto her tray. There was a half-full drink that another customer had left sitting on the bar, and Sydney paused long enough to slosh it onto the melted ice in Henry Lee's glass.

Henry Lee squinted at the pale liquid. "Is this what I'm drinking?" he asked.

"It is now," Sydney informed him as she watched Sister Tucker stand and say good-bye to Cole Brackner. Then the Primary teacher turned and waved to Sydney before walking toward The Lure's front entrance. Sydney spent the rest of the evening trying unsuccessfully to think of a good excuse not to go to church on Sunday morning.

She kept Sarah home from school on Tuesday even though her fever was gone. Sarah said her throat was still hurting a little, and Sydney didn't want to take any chances. The child was harder to entertain now that she felt better. Sydney read books, suggested videos, and drew pictures, but Sarah lost interest in each activity quickly.

At noon Grandma came into the den and informed them that a police car was parked next door at Miss Glida Mae Magnanney's house. Grandma said she would heat up some soup for Sarah while Sydney went next door to check on Miss Glida Mae.

The neighbor's yard was dotted with concrete statuettes, so Sydney had to weave her way around a birdbath, two cherubs, and a life-sized deer. A Eureka patrolman stood on the front porch talking to the older woman. "Sydney, I'm so glad you're here," Miss Glida Mae said breathlessly as Sydney climbed the wide stone steps. "I have become a victim of crime, and since you live next door you need to be on your guard as well. We have criminals in our midst!" she proclaimed with feeling.

Familiar with Miss Glida Mae and her delicate grasp on reality, Sydney looked at the patrolman. "Miss Magnanney seems to think that some things are missing from her storage shed out back," the man said with careful neutrality.

Miss Glida Mae's head bobbed vigorously. "I had asked Elvis Hatcher to come over and put some sheet plastic over my windows before the cold weather gets here," the neighbor explained. "So I went out into the shed this morning to make sure everything was ready."

"Someone stole the plastic that you use to cover your windows during the winter?" Sydney asked with obvious skepticism.

"Oh, no! The plastic sheeting was right where I left it last spring. It's my duct tape that's missing."

Sydney risked a glance at the policeman. "You called the police because you can't find a roll of duct tape?"

Miss Glida Mae gave Sydney a disappointed frown. "It doesn't matter what was stolen. It's the idea that someone has been in my storage shed that concerns me."

Sydney started to speak again, but the patrolman intervened. "I'll take a quick look," he addressed Miss Glida Mae.

Sydney followed the policeman around the side of the house to the small storage shed in the corner of the yard where Miss Glida Mae's property met Grandma's. "You don't really think that someone came in here and stole her duct tape?" Sydney demanded when she was sure that Miss Glida Mae couldn't hear them.

The patrolman didn't laugh. "It's unlikely, but I don't want to take any chances."

The young man was obviously new and didn't have much experience with elderly women. "She thought somebody had stolen her glasses last week, but they were hanging around her neck," Sydney told him. "And during the summer she spent days searching for a cat that died before I was born."

The patrolman nodded as he opened the storage room door and looked inside. Sydney glanced back over at Grandma's house while the policeman went through the motions of his job. She could see Grandma and Sarah eating soup in the kitchen. She looked longingly up at her own bedroom window and wondered if she would get any sleep at all that day.

"I don't see anything suspicious in here." The young man backed out of the storage room and walked toward the porch where Miss Glida Mae was waiting.

"It was the red duct tape that I use to put up my Christmas lights," Miss Glida Mae whimpered.

"They have more at Wal-Mart for $1.97," Sydney said impatiently.

Miss Glida Mae sniffed and the young policeman started across the backyard. "You ladies keep an eye out, and if you have any more problems, give us a call."

Sydney felt sorry for the poor man. He didn't realize it but he had just set himself up for a daily phone call from Miss Glida Mae. Sydney walked back home and found that Grandma had Sarah lying contentedly on the couch reading a book. Disgusted that Grandma had accomplished in ten minutes what she had failed to do all morning, Sydney went upstairs for a short nap.

When she picked Ryan up after school he informed her that he had a special soccer practice from three-thirty to six at a baseball field close to the elementary school. "I thought you were only allowed to practice once a week." Sydney looked at Ryan in surprise.

"Well, it's not a real practice. Preston said that if anybody asked, to say that a few friends were just getting together to kick the ball around. But he also said anybody who doesn't come won't play in the game on Saturday."

Sydney digested this information. Determination to win was a good thing. The coach might be stretching the rules a little, but it was early in the season and the boys undoubtedly had a lot to learn. She dropped Trent off at Grandma's house and waited in the car while Ryan ran inside to grab his cleats.

By the time they got to the baseball field, it was 3:35 and the coach already had the other team members running through a series of drills. Sydney watched Ryan approach the coach. The man spoke to her son, the boy nodded and then took off running around the field. Sydney was upset that Ryan was apparently being punished for arriving five minutes late for an unscheduled, possibly illegal, practice. She got out of the car to give the man a piece of her mind and was just walking onto the field when Ryan came around to complete his first lap.

"Don't do it, Mom," he pleaded. "You'll make him hate me."

Sydney stared after him as he ran past her and up the far side of the field, feeling almost as helpless as she had the night Craig walked out of her life. Frustrated and discouraged, she headed back to the car and drove home.

When she picked Ryan up at six, she asked him how many laps the coach made him run and he said just a few. He wouldn't meet her eyes, and she had the feeling he was minimizing his punishment for her benefit. That gave her something new to worry about as she prepared for work.

CHAPTER THREE

Sydney was so upset about Ryan and his soccer situation that she actually nodded to Cole Brackner when she walked into The Lure. Then she remembered that she was supposed to resent his presence and was berating herself when Carmella came in.

"I talked to some of your bicycle boys this afternoon and they were cute enough to make me consider religion." Carmella smiled at the memory, and Sydney rolled her eyes. "But I'm not willing to give up men quite yet," Carmella added as she organized pens and pads in her waitress apron.

Sydney made a face. "If you joined my church you wouldn't have to give up men entirely, but you would have to settle on just one."

Carmella sighed at the thought. "Well, bicycle riding is a good way to get exercise anyway. I might take it up as a hobby even if I don't join the Mormons."

"All Mormons don't ride bicycles," Sydney said in exasperation.

"Who rides bicycles?" Starla asked as she walked in.

"Mormons," Carmella answered before Sydney got a chance.

Starla risked a quick glance at Sydney, obviously remembering their last religious discussion. "I've always wondered how the women keep those long dresses and their knee-length hair from getting caught in the spokes," Starla ventured hesitantly.

"Mormons don't have to wear long dresses and we can cut our hair," Sydney responded. "You're thinking of some other religion. Maybe the Pentecostals."

"Can they ride bicycles?" Starla asked, then ducked her head as Sydney glared back.

"I don't know if they ride bicycles or not," Sydney returned. "And I don't care. Let's get to work."

Tuesday nights were usually slow and this one was no different. By seven-thirty there were only a handful of people in the big room. As Sydney loitered by the kitchen door, waiting for someone to sit at one of her tables, she wondered wryly if Cole Brackner would turn out to be Starla's best source of tips that night.

Because of the meager crowd, the manager suggested that one of the waitresses could go home at nine. Starla was taking a computer applications class at a local technical college and said she could use the time to study. So her tables were split up and Carmella took over number eight. Several times during the evening Sydney heard her friend's booming laugh and looked up to see her engaged in lively conversation with Cole Brackner. When Carmella sat at the bar for her break, Sydney asked what could possibly have been so funny.

"That Cole Brackner is a doll! I like him even better than the bicycle boys," Carmella said with a smile. "I'm going to try and talk Starla into switching tables with me."

"Starla will never give him up. She's crazy about him too. And aren't you a little old for him?" Sydney asked, more irritated than the situation warranted.

"Age is irrelevant in matters of the heart," Carmella pronounced.

"I don't understand why either of you waste your time on men!"

"That may be the biggest tragedy in your life," Carmella replied with unusual seriousness.

"What?" Taken back, Sydney stared at her friend.

"That after more than ten years of marriage you don't have any idea how beautiful love can be."

"All that love stuff is just like Christmas," Sydney scoffed. "I mean it's commercialized, blown out of proportion, exaggerated beyond reason. Nothing could live up to the movies and magazines and romance novels."

Instead of answering, Carmella gave her arm a squeeze and went back to check on her customers. Just before ten o'clock, Sydney noticed Bishop Middleton sitting by Cole Brackner, sipping a Sprite.

When he saw her look in his direction, he waved her over. With a deep sigh, Sydney crossed the room and took a seat.

"Trent's birthday isn't until March," she said wearily. "And Sarah's is in July, so I know you didn't come here to remind me about family holidays."

The bishop smiled. "No, this evening I came to talk to you about the Young Men program and scouting."

"Ryan probably won't have any interest in scouting," Sydney dismissed this. "He's not much of an outdoors type."

"Scouts is more than just camping and Ryan tries very hard to please you. If he thinks you want him to like it, he probably will," the bishop predicted. "We have a temple trip scheduled for early December, and we've planned a two-night Scout campout over Thanksgiving. I've written down the dates of each activity and the items Ryan will need."

Sydney stared at the carefully prepared list in front of her. Ryan was growing up. He would now have activities that didn't include her, and places to go without her; he would depend on other people besides her. Dazed, she looked back up at the bishop. "I can get him to the church on Wednesday nights for Scouts," she said uneasily. She took great pride in taking care of her own and hated to ask for help. "But I'll be at work when it's time for him to come home."

"The Fords live a few streets over from you, and they have a son Ryan's age. I'm sure they'll be glad to drop Ryan off on Wednesdays, and it will be good for the boys to get to know each other better." The bishop made it sound simple.

Sydney wanted to decline. She didn't like the idea of Ryan riding with strangers, but the truth was that in order for Ryan to participate in youth activities, she was going to have to accept assistance. So she forced herself to nod. "Thanks," she added grudgingly. For the rest of her break she listened to Lauren Calhoun sing and carefully avoided looking at Cole.

On Wednesday Sarah went back to school and the house seemed lonely. Sydney slept fitfully in spite of her chronic exhaustion and left early to pick up the kids. She brought Ryan's cleats along, just in case, and was glad that she had when he said that Preston had announced another non-practice. During the short trip to the baseball field,

Sydney told Ryan about the activities the bishop described, and he seemed pleased with the arrangement to have the Fords bring him home on Wednesdays.

Sydney fixed a chicken pot pie for dinner and picked up Ryan at six. On the way home she stopped at the Piggly Wiggly to buy poster board for a project Trent had due on Friday. Then she rushed to feed the kids before taking Ryan to Scouts and going on to work.

On Wednesday night most of Eureka went to the church of their choice, so it was always dead at The Lure. Except for two traveling salesmen and a few couples eating the "buy-one-get-one-free" country fried steak dinner, the room was deserted. Table eight looked particularly lonely.

Henry Lee came in at seven-thirty and took his regular seat at the bar. The two salesmen were sitting at table five, trying to drink their cares away. One was overly friendly to Sydney, and Henry Lee finally complained that she was giving the man preferential treatment. She told Henry Lee to mind his own business. Then Lauren Calhoun started to sing from the stage, and a quick glance at table eight confirmed that Mr. Brackner had taken up residence.

When it was time for her break Sydney stepped out into the big room and headed toward an empty table in the corner. Cole looked up as she walked by. "No company tonight?" she asked lightly.

"I guess your family and the second ward members are all busy," he returned with a smile. Sydney was trying to think up a clever reply when he pushed out a chair. "Have a seat." Sydney was going to refuse but saw the friendly salesman approaching her. Choosing what she hoped was the lesser of two evils, she sat down beside Cole. The salesman stopped in his tracks, then turned and went back to table five. "Looks like you have an admirer," Cole said as his eyes followed the man.

"He wouldn't like me once he got to know me," she assured him, wondering how she was going to make conversation with this virtual stranger until her break ended.

"So, how's the forty-sixth anniversary party for your parents coming along?" he asked, confirming in those few words that he listened to her personal conversations.

She wanted to be mad, but since these discussions, though private, had taken place at his table, it didn't seem reasonable to complain. "That was just an excuse for Rachel to come see me. They think I'm avoiding them," she said and he looked up. "Which of course I am."

He smiled in response. "Sisters can be a pain. Mine both drive me crazy."

"Mine are perfect," Sydney mused quietly. "It's hard to be part of a perfect family, especially if you're not."

Cole opened his mouth to reply, but Carmella came up to the table and told Sydney that she had a phone call. She stood quickly, expecting the worst, and rushed toward Pinkie's office. It was Ryan letting her know that he had made it home safely. He reported that he had taken a bath and completed his homework. He didn't want her to worry and hoped her boss wouldn't mind that he called.

Sydney told him that it was fine for her to get phone calls during her break, then asked all about Scouts. He talked enthusiastically until the relief waitress came to find her. After they hung up, Sydney resumed her post by the kitchen door waiting for customers and watching Henry Lee get drunker.

When she passed Cole on her way to deliver a plate of potato skins to a group of college students, he asked her if everything was okay at home. Surprised, she nodded. "When you got that phone call during your break, I was afraid that something might have happened," he explained.

Sydney shifted the appetizers to her other hand. "My oldest son went to Scouts for the first time tonight and he was just checking in."

"It was considerate of him to call," Cole commented.

Sydney felt some of the tension drain from her shoulders. "I've managed to mess up every other aspect of my life, but my kids are great."

Cole smiled at her caustic humor as Starla walked over with a proprietary attitude and gave him a fresh Sprite. Sydney rolled her eyes at the possessive waitress and went back to work. She saw Cole and his girlfriend leave at eleven-thirty and called a cab for Henry Lee at midnight.

On Thursday morning Miss Glida Mae Magnanney was waiting for Sydney when she got home from taking her children to school. Sydney was exhausted and wanted desperately to go to sleep. Dealing with Miss Glida Mae was frustrating under any circumstances, but especially so when she was tired. "Good morning, Miss Glida Mae," Sydney said as the older woman walked up to her car door.

"'Morning, Sydney." The actress tossed her golden curls. "I found something out by the storage shed a little while ago and I wanted to show it to you, to see if you think I should call that nice young policeman and ask him to come back." Miss Glida Mae opened her palm to reveal a tiny piece of tinfoil.

"It looks like part of a gum wrapper," Sydney said blankly.

"I think so too, or maybe candy." Miss Glida Mae studied the scrap. "And I found it right in front of the storage shed," she added with emphasis.

Sydney pushed open the car door and stood up wearily. "The wind could have blown it there," she said. "Or the meter man might have dropped it."

"The meter hasn't been read yet this month and this paper didn't have a speck of dust on it like you'd expect if it had been blown around. It was lying right there in front of my storage shed, just like new."

"So, what are you saying?" Sydney was quickly losing patience.

"I think I have a stalker," Miss Glida Mae whispered, shuddering delicately. "I've seen cases on *America's Most Wanted* and famous actresses are particularly vulnerable," Miss Glida Mae paused and Sydney realized that she considered herself in this category. "Once these men get a fixation on a woman, their obsession causes them to follow the victims continuously. Sometimes they even search her garbage and watch through her windows at night."

Sydney had trouble conceptualizing a person perverted enough to want to see Miss Glida Mae in her underwear. "Well, call the police if you want to, but I think the wind just blew some trash into your yard."

Grandma met Sydney at the door and wanted to know what Miss Glida Mae had to say. "She thinks someone is stalking her, chewing gum in her backyard, stealing her Christmas duct tape, and trying to watch her undress at night."

"Oh dear," Grandma gasped.

"For heaven's sake," Sydney replied in exasperation. "No one is crazy enough to want to see Miss Glida Mae in her underwear!"

That afternoon, as Sydney was leaving to pick up the kids, she waved at Mr. Camp, who was standing by his car.

"Hey Sydney," he greeted her as he lifted a grocery sack from the front seat. "Just got back from the grocery store."

"I see that," Sydney said, walking over beside him. "You need some help?"

"No, all Mayme wanted was milk." He shuffled toward the front door as Miss Mayme Camp stepped out onto the porch.

"Camp! Gracious sakes alive, I was about to call the police! How long can it take to get a gallon of milk?" his wife demanded. "Hey Sydney." When she saw Sydney her tone changed to cordial instantly. She walked to the porch railing. "Heard Miss Glida Mae has a stalker."

"She's missing a roll of duct tape and found a piece of foil in her backyard. I don't think we need to call the National Guard," Sydney replied.

"This is a crazy world we live in," Miss Mayme pointed out, ignoring Sydney's sarcasm. Mr. Camp had just put his foot on the bottom step when his wife spied the milk label through the white plastic bag. "What in this world?" She descended toward her doomed spouse. "You got two-percent milk!" she screeched as if he'd brought home a pint of blood. "I told you to get whole milk!"

Mr. Camp turned around and started back to the car without complaint.

Unable to help herself, Sydney stepped forward. "You still drink whole milk?" she asked Miss Mayme in false amazement.

"I like it on my breakfast cereal," the woman admitted, her voice cautious. "Why?"

"Well I'm not sure where, but I think I heard that drinking whole milk increases your chances of having a heart attack by like . . ." Sydney searched for an appropriate number, "at least fifty percent," she claimed.

Miss Mayme's mouth opened, exposing both rows of dentures. "Really?"

Sydney nodded. "So the low-fat milk would be much better for your health."

"Well, I had no idea," Miss Mayme stammered. "Camp!" she yelled as her husband opened the car door. "Didn't you hear Sydney say that whole milk will kill you! Bring that two percent in the house before it spoils."

With a smile, Sydney climbed into the Crown Victoria and drove to the elementary school. When she dropped Ryan off at the baseball field, she waited for a few minutes, watching her son stand along the sidelines.

She had intended to talk to Ryan about the soccer coach that evening, but Pinkie Howton from The Lure called and asked her to work for Starla, who had called in sick. Sydney really wanted to decline since she no longer had a computer to pay for, but she thought about the new charges on her credit card and agreed. She had to rush to get ready and was halfway to The Lure before she realized that she had forgotten to discuss the coach with Ryan.

Cole Brackner was already at table eight with another man when she hurried into the large room. Assuming that he was the Young Men president or the Scoutmaster, there to talk to her about Ryan, Sydney walked over. "So, who's this?"

Cole seemed surprised when she spoke to him from behind, but recovered quickly and offered her a seat. She declined, explaining that she was working. Then she turned to stare at the other man and Cole introduced him as Darrell Calhoun, his brother-in-law and Lauren's husband.

It took every ounce of self-control that Sydney possessed to keep her mouth from falling open in astonishment. Her shock changed quickly to embarrassment. How could she have misjudged Cole Brackner's relationship with the blonde singer so completely? And why had she assumed that the stranger sitting at table eight was there to see her?

"Oh, I'm sorry to interrupt," she began as heat rose in her cheeks. "I just thought or well that he was maybe . . . ," her voice trailed off in confusion. She knew Cole's brother-in-law probably thought she was an idiot, and who could blame him?

Cole cleared his throat and spoke into the awkward silence. "Darrell usually works late, so I bring Lauren to The Lure and watch her performances," he supplied compassionately. "This is the first chance he's had to hear her sing." Sydney's face was flaming, but she acknowledged the information with a nod. Turning back to Darrell, Cole continued, "This has become sort of the Mormon table."

Darrell looked over at Sydney and immediately asked her to get him some barbecued ribs. Put firmly in her place, but glad for any chance to escape, she promised he'd have them soon.

"Who's the guy with your friend at table eight?" Carmella asked appraisingly when Sydney turned in the ribs order.

"Apparently he is Lauren Calhoun's husband," Sydney admitted.

Carmella studied the men. "He doesn't look upset. Do you think he's here to confront Mr. Brackner about trying to steal his wife?"

"Cole Brackner is the blonde's brother," Sydney said reluctantly. She could still hear Carmella's loud laughter as she went to check on her own tables.

The Braves were playing in the first game of the World Series that night, so the crowd was big and rambunctious. Sydney ran herself ragged trying to keep up with the continuous orders for her tables. Henry Lee was drunk and asked her several times for refills. She pointed out that she was not the bartender and told him to ask Vernon, but Henry Lee whined that Vernon was always fixing drinks for someone else. She was relieved when a group of Auburn students vacated table three, but irritated when she walked by a few minutes later to see that Henry Lee had stationed himself there.

"Now you have to wait on me," he told her. "Since I'm at one of your tables." He seemed very pleased with his idea. Unable to refuse, she brought him a fresh drink, then told him not to bother her again. "It's almost ten." He pointed to the big clock behind the bar. "Why don't you sit here during your break since table eight already has company?"

Sydney studied Henry Lee carefully. His thin, greasy hair had fresh ridges, as if he had just combed it, and he was vigorously smacking gum in an obvious, if vain, attempt to cover his alcohol breath. Trying not to laugh, Sydney declined.

"Why won't you sit with me? You sit with him all the time." Henry gestured angrily toward Cole Brackner.

Sydney stepped closer to keep the entire room from hearing their ridiculous conversation. "I don't sit with married men during my breaks," she told him firmly. "Now behave yourself or I'm calling your wife."

Henry Lee pouted for a while, then went back to his seat at the bar and eventually left The Lure under his own power. The crowd

dwindled quickly after the Braves game ended in an Atlanta defeat, so
Sydney had no trouble finding a quiet table to count her tips. When
she was finished, Carmella came by and told her she would handle
any last-minute customers. "Pinkie said to tell you thanks and that
you could go on home."

Gratefully, Sydney got her purse and walked out the back door of
the nightclub. As she headed down the alley, she heard a noise and
looked behind her, but didn't see anyone. Spooked, she hurried to
Grandma's car. Once inside she locked the doors and glanced around
the deserted streets. There was not a soul in sight, so she inserted the
key in the ignition and turned. Nothing happened.

Sydney groaned. The car had been overheating for weeks and she
knew that it might have a leak in the radiator, but never dreamed it
was anything serious enough to keep the car from starting. Her
mother was always begging her to get a cell phone, but she'd never felt
like she could afford one. As she looked across the empty expanse of
parking lot that separated her from The Lure's back entrance, she seriously regretted her decision.

Accepting that she really didn't have any choice but to go inside
and find some help, she opened the car door and stepped out. The
sound of a loud motor from behind her scared years off her life. She
turned around to see a huge red truck with dual wheels and a double
cab coming down the street. She waved, hoping that the driver would
have a set of jumper cables. The truck roared to a stop beside her and
Cole Brackner climbed down.

"Couldn't you find a truck that was any bigger or more obnoxious?" she asked as he approached her.

Cole shook his head. "It's generally a good idea to be nice to the
people who stop to help you," he said, walking to the front of
Grandma's car. "It won't start?" He gestured toward the vehicle.
Sydney considered another smart remark but shook her head instead.
"Pop the hood," he instructed and she complied.

"Do you know anything about cars?" she asked dubiously.

"You're in my light," he responded and she stepped back. "I'm not
an expert, if that's what you mean. But my dad and I used to work on
all the farm equipment and usually kept it running." He studied the
rusty bowels of the old Crown Victoria. "Unfortunately, I can't see

well enough tonight to find your problem. So, why don't I just take you home and I'll come back and look at it tomorrow?"

Sydney hated to accept assistance from anyone, especially Cole Brackner. But after rapidly calculating how much it was going to cost to have the car towed and repaired, she decided to compromise and save herself a taxi fare. "I'll take the ride, but don't worry about my car. I'll have it towed somewhere tomorrow."

"It might be something simple and then you would have wasted a lot of money."

"Whether it's something simple or complicated, it's not your problem."

"Actually, that's not quite true. As of Sunday, I've been assigned as your home teacher," he announced and Sydney stared back, speechless. "The bishop said it was the obvious thing to do since I see you every night at The Lure. So if you let me fix your car, I can count you as visited and served."

"The elders quorum president will be so impressed," Sydney found her tongue at last.

"And he's not easy to please," Cole agreed with a nod.

"Well." Sydney considered the situation. "I guess I'll let you look at the car tomorrow, but if it's anything big, don't try to fix it. I can't afford to pay for what's wrong with it now and what you break too." With this gracious comment Sydney walked around and climbed up onto the running board of the huge truck and slipped into the seat. She gave Cole some brief directions, and in a few minutes they pulled up in front of Grandma's house.

"I've got some work to do on the farm in the morning, but I'll pick you up about one-thirty and we'll check on your car."

"Why do you need to pick me up?" Sydney asked.

"How else will we get the car home after I fix it?" he returned logically. Too exhausted to argue, Sydney nodded and got out of the truck.

Once inside Sydney wearily went through her regular routine. She checked on Sarah, but the little girl had no fever. As she ironed clothes she worried about how she was going to get the children to school the next day. She could call one of her sisters, but she hated to put them on the spot with a desperate request so early in the morning. And she would call a cab before she begged Craig for help. Finally she accepted that the only reasonable solution was to let the kids ride the bus. She hated the thought, but it would just be for one day.

She told Grandma about the car during breakfast. "Granddaddy used to take it to McCrory's on Fourth Avenue for service. They would probably send someone to look at it if I call," Grandma offered.

"A customer at The Lure gave me a ride home last night, and he's going to try and fix it this afternoon. If it's something he can't handle, we'll call McCrory's," Sydney said. "And why do you keep sending people to talk to me at work?" she asked, slicing bananas onto Sarah's Cheerios.

Grandma looked up in surprise. "You said that was the most convenient time for you."

"Well, from now on, please just take a message."

Once the children were fed Sydney walked them to the bus stop although both boys begged her not to. She stood beside them as they waited, eyeing the other children suspiciously. "That little boy has a runny nose," she whispered to Sarah. "Make sure you don't sit by him." Sarah nodded as the big yellow vehicle rounded the corner and came to a stop. Sydney watched as her children climbed on board, then returned to the house feeling like the world's worst mother.

When Sydney glanced out the front window at one o'clock, Cole Brackner's ostentatious truck was already parked at the curb. She hastily said good-bye to Grandma and grabbed a sweater on her way out the front door. "You're early," she said irritably as she hauled herself into the passenger seat.

"Sorry," he replied with a smile. "I got through at the hardware store sooner than I expected." He pulled onto the street and headed toward downtown. "Hungry?" he asked and she turned to him with a blank stare. "I haven't had lunch yet and wondered if you'd like a sandwich or something."

"No, thanks."

"Well, I'm starving so I hope you don't mind if I stop," he said as he parked in front of The Pork Belly restaurant without waiting for her response.

"Can't you just get a sandwich from the drive-through?" Sydney asked.

"I can't eat and drive at the same time," Cole pointed out. "Come on in. It will only take a minute and like you said, we're ahead of schedule."

Sydney followed reluctantly through the door of the small restaurant and took a seat across from him. The waitress knew Cole by name and wrote down his order carefully. He offered again to buy her lunch, but Sydney shook her head. "I'm on a diet."

Cole seemed sincerely startled by this information. "Why would you be on a diet? You're not fat!" He flushed with embarrassment. "I'm sorry," he tried to apologize, but Sydney waved his words aside with a smile.

"It's okay." Her weight was a constant concern and she was secretly pleased by his comment. Cole's food was delivered and he told the waitress to bring Sydney a Sprite. "Make it a water," she corrected as the woman hurried off. While he ate, Cole asked about her kids. Since that was the one subject she couldn't resist, she gave him a detailed description of each child's activities. She got so carried away with her favorite topic that she ate a few fries off Cole's plate before she realized what she was doing.

On the way out of the restaurant Cole put a toothpick in his mouth and offered her one. "No, thanks. I've discovered dental floss," she said as they walked back to his truck.

Once they reached The Lure, it only took Cole a few minutes to get the car running. "Your battery cable was disconnected," he told her, wiping his hands on a handkerchief.

"It's been running hot, so I thought it might have something to do with the radiator." Sydney leaned over to look under the hood.

Cole inspected the radiator and reported that it was wet on the bottom. "You probably do have a leak. It might just be a hose, but I'll have to put it on some blocks to tell." He continued to frown at the Crown Victoria.

"I know it's an old piece of junk, but I can't afford to start making car payments right now. Do I need a new battery or what?"

Cole looked up. "There's nothing wrong with your battery, and I can't see any reason that this cable would come loose. I think someone did it on purpose." His tone was grim.

"Why would anyone do that?" Sydney looked at him in disbelief.

Cole shrugged. "I don't know. Maybe it was a practical joke, or maybe you made someone mad and they wanted to scare you." Sydney studied his serious eyes. "Or maybe someone wanted you to be stranded in this empty parking lot late at night."

A little shiver ran down her spine. "It was probably just a joke or a dissatisfied customer." The thought of Henry Lee ran through her mind, but she quickly dismissed it. He barely had enough equilibrium to walk by the time he left The Lure each night. Disabling a car would be well beyond his abilities.

"You need to be careful from now on. You should park in the front and get someone to walk out with you at night. It's pretty isolated back here." He glanced around the open space and even in the light of day, Sydney felt a chill. "I'm going to drive behind you until you're back at home," he said as he closed the hood.

"That's not necessary."

"Think of the brownie points I'll earn with the elders quorum president when I tell him about all my selfless service," he said, swinging up into the big truck.

Sydney frowned as she put the Crown Victoria in gear. The car was completely out of gas, so she had to pull into a Chevron station a few blocks from The Lure. Cole offered to pump the gas, but she told him she could handle it. He waited patiently in the cab of his truck and watched every move she made. Once they reached Grandma's house Sydney expected him to drive on by, but he stopped and got out.

"I'd be glad to take a look at that radiator, but you'll need to bring it out to the farm so I'll have my blocks and tools."

Sydney refused further assistance. "You've done enough for us. My grandmother has a regular mechanic who can take it from here," she said as they stood awkwardly beside the old car. Then the school bus pulled around the corner and Sydney forgot everything else as she rushed toward the bus stop. She searched the windows anxiously for her children, but didn't see them until they climbed happily off the bus.

"That was so fun!" Sarah declared with a big smile. "Can we ride the bus every day?"

"Eddie Sellers from my class rides this bus too, and he sat by me on the way home!" Trent endorsed Sarah's comments as he ran past Sydney toward Grandma's front yard.

Sydney turned to Ryan as he stepped down beside her. "So you didn't have any problems?" The boy shook his head. "No one tried to steal your milk money or sell you drugs?"

Ryan smiled. "Not today."

By this time the children had noticed Cole. "Hey, Brother Brackner!" Trent hollered as he skidded to a stop in front of the truck. "Is this yours?" The boy ran a hand along the sleek red paint, and Cole admitted that it was. "Wow!"

Even Ryan was impressed. "Does it have two gas tanks?" he asked and Cole nodded.

"You want to come in and see Grandma?" Sarah offered and Sydney wanted to strangle her. "She likes it when we have company."

"We have already wasted enough of Brother Brackner's time," Sydney declined for him.

"It will only take a minute and Grandma probably made some cookies," Sarah persisted.

Sydney looked to Cole for help. "I really need to go inside the house in order to count this as an official home teaching visit," he said with a grin.

Defeated, Sydney led the way through the back door. Grandma did have homemade cookies and milk on the table. She greeted the children warmly, but when she saw Cole Brackner she absolutely quivered with delight.

"Cole isn't making a social call, Grandma. He just helped me with the car," Sydney explained. Everyone was watching her and she forced herself to continue. "He's also our home teacher, and we had to let him in the house so he can get credit for visiting us."

Grandma smiled at Cole. "Don't mind Sydney. She loves to be outrageous." Grandma rarely criticized her, and Sydney was stung by this remark. Then she watched in horror as Grandma settled Cole Brackner at the table and insisted he stay for dinner.

"I ate a late lunch so I'll pass, but I appreciate the invitation."

"Well, at least have some of these cookies. They're fresh out of the oven." Good manners demanded that he eat at least one, so Sydney couldn't be too mad at him when he took a cookie off the plate. Grandma pulled out chairs for the children and piled their backpacks in the corner as Sydney turned her back on the table and began preparations for dinner. Cole asked the kids about school, and Sydney had to hear indirectly that Trent made an A on his spelling test and Ryan's nature poem was being submitted to a statewide writing contest.

"Do you live by us?" Sarah asked with her mouth full of cookie.

"I'm not too far away. I have a farm over by the lake and Bishop Middleton is my neighbor," Cole answered, then drank his entire glass of milk as Sydney watched from the corner of her eye.

"Do you have a fish farm?" Sarah asked.

"No, I raise cows and horses and kittens," Cole replied.

"Horses!" Trent cried.

"Kittens!" Sarah squealed.

Cole laughed. "Really I only have a few horses that we use to work the cows. But there are several cats that help keep the mice out of our hay barns, and one of them just had a litter of kittens about a week ago."

"Are they cute?" Sarah asked softly.

"They are real cute," Cole confirmed. "One is solid black and one is kind of yellow, like a little lion." This made Sarah giggle. "One is striped and one is polka-dotted."

"A polka-dotted cat?" Ryan was skeptical, but Cole nodded.

"It's white with little black and brown spots," he promised.

"Oh, Mom!" Sarah cried and Sydney braced herself for the obvious request. "Can we go see Brother Brackner's kittens?"

Before she could respond, Cole graciously issued an invitation. "You're welcome to come."

"Thanks," Sydney said. "But we're busy right now."

"Oh Mom!" Sarah wailed, but Sydney spoke with unusual firmness, telling her to go to her room and start her homework. Then she instructed the boys to do the same. Turning back to Cole, she started clearing the table. "I hate to rush you off, but I've got to get dinner ready. You can take some cookies with you for later if you want."

Cole stood and pushed his chair under the table. "No, thanks. I've had plenty and they were delicious." This he directed toward

Grandma. The older woman accepted his compliment and walked him to the door, apologizing for Sydney's "atrocious manners."

When Grandma came back into the kitchen, she approached Sydney with purpose. "That young man went out of his way to help us and you were rude to him."

"All he wanted was to be able to tell people at church that he visited us, Grandma. He'll get his gold star on Sunday, so don't feel too bad for him." Sydney continued to chop onions, unconcerned about Cole's feelings. Her grandmother's anger bothered her though, and after Grandma left, her conscience continued to nag her.

Everyone was subdued as she served the meal, and she left them picking at their food while she went to get ready for work. Mr. Warren was burning leaves in the corner of his yard, and Sydney waved as she passed him.

The crowd at The Lure was light for a Friday night, probably because of the various high school football games. So Sydney had plenty of time to stare at table eight, which was empty, and formulate what she would say when Cole arrived.

All her carefully planned words left her when he walked in with a tall, and incredibly beautiful, blonde woman. Sydney's chest tightened as Cole pulled out a chair and seated his guest at his regular table. For the next two hours Sydney waited on occasional customers and stared at table eight.

"I see your sweetheart has come with another woman tonight," Carmella teased as she turned in an order for table twelve. Sydney ignored the remark and asked why her friend had been late for work.

"Oh, Sydney! I've got the cutest new UPS man!" Carmella exclaimed. "He looks like Tom Cruise and he wears shorts! I was his last stop and we got to talking. I was having so much fun I lost all track of time."

Sydney shook her head in despair as she put the soft drinks for table five on her tray. She glanced back at table eight in time to see the beautiful woman stand and walk into the lobby, apparently going to the restroom. It was close to ten so Sydney looked around for a good table to sit at during break since she couldn't join Cole Brackner and his date. She spotted one in the corner just as Craig walked in.

He looked around the room and nodded in her direction but didn't approach her. Instead he walked over to Cole, who was temporarily sitting alone at table eight. Sydney watched in horror as Cole stood and extended his hand to Craig, then offered her ex-husband a seat at the table, which he accepted by pulling out a chair. Cole got Starla's attention and she came over to take Craig's order. Then the men talked quietly until Craig's Sprite arrived.

"Sydney," Henry Lee's whine interrupted her surveillance. "We're out of peanuts down here!" She walked around behind the bar and picked up an eight-pound container of roasted peanuts. She put the whole can in front of Henry Lee, then removed her apron and headed for table eight.

The men were laughing about something when she got there. "You two know each other?" she asked abruptly.

"We met when Craig attended our meetings last Sunday," Cole replied.

"So, why are you here?" she asked Craig.

His smile disappeared as he faced her. "The kids told me your grandmother's car was broken, and they had to ride the bus today. I was coming to see if you needed the van or wanted me to have someone look at the car."

"Thanks, anyway, but Cole is going to fix it for me." The home teacher looked a little startled but recovered instantly.

"Oh, yeah. I think it's probably just a leak in the radiator hose. Nothing major."

Before Craig could comment, the blonde stepped into the doorway and Sydney's heart almost stopped beating when she saw the look on her ex-husband's face. His eyes followed her as she approached and both men stood as the blonde arrived at table eight. She took the chair beside Craig, and Cole introduced her as Peyton Harris from Nashville.

"She's a property acquisitions specialist sent here to torment me into selling my farm to some developers who want to build a western theme park," Cole explained and the woman laughed good-naturedly.

"I'm trying to make Cole a very rich man, and eventually I will convince him that the deal I am offering him is in his best interest, as well as my client's," she said. Her voice had a sultry, seductive quality, and while Cole seemed unaffected, Craig was staring openly. "And

Cole is wasting his time by resisting. I am very good at what I do and have never failed to close a deal."

Sydney listened with increasing discomfort as Craig questioned Peyton about Nashville, her occupation, her employers, and the theme park. Cole sat back quietly, his eyes on the band as the woman described her conversations with him over the past few days. "You seem very dedicated to this project," Craig said finally.

"I won't rest until I make Cole a millionaire," she agreed.

The relief waitress finally came to get Sydney, and it was with reluctance that she left the cozy group at table eight and went back to work. Business picked up a little after her break so she didn't have time to stare at Cole's companions, and it was too noisy for her to hear any of their conversation. Occasionally she would hear them laugh, and every time she glanced in that direction she saw Craig watching the blonde with open admiration. At eleven-thirty Craig stood. Sydney grabbed a pitcher of water and refilled the glasses at table nine so she could hear what was said.

"It was nice to meet you, Peyton," Craig used her first name very naturally. "And good luck with this project. I've never been to the Brackner place, but from what you've described, it must be great." This was an obvious attempt to get an invitation, and Cole cooperated by telling him to visit anytime.

"Cole is going to give me a tour tomorrow. You should come with us," Peyton suggested.

"I hope that when she sees how beautiful and undisturbed the place is that she'll give up and go home," Cole said.

"I'm sure the integrity of the land can be preserved. The people I represent aren't like strip miners! They want to keep the area beautiful. That's what will attract the tourists."

"I'd love to come," Craig interrupted. "What time is the tour?"

This elicited a delicate yawn from Peyton. "Not too early, I hope."

"I have a soccer game at eight. How about ten?" Craig proposed.

Sydney stepped forward with the pitcher of water still in her hand. "Cole has to fix my car tomorrow," she said desperately. "And what about Brittni?" she demanded, suddenly feeling a kinship with the other woman in Craig's life. As angry as she was with Craig, in the recesses of her mind there was the faint hope that someday, after he had suffered sufficiently, they might get back together. Her female intuition warned her that Peyton Harris represented a serious threat to her dream of reuniting her family.

Everyone turned to stare at Sydney. "Brittni and I are just good friends." Craig flushed with embarrassment and Sydney wondered if the nurse was aware of this.

Finally Cole spoke. "I did promise Sydney I'd look at her car."

Sydney exhaled and Peyton pressed her lips together in irritation. "Well, how long will that take?" Her sweet tone was in direct contrast with her hard eyes.

"Not long," Cole conceded.

"Why don't we come after lunch so you'll have the morning to handle free car repairs?" she suggested.

Sydney let the insult pass, standing aside with the pitcher of cold water in her hands while the others left together. Her mind was reeling as she went around wiping her tables. Somehow she had to find a way to keep tabs on Craig and Peyton during the tour of Cole's farm. By the time she left The Lure, her head was pounding.

At home she took some Tylenol and decided to skip her regular routine of laundry, baking, and cleaning. She knew she would need a clear head and sharp wits to contend with the beautiful Ms. Peyton Harris in the morning. So she put on a nightgown, read 2 Nephi 31, and crawled into her bed.

CHAPTER FOUR

On Saturday morning Sydney woke up at seven and took a fast shower. Then she checked Ryan's soccer schedule, hoping he had an early game. She ground her teeth together when she saw that his game didn't start until eleven. At 8:30 she called Cole and told him that she'd be late. He said to come when she could and gave her directions to his farm.

She made breakfast and tried not to think about Craig and his interest in Peyton Harris. At 10:15 Sydney loaded Grandma and all the kids into the car. She wanted to get to the field early in case the games were ahead of schedule. They stopped by the Quick Mart and she bought Ryan a liter of Gatorade, then hurried on to the baseball field, where the games were running late. She met Ryan's coach briefly and, as she walked to the bleachers, heard him criticize the Gatorade. "That stuff is for sissies," he said scornfully. "Serious athletes drink water during games."

Sydney regretted purchasing the sports drink as she watched Ryan drop it into the fifty-gallon drum that served as a garbage can. Ryan's team won by a landslide but he only played for about two minutes of the second period, and Sydney was furious when the game ended. "The rules specifically state that all the players get to play at least half the game and there was no reason for him to keep the more experienced kids in since he was already winning," she fumed as they walked back to the car. "I'm going to talk to Mr. Roosevelt on Monday—"

"Please don't, Mom." Ryan took her arm and pulled her to a stop.

"It's like cheating for him not to play everyone half of the time," she tried to explain. "The purpose of this league is for all the team members to learn the game."

"Please, Mom. I don't care. Really."

By this time Grandma had hobbled up to congratulate Ryan. She patted the boy's back, then offered to buy hamburgers for lunch to celebrate. Sydney hated the delay, but couldn't refuse, so she took them to Burger King and ordered four whoppers at the drive-through line. The kids wanted to go inside, but she told them she had to get the car fixed and couldn't spare the time.

"McCrory's is closed on Saturdays," Grandma said as they headed home.

"Cole Brackner is going to try to fix the leak," Sydney supplied absently.

"You're going to his farm?" Trent demanded. "I want to go too, so I can see his horses."

"And I want to see the polka-dot kitten," Sarah added.

"I can't take you today," Sydney replied, and they responded with simultaneous complaints.

"Brother Brackner said we could come!" Sarah wailed.

"I'll take you to see his animals another time. Today we'll be concentrating on the car and won't have time for anything else," Sydney explained briefly as she pulled in front of the house. "Go inside with Grandma and eat your hamburgers,"

"You promise you'll take us another day?" Sarah insisted and Sydney nodded reluctantly. "Okay then, but say hi to the kittens for me!" she called as she climbed out of the car.

Mr. Warren was putting a new coat of orange and blue spray paint on his garbage cans and crossed the road to speak to Sydney as she pulled out of the driveway, further delaying her arrival at the Brackner farm. Her neighbor asked for a report on the soccer game, and Sydney filled him in quickly. Then she suggested that he get more details from Ryan personally and eased away from the curb.

She was not very familiar with the west side of town, but followed Cole's directions and found the gravel drive that led up to his farm- house without much trouble. Glancing at her watch as she bounced up the pitted surface, she saw that it was 1:15. When she pulled out of the trees a white house with dark green shutters came into view. A big barn towered behind it, and several large pieces of farming equipment were lined up neatly to the side.

She parked the Crown Victoria between a silver Pathfinder with an Avis Rental sticker and Craig's van. The farm seemed too quiet, almost deserted, as she climbed the wooden steps to knock on the front door. No one answered and she tried to peer through the oval of etched glass. "Looking for me?" Cole said from close behind her, startling a little scream from Sydney.

"Why did you sneak up on me like that?" she demanded.

He shrugged. "I just walked over to meet you. I thought you'd hear me coming, but I guess you were too busy trying to peek inside my house."

Sydney ignored him as she scanned the immediate area. "Where's Craig?"

"My foreman took Peyton and him on ahead," he replied. When he saw Sydney's horrified expression, he assured her that she wasn't going to miss the tour. "I'll take you around the farm as soon as I fix your car," he promised.

"Forget the car," she called over her shoulder as she ran toward his huge truck. "We've got to catch up with my husband and that woman!"

The door was locked and Sydney had to wait for Cole to open it. "I thought you were divorced," he said when he reached her.

She waved this remark aside impatiently. "That's just a legal term. He's still the father of my children."

Cole watched her climb in, then walked around and settled himself behind the wheel. His expression was grim. "But you're not married, so he can drive around the farm with Peyton, he can go on a date with her," Cole itemized. "In fact, he could even—"

"Not if I have anything to say about it!" Sydney interrupted him quickly.

Cole was quiet for the next few minutes as they traveled down a dusty dirt road. Finally he pointed out some cows in a pasture to the left. "That's our breeding stock. And up here," he pointed to the neighboring pasture, "are the yearlings that have recently been separated from their mothers."

Afraid that he was about to begin a cattle lesson, Sydney held up her hand. "I don't really care about your cows, Cole. I just came so I could keep an eye on Craig." She craned her neck and studied the landscape. "Surely something so big can go faster than this," she added with an impatient gesture at the truck.

Cole immediately slowed down and she shot him a glance. "The road is bad and I don't want to damage my shocks," he offered as a lame excuse. "And there's really no point in rushing. The farm is almost three hundred acres, and I have no idea where Lamar took them."

Sydney sighed and leaned back against the seat.

"So, should we go back to the house and work on your car?" he asked.

Sydney shook her head. "Let's drive around some more and see if we run into them. Maybe I'll get lucky." She turned discouraged eyes to the passenger window. "There's a first time for everything." They rode in silence for a while, then Cole turned off the dirt road onto a path so narrow that tree branches scraped along both sides of the truck. "You're going to ruin your paint job!" she warned him.

"I don't care. I hate this truck anyway."

"Then why did you buy it?" Sydney asked.

"I didn't. My brother-in-law bought it while I was on my mission. When I got home my mother took it away from him, and now I'm stuck with it."

Sydney inspected the truck's interior, then raised her eyes to study Cole's profile. "It still looks new." And Cole certainly didn't look like a twenty-one-year-old boy.

He smiled, sensing her skepticism. "My father died while I was in college, which left me running the farm. I didn't think I'd be able to leave long enough for a mission, but right before I turned twenty-eight, our bishop worked it out with the stake president and area presidency. So I've only been back a little over a year, and Darrell and Lauren bought this obnoxious truck while I was gone."

Sydney considered this as they emerged from the woods into a large meadow. The truck bumped over the open space until Cole parked at the base of a tree-covered hill. "We have to walk from here." He opened the door and offered her a jacket from behind his seat, but she shook her head.

He stepped into the dense forest and she followed. "Where are we going?"

"You'll have to wait and see," he replied.

There was no path to speak of, and the ground was littered with damp leaves and broken branches so Sydney had to watch her feet. She was breathing heavily by the time they reached the crest of the hill. "Do you think your foreman took Craig and Peyton up here?" She was gasping for air as she stopped beside him.

"I'm absolutely certain that he didn't. Nobody comes here but me," Cole said and she followed his gaze to the scene below, where a little cabin was nestled in the woods with a small, overgrown garden to the side. The backwaters of Lake Eureka slapped against a pier built along the shore in front.

"It looks like a painting," Sydney whispered.

"It's my dad's fishing retreat. He and I spent a lot of time here."

"He liked to fish?"

"And hunt and birdwatch. Sometimes we just came to get away from my mom and my sisters," he admitted with a smile. "My dad understood how tough it could be living in a house full of women."

"You miss him a lot," Sydney observed quietly.

Cole continued to look down at the little cabin. "A father is the most important thing in a boy's life." Sydney opened her mouth, but before she could comment, he took her hand and pulled her down the hill. "Come on, I'll show you around."

She clasped his hand for balance as they made their hurried descent. At the bottom of the hill, both became aware of the physical contact and she pulled free of his grasp. He gave her a tour of the small cabin, then they walked out and stood on the pier.

"It must be nice to be able to swim around all day without worrying about anything," Sydney said as she watched the tiny fish in the clear water.

"Except bigger fish," Cole pointed out.

They returned to the truck at a leisurely pace, and as they were driving back to Cole's house, Sydney noticed field after field with bales of hay stacked in the corners. "You need that much hay to feed your cows?" she asked with mild curiosity.

"No, we raise more than we need and sell it to Hawkins Feed and Seed in Columbus. That's how we get our operating cash. All of that's ready to go." He waved toward yet another field full of hay. "My foreman and I will start delivering it next week."

The bouncing of the truck lulled Sydney to sleep, and she startled awake when the roaring of the large engine ceased. She stretched as Cole climbed out of the truck. Craig's van was gone, but the Pathfinder was still parked in front of the house. Pleased that Craig had apparently left without the lovely acquisitions specialist, Sydney followed Cole to the barn. A tall, thin man wearing overalls and a faded Braves cap met them at the door.

"Hey, Lamar," Cole greeted him. "This is Sydney. Sydney, this is my foreman, Lamar." Sydney nodded absently as the man took off his hat, revealing sparse gray hair.

"Nice to meet you, ma'am," he said, replacing the cap.

"How did the tour go?" Cole asked as he began arranging automotive blocks in preparation for the car repairs.

Lamar shook his head. "Went fine until we stopped to look at the calves. Ms. Harris stepped in a hole and twisted her ankle. Sure is a good thing Dr. Cochran was here. He had to take her to the hospital to have it x-rayed."

Ignoring Sydney's stricken look, Cole picked up his toolbox and opened it on the ground. "Too bad she left her rental. Now she'll have an excuse to come back," Cole said, causing Lamar to chuckle. Sydney leaned against the door for support. "Are your keys in the car?" Cole asked and she nodded dumbly. He walked over and slipped in behind the wheel. Seconds later the old Crown Victoria was up on the blocks and both men were peering underneath.

Sydney trudged to the front porch steps and sat down. Dejected, she watched brightly colored leaves fall off the trees in Cole's front yard. The sun went behind some clouds and she shivered as Cole walked up. "It was a leaky hose. We repaired it with duct tape, but eventually you'll want to replace it." Sydney nodded morosely and shivered again as a fresh gust of wind blew by. "Come on inside," he instructed, pulling her to her feet. Too depressed to argue, Sydney followed him.

The house was dark and silent. "Your mom's not home?" she asked.

Cole shook his head. "My mom died a little over a year ago."

Sydney winced. "I'm sorry."

"It's okay." The wood creaked as they crossed the small foyer and Cole smiled. "My dad used to say these old boards were his security system. He never had to worry about us sneaking out at night." He paused in the next room to turn on a crooked floor lamp. The carpet was a nice neutral tan, but the furniture was awful. "I know it looks pretty bad. Lauren and Darrell bought new furniture while I was on my mission, but they took it with them when they moved to town." He rested his hand on the back of a green vinyl couch that looked like it belonged in a bad dentist's office. "I moved this stuff down from the cabin."

The kitchen was very modern in contrast, with expensive-looking stainless steel appliances. There was no table, but Cole pointed to a set of barstools and told her to have a seat at the counter. "I'll make you a cup of hot chocolate before you go."

Sydney glanced at her watch. "I really should go on now. It's almost three and I have to work tonight."

"You've got a few minutes." He took two mugs and a box of doughnuts from a cupboard. "You want one?" He extended the box of Dolly Madison powdered sugar-covered doughnuts. They were her favorite, but she shook her head resolutely. "I thought we agreed yesterday that you don't need to lose weight."

"You decided that. I'm the one who has to get into my work pants." Sydney's mouth watered as she watched him lick sugar from his fingers. Clearing her throat, she turned away and looked out the kitchen window. "Are you coming to The Lure tonight?"

He nodded. "It's just a part of my regular nightly routine now." "It's nice of you to support your sister like that," she said and he laughed.

"I'm a real nice guy." He put a cup of steaming chocolate in front of her and sat down on another barstool. "And the waitresses at The Lure are the best."

Sydney accepted the compliment with a brief nod. "At first I thought you and Lauren were engaged," she admitted as she took a sip.

This made him grin. "I've never been engaged, especially not to my sister," he said. "I dated when I was a teenager, but after my dad died I didn't have time for a social life. Then I went on a mission, and now all the women my age are married. Lauren keeps trying to fix me up with girls she knows, but they're so young I'd feel like a criminal asking them out."

"There's a lot to be said for staying single," Sydney advised. "This is pretty good." She lifted her cup to him.

"Old family recipe. One cup of hot water, four tablespoons of Carnation Hot Chocolate Mix, two marshmallows." This earned him half a smile. "So how did your son's soccer game turn out?" he asked.

"The team won but Ryan didn't get to play much. I wanted to talk to the coach, but Ryan asked me not to."

Cole cringed. "If you do, you'll give him a reputation as a mama's boy."

"Is that really bad?"

"Worse than being an awful player," Cole promised.

She considered this for a minute. "Did you play soccer?"

"Naw, I never cared much for sports. I played a little football in junior high, but I was one of the awful players." This earned him a whole smile.

"With your upper-body development, I thought you were probably a weight lifter."

He laughed so hard that he spit hot chocolate across the counter. "Sorry to disappoint you Sydney, but any muscles I have were earned the old-fashioned way." She stared blankly as he pulled a dish towel from the drawer and cleaned up his mess. "Work. Long hours of hard work."

"Oh." She was nonplussed. "Well, thanks for the hot chocolate and the car repairs and the farm tour, but I really do need to go." She stood and Cole followed her through the room with the ugly green couch and crooked floor lamp. "And I guess you'll be the star of the elders quorum tomorrow."

"They might even let me sit on the front row." He pulled the front door open and she stepped outside. "See you tonight," he said warmly. With a nod Sydney got into Grandma's car and drove home.

* * * * *

The Lure was crowded by the time she arrived and Sydney worked steadily. Cole came in at seven-thirty and waved as he sat in his regular seat. She took advantage of a momentary lull in orders to walk over on the pretense of taking fresh onion rings to table seven.

"Starla taking good care of you tonight?" she asked as she balanced the appetizers.

"She always does." He pointed to a plate of cheese fries and a pitcher of Sprite that had already been delivered.

"She thinks you're cute," Sydney revealed and he smiled.

"And what do you think?" he asked. Sydney opened her mouth to reply but was interrupted by the arrival of Craig and Peyton Harris. The latter was wearing one white leather ankle boot, but the other foot was clad only in a thin sock. She was leaning heavily on Craig's arm, and Sydney noted that several strands of her silky blonde hair draped across his shoulder as he settled her tenderly into a chair.

"We've been at the hospital for hours," Craig reported once Peyton was seated.

"Were they all out of crutches?" Sydney asked, eyeing the woman's hand that was still clutching Craig's arm.

"The orthopedist said she didn't need a cast or crutches since the x-rays didn't show any fractures. It's just sprained and he told her to keep pressure off of her ankle for a few days," Craig replied, and Sydney rolled her eyes at his denseness.

"I hope my rental car won't be in the way until I can come back and get it," Peyton said to Cole and he assured her that he could work around it. "I've called my employers and told them that I'll have to take a few days off to let my ankle heal."

"Does that mean I get a break from your constant negotiations?" Cole asked and she laughed.

"Yes, but don't relax too much. My client is working up a new proposal, and I'll be preparing one of my own while I'm trapped in my hotel room."

"New proposals are a waste of everybody's time. I'm not going to sell the farm," Cole said in exasperation.

"Well, even if the whole thing is hopeless I want to drag it out as long as I can. This is the closest thing to a vacation I've had in years, and I'm not going back to Nashville until I have to. And I'd be crazy to leave when I have my own personal physician here." Peyton's smile lingered on Craig, and Sydney almost dropped the onion rings. Afraid that she might be moved to physical violence if she stayed a second longer, Sydney turned abruptly and walked to the kitchen.

From a safe distance she watched as Craig ordered dinner for himself and his patient. Then he cut Ms. Harris's steak for her as if she had two broken arms instead of a sprained ankle. Throughout dinner they leaned close to speak to each other and left together just before Sydney's break. When her relief arrived, Sydney walked over to table eight and sat down heavily.

"He likes her," she stated the obvious. "A lot."

Cole nodded. "I would say so."

"Oh gosh!" Sydney put her elbows on the table and rested her face in her hands. "Why did you have to bring her here!"

"He was bound to meet someone else eventually," Cole told her gently. "I don't know why you care. You shouldn't waste any more time on Craig." This remark caused Sydney to whimper. "You should invest your energy in improving your own life instead."

She peeked between her fingers at him. "Look who's talking. You work yourself to death all day and watch your sister sing at night. That's not exactly what I call a dream existence."

"You're right. I need to find a wife and start a family," Cole agreed with a sigh. "And I'm going to start looking for someone . . . soon."

They were sitting there in various stages of depression when Sister Tucker walked up to table eight. "Hello Cole, Sister Cochran," the Primary teacher greeted them cheerfully as she took a chair beside Sydney. "I wanted to stop by and remind you about the presentation practice tomorrow so you wouldn't forget."

"That *was* my plan," Sydney admitted and the teacher laughed.

"Not every parent has the opportunity to make their child's dream come true," she said and Sydney nodded in defeat.

"I'll try," she promised as she went back to work.

That night after she had cleaned and ironed, Sydney laid out the children's Sunday clothing, then faced her own closet. She shuffled through her old dresses but couldn't imagine putting one of them on. They were a little out of style, maybe even dowdy by some standards. The kind of dresses women who were still married to their husbands wore to church. Since she no longer fell into that category, she would have to find something else.

She thought she had found her excuse to stay home but then she came across the black suit she had bought for her interview at The Lure.

The skirt was a little short and the jacket tight-fitting. It was perfect, and with a sigh of resignation she laid it on her bed beside Sarah's dress.

Sydney dozed in a living room chair for a couple of hours until daybreak, and when she went in to wake up the children, she saw the black suit and her courage failed. She picked it up to hang it back in the closet. "You're coming to church with us, aren't you, Mom?" Sarah whispered from behind her.

Sydney stared at the suit in her hand and tried to think of another reason that she would be holding it. "I want to hear you sing, Sarah," she said. "But I'm not sure I can go to church."

"We'll help you, Mom," Sarah promised as she jumped out of bed and wrapped her arms around her mother. "And can I have Corn Pops for breakfast?"

Once the children were fed, Sydney sent the boys to their room to get dressed and then assisted Sarah. When the little girl was completely ready, she sat on the end of her bed and stared at her mother. "Now it's your turn, Mom."

Nodding grimly, Sydney dragged her clothes into the bathroom. She took a shower and dried her hair, then examined herself ruthlessly in the mirror. The highlights Carmella had given her last month were fading and her permanent was finally relaxing, so her hair didn't look bad. After applying makeup and wiggling into a pair of control-top pantyhose, Sydney put on the black suit. It seemed tighter than she remembered, and she determined to ignore Cole Brackner and cut back on calories in the future.

Grandma didn't bat an eye when Sydney walked into the kitchen dressed for church for the first time in over a year. Ryan hated to be late and hurried them all out to the car. Sydney's anxiety increased as she drove. After dropping Grandma off with the Baptists, she started thinking about her Primary teachers and Young Women leaders and how she had let them down.

By the time she parked beside the church Sydney was trembling so badly that she knew she wouldn't be able to go inside. She told Ryan that she wasn't feeling well and would have to go home. "Can't you at least try?" he asked, but Sydney shook her head.

"Oh, Mom!" Sarah wailed, tears filling her big eyes. "Please!"

"I just can't do it." Sydney felt her throat tighten with emotion.

"Come on, Trent, Sarah," Ryan said firmly from the back seat. "We're going to be late." He took Sarah by the hand and pulled her out of the car. Sydney watched in despair as her children walked toward the building. Sarah turned around and gave her a brave little wave just before she went inside.

Sydney rested her head on the steering wheel, feeling ill and miserable. Taking deep breaths, she tried to regain enough composure to drive home. Before she reached that point, however, the front passenger door opened, and Maralee Tucker slipped into the car.

"I'm sorry." Sydney knew she didn't really owe the teacher an explanation, but the woman had tried to help Sarah. "I tried, but I can't."

For a minute the only sound in the car was Sydney's ragged breathing. Then Maralee Tucker spoke. "Sometimes if we look at a big task all at once, it overwhelms us. By taking it one step at a time, it's easier."

Sydney turned her head to stare at the woman. "What do you mean?"

"I mean, instead of thinking about going inside the building, why don't you concentrate on opening the car door? Once you accomplish that, we'll worry about the next step."

Sydney laughed at this simplification of her problem. "You have no idea how I feel."

She expected Sister Tucker to claim understanding. Instead the woman shook her head. "You're right. I don't."

Sydney sat up a little straighter.

"I have a wonderful husband and I've never been estranged from the Church," she admitted with total honesty. "But I have been afraid many times, and the Lord has always pulled me through." She paused, then continued, "I'd like to say a prayer, if you don't mind." Sydney nodded her acquiescence and the teacher bowed her head. When the prayer was over, Sydney opened her eyes and stared out the window. "You have done so much for your children, made so many sacrifices. I know you can do this too," the teacher whispered.

"All I have to do is open the door?" Sydney asked.

"That's all."

Sydney pursed her lips. "This could take a while. Won't your class be running irreverently up and down the halls without you there to stop them?"

Sister Tucker laughed softly. "They're in opening exercises now, and then they'll practice for the program with the others. So we have almost an hour to get you inside. After that, the eternal salvation of eleven seven-year-olds may hang in the balance if I'm not there to teach them about the Good Samaritan."

"You're wasted teaching Primary," Sydney told the other woman.

"Try to open the door," Sister Tucker said and waited patiently as Sydney reached for the handle with a trembling hand.

By the time they made it to the Primary room, Sydney was sweating and Sarah had already performed her solo. Disappointed, Sydney collapsed in a plastic chair on the back row. Sister Tucker spoke to the chorister and moments later the Primary president announced that Sarah was going to run through her song just once more. With a grateful smile at Sister Tucker, Sydney turned her attention to her daughter.

Somehow the musical talent possessed by the rest of her family had skipped a generation and settled on Sarah. The child sang in a beautiful, clear tone, and tears pooled in Sydney's eyes. When the song was over, Sarah ran to the back row and embraced her mother.

"That was so wonderful!" Sydney praised her.

Sarah laughed as the Primary president began dismissing the children by classes. When she called for Sister Tucker's CTRs, Sarah took Sydney's hand and pulled her toward the door. "Sister Tucker said you could come with us."

"We're just right here." Sister Tucker pointed to the adjoining room, and Sydney slipped inside quickly. The walls of the room were plastered with pictures, and a big vase of sunflowers adorned the little table. Once the children were seated, Sister Tucker introduced Sydney as Sarah's mother and Sarah beamed with pride. "We're going to go through the story of the Good Samaritan, and afterward we are going to act it out. I'm hoping Sarah's mother will help me with costumes."

The class time flew by, and when it was over Sister Tucker pushed her hair from her face in exhaustion. "See what I mean! They'll kill you, but you'll die smiling!" The teacher began removing pictures from the wall. "Next week as part of the lesson I'm supposed to show them the difference between leavened and unleavened bread. You don't by any chance bake bread, do you?" Sister Tucker asked as she stacked up her teaching supplies.

"My mom bakes bread all the time!" Sarah answered for her.

"With your work schedule and all, you might not have time . . ." The teacher hesitated.

"She'll do it! Won't you, Mom?" Sarah was determined.

"Do what?" Trent asked as he stuck his head in the door.

"Mom's going to make level bread for my class next week," Sarah reported proudly.

"Hey! Can you make something for my class too?" Trent wanted to know. "Something better than bread?"

"Maybe. I'll have to see," Sydney replied as they stepped out of the classroom. The halls were crowded with children trying to get to their parents in the chapel, and the Cochrans were pulled along with everyone else. "I'm going to have to go now," Sydney told her children.

Bishop Middleton came around the corner at that moment and almost ran into them. "It's wonderful to have you with us today." He trapped Sydney in a big hug. "Nancy!" he called to a woman across the room. "Nancy, this is Sydney. Sydney, this is my wife, Nancy."

"You're Sarah's mother," Sister Middleton said with certainty. "She looks just like you."

Pleased, Sydney accepted her outstretched hand. "And this is our daughter Stephanie," the bishop continued. "She's working on her degree in entomology."

"Bugs," the daughter provided helpfully as the bishop spun Sydney around to meet the Young Men president, Brother Ingram.

"I'm glad I ran into you." The youth leader pulled out a pocket calendar. "We're in charge of refreshments for the fireside next Sunday night. Can you send a plate of brownies?" Sydney nodded and the man made a quick note.

"I gave Ryan a list of activities for the month of October. He'll probably lose it," Brother Ingram added as he put away his calendar. "The deacons usually do."

As they reached the chapel doors, Sydney tried again. "I've got to go—"

"Mom!" Ryan spoke from beside her. "Sit over on the left side toward the back 'cause that's where I'm passing. I'll try not to spill any water on you," he promised as he rushed off.

Sydney allowed Sarah to drag her a few feet inside the chapel doors, then dug her feet into the carpet and shook her head. "I can't stay here. I have to go . . ." A member of the bishopric stood up, and the organist moved smoothly to the last line of the song she was playing.

"Sydney, you've got to save me," Cole's voice whispered in her ear as he stepped up behind her. "Lauren is trying to fix me up with a girl who just graduated from BYU. She's taller than me and outweighs me by fifty pounds," he added urgently. "I told her that you and I were dating. If I sit by you during sacrament meeting, maybe she'll believe me."

"You lied?" Sydney was so surprised she allowed Sarah to pull her onto the last pew.

Cole slid in next to her and shrugged. "Some people would consider lunch at The Pork Belly and a drive around my farm to be dates."

"You lied." She couldn't get over it. Cole Brackner wasn't perfect.

"The ox was in the mire," he tried, but Sydney shook her head.

"That only goes for working on Sunday, not lying." The organ started playing again and Sydney realized that she was sitting in the chapel and sacrament meeting had started. Leaning forward, she whispered, "I've got to go."

"If you leave now, Beulah might come and sit by me!"

"Her name cannot be Beulah." Sydney was positive about this.

"Actually it's Tiffany, but her parents should have gone with Beulah," Cole insisted. Sarah found the page in the hymnbook and held it over to share with her mother.

Sydney saw the words and automatically her mouth opened. Cole's gravelly base joined her nervous soprano and a peace settled over her heart. She had forgotten how beautiful the hymns were. After the sacrament song, Ryan stood with the deacons to pass the bread and Sydney's chest constricted. He was so perfect and wonderful. He deserved so much better than divorced parents. She clawed at her throat, gasping for air. Then she felt Cole's hand on her arm.

"Relax. Take slow, deep breaths," he whispered.

Humming the sacrament song in her mind, she forced herself to breathe, and by the time Ryan got to their row she was able to give him something approaching a smile. When the Aaronic Priesthood was dismissed, the Cochrans and Cole shifted up the bench to make room for Ryan, and Sydney noticed that her son was the only deacon wearing a complete suit.

"None of those boys have on coats, and some of their shirts look like they came straight out of the dryer," Sydney said to Cole, who was now pressed close against her.

He gave her an amused look. "I hope my shirt passes your inspection," he murmured and she studied his collar, crisp and white against the dark tan of his neck. She saw a pulse beating under his skin and dropped her eyes.

"I guess it will do."

The speakers had been assigned to talk on preparing for baptism, and since Sarah would be eight in July, Sydney listened closely. Afraid she wouldn't be able to remember all the suggestions, she got out a pen and jotted down ideas on the back of her program. After they stood for the rest hymn, the concluding speaker was a high councilor, so she and Sarah played tic-tac-toe until the meeting ended.

Afterward they waited their turn to file out the chapel doors. They had almost made it when an older woman pointed a finger at Sydney and approached with determination. Stomach acid churning, Sydney stood and awaited her fate. The woman reached her and opened her mouth to speak, then squinted her eyes in confusion.

"I'm sorry, dear. I thought you were Fiona Whatley, but you must be Sarah's mother." She patted the child on the head. "You look just like her." With that pronouncement, the woman hurried off in search of the missing Sister Whatley.

"You did it, Mom!" Sarah praised as they stepped outside.

"It was . . ." She searched for the right words. "I enjoyed it." Cole smiled and she narrowed her eyes at him. "The bishop must have told everyone to leave me alone."

"Maybe," Cole hedged. "Probably," he finally admitted. "Don't be mad. He just wanted you to feel comfortable."

"I'm not mad." And she wasn't. In fact, she appreciated the bishop's thoughtfulness. She was so distracted by this concept that she didn't hear Sarah inviting Cole to eat with them until it was too late. He did try to decline, but Sarah was insistent. "Grandma told me to be sure and bring you."

"He might have other plans," Sydney spoke quickly.

"But Grandma will be sad if he doesn't come." Sarah wouldn't give up.

"I don't have other plans," he said with a smile.

Sydney thought of the lonely farm and shrugged. "I guess we owe you a free meal after all the things you've done for us. Even if you are just trying to get Home Teacher of the Year."

Cole waited until the children had walked ahead. "If you want me to, I'll think of an excuse and go home."

Sydney shook her head. "It's nothing personal. After Craig, I'm just not crazy about men."

Cole lifted an eyebrow. "Well, you'd better learn to like them, since you're raising two."

She ignored this remark and said they'd meet him at the house after they picked up Grandma. Cole was waiting in his truck when Sydney pulled into the driveway. He followed along behind as she ushered the children inside and told them to change. Then she left Cole with Grandma while she went up to her room and peeled off her black suit.

By the time she put on jeans and made it into the kitchen, Grandma had Cole firmly entrenched at the head of the table. He had taken off his coat, the top button of his perfectly pressed white shirt was undone, and his tie hung loosely around his neck. He gave her a big smile and Sydney rolled her eyes.

The kids fought over the seats next to Cole until Ryan finally gave in to keep the peace. Grandma sat in Sydney's chair, forcing her to sit at the other end of the table, facing Cole. She put a little salad and some Jell-O on her plate as they passed dishes around. "You don't want any roast or potatoes?" Cole asked as he served himself a generous helping of each.

Sarah took a roll. "Mom's always on a diet."

"It makes me nervous when the cook doesn't want to eat her own food," Cole said, eyeing the roast suspiciously.

"There is nothing wrong with the food!" Pride forced Sydney to defend herself.

Sarah nodded in agreement. "Mom makes good food; she just doesn't eat it."

"So, how do you like soccer?" Cole questioned Ryan.

"It's okay," the boy answered guardedly.

"Ryan doesn't even know how to play!" Trent scoffed. "I told Mom she should let me be on a football team instead."

"Do you know how to play soccer, Brother Brackner?" Sarah asked with her mouth full of potatoes.

"Sarah, mind your manners!" Sydney reprimanded her daughter.

"I never liked soccer, or any sport really," Cole answered as he helped himself to more black-eyed peas.

"You don't like sports?" To Trent this was comparable to professing atheism. "You don't even watch games on television?"

"Hardly ever," Cole affirmed. "I watch an occasional Braves game."

"Wow." Ryan was impressed. "And you're not even a wimp."

"Ryan!" Sydney objected but Cole laughed.

"It's okay. I'll take that as a compliment. I started working on the farm with my dad when I was about your age. Lifting hay bales and dragging cows around makes you pretty strong, but it doesn't get you dates with cheerleaders. That's where sports come in handy."

"I don't want to get dates with cheerleaders!" Ryan assured them all.

"That will change," Cole predicted as he dished more roast onto his plate.

"When can we come to your farm to see your kittens?" Sarah asked and Sydney sighed.

"Why don't you come over after dinner today?" he suggested. "I'll show you the kittens and let you feed the horses. We could even go for a ride and look at the cows."

Sydney watched rapt expressions develop on the children's faces and raised her hand. "We'll have to come another day. I'm too tired."

All eyes turned to stare at her, and Cole spoke for everyone. "You don't have to work tonight, so you can sleep then."

The children started begging again, and finally Sydney nodded. "We can't stay long . . ."

Grandma stood and began clearing the table. "You go on. I'll clean the kitchen."

Sydney told everyone to get a coat and the children groaned. "It's eighty degrees outside, Mom," Ryan protested.

"It's also October and the weather can change at any minute." She would not be swayed. All the children wanted to ride in Cole's huge truck, but only Ryan was given permission. Trent and Sarah sulked in the old Crown Victoria, but after a few minutes their excitement overwhelmed them and they watched out the windows for Cole's farm.

Sydney parked next to Peyton's rental car and frowned at the reminder. Cole and Ryan went into the barn and the other children ran to join them. By the time Sydney walked in, Sarah had a kitten under each arm and Trent was shoveling hay into the horse stalls. "Brother Brackner says I can have one!" Sarah reported ecstatically.

"Sarah, you know we can't have pets at Grandma's house," Sydney said.

Sarah's jaw jutted out stubbornly. "I'll keep it at Daddy's."

"Why don't you just keep your kitten here?" Cole knelt beside her. "They are too little to leave their mama anyway. You can name it and then come visit."

"Can I have a boy and a girl?" Sarah saw an opportunity to negotiate a better deal.

"You can have them all," Cole offered generously.

"Can I have a horse?" Trent called from the back of the barn.

"For heaven's sake!" Sydney was losing patience.

"How about I loan you one?" Cole suggested as a compromise.

After the horses were fed, Cole told everyone to get in the truck for a ride around the farm. The children cheered, but Sydney felt it necessary to raise an objection. "There won't be enough seat belts!"

"I won't go over five miles an hour. Impact at that speed wouldn't even give them a bruise," he said as he herded them toward the barn door. Ryan paused briefly to examine some fishing equipment stacked in a corner. "You like to fish?" Cole asked and the boy nodded. "Do you have a pole?" Ryan shook his head. Cole looked through the assortment. Finally he untangled a rod and reel from the rest. "This was my favorite when I was a boy. You can have it."

Ryan accepted the gift and Cole told him about the little cabin up on the lake. Sydney rarely let her children spend the night away from home, but as Cole described the cabin and trips he took with his father as a boy, she realized that Ryan did need a good male role model. Cole Brackner would provide that, so Sydney decided to agree when he invited Ryan to go fishing with him at his cabin. "I'll talk to your dad and maybe one weekend he can take you up there." Sydney glared at Cole, but Ryan was smiling as they went out to the truck.

"Can I bring Brownie and Whitie with me?" Sarah asked, holding up two kittens.

"You're not bringing those stinky cats." Sydney shook her head.

"You can't name your kittens Brownie and Whitie," Trent moaned.

"They need to stay with their mother." Cole put the squirming fur balls back into the box with their siblings.

As he had promised, Cole drove slowly. He pointed out the various types of cows and actually pulled into a pasture with the mothers who had young calves. When they stopped outside the yearling pasture, the little cows ran toward the truck. "They think I'm here to feed them," Cole explained as everyone got out and stood by the fence. Trent immediately climbed to the top slat and Sydney told him to get down.

"Where are the daddy cows?" Sarah asked, peering through the boards.

"We don't keep any bulls. They are too expensive to maintain," Cole replied.

Sydney digested this information, then turned to him. "How do you get babies if you don't have daddies?"

"Artificial insemination. We buy frozen . . ."

"Never mind," Sydney waved his explanation aside.

"It's more time and cost efficient," he continued with a smile. "Although not very romantic . . ."

Sydney ignored him as she pulled her children from the fence and told them to get inside the truck. Sarah climbed up onto the running board, then pointed to the far corner of the yearling pasture. "Is that the door where these calves can go back and visit their moms?" she asked.

Cole shielded his eyes with his hand and looked at the corner of the pasture. "There isn't supposed to be a door there. Let's go take a look." When they drove around to the broken fence, they saw that several wooden slats had been removed and thrown to the side. Cole got down on his knees and fingered the ground. "It looks like someone stole some of the yearlings."

"Why would someone steal your little cows?" Trent asked.

"For all kinds of reasons. To sell or eat, or just for the fun of it." Cole's tone was light, but his eyes were serious.

"Is this really bad?" Sydney asked on the way back to the truck.

"Losing a cow or two won't hurt us, but Lamar says he's found other evidence that people have been on the farm. Campfires, beer cans, unusual tire marks. It makes me a little uneasy." Cole looked across the pasture. "When my father was alive we had a lot of farmhands around to discourage trespassers. Now," he shrugged, "it's just Lamar and me."

"Do you have a fence around your property?"

"Yes, but anybody who wanted to could get in without a problem."

"You should call the police," Sydney advised. "It's their job to protect citizens from trespassers," she added, thinking about Miss Glida Mae and her frivolous calls.

"I will if it gets any worse," he promised.

Sarah was asleep by the time they got to Cole's house, and he carried the child to Grandma's car. "Can we come back tomorrow, Mom?" Trent asked as he put on his seat belt.

"Not tomorrow," Sydney said. "You've got school and I have to work."

Cole walked around and spoke to Sydney through the driver's window. "If you want me to put a new hose on the radiator, I'll pick one up in town."

"I'll let you know. And thanks for today," Sydney forced the words out. "The kids had a good time and you probably really will get Home Teacher of the Year. Maybe of the decade."

"Who won it last year?" Trent leaned over the front seat to ask.

Sydney frowned. "Won what?"

"Home Teacher of the Year," Trent clarified.

"Your mother was kidding. There's no such thing," Cole said as Sydney started the car and pulled away. The children waved to Cole until he disappeared from sight.

CHAPTER FIVE

When they got home, Sydney sent the boys to take baths. Grandma made Sarah a peanut butter sandwich and asked if they had a fun afternoon. "I had a great day," Sarah said. "I have four kittens named Softie and Fluffy and Furry—"

"Mom! Don't let her name them stupid stuff!" Trent wailed from the stairs.

Sydney smiled in spite of her exhaustion. "We'll talk about some good cat names later, Sarah. Just eat your sandwich."

"It was nice of Cole to give you four cats," Grandma said as she poured a glass of milk.

"They will continue to live on the farm. Sarah just gets to name them and visit occasionally," Sydney assured her grandmother.

Grandma offered to make Sydney something to eat, but she declined, saying she was too tired to swallow. "Oh, Sydney, some visiting teaching ladies called you this afternoon. They want to meet you and I know I'm not supposed to send people to your work anymore. But you're terribly busy and I worry that you don't get enough sleep," Grandma paused, "so I told them you have a break at ten o'clock every night."

Sydney shook her head with a smile. "Grandma, if you keep sending people to visit me at The Lure, Cole may have to expand to more than one table." Sydney laughed at her grandmother's blank look. "Never mind. I'll call the visiting teachers tomorrow and tell them they can come here on Wednesday."

She was so exhausted she could barely breathe and expected to fall asleep immediately, but after reading her scriptures Sydney lay awake, staring at the ceiling. She thought back over her morning at church and her afternoon at Cole's farm. Now that she had made it through an entire sacrament meeting, she couldn't remember why she thought it would be so hard. And she was looking forward to showing Sarah's class the difference between leavened and unleavened bread the next week. Of course they couldn't go out to Cole's farm regularly, but an occasional visit would be good for the kids.

Then her mind strayed to Craig and the threat that Peyton Harris posed to the delicate balance of their lives. She wondered if Craig had spent the day nursing his patient back to health, and the thought made her shudder. She needed to get Peyton out of Eureka and fast. Since the only person who wanted her gone almost as much as she did was Cole Brackner, Sydney would have to think of a way to convince the cow farmer that they should work together.

* * * * *

On Monday morning Sydney called Carmella as soon as she got home from taking the kids to school. "I have a cosmetology emergency," she told her friend. "I need to be blonde."

"I've always liked your hair color," Carmella responded doubtfully.

"Well, Craig likes blondes so I've got to be one."

"Last month you said he liked curly hair so I gave you a body wave," Carmella reminded her. "And you can't stand Craig, so I don't know why you want to be attractive to him."

"Before, I just wanted to make him sorry he'd divorced me. Now it's serious. I have to look good enough to distract him until I can get rid of Peyton Harris."

"Oh, Sydney. I don't think this is a good idea," Carmella's anxiety came clearly through the phone lines.

"Are you going to help me or not?" Sydney demanded.

She heard her friend sigh. "I guess I'm going to dye your hair, but I'm not sure if that will be helping you."

"I don't mean blonde, blonde. Just a few shades lighter than it is now. Tell me what to get and I'll run by Wanda's Beauty Supply after

I go to the grocery store. Then I'll come on out to your place."
Holding the phone in the crook of her neck, Sydney wrote down the
instructions.

Three hours later she was sitting in Carmella's tiny kitchen
watching *Top Gun* and breathing ammonia fumes. "How long did the
box say this stuff is supposed to stay on my hair?" Sydney asked.

"What hair?" Carmella pulled her eyes away from Tom Cruise.
"Oh, it said fifteen minutes."

Sydney continued to read on the box. "It says fifteen minutes for
first applications. For permed or tinted hair, it says to leave it on for
five minutes." Carmella's eyes still had a glazed look. "Carmella! My
hair is permed *and* tinted. Get this stuff off fast!"

Carmella worked as quickly as possible, but when Sydney looked
into the bathroom mirror she screamed, then touched her white-
blonde hair in morbid fascination. "I look like Dolly Parton," she
whispered. "Without the chest."

"It's a nice look for you," Carmella attempted to minimize the
disaster, then burst into tears. "I'm so sorry, Sydney. You know I never
made it all the way through cosmetology school! You never should
have trusted me!"

Sydney reassured her friend repeatedly and Carmella finally
regained her composure. "Maybe I could run over to Wanda's and get
a Rich Chestnut rinse," Carmella suggested without enthusiasm.

Sydney shook her head. "I don't have time for that today. I've got
to be at the elementary school in an hour, and after that there's Ryan's
soccer practice, then work. I'll come back tomorrow and see what you
can do."

"Maybe you should make an appointment with someone at Shear
Delight. This is probably a job for professionals," Carmella suggested
tremulously.

"I'll think about it." Sydney gave her friend a final hug and
walked to her car.

Carmella followed her as far as the front door with a damp hanky
pressed to her lips. "You are the bravest woman I've ever known," she
said with feeling, then hurried back inside.

Sydney avoided the rearview mirror until she was safely parked in
front of the elementary school. Then she took a deep breath and

faced her reflection. Her hair was very blonde and startlingly different from her natural color, but it didn't look exactly bad. It might take some getting used to but . . .

"Mom?" Sarah's voice spoke with wonder from the passenger window. "You look just like Barbie."

Trent was less charitable. "What did you do to your hair? You look like a poodle!"

Ryan made no comment at all when they picked him up, a sure sign that he hated it. After dropping him off at the baseball field, Sydney was tempted to stop in at a drugstore and buy some Miss Clairol, but she was afraid that she'd only make herself look worse. She explained this to Grandma when she got home, and Grandma assured her that would have been impossible.

Miss Glida Mae knocked on the back door as Sydney started chicken and dumplings for dinner. "Is that you Sydney?" she shrieked when Grandma led her in. "Mayme Camp called and said y'all had company. She didn't even recognize you."

"They say blondes have more fun," Sydney replied sarcastically. "Life as a brunette has been pretty rotten, so I thought I'd give it a try."

"Well, if I were you I'd call one of the girls at Shear Delight and see if they can reverse that," Miss Glida Mae advised.

"I'll think it over," Sydney said, stirring her dumplings. "Grandma, can you keep an eye on this while I get ready for work?" she asked when Miss Glida Mae took a seat at the table.

Sydney left the dumplings in her grandmother's care and went upstairs. She washed, conditioned, and dried her hair, then looked in the mirror hoping for a miracle. Instead she saw Waitress Barbie. She could still hear their neighbor in the kitchen talking to Grandma, so she quietly said good night to her children and slipped out the front door.

Starla didn't mention her hair when she walked in, so Sydney knew that Carmella had warned everyone. "It's okay to laugh," Sydney told the girl. "I know you want to."

"It's not that bad. It looks real . . ." Starla dissolved into a fit of giggles. Sydney squared her shoulders and began waiting on customers. She tried to forget about her appearance, but it was hard since every time Carmella walked by, her eyes filled with tears.

"Would you quit worrying about my hair!" Sydney finally said. "The only person I wouldn't want to see me like this is Craig, and he always stays at the hospital on Monday nights."

This thought seemed to comfort Carmella, and both women went about their duties. Henry Lee came in at seven-thirty and almost tripped over his own feet when he saw Sydney.

"Oh, Sydney," he said reverently. "You look beautiful."

"Don't talk to me," she bit out between clenched teeth. Cowed, Henry Lee took his regular seat and started eating beer nuts. Taking her at her word, for the next hour he wrote his orders on cocktail napkins and handed them to her when she passed by. She kept an eye on table eight until Cole arrived, then rushed over.

"I'm so glad you're here," she told him.

Cole's eyes widened when he looked up, but he made no comment about her hair or her unusually friendly greeting.

"Are you taking your break early tonight?" he asked warily.

"No, but I do have something important to talk to you about. I'll be back at ten," she warned him, then hurried back to her tables.

Sydney endured the good-natured teasing from the regulars and had almost quit shuddering every time she caught a glimpse of herself in the big mirrored wall behind the bar when Carmella rushed up. The tears were back and Sydney sighed. "Carmella, I told you—"

"Oh Sydney," her friend began, then pressed a trembling hand to her lips.

"Excuse me," Craig's voice said from behind her. "I'm looking for Sydney, one of the waitresses who works here."

Sydney was tempted to walk straight into the kitchen and out the back door, leaving Carmella to make up an explanation. But he'd be bound to find out sometime, so she turned to face her worst nightmare. Standing next to the bar was her ex-husband with his arm draped gently along the shoulders of the naturally blonde Peyton Harris.

"How's the foot?" Sydney asked the other woman when it became obvious that Craig had lost his powers of speech.

"Do I know you?" There was a haughty quality to her cultured voice.

"Sydney Cochran, Craig's ex-wife. We met briefly on Friday and then again on Saturday after you conveniently twisted your ankle."

Peyton's eyes darted to Craig, who was still paralyzed, then back to Sydney's hair. "Oh yes, I didn't recognize you," she replied. "And my foot's much better, thank you."

Sydney looked at Craig and sighed. "I guess you'd better take him over to table eight. If he ever remembers what he wanted to talk to me about, send him back."

"This Saturday is my day to have the kids," Craig croaked. "I need to arrange for a time to pick them up." He still couldn't drag his eyes away from her hair, and Sydney was starting to wonder if he liked it. Then he met her gaze, and she saw horror and pity in equal measure.

"Ryan's game is at nine. You can take them afterward." Sydney just wanted them to go.

Craig nodded mutely and Peyton led him over to speak with Cole. They didn't sit down, but left The Lure a few minutes later. The crowd was sparse and by ten o'clock, Henry Lee was the only customer sitting at the bar. He ordered a plate of chicken fingers before she took her break, and when she delivered it, he asked if he could bring a camera on Tuesday night and take her picture.

"Don't make me hurt you, Henry Lee," she responded on her way to table eight.

"Your new hair is the talk of the place tonight," Cole said as she sat down.

"I know I look awful," Sydney sighed.

"You don't look awful," Cole disagreed. "I'm not partial to blondes, but—"

"But what do you know!" Sydney pounced on his words. "You look at cows all day."

He acknowledged the truthfulness of her words with a nod. "I saved you some cheese fries." He pointed to the plate where four or five stone cold fries lay covered in oil-dotted cheese.

"You're too good to me," she replied with half a smile. "What did Peyton want?"

"To tell me that she and Craig were going to ride out to the farm to pick up her car."

"She's leaving?" It seemed too good to be true, but her luck had to change sometime.

"Naw. She'll be back out to present her new proposal tomorrow."

"Somehow we've got to figure out a way to get rid of her before she ruins what is left of my life," Sydney lamented.

"I don't know how I can help you there," Cole said. "The only thing I could do that would make Peyton go back to Nashville is sell her my farm." Sydney raised an eyebrow. "There is nothing you can say that will convince me to do that."

"Oh well." She risked a glance at Cole, but he seemed distracted and she asked if something was wrong.

"I got some bad news today," he admitted. "I told you that I always sell my extra hay to Hawkins Feed and Seed in Columbus." He paused and Sydney nodded. "Well, I called them today to arrange delivery, and they said they didn't want it. Another supplier offered them all the hay they could use at half the market price. I couldn't blame them for taking a crazy deal like that, but it's really going to hurt me."

"Because you need the money?"

He nodded. "Under ordinary circumstances it wouldn't be that bad, but my cash reserves are low and I'm trying to prove myself to the bank. Hay rotting in the field can't really be considered an asset." She gave him a blank look and he sighed. "Darrell ran the farm while I was on my mission. He didn't have any experience, and when I got home things were in bad shape. He had spent all our savings and there were some loans . . ."

"He bought the big truck," Sydney remembered.

"The barn, a tractor and hay baler, new roof on the house . . ."

"Put in new carpet and a great kitchen," Sydney added.

"So I had to mortgage the farm. The loan is renewable annually, but if the bank thinks I'm not managing things well, they'll pull the rug out from under me," Cole finished morosely.

Sydney picked up a cold cheese fry. It had been a long time since she had thought about a problem that she wasn't emotionally involved in. "Who buys the hay from Hawkins Feed and Seed in Columbus?"

"Other farmers who don't have enough pasture land to grow all the hay they need."

"Local folks?" Sydney asked.

"Mostly."

"What if you contacted the farmers directly and offered a better price than what they'll get from Hawkins and say you'll deliver, as an added incentive," Sydney suggested.

"They might think I'm crazy."

"They might buy your hay," she countered.

He considered this for another minute, then smiled. "I thought blondes were supposed to be dumb."

Sydney stood and pushed her chair up under the table. "That's just real blondes," she said as she walked back to the kitchen.

On Tuesday morning Carmella put a rinse on Sydney's hair and turned it a brassy blonde shade that closely resembled Miss Glida Mae Magnanney's. It was a moderate improvement at best, but Sydney assured Carmella that she loved it.

After a short nap, Sydney picked the children up at school. Sarah was disappointed that she had changed her hair color since she had thought they could be Barbie and Skipper for Halloween. Trent said she now looked like a cocker spaniel, and Ryan again made no comment. She had been too wrapped up in her own worries lately to ask about his coach, but as they rode to practice that afternoon, she brought up the subject.

"I don't like Mr. Lydell," Ryan said slowly. "But I don't blame him for not playing me in the games. I'm terrible at soccer, Mom. Really terrible."

"It might take some time . . ." Sydney was completely at a loss. She had been a natural at every sport she ever tried. All they had to do was tell her the rules and she excelled. Craig was a graceful and talented athlete as well. How could it be that the two of them had produced a klutz?

"Why do I have to do it?"

"You can't just quit now and desert your team." Bad sportsmanship was unthinkable.

"They'd be glad!" Ryan guaranteed her.

"Well, let's finish out this year, and then we'll have months to decide about next season," she proposed as a compromise. Ryan nodded without enthusiasm and climbed out of the car.

When Sydney arrived at The Lure that night she braced herself for more hair comments and she was not disappointed. "Is your hair color going to be different every night, sort of like the daily lunch special at The Pork Belly?" one man asked.

"Sydney, we're going to have to start making you wear a name tag since we never know what you're going to look like," Pinkie Howton said with a smirk.

Carmella didn't say anything, just dabbed at her eyes with a fresh Kleenex. Henry Lee had his camera, and Sydney resentfully stood for a photograph, but only because Pinkie was nearby when he asked. "Thanks," Henry Lee said with a smile as he advanced the film. "You look nice tonight, but yesterday you were beautiful. Your hair was just like Marilyn Monroe's."

"Making comments about my hair could be dangerous," Sydney warned him ominously.

The Lure was almost deserted when Cole Brackner came in at ten. He walked past table eight and sat beside Sydney, who was taking her break at the bar. "I tried out your idea," he told her as he helped himself to the peanuts. "I called around and sold all my extra hay."

"That's great!" Sydney was genuinely pleased. "So now you're rich!"

Cole smiled. "Not exactly rich. Some of the other farmers are short of cash themselves, so about half of my sales were on a deliver now/pay later basis."

"That won't help your cash flow, but an account receivable will look better to the bank than hay rotting in your fields," Sydney pointed out.

Cole nodded. "I'm going to need some help for the next week or so, and I thought Ryan might be interested in a part-time job."

"What would he have to do?" Sydney asked.

"Lamar and I will be tied up with the hay, so I thought he could feed the horses, clean out the stalls and take food out to the yearlings."

"How would he do that?"

"We have a little four-wheeler . . . ," Cole explained and Sydney started shaking her head. "It's old and won't go over ten miles an hour. If he fell off and it ran over him, he wouldn't get more than . . . two bruises." She gave him a dubious look. "Lamar or I would be nearby all the time. You know he'd love to do it, and it would give him a little spending money for Christmas."

"How are you going to pay him if you're broke?" Sydney was weakening and he knew it.

"I'll roll pennies if I have to."

"Hey!" Henry Lee's strident voice sounded from down the bar. "He's not supposed to sit up here if he isn't drinking!"

Sydney leaned forward and asked Vernon for a Sprite. When the bartender placed it in front of Cole, she picked up a slice of lime and dropped it into the glass. "Now he's drinking," she said to Henry Lee. "Unfortunately that Sprite served with lime at the bar is going to cost you $2.50," she said to Cole as she stood to go back to work.

Cole was still sitting at the bar hours later when Sydney was ready to leave. "What are you doing here this late?" she asked him.

"You didn't park in front, so I stayed to walk you to your car."

"I'm a big girl." She frowned as he fell into step beside her. "Anyway, whoever is out to get me probably won't recognize me with this hair."

Once he had her safely beside Grandma's car, he offered to come over after school the next day and pick up Ryan. "And I'll have him back in time for dinner and Young Men."

"You don't have to come get him. I'll drop him off on the way home since we'll already be out," Sydney replied. "And you'd better have him home in time for dinner and church."

Ryan was still awake when Sydney went in the boys' room and his eyes shone with happiness when she told him about Cole's job. "It's just for a week or so, until they get their hay delivered." She didn't want him to get too excited.

"So I guess I'll have to quit soccer," he assumed, but Sydney shook her head.

"I don't want you to quit, but I won't make you go to the illegal practices. Tell Preston tomorrow that you have a job and can only attend the Tuesday afternoon practice. If the coach doesn't play you on Saturday—"

"Who cares!" Ryan finished for her. "Cole said I'll get to drive a four-wheeler!"

This thought still made Sydney's stomach quiver, but Ryan was not a baby anymore and Cole would be nearby. "That's what he said."

"Man! I never would have thought something so good could happen to me!"

Sydney kissed him, then moved over to Trent. The younger boy had turned sideways in his bed, so she twisted him around and kissed him too. Then she picked up their dirty clothes and headed toward the laundry room.

On Wednesday morning the visiting teachers came. They were friendly and didn't mention her hair, so Sydney made an appointment for them to come back the next month. After they left she worked on her hair for almost an hour before giving up. As she walked outside to pick up the kids, Mrs. Camp called from the front porch. "Yoo-hoo! Oh Sydney! I thought you were Glida Mae! Why do you keep turning your hair different colors?" She leaned over the railing and peered at Sydney's new shade.

Sydney took a deep breath. "I didn't have anything better to do."

Miss Mayme lowered her voice to a conspiratorial whisper. "Did you hear that Miss Glida Mae saw somebody looking in her dining room window last night?"

"The kids told me that the police came again," Sydney admitted.

"It's a crying shame when a woman can't eat a meal without perverts watching her," Miss Mayme fumed. "I've got Camp nailing up plywood over our ground floor windows now." She pointed toward her husband, perched precariously on a stepladder.

"Be careful, Mr. Camp," Sydney admonished, then climbed into the Crown Victoria.

She picked up her children at school and then instructed everyone except Ryan to remain in the car when they reached Cole's farm. They all ignored her. Sarah ran into the barn to check on her kittens, and Trent said he was going to pick out which horse he wanted Cole to loan him. Ryan walked shyly up to his new boss, who was standing by the front steps of his house. Cole was wearing work gloves and a faded flannel shirt covered with hay. He wiped the sweat from his face with his sleeve, then gave them a weary smile.

"Lamar just left with the last truckload of hay for Simpsons' Bar S Ranch." He turned to Ryan. "You ready for me to show you your duties?"

The boy nodded and Cole led him to the barn. Rather than stand by herself, Sydney followed. "You might want to pull on some of those rubber boots." Cole pointed to a row of protective footwear by the door. Ryan found a pair and Sydney did the same. As she leaned forward, her caramel-colored hair fell into her face, blocking her view. Cole watched her struggle blindly for a few seconds, then handed her a thick rubber band. "Try this," he suggested. She twisted her hair back into a tight ponytail, then put on her other boot without interference.

Cole waited patiently until they were ready, then he showed them where to find the various feeds and fresh hay. "Each animal has a slightly different diet. Their daily feeding schedule is posted outside the stall." He tapped a plastic-covered card stapled to the wood.

"Don't try to move any of the horses yourself," he added, to Sydney's relief. "Lamar and I will put them out to run in the corral while you rake the stalls." Sydney's mind wandered as Cole continued to instruct her son. Trent was being awfully quiet, so she walked down to the end of the barn to investigate. The boy looked up guiltily as she approached.

"What were you doing?" she asked, and his hand slipped from the stall door. With some type of sharp instrument he had scratched "This horse belongs to Trenton Edward Cochran." Sydney stared at the vandalism, unable to speak.

"I'm sorry, Mom," Trent said.

Cole walked up at that moment. "This is the horse you want?" He glanced at the words engraved in the wood, and Trent nodded. "His name is Old Joe."

"I'm sorry I messed up your door," Trent offered miserably.

"It's okay," Cole responded. "And this way I won't forget which one is yours." He opened the door to an empty stall to the left. "Climb up here and you can brush Old Joe's back." He removed a big brush from a hook on the wall. Sydney started to object, but Cole held up his hand. "Old Joe is gentle, and as long as Trent keeps both feet on this board," he gave the boy a stern look, "he'll be perfectly safe."

Sydney stepped back and watched her son as he lovingly drew the brush along the animal's back. Old Joe raised his nose into the air and gave them the horse equivalent of a sigh. Cole took her arm and led her to the front of the barn where they found Sarah trying to rock her kittens to sleep. They kept escaping and Sarah giggled as she retrieved one and lost another.

Leaning against the wall, Sydney watched Ryan measure horse feed and thought how different things might have turned out if she and Craig had chosen a more simple life. Farming, raising cows, eating meals around a big kitchen table. Maybe Craig would have been happy. Maybe they would still be together. Maybe . . .

"That pretty much wraps it up in here," Cole interrupted her thoughts. "Ryan's going to drive the four-wheeler to the yearling pasture, and I thought we'd follow him."

Sydney nodded and walked out where Sarah and two of her kittens were already settled in the back of the truck. "Oh no," she protested, "That is completely unsafe."

"Why don't you sit back here too?" Cole said as he put his hands around her waist and lifted her up onto the tailgate. She glared down at him, but he just smiled. "I promise to go slow, and bouncing around in the back of my truck can't possibly give her more than," he pretended to consider as his hands lingered around her waist, "three bruises at the most." Rolling her eyes, Sydney scooted next to Sarah and reluctantly took the kitten her daughter extended.

Ryan drove the little tractor competently and when they passed him, the look on his face was worth all her worry. Cole parked the truck, but didn't get out. Instead he watched from the cab as Ryan followed his instructions with exactness, then turned the four-wheeler around and headed back. By the time they had the equipment parked, the barn straightened, and the kittens snuggled against their mother, it was starting to get dark. Sydney glanced at her watch and told the children to get into Grandma's car. They all complained, but she told them they still had to eat before she left for work.

"I was hoping you'd eat supper with me," Cole offered quietly, and she turned around to stare at him. "I made a big pot of chili."

Sydney was touched by his thoughtfulness and moved by the isolation of the farm. It probably got pretty lonely out there. So she nodded and the children cheered. "We'll have to hurry, though."

They followed Cole into the house and he stopped to turn on the crooked lamp. "Have a seat," he invited, pointing toward the ugly green couch.

"Is that your only television?" Trent asked, waving at the old console in the corner.

"That's it," Cole affirmed.

"Is it cable-ready?" Ryan was dubious.

"I doubt it, but I don't have cable so it doesn't really matter."

"You don't have cable?" Trent was amazed. "And no VCR either?"

"Not even a Nintendo!" Ryan reported from the corner.

"What do you do?" Trent demanded and Sydney told him it was none of his business.

Cole laughed. "I work until dark, then go listen to my sister sing at The Lure. I just turn the TV on in the mornings to check the weather."

"What about when you were a kid?" Ryan inquired.

"I lived in Atlanta when I was a kid and we had cable there," Cole said, and Ryan's face registered relief. "Once we moved here we worked hard until dark and at night we would read books or look at the globe or play chess." He showed them the set in a box on the bookshelf. "Do you two know how to play?" he asked the boys and Trent nodded.

"Sort of," Ryan hedged.

"Then why don't you try a game while I dish up the chili." Cole put the box on the floor in front of the couch.

"Can I play?" Sarah asked and the boys objected vehemently.

"Only two people can play at once, but here's something you might like." Cole opened a cabinet and pulled out some puzzles. Once the kids were settled, Sydney followed him into the kitchen and watched as he set up a card table and four folding chairs. "I don't have company often," he explained. "And lately I've been living off cheese fries and Sprite." This was said with a smile.

"I'll bet if you asked her, Starla would bring you a free, well-balanced meal," Sydney suggested as she took a seat at the counter.

Cole ladled some chili into a bowl and put it in front of her. Then he took a metal canister from the cupboard and handed her a package of crackers. "Go ahead and try it, but be careful, it's hot."

Sydney scooped up a spoonful and blew on it several times, then put it in her mouth. She considered it for a few seconds, then smiled. "Very good. You're not going to tell me it's out of a can, are you?" she asked, remembering his hot chocolate formula.

He laughed. "No, it's my mother's recipe."

Sydney's expression became serious. "I'm sorry about your mother." He nodded. "How did she die?"

"Cancer."

Sydney couldn't think of an adequate response, so she ate quietly as Cole filled bowls for her children. He let the chili cool for a few minutes, then called the kids. During the meal, Ryan asked Cole questions about chess strategy. Sydney was rinsing their bowls when Cole surprised her by pulling a chocolate layer cake out of the refrigerator. "Did you make that too?"

"Actually I bought it at Marsh's Bakery," he admitted as he cut her a big slice.

"I can't eat cake!" Sydney put her hand up as if to ward him off.

"Just one piece? Please?"

She continued to shake her head, but further negotiations were suspended by the slamming of the front door. Sydney and Cole exchanged a startled look, then Cole took two steps toward the living room.

"Anybody home?" a strange woman's voice called and Cole halted in the doorway. "Well, there you are. I see I've interrupted your party. Happy birthday, little brother," the woman gave Cole a quick kiss on the cheek, then hung her sweater on the hook behind the door.

"Today is your birthday?" Sarah demanded and Cole nodded reluctantly. "And we didn't even sing to you before you cut the cake."

"It's not too late." Cole's sister got a bowl from the cupboard and spooned some chili into it.

Cole finally spoke. "I didn't know you were coming."

"If you ever answered your phone, you would have," she said, then turned to Sydney. "Apparently Cole isn't going to introduce us. I'm his sister Michelle, from Atlanta, and I've come to visit him for a few days."

Sydney provided her name, then looked back at Cole. Today was his birthday. He had made chili and bought a cake, then invited them to dinner. It was so sweet and yet sad. It made her wish she hadn't refused a piece of his cake.

"These your kids?" Michelle asked, looking around and Sydney nodded.

"I thought we were going to sing to Brother Brackner," Sarah reminded everyone and Michelle laughed.

"I'll start us off," she volunteered, then began singing a boisterous, if off-key, version of "Happy Birthday to You." Everyone
joined in and Cole stood uncomfortably until it was over.

"Hurry and eat your cake," Sydney told her children. "I've got to
get to work."

"I'm sorry you have to rush off." Michelle eyed Sydney specula-
tively. "I didn't know Cole had a lady friend, and I'd like to get to
know you."

Sydney opened her mouth to correct this gross misconception.
Then an idea occurred to her. Cole said his sisters were always trying
to fix him up with women, and he particularly objected to their latest
candidate, Tiffany also-known-as Beulah. If she helped him with his
sisters, he might be more cooperative in her campaign to get rid of
Peyton. "We've only dated a few times." She was glad that Michelle
couldn't see the astonishment on Cole's face. "And we can talk this
evening if you come to The Lure to listen to Lauren sing."

"Are you a singer too?" Michelle wanted to know.

"No, I'm just a waitress," Sydney said as she collected her children.

By the time they got home, Sydney only had time to take a quick
shower and pull her damp hair back into a ponytail. She dropped
Ryan off at church, then drove on to The Lure.

"Same color, new style," Pinkie said as she walked by.

"Same face, still ugly," Sydney replied without pausing.

"The ponytail is a good idea!" Carmella was pleased. "That way
your hair is kind of hidden behind your head. You might want to
wear it like that for a while."

"I'll add that to my list of helpful suggestions," Sydney promised
as she tied on her apron. "I see we've got a record crowd tonight." She
counted three people in the whole big room

"Wednesday is always slow, but the Braves play again tonight, so
it will fill up," Carmella assured her.

Cole arrived at nine and, after settling his sister at table eight, he
walked up to the food counter where Sydney was waiting for an order
of nachos. "Michelle has interrogated me about you for the last two
hours. Why did you tell her we were dating?"

Sydney smiled. "I thought I was doing you a favor." His eyebrows
shot up. "Saving you from Beulah," she clarified.

Some of the suspicion left his face. "I was afraid you were starting a rumor about us to make Craig jealous."

Sydney considered this. "That might be a good side benefit."

When Henry Lee came in, he asked why Sydney had all her hair pulled back, and she told him that her grooming decisions were none of his business.

"Why are you so mean to him?" Cole asked when Henry Lee was gone.

"Henry Lee?" Sydney was surprised by the question.

"I understand why you wouldn't want to encourage his obvious infatuation, but it seems like you're unnecessarily harsh."

"His family does without because he drinks up most of what he earns." Sydney's tone was curt. "Believe me, he deserves much more grief than what I give him."

Cole glanced down the bar at Henry Lee who was slurping loudly. "I guess you're right."

The hostess seated customers at table three, so Sydney went to take their orders while Cole returned to table eight and his sister. As Carmella had predicted, the crowd grew steadily. Sydney was trying to keep up with the Braves game as well as her tables and didn't see Rachel come in until her sister was standing by the bar.

"Are you here to discuss the big forty-sixth anniversary party again?" Sydney asked, looking over to see Rachel's husband, Bill, sitting with Cole and Michelle at table eight.

"No, Michelle called and asked us to meet them here." Rachel waved toward Cole's sister. "Bill was worried about going someplace where alcohol is served, but I told him lots of ward members come here now that Lauren is a regular performer." She popped a cocktail peanut into her mouth. "I'm excited about visiting with Michelle. I haven't seen her for years. And why didn't you tell me that you and Cole were dating?"

"It's a recent development," Sydney replied absently. "Why is Michelle here?"

"She said she came to convince Cole to sell the farm to some people from Nashville."

"She knows Cole wants to raise cows. Why would she ask him to sell the farm?"

"Because the folks from Nashville have offered almost a million dollars for the land, and they all own equal parts of it!" Rachel exclaimed. "Their mother made arrangements for Cole to work the farm, but if he sells, they all get a third. She thinks it's ridiculous and selfish of Cole to squeeze out a meager living on the farm when he could sell it and make them all rich."

Sydney's eyes narrowed as she listened. "But they shouldn't pressure him to sell. His sisters ought to care more about his happiness and less about money."

"Things like this often cause problems in families. There was a similar discussion when you moved in with Grandma," Rachel said. "Rebecca thinks Grandma might leave her house to you when she dies, which wouldn't be fair."

Sydney ignored the sudden ache in her chest. "I can't believe that during the worst time of my life, the two of you were worried about a house you don't need." She wasn't close to her sisters, but she had never doubted their love. And Grandma's eventual departure from this earth was not something she ever allowed herself to think about.

"Of course we care about you more than the house!" Rachel answered with feeling. "But the subject did come up."

"How much could that house possibly be worth?" Sydney demanded. "Fifty thousand?"

"Rebecca had it appraised at $64,500," Rachel admitted reluctantly. "Now don't get mad!" She spoke quickly in response to Sydney's murderous expression. "Divided three ways that's over twenty thousand each. Then there's the furniture, a lot of which has sentimental value. Rebecca learned to play on that old piano, and Grandma told me years ago that I could have her antique bedroom suite."

Sydney put a hand to her head. It was beyond morbid to think that they had made plans for Grandma's furniture while she was still very much alive, and more painful than she could bear that they begrudged her an old house full of old junk when she had nothing of her own.

Swallowing her hurt, Sydney squared her shoulders. "I've got to get back to work."

"I'm sorry I brought it up." Rachel reached out and touched her hand. "Please don't say anything to Rebecca. She'd be so mad at me."

Sydney murmured that she wouldn't mention it. "I was only trying to point out that it's not unreasonable for Michelle to take an interest in her inheritance." Sydney continued to stare in stony silence and finally Rachel sighed. "Don't you take your break at ten?" At that very moment, the relief waitress walked up.

Bill and Cole stood as the sisters approached table eight. "We thought you two were going to spend all night talking to each other," Michelle said.

"We were just going over a little family business," Sydney replied shortly. She didn't exactly dislike Michelle, but the woman had that irritating, big sister, I-know-more-than-you-ever-will kind of attitude.

Sydney had mentioned to Carmella that it was Cole's birthday, and she had obviously shared this information. As soon as they were seated, Starla brought Cole a piece of fresh peach pie with a candle in the middle. Then all the waitresses surrounded his chair and sang to him. Cole looked embarrassed by the attention, but he was a good sport about it. When the singers left, Michelle begged Cole for a bite of his pie, and he pushed his plate across the table to her.

"Did you ask Cole about the witches?" Rachel said to her husband.

"Rachel!" Bill protested.

"Well you know everybody in town is talking about it. I might as well get the story straight." Rachel was unrepentant.

"What witches?" Sydney and Michelle asked almost in unison.

"On Monday we found a couple of our yearlings shot and partially burned. The area was littered with beer cans, so I think it was some drunk teenagers," Cole explained reluctantly.

"The broken fence?" Sydney gasped, realizing the correlation.

"Probably," Cole acknowledged.

Rachel rejoined the conversation. "I saw Edith Wilkerson, the police dispatcher, today and she told me that she heard from an unimpeachable source that the cows were killed by witches making burnt offerings on Cole's farm."

"Why are you talking about witches?" Lauren Calhoun asked as she walked up.

"Because Cole has some," Michelle said. Lauren paled and turned to Cole.

"I don't have witches," he denied.

"Edith Wilkerson is the police dispatcher, and she says he does," Michelle told her sister.

"Edith Wilkerson?" Lauren's voice was barely above a whisper.

Rachel shrugged. "Edith says that the Civitan Club discussed it on Tuesday night, and the Presbyterians started a petition for the mayor this morning. Everyone is afraid that if a few witches take up residence here, before long we'll have a coven."

"A coven?" Cole raised an eyebrow.

"That's a bunch of witches living together," Rachel provided knowledgeably. "Edith says they could take over the whole town and cause our property values to drop."

"For heaven's sake," Sydney scoffed.

"You can make fun of me if you want to, Sydney, but the whole town is talking about it and people are really worried," Rachel insisted.

"Is witchery a religion?" Michelle asked the group. "Because if it is, they would be protected by the Constitution to practice what they believe."

"The Constitution does not give anyone the right to steal my cows and burn them on my property," Cole said. "But I think it was just kids. As soon as we get this hay delivered, Lamar and I are going to set a trap and see if we can catch them."

"Let me know when you're going to be watching, and I'll send Darrell over to help," Lauren offered.

Cole shook his head. "Lamar still hasn't forgiven Darrell for firing him while I was on my mission, and I'm afraid if they get together I'll have more trouble. But thanks anyway."

When Lauren walked to the stage for her first performance, Sydney excused herself and went back to work. Bill and Rachel stayed until eleven, then left saying they had to get up early the next day.

After clocking out at midnight, Sydney passed through the main room and saw Cole standing by the door. "Where's Michelle?"

"She rode home with Lauren. They're going shopping in Columbus tomorrow."

"I thought Lauren's car didn't work, and that was why you have to bring her every night."

Cole shrugged. "She bought a new car a week ago, but I'm in the habit of coming and we've established that I don't have anything better to do." Cole held the door open for her. "I'm sure they are planning to ambush me during dinner tomorrow about selling the farm and marrying Beulah. So, I was thinking that maybe the two of us could do something," he suggested casually, and Sydney gave him a startled look. "Since we're dating and all."

"Like what?" Her tone was cautious.

"We could go out to dinner, and maybe Craig will find out and get insanely jealous," he broadened the possibilities. "And if I get home late enough, I'll avoid a family confrontation."

"They'll catch up with you eventually."

"I know, but I want to delay it as long as possible."

"I can't very well say no on your birthday," Sydney grumbled. "Will you pick me up or what? I never dated anyone but Craig and that's been years, so I'm rusty on this type of thing."

"I'll pick you up when I bring Ryan home," Cole said. She nodded, then got into the car.

All the way home to Grandma's she regretted her acceptance. What could she have been thinking? She couldn't possibly go on an actual date. Then she remembered Cole's remark that a date with him might make Craig jealous. It was a long shot, but at this point anything she could do that might distract Craig from Peyton Harris was worth a try. So by the time she walked in the front door, she had talked herself back into going.

CHAPTER SIX

On Thursday morning Sydney dropped the kids off at school, then drove to Carmella's house. Her friend walked out in a broad-brimmed straw hat and sunglasses. "I'm not a morning person," she said in response to Sydney's arched brow. "And I can't believe you even want me to help you shop after our hair disaster."

"I'm bringing you along so I'll know what not to buy," Sydney teased. "Whatever you like, I won't even try on."

"You never did tell me why you have suddenly decided to improve your wardrobe." Carmella used the vanity mirror under the passenger side sun visor to apply lipstick.

Sydney grimaced. "That's because I'm afraid you'll jump to the wrong conclusion."

Carmella turned to face her, the Mary Kay Rustic Coral suspended in air. "You're going out on a date?" Her tone was incredulous.

"Yes and no."

Carmella squealed.

"I knew you'd misinterpret things! I'm just helping out a friend and hoping to drag Craig's attention away from the lovely Peyton Harris for a little while."

"Who's the guy?" Carmella put away the cosmetics and gave her full attention to Sydney.

"Cole Brackner," Sydney admitted reluctantly and Carmella screamed again. "I told you, it's just a friendly date," Sydney reiterated.

"Starla's going to be furious," Carmella predicted with relish as they pulled into the new shopping center called Lakeside Place.

Carmella proved to be a tenacious bargain-finder with a good sense of style. Besides that, she was brutally honest. "You're too old for that," she said about a skirt and knit top. "That makes your hips look huge," about a pair of jeans, and "even my grandmother wouldn't wear that," about a sweater.

They left the mall at noon with two new dresses appropriate for church and a pants outfit for her date. "You've been so helpful, I'm going to take you out to lunch," Sydney offered magnanimously. "Where would you like to go?"

Carmella declined twice, as southern etiquette required, then suggested they go to Lorene's Tea Room. Lorene's was a new restaurant built inside an old house in downtown Eureka. It was a prissy, feminine place that only served lunch, and Sydney would have preferred to go elsewhere. But it was Carmella's reward, so she agreed.

Sydney started feeling claustrophobic the minute they walked into the restaurant. Tiny tables were jammed into every available inch, indicating that Lorene was determined to make the most of her luncheon crowd. Sydney and Carmella were already seated in the Wisteria Room before they noticed that Peyton Harris and another woman were at the adjacent table. All the women exchanged wary nods.

A harried waitress dropped off abbreviated menus showing five lunch specials. Sydney studied her options, trying to ignore Peyton, who was sitting so close that their elbows almost touched. Carmella asked what she was having and Sydney shrugged.

"The vidalia chicken was good," Peyton Harris said waving toward her partially empty plate. "It comes with a broccoli rice casserole and glazed carrots."

"That sounds okay." Carmella scrutinized both plates on the neighboring table.

"Cajun shrimp," the other woman provided. "With wild rice and green beans. Not bad, but the chicken looked better."

The waitress skidded to a halt by their table, and they both ordered the vidalia chicken. As the waitress rushed off, Peyton introduced her companion as Marcie Heinz, her valued personal assistant.

"Marcie just drove in from Nashville," she added as Sydney and Carmella supplied their names.

"Has she come down to help you pack to go home?" Sydney asked hopefully and Carmella kicked her under the table.

Peyton smiled. "No, actually we're going to set up a temporary office at the hotel. Mr. Brackner's stubbornness and my injury have caused us to get behind on our other clients. Rather than give up, I asked Marcie to come here so we can conduct business as usual."

This was a tremendous blow, but Sydney kept her face blank. Carmella asked about their business, and the women began an in-depth explanation of the property acquisition market. Their food arrived and they ate while listening to Peyton and Marcie describe how they had built their business from nothing. By the time her plate was clean, Sydney had to admit that if she didn't have a preexisting prejudice against the woman, she would have admired Peyton Harris.

"As soon as the Brackner case is settled, Peyton is going to join the biggest acquisitions firm in Nashville," Marcie related with obvious pride. "And we'll have a nice office downtown."

The waitress hurried over and asked if she could get them anything else. Sydney was dying for a piece of praline pecan pie, but resisted the self-destructive urge. The waitress passed out the checks, and the women walked together to the cashier counter. After paying for their meals, they gathered on the small front porch.

"Well, it was nice to meet you," Carmella told the secretary politely. "And to see you again, Ms. Harris," she added.

"Please call me Peyton," the blonde invited her. Before Carmella could respond, the roar of an engine followed by several backfires interrupted them. They watched in fascination as an ancient blue car pulled up to the curb. The driver's side window was covered in opaque plastic so they couldn't see the only occupant until he stepped out onto the sidewalk. Sydney gave him a cursory glance, but Carmella continued to stare as he peered toward Lorene's.

"I wonder who in the world that is?" Carmella breathed as she examined the man's dusty work pants and stained T-shirt.

Sydney wasn't interested in the man's identity, but she did want to put some distance between herself and Peyton Harris. "Probably a bum from the rail yard," Sydney guessed as she moved toward the steps, but Peyton was blocking her exit and seemed paralyzed by the man on the sidewalk.

"Unless I'm badly mistaken," Peyton whispered finally. "I think he's my father."

Carmella and Marcie gasped in unison, and Sydney swiveled her head back to study the tramp. The man was tall and thin, probably around seventy, with snow-white hair that brushed the collar of his dirty shirt. Peyton stood her ground as the man approached.

"You wouldn't return my phone calls," he said when he was close enough. "I went to your office and saw the note on the door about you working in Eureka for a while. So I called the number where you could be reached and got the name of your hotel, then headed down here. Had a flat tire just outside of town, and it took me forever to get the lug nuts off." He wiped his greasy hands against his pants self-consciously. "Woman at the hotel desk told me she had recommended this place." He waved at Lorene's. "So I came over."

Everyone waited for Peyton to respond, but she didn't. Instead she turned and walked to the parking lot. Marcie followed right behind her, risking one quick look over her shoulder before climbing into the rental car with her boss. After Peyton drove out of sight, Sydney turned her eyes back to the old man, who was standing dejectedly on the sidewalk. "Would you like a piece of praline pecan pie?" She pointed at Lorene's and he cocked his head to one side.

"You a friend of Peyton's?" he asked.

"In a manner of speaking," Sydney replied carefully. Peyton's obvious aversion to her father seemed like a hopeful sign. Maybe if this bum stayed in Eureka, Peyton would be encouraged to leave.

"I can't go in a fancy place like that dressed like this." Dust billowed off his pants as he patted a leg. At that moment a group of middle-aged women came out of Lorene's and gave him collective contemptuous glances while passing by at a safe distance.

"There's a Dairy Queen down the street, and their grilled chicken combo is delicious," Sydney said.

Peyton's father smiled. "Now you're talking."

"I'm in the Crown Victoria." Sydney descended the steps to stand beside the old man. "Follow me and I'll buy you lunch."

"What are you doing?" Carmella hissed as they climbed into Grandma's car.

"Trying to get that woman away from my husband," Sydney replied.

"You don't have a husband!" Carmella whispered, looking stealthily in the vanity mirror. "Oh gosh! He's right behind us!"

"I told him to follow me." Sydney was unconcerned. "I'm going to invest a couple of dollars in a cheap meal and find out why his daughter won't even speak to him."

Against Carmella's advice and finally pleadings, Sydney pulled into the Dairy Queen, then waited by the door for Peyton's father.

"Clyde Harris," he said, extending his hand when he joined them. Sydney made introductions on the way inside. Clyde stepped up to the counter and ordered the grilled chicken combo and after Sydney paid, they settled into a booth in the back. Mr. Harris took several big bites out of his sandwich, then apologized to the ladies.

"Sorry. I haven't eaten since last night when I boiled a few eggs on my campfire."

"You spent the night outside?" Carmella was shocked into the conversation.

"No point wasting money on a hotel room when it's only me. Besides, I like to camp. I just pull off the road, park my car, and roll out my sleeping bag."

Carmella continued to stare at him in horror, but Sydney was unconcerned about his sleeping arrangements. "Peyton didn't look too happy to see you," she said bluntly, and Carmella turned to include Sydney in her scandalized gaze.

Mr. Harris put down his sandwich and sighed. "I was a terrible father," he said sadly. "I married late in life and had a hard time adjusting to a family. It's not much of an excuse . . ." He shrugged. "I loved Peyton's mother, but having to answer to someone for everything I did was hard to get used to. Then the baby came along." He shook his head. "She cried all the time and Maxine was always after me for money to buy clothes or some baby gadget or to pay a doctor bill. It got to where I dreaded going home." This comment brought Craig to mind, and Sydney controlled a shudder.

"So I took a job down in Louisiana on an offshore oil rig. The pay was good, but you had to sign up for eighteen months at a time.

Maxine hated it at first, but after a few years she quit complaining. For a while I came home to visit during my time off, but it was uncomfortable for everyone and finally I stopped. Maxine never divorced me until a couple of years ago when she wanted to marry someone else."

Sydney gleaned the basics from his discourse. "So, Peyton doesn't even know you? She hasn't seen you in years?"

The man nodded. "I'm a solitary kind of person, never been unhappy alone. But after I got the papers saying Maxine and me was divorced, it made me start thinking. Peyton is all I have in the world as far as family. So I called her, but she won't talk to me. Been trying for months. I'm hoping it will be harder for her to dodge me here."

The possibilities seemed endless, and Sydney's mind was reeling as she patted the old man's hand. "Stay here and finish your lunch, Clyde. I have an idea." She went to the pay phones and called Lakeside Hospital. When the operator answered she identified herself, then asked the woman to page Dr. Craig Cochran and tell him it was important. She waited impatiently until Craig's anxious voice spoke into the phone.

"Sydney?" he said urgently. "Did something happen to one of the kids?"

"The kids? Oh no." She realized that this was a reasonable conclusion. "The kids are fine, but I do have another little problem. You remember Peyton Harris, the woman who's trying to get Cole Brackner to sell his farm?" she questioned with exaggerated naiveté.

"Of course I know Peyton," Craig responded.

"Well, her father has just arrived in town and he needs a place to stay . . ."

"Peyton's father is in Eureka?" Craig asked and Sydney confirmed that he was. "She didn't mention that he was coming."

Sydney ignored the racing of her heart at the revelation that Craig and Peyton had talked about things of a personal nature. "His visit is sort of unexpected, I think. But he was trying to decide the best way to meet up with Peyton, and I had this idea. I thought maybe you could invite her to The Lure tonight for a surprise reunion with her dad."

"Sure," Craig agreed, so stupidly pleased to have a reason to call Peyton that he didn't sense any danger.

"I don't know that much about hotels and stuff. I was hoping you could recommend a good, cheap place," Sydney hinted.

"He can stay with me," Craig offered like an idiot. "I have plenty of room and they can come over and visit after we eat at The Lure."

"I'm sure it will be an evening Peyton will never forget." Sydney smiled. "Where do you want Mr. Harris to meet you?"

"Where are you now?" Craig asked and Sydney told him the Dairy Queen downtown. "Bring him out to the house. I can be there in fifteen minutes," he said, then ended the call.

Trying to keep the satisfaction from showing in her face, she walked back to the booth. She explained the arrangements on the way out to the parking lot, and Carmella sat in stony silence as they rode to the house where Sydney had planned to live for the rest of her life. Craig was standing in the driveway, still dressed in his hospital scrubs, and if he was surprised by Mr. Harris's appearance, he was too polite to say so. Sydney watched as they shook hands, then Craig helped the old man get two battered duffel bags from the trunk of the car. It took Clyde several tries to get the trunk lid to stay closed and then they walked toward the house.

"I'll make reservations for eight at The Lure!" Sydney called after them and Craig nodded.

"You ought to be ashamed," Carmella scolded as they drove away.

"Have you lost your mind?" Sydney demanded. "After all he's done to me?"

"But that poor old man hasn't done anything!" Carmella pointed out. "He's lonely and trying to win Peyton's love. You could ruin all his hopes by your little surprise meeting."

"Well, I guess it was just his bad luck to run into me today," Sydney answered. Carmella refused to speak to her the rest of the way to her house, but as she got out of the Crown Victoria, Carmella leaned down.

"You're not a mean person, Sydney," she said through the window. "You've been hurt, that's all. But this latest scheme is beneath you and I hope you'll change your mind."

"See you tonight," Sydney replied, putting the car into reverse.

Cole Brackner was gone delivering hay when Sydney dropped Ryan off after school, but Lamar promised to take good care of the boy until Cole returned. Reassured but still uneasy, Sydney headed home. Miss Glida Mae met her in the driveway.

"Heard you've got a date tonight," the neighbor said without preamble. "First one since your husband left you. That's good. It's a healthy sign." The butterscotch curls bobbed. "If there is anything I can do to help—makeup, hairstyling, whatever—let me know. I'd be glad to give you the benefit of my experience."

"Thanks," Sydney said as she took her purchases from the back seat. "But it's nothing special. Just dinner with a family friend."

"New clothes." Miss Glida Mae's eyes zeroed in on the shopping bags.

"Hey, Sydney, Glida Mae," Miss Mayme hollered from her porch. "Heard you're going on your first date since the divorce," she said loudly enough for everyone on the street to hear. "Been shopping too, I see."

Since she didn't trust herself to speak, Sydney walked briskly into the house and left the old women to discuss her private life. "Oh, let's see what you got," Grandma said, turning from the stove when Sydney entered the kitchen.

"Why did you tell everyone I was going on a date?" she asked crossly as Sarah dug through the bags.

"I didn't know it was a secret and I'm so glad for you," Grandma answered.

Sydney took the new clothes from her daughter. "It isn't a secret, but I don't want you to get your hopes up. I'm just doing Cole a favor."

After a shower Sydney put on her new outfit. The dark green color was reflected in her eyes, which encouraged her to apply makeup with more enthusiasm than usual. Finally she was satisfied with her face, but there was really nothing she could do about her hair. There was a knock on the door and she opened it to find Grandma standing in the hallway.

"Don't you look lovely." She put a soft hand to Sydney's cheek, then picked up a damp, goldish curl thoughtfully. "It looked nice last night when you had it pulled back. Give me your brush."

Sydney sat in the chair and enjoyed the sensation of having her hair brushed. Closing her eyes she could almost believe that she was a little girl again, safe at Grandma's house without crushing responsibilities or tragic mistakes in her past. Afraid that if she got too comfortable in the memory she wouldn't be able to face reality again, Sydney opened her eyes and stared at her reflection. Grandma had pulled her hair into a loose bun at the back of her head. The brassy color was less obvious and she looked almost . . . good.

"Thanks, Grandma." Sydney caught the old hand and squeezed for just a second.

"Have fun tonight, dear. And try not to say anything inexcusable."

When Cole and Ryan arrived at seven, Sydney had some Bulk-Up mixed and ready for her son. The boy drank it in one big gulp, then smiled at his mother. "You probably won't have to give me this stuff too much longer," he predicted. "Now that I'm a farmhand I'll be getting all kinds of muscles." His eyes shone, his cheeks were flushed, and he couldn't keep the smile off his face. Sydney knew she should remind him that his farmhand job was only temporary, but she couldn't bring herself to dampen his spirits.

Trent and Sarah came in to hear about his first day of employment, and Sydney asked if he wanted anything to eat. "Naw, Lamar and me ate chili dogs and cheese toast," Ryan reported with pride.

"I," Sydney corrected absently, trying not to stare at Cole, who stood in the doorway looking wonderful in jeans and a dark blue shirt.

"I what?" Ryan asked in confusion.

"Lamar and I, not Lamar and me," she explained.

Ryan laughed, "Sorry, that's the way cowboys talk."

"Tell me more stuff cowboys say," Sarah begged as they walked into the living room.

"You look nice," Cole said as she returned her attention to him. "New hairstyle?"

"Grandma fixed it for me. She's more excited about this than I am."

"Then maybe I should take her," Cole muttered as he led the way out to his truck. He opened the door for Sydney, but she batted his hand away when he offered to help her up.

"I've been climbing into vehicles without assistance for years," she told him.

Cole clasped her fingers and held on tight. "But tonight you are my date and I am a gentleman, even when I'm not dealing with ladies."

Sydney considered his words as she put on her seat belt. "I'm a lady," she said as soon as he was settled behind the wheel.

"Then prove it." He pulled away from the curb and they drove in silence for a few minutes. As they approached the business district of Eureka, Cole glanced over at her. "So, where do you want to eat?"

"I thought we could go to The Lure," she proposed carefully. Cole slammed on his brakes and Sydney fell forward against the restraining safety belt.

"You want to go to The Lure on the one night you're not working there?" he demanded and she nodded. "I thought that was the last place you'd choose."

"The food is good, and it will be nice to be there when I don't have to serve anyone."

"You're sure?" A car behind them honked and Cole moved forward slowly.

Sydney nodded. "I'm sure,"

With a shrug, Cole turned at the next intersection, heading toward Lake Eureka and The Lure.

Sydney got several whistles when she walked into the club. She ignored the compliments but was secretly pleased. Vernon waved from the bar and Starla dropped her tray, which was thankfully empty. Carmella passed by without saying a word, and Henry Lee gave Cole a malevolent look as they seated themselves at table eight.

Starla came up, clutching her pencil in trembling fingers, her expression murderous. "Good evening, Starla," Sydney began. "I think I'll have the chef salad, dressing on the side and a large ice water." The younger woman wrote down the order, her lips compressed in anger. "And I'm going to let Cole taste test it for me, just in case you were planning to sprinkle it with arsenic or something."

Cole gave Sydney a sidelong glance, then ordered a T-bone steak, medium rare, with baked potato. "Why did you say that about the arsenic?" he asked after the waitress left.

"Starla's had a crush on you since the first night she waited on you. She thinks that since you sit at her table I shouldn't go out with you." Cole was still staring at her blankly. "It's like in grammar school when you said you liked somebody, then your friend couldn't like them because you said it first."

"That's ridiculous," he said.

"What about love and romance isn't?" Sydney asked, lifting her shoulder. Starla delivered their drinks, and as Sydney took a sip of her water she saw that Carmella had scribbled a note on the cocktail napkin. "It's not too late."

"What does that mean?" Cole wanted to know.

"Carmella is still upset about my hair. I'm over it, but she can't forgive herself." Sydney angled her chair so that she could see the entrance. While they ate she fantasized about the confrontation between Peyton and her father. Craig and Mr. Harris would arrive first and Sydney would graciously offer them seats at table eight.

They would share some small talk, then Peyton would walk through the door. She would smile at Craig, her newfound friend, and cross the room to meet him. Then she would see the father she hated. Craig would announce that her long-lost daddy was staying at his house. Peyton would react with fury and run from the room, telling Craig never to speak to her again. She would rush to her hotel room, pack her bags, and leave Eureka forever. Cole interrupted her pleasant thoughts by asking her to pass the salt.

Or maybe Peyton would arrive first. She would be seated comfortably at table eight, conversing politely. Craig would walk through the door and his eyes would find Peyton's. Then Mr. Harris would jump out and yell "Surprise!" The smile would freeze on Peyton's lovely face. She would turn confused eyes to Craig. He would explain that her father was living with him and that he had planned a nice little reunion after dinner. Peyton would stand, her eyes cold and her face pale. "You are no friend of mine," she would tell Craig. "I never want to see either one of you again as long as I live." Then she would storm out into the night . . .

"Sydney," Cole's voice penetrated her dream. "You seem distracted tonight."

"What makes you say that?" she returned casually.

"Well, I've asked you three times when Ryan plays soccer on Saturday, and you haven't answered me yet."

She felt heat rise in her cheeks. "I'm sorry. Why do you want to know?"

"I thought I might come. Get more points toward Home Teacher of the Year."

"He plays at nine." She checked her watch and saw that it was 7:50. Someone should be arriving soon. Cole glanced over his shoulder at the door just as Craig and Mr. Harris walked in. Cole turned accusing eyes back to Sydney, but she was too entranced to notice. Craig nodded in greeting and she waved them over.

"Hey, Craig, Mr. Harris," she said cheerfully.

"Call me Clyde," the older man insisted.

"I didn't know you were going to be here tonight," Craig added.

"Cole and I are on a date," she announced, and waited for a reaction.

"Oh, well we don't want to impose." Craig took a step back from table eight.

"Nonsense. There's plenty of room. Have a seat, Clyde." Sydney pulled out the chair next to her, and Peyton's father sat down. Left with no real options, Craig took one of the other empty seats. After introductions, Starla took the new drink orders and then Peyton walked through the door. Sydney felt Cole's eyes on her again, but all her attention was riveted on the woman from Nashville.

Craig's back was to the door, but he seemed to sense her arrival. He turned and went over to meet her. They were a beautiful couple, and Sydney's heart flipped as Craig held Peyton's chair while she sat down. Peyton spoke to Sydney and Cole, then nodded to her father. There were no screams, no recriminations, no hysterics. Nothing. Sydney was devastated.

"So, Mr. Harris, are you going to be visiting long?" Cole said into the awkward silence.

"Not long. I just came here to see Peyton. She takes her job real serious, and I've had a hard time catching up with her."

"She has certainly left no stone unturned in trying to make me sell my farm," Cole agreed. Peyton was too busy looking into Craig's eyes to respond. "Are you from Nashville?" Cole continued as the lovebirds gazed at each other and Sydney watched in horror.

"I don't know if I could say I'm really from anywhere. Born in Tupelo, but my folks moved around a lot. Ended up in Nashville working construction during the late sixties. That's where I met Peyton's mom. Lived there for a few years, then started working on oil rigs off the Louisiana coast. Since I retired I just drive around. Been out to the Grand Canyon, even stayed in Hollywood for a while."

"Did you see any movie stars?" Starla wanted to know when she came to take orders.

"Lots of them," Clyde affirmed. "Then I drove up to Canada, but when the weather turned cold I headed south. Ended up back in Nashville and decided to try to make things right with Peyton. But she took off to Eureka, so here I am."

Orders were placed and Starla left. Sydney cleared her throat. "I thought you didn't want to see your father," she reminded Peyton and the other woman nodded.

"I didn't, but Craig convinced me to at least talk to him." Peyton laughed at Sydney's startled expression. "He told me you thought it would be nice to surprise me, but he decided that we should discuss it first." Peyton turned adoring eyes back to Craig for a few seconds.

"Clyde doesn't have long to live," Craig disclosed solemnly, and Sydney looked at the old man, who inclined his head in acquiescence.

"I've agreed to talk." Peyton pointed a finger at her prodigal parent. "But I'm not making any promises about the future."

Another uncomfortable silence settled over the table. Finally Cole asked a question about the Grand Canyon, and Clyde was off, moving from one adventure story after another. Soon everyone was laughing except Sydney, who was trying hard not to lose her dinner. When Starla arrived at her elbow and placed a Sprite by her plate, she shook her head. "I didn't order that."

"It's on the house," Starla replied. Sydney glanced down to see "Serves you right" written on the accompanying cocktail napkin. Starla asked if anyone wanted dessert, but only Clyde did. He ordered a piece of pecan pie with vanilla ice cream on top.

"Ever since you mentioned pecan pie this afternoon I haven't been able to get it off my mind," Clyde told Sydney and she responded with a weak smile.

"Well, if you don't want anything else to eat, I guess we'll be going," Cole said to Sydney. His voice sounded cold and unfriendly.

Sydney didn't want to leave. If she stayed maybe she could somehow think of a way to distract Craig from Peyton Harris and avert disaster. But Cole stood up and pulled her chair back. "Thanks for your help, Miss Sydney," Clyde Harris said as his pie arrived. "This sure is a nice, friendly town."

Cole led Sydney outside and opened the door of his big truck. She expected him to condemn her actions, but instead he drove in determined silence. Sydney was uncomfortable at first and angry by the time they pulled up in front of Grandma's. "Well, have you got anything to say for yourself?" he finally asked as they sat in the dark.

All her frustration and hurt welled up, and she lashed out at him, "I don't owe you any explanations!"

He considered this for a few seconds, then closed the distance between them. Sydney was too stunned to resist as his arms went around her and his lips pressed against hers. As the shock wore off another, a much more unsettling sensation took its place. Her limbs grew languid, her head heavy, and her mouth met his eagerly. When her hands moved up behind his neck, he pulled away. Embarrassed, she glared at him. "Why did you do that?"

He met her eyes with a hard look of his own. "You used me tonight and I figured you owed me something."

Sydney tried to laugh, but it came out more like a strangled cry. "Well, I hope that kiss was worth it."

"Why don't you tell me?" he replied.

With a snarl she pushed open the passenger door and rushed into Grandma's house.

"You're home sooner than I expected," Grandma said as Sydney hurried through the kitchen.

"Cole has to get up early tomorrow," she answered briefly, then went up to her room and closed the door. She wrapped her arms around herself and tried to regroup. The evening at The Lure had been a catastrophe. Now Craig and Peyton were closer than ever. Cole, Starla, and even Carmella were mad at her. But worst of all, she'd been kissed by Cole Brackner, and she had liked it. She needed time to think, to pray, and possibly to call a 1-900 help line. But before she could decide upon an immediate course of action, Sarah and Trent called to her from the hall.

"Let us in, Mom," Sarah demanded.

"Tell us about your date," her son added.

"Did you bring me anything?" Sarah continued to pound on the door.

Sydney reluctantly turned the knob and admitted them both. She apologized for not bringing Sarah a souvenir and told Trent that her date was nice. "So, are you and Brother Brackner going to get married?" he wanted to know and Sydney laughed, remembering Cole's expression as she left the truck.

"No, Brother Brackner and I will not be getting married."

"Darn!" Trent said and Sydney reprimanded him for his language. "Well, if you marry Brother Brackner I can keep Old Joe forever."

"You did have fun, though?" This from Ryan, who was now standing in the doorway. "I thought he might come in for a while."

"He was tired," Sydney answered briefly. Then she checked homework and rushed the kids through their baths with a reminder that it was a school night. Throughout the evening, as she scrubbed the tub, kneaded bread dough, and ironed clothes, her fingers kept straying to her lips. It had been so long since she had been kissed. That had to be why she couldn't forget the feeling of Cole's mouth on hers.

On Friday morning Sydney met Mr. Camp heading to his car when she came back from dropping the kids off at school. "You're up and out awfully early," she commented and the little man nodded.

"Mayme wants a paper."

"Morning, Sydney," his wife bellowed from her front porch. "How was your date last night?"

"It was fine, thank you."

"Glida Mae said you and that Brackner boy were necking in his truck."

Blushing scarlet, Sydney shook her head. "It was just a friendly good-night kiss."

"Cole kissed you?" Grandma stepped down from her porch and out into the yard. "I can't believe you didn't tell me."

"It was nothing Grandma," Sydney insisted.

Grandma didn't look convinced, but she turned from Sydney to Mr. Camp. "Where you off to so early, Woodrow?"

"Miss Mayme wants a newspaper," Sydney provided.

"I've got a morning paper in the house you can have, Mayme," Grandma called over to her neighbor.

"Camp!" Miss Mayme shrieked. "Nelda has a paper so you don't have to go to the Quick Mart!" Mr. Camp closed the car door and shuffled back toward his house. "Glida Mae said there was a coupon for buy-one-get-one-free toilet paper at the Piggly Wiggly," Miss Mayme yelled.

"Oh, I've already cut that out," Grandma said regretfully.

"That's all right. Camp can go get me one." Miss Mayme rounded on her spouse, who was on the second porch step. "Camp! Nelda's already cut the coupons out of her paper. Go on to the Quick Mart and get me another one!" Mr. Camp turned and descended the stairs.

"I don't really need toilet paper this week," Grandma said after brief consideration. "I'll give you the paper and the coupons."

"You sure you don't need them?" Miss Mayme demanded.

"Absolutely."

"Camp! Nelda says we can have the coupons!"

Mr. Camp was almost back to his car when his wife screamed again. He looked up at Sydney. "Am I going or staying?" he asked wearily.

"I think you're staying," Sydney whispered. "I'll bring you the newspaper in just a minute, Miss Mayme," she called over her shoulder.

When Sydney got back from delivering the paper, she found Miss Glida Mae sitting at the kitchen table. With a sigh of despair, she braced herself for the verbal onslaught.

"So, when are you and Cole Brackner getting married?" was Miss Glida Mae's first question. Sydney assured her that they had no such plans. "Hmmm," she mused. "You're not getting involved in those witchcraft doings out at his place, are you?"

"I've never seen a witch on his farm," Sydney said, then thought about Peyton and wondered if she was lying. "Has your stalker been around lately?" she changed the subject.

"Oh, I see signs of his presence all the time. I know he comes to my house almost every night, but I've decided that he is motivated by love and means me no harm. It's something that people in the public eye have to learn to live with." Grandma came in then, and Sydney made her escape before she laughed out loud.

When she picked the kids up at school they reminded her that Monday was Halloween. Sarah begged for a Little Mermaid costume, complete with the fishtail, but Sydney convinced her to wear the generic princess ensemble from the year before. "It still fits you and everyone thought you were so cute!" Trent said he was just going to be a dead guy, and Ryan claimed that middle school students were too mature for Halloween.

Sydney was relieved that Cole was gone on an errand when she dropped Ryan off at the farm that afternoon. Then she got ready for work and left a little early so that she'd be sure to miss him when he returned her son.

Starla wasn't speaking, which didn't bother Sydney in the least. Carmella spoke but was distant, and that bothered Sydney a great deal. The Lure filled up quickly, and when a group of Auburn students sat down at table eight, Sydney decided that Cole wasn't coming. A few minutes later he walked in and took a seat at table nine.

"You let someone else sit at my table," he said when she stopped by for his order.

"We don't save places here. Just ask Henry Lee." She tipped her head toward the man staring blindly into his half-empty glass. "What are you having?"

"Give me another one of those Sprites with lime for $2.50," he requested and she had to work hard to control a smile. When she returned and placed the glass in front of him, he reached out and clasped her hand. "Last night we were both wrong. What do you say we call it even?"

Sydney sighed. "I guess dating wasn't a good idea."

"We *have* to keep dating," Cole corrected. "My sisters had Beulah waiting at the house when I got back last night, and I had to tell them that we were getting pretty serious to get them to take her home."

"Cole!"

"It'll be fine," he soothed. "And there's no downside for you. You get a few free meals and have someone to sit by at church." Sydney was still frowning as she nodded in reluctant agreement. He gave her a sweet smile and leaned forward. "Just out of curiosity, on a scale of one to ten, how would you rank my kiss?"

She thought for a few seconds. "I'd probably give you a seven, but I'm not a good judge of that sort of thing."

"Just a seven?" he asked and she shrugged. "Well, that gives me something to look forward to," he said, and her brow creased. "Eight, nine and ten!"

She shook her head and went back to work.

The War Eagles never relinquished table eight, so Cole remained in Sydney's section until eleven-thirty, when he waved her over and said he was headed home. Once he was gone the night seemed to stretch out endlessly. She was surprised and pleased a few minutes later when he was back beside her. "Couldn't leave without one more Sprite with lime?" she teased.

He didn't smile. "Someone slashed all of my tires."

"Cole!" Sydney cried. "Did you tell the security guard at the door?"

He nodded. "I told him and he said he'd call the police. I doubt they'll be able to find anything though. It's dark and whoever did it is probably long gone."

"I'll bet all those tires for that huge truck cost a fortune." Sydney thoughts jumped to the practical. "I don't guess they could be patched?"

"Not a chance," Cole reported grimly. "The insurance company will reimburse me for most of the expense, but what's worse is the time it's going to cost me. I'm supposed to make a delivery out of town tomorrow, and I can't do it without my truck."

"Can Lamar deliver it for you?"

"He drives an old Mazda. It doesn't have a trailer hitch and I don't think it could pull a trailer full of hay." Cole sighed. "I'll have the truck towed to the tire place first thing tomorrow morning and hope it won't take them long to put on new ones."

The security guard from the front entrance walked over and told Cole that the police had arrived. With a wave at Sydney he followed the man outside. Sydney wiped off her tables, then found Pinkie and explained the problem. "I was wondering if I can go ahead and leave a little early."

"Why does a customer's tires getting slashed mean you need to leave early?" the restaurant manager asked irritably.

Sydney momentarily regretted some of the harsh words she had spoken to the man in the past, but there was nothing she could do about that now. "I was going to drive him home." Pinkie lifted an eyebrow. "We're dating," she added, but he remained unimpressed. "It's pretty serious," Sydney tried and the ex-fullback sighed.

"I'll have to dock your pay," he warned and Sydney nodded. "And don't make a habit of leaving early just because you have a boyfriend."

"Hopefully he won't get his tires slashed in The Lure's parking lot very often," she replied pertly as she hurried to the back to get her purse. There was a small crowd of people gathered around Cole's huge vehicle by the time she got outside. Two Eureka policemen were examining the damage as Sydney stepped up beside Cole. "Are they going to dust for fingerprints?"

He looked over at her then down at his watch. "You leaving early?"

"Pinkie's letting me go now so I can take you home." Cole's eyes widened, and Sydney couldn't resist adding, "Never say that The Lure doesn't provide excellent customer service."

Cole turned his attention back to the truck. "I doubt if they'll try for fingerprints. Whoever did this wouldn't have touched anything except the knife they used." One of the policemen walked over a few minutes later and confirmed this. He said it looked like a small sharp instrument, something on the order of a pocketknife or switchblade, had punctured the tires. He offered to call in a fingerprint team, but admitted that results were unlikely.

Cole asked for the police report for his insurance, but didn't see any point in a further investigation. Papers were signed, the truck was locked, and then Cole walked with Sydney around to Grandma's car in the back parking lot. He was quiet as they drove and finally she asked if he was upset about his tires.

"It's not just the tires. Have you ever had the feeling that everything is going against you?"

Sydney gave him an incredulous look. "That describes my whole life."

Cole ignored her dark humor. "I've had my share of problems in the past, but lately it seems like there's a cloud over my head that I can't shake."

"You mean the witches and your tires."

"And the mortgage at the bank and Peyton Harris with her endless proposals and my sisters badgering me to sell the farm and date women I don't even know. Then the feed store didn't want my hay, and this afternoon the mayor called and asked me to stop by his office. He had a petition signed by the Presbyterians and letters of concern from two women's groups about the 'occult activities' that they claim are taking place on my property."

"Surely they don't think you could help it that people burned your calves!"

"They think I'm the head witch!" he said wryly.

"That's ridiculous."

"Apparently the mayor doesn't think so. He said the whole community is in an uproar. The Civitan Club is pressuring him to call the FBI, and the Presbyterians have arranged for a specialist from Pittsburgh to come down."

"I didn't know there was such a thing as a witch specialist."

"Well there is," he assured her as they pulled in front of his house. Every light was on and three cars were parked in the front yard. "And on top of that, I have more company," he muttered. Then he looked over at her. "I don't guess you'd be interested coming in?" She shook her head. "How about trying for a higher-rated kiss?"

She smiled but declined again and he sighed.

"It's probably just as well. The way things have been going I'd be lucky to get a two or three on the passion scale." He opened the door and stepped out of the car. "Thanks for the ride."

Sydney waited until he closed the big front door of his house, then turned around and headed home.

CHAPTER
SEVEN

On Saturday morning Sydney got the kids ready to spend the day with their father, then loaded them into the car for the soccer game. Craig's team was just finishing a victory when they arrived. Brittni was nowhere in sight, but Peyton was sitting on the bleachers. Sydney chose seats far away from the beautiful blonde.

Cole walked up just as Ryan's game started. "How'd you get here?" Sydney asked when he sat down beside her.

"Michelle dropped me off. I had the truck towed in to the Tire Warehouse, and I'll call them after the game to see if it's ready."

The game went much as the others before it. The team won, but Ryan only got to play for a few minutes and spent the rest of the time watching from the sidelines. Sydney saw Craig join Peyton during the first period but carefully ignored them. When the game ended Ryan ran to the field gate where Sydney and Cole were waiting. Craig brought his guest over and introduced her to his children. Then he turned to Ryan.

"Good game," Craig told his son.

"I guess," the boy replied without enthusiasm.

"I'd never been to a soccer game before, but it was really exciting," Peyton contributed.

"Well, is everybody ready to go?" Craig asked, rubbing his hands together. "We've got a big day planned." Sydney realized with a sinking heart that Peyton was included in the festivities.

"What about my job at Brother Brackner's farm?" Ryan's features clouded with concern. "I've been feeding his animals, cleaning out their stalls and stuff," he explained to his father.

"And today is payday." Cole pulled an envelope out of his shirt pocket.

"I wouldn't feel right taking your money if I don't do my work today," Ryan said firmly.

"If you're obligated to work for Cole, you go ahead," Craig offered. "Just call me on my cell phone when you're through and we'll come pick you up."

Ryan was pleased, but Sydney refused to be impressed. Craig was just showing off in front of Peyton, playing the benevolent parent. Cole excused himself to call the tire place while arrangements were made for returning the children that night.

"Your time is up at six o'clock," Sydney reminded Craig and he nodded. Then he took the two younger children by the hand and led the way to the parking lot. Sydney watched Peyton glide gracefully beside them.

Cole walked back over with a worried look on his face. "Trouble?" Sydney guessed.

"The Tire Warehouse doesn't have tires to fit my truck. They said they've checked and no one in town has the right size. They'll have to be ordered and probably won't get here until Tuesday or Wednesday of next week."

Sydney told Ryan to get in the car. "I'll take you out to the farm," she offered and Cole accepted with a curt nod. She questioned Ryan about the coach during the ride, but he answered in monosyllables. When they reached the farm, Ryan ran over to the barn where Lamar stood waiting. Cole thanked Sydney for the ride and said he'd go call the other farmer and cancel the hay delivery. He looked so discouraged that even Sydney felt sorry for him.

"How far away is this other farm?" she asked. Granddaddy Lovell had been an avid fisherman, and the Crown Victoria had a trailer hitch used in days past to pull his shallow-bottom boat to the lake.

"About an hour to the north," he responded dully.

"So, if I were to lose my mind and offer to drive you there, I'd be back in time for work?"

Cole gave her a weary smile. "Thanks anyway, but this is my problem."

"There's no question about that," she agreed. "But if you go bankrupt you won't be able to pay my son, and he's got big plans for the money he's earning as your farmhand." Cole watched her closely as she added, "And think how impressed Beulah would be if she were to find out we're not only dating, but I'm helping you around the farm." Her comment caused his expression to become almost hopeful. "And imagine telling the elders quorum president that in addition to visiting the less-active, divorced, single mother assigned to your route, you've actually gotten her to perform a deed of selfless service," she taunted him gently.

This finally earned her a smile. "I'll pay for your gas and buy you lunch," he insisted and she nodded. "Let me get the trailer ready and tell Lamar." He was already walking toward the barn.

Sydney leaned out the window and reminded Ryan to call his father as soon as his chores were finished. Then she moved across to the passenger seat. When Cole came back to the car, he gave her a quizzical look. "I'm loaning you the car, but I'm not going to be your chauffeur," she indicated dryly. He slid behind the wheel and backed over to the barn. It only took a few minutes to attach the trailer full of hay and they were on their way.

Once they were driving peacefully down the highway, Cole glanced over at Sydney. "This is really very nice of you," he said.

"What are friends for?" Sydney controlled a yawn.

Cole gave her another quick look. "If we're going to be real friends, I need to know a little more about you. Why don't you start with your birth and tell me your life story?" Sydney frowned. "Otherwise I might fall asleep and kill us both." She was still reluctant. "You can leave out all the painful parts," he offered. "Just tell me the good stuff."

"That will make for a very short story," she replied and he laughed. Turning sideways in the seat to face him, she began with her conception in Australia and had made it to the sixth grade by the time they stopped for gas. When Cole got back in the car she hoped he'd forget, but he told her to pick up where she had left off. She described high school, her sports careers, the satisfaction she'd found in motherhood. She finished with an exaggerated account of her recent hair-color disaster and had him laughing again before she fell silent.

"You see, you've had some good times," he said. "And what's interesting to me is that none of them involved Craig."

"I purposely didn't mention him."

"Because those memories fall into the painful category." He carefully passed a car that was going even slower than they were. "That's why I can't understand why you care about him and Peyton. You know he doesn't love you and I don't think you love him. So why don't you forget him and look for someone else?"

Sydney stared out the window. "All my life I was taught to grow up and get married in the temple. I thought that if you did that and lived a good life, everything was supposed to work out fine."

"Your righteousness couldn't take away Craig's agency."

Sydney closed her eyes briefly. "I don't want my kids to have to say words like stepmother or half-brother. I want them to have one home, not two."

"I want my financial problems to disappear," Cole spoke softly. "I want my parents to be alive. I want a wife who loves me." He glanced at her, then returned his attention to the road. "We can't always have exactly what we want."

Sydney was still searching for an answer a few minutes later when he pulled off the highway onto an access road that led them to the B&L Ranch. She stayed in the car while Cole arranged for the hay to be unloaded, and by the time he got back, she had a plan. She waited until they were driving back toward Eureka, then sprung her trap. "Okay, now it's your turn. I want the story of your life, starting at your conception."

Cole gave her a startled look. "My parents never shared that particular story with me."

"Well, tell me how they met and when they married. I'll read between the lines." She settled against the old car seat and waited for him to begin. They had just reached his teen years, and Sydney was questioning him closely about early romances, when he pulled into a McDonalds and insisted that he was starving. "Your appetite certainly did manifest itself at a convenient time," Sydney muttered as she climbed out of the car. "And I wish you had told me that I had a Big Mac in my future. I could have been counting the minutes."

He ignored her and opened the restaurant door. When they finished lunch and got back in the car, Cole suggested that Sydney take a nap.

"Oh no you don't. Now, who was your first girlfriend?"

"You mean a girl I liked or one that actually liked me back?" he asked.

She considered this for a few seconds. "Let's skip the puppy love stage and go straight to your first kiss." Cole groaned. "Come on, you didn't make it to a level seven kisser without some practice. Who was it?"

Cole spent the next thirty minutes divulging his love life up to and including his current pursuit by Beulah. Feeling more light-hearted than she had in years, Sydney let out a sigh. "So, after an idyllic youth, you've had a stinky adulthood," she summed up.

"I wouldn't call it 'stinky.'"

"You're over thirty years old, no wife, no kids, and flat broke. And if you've told me the truth, the only kiss you've had in almost five years was from a plump, bleach-blonde divorcée."

"Do you ever give anyone a break?" he pleaded and she shook her head. "I guess my adult life has not been what I would have hoped. But I'm not unhappy."

"You're lonely."

"Only sometimes," he hedged. "And there are worse things than being alone."

"Maybe." They rode in silence for a few minutes, then she slammed her hand on the dashboard, causing Cole to swerve and the trailer to fishtail.

"Why did you do that?" he demanded when he had the vehicle under control.

"Life is just so unfair!" Sydney railed. "And the simplest things could have made all the difference. If I had been born a blonde, for instance." Cole glanced up at her hair. "I mean a real blonde, with a cultured voice and a naturally thin frame."

"Peyton?"

"Then I would have been Craig's type, and he would have loved *me*!" She turned her face to the window, appalled by the emotion in her voice. After a few deep breaths, she continued. "He really likes her. A lot."

"It looks that way."

"Why did she have to be so beautiful?"

"You think that Craig is just attracted by her appearance?" he asked gently.

"What else?"

"I've been around Peyton almost as much as Craig and I'm not in love with her."

"You think he's in love with her?" Sydney cried.

Cole shrugged. "It seems like a distinct possibility, but I doubt that her beauty is all that matters to Craig. You're very pretty—" Sydney interrupted him with a short laugh. "I may spend most of my time with cows, but I know a pretty woman when I see one," Cole insisted and Sydney shook her head in disagreement. "Do you think Sarah is pretty?"

"Sarah is beautiful."

Cole smiled in triumph. "And how often does someone say that you look just like her?"

Sydney waved this aside. "I hate the thought of Craig remarrying, going on happily with a new life and leaving us behind. I have to think of a way to come between them . . ." She sighed. "And on top of everything else, I ate too much at lunch, so I'll probably pop the seams on my waitress pants when I try to squeeze into them tonight."

"If you'd cash Craig's checks you wouldn't have to work at The Lure anymore," Cole reminded her. "You could buy yourself some one-size-fits-all stretch pants and eat as much as you want." Sydney glared at him as they pulled onto the gravel driveway that led up to his farm.

A truck Sydney didn't recognize was parked in front of Cole's house. "The vet's here," he said as he turned off the ignition. "Something must be wrong."

Lamar walked out to the car and sadly reported that when he made his midday rounds he had found twenty cows dead. "About that many more are sick. Doc Gray is up in the west pasture now, trying to see what he can do."

Cole quickly unhooked the trailer. "Any idea what happened?"

"Doc says poisoning of some kind. He's taken samples of the water sources and the feed to send to Auburn. In the meantime we've moved the ones that ain't sick across the road to the winter pasture."

"Do you think Ryan did something wrong . . . ," Sydney began as the horrible thought occurred to her.

"Oh no, ma'am," Lamar said with certainty. "The boy don't go near these cows."

"Ryan feeds the horses and the yearlings. The affected cows are our breeding stock." Cole's mouth was grim and his face pale.

"They're valuable?" Sydney hated to ask.

"Very, some of them almost irreplaceable."

"Doc says he suspects the water. Says it could be gasoline or some other toxic chemical," Lamar said. "Maybe somebody dumped out something nearby and it ran into the creek that feeds the pond."

Cole climbed back into the car, and since the Crown Victoria belonged to her grandmother, Sydney didn't feel that she needed to wait for an invitation. She jumped in beside him and held on as Cole drove toward the pasture. He made a particularly sharp turn, and Sydney slid across the seat and into his arm. She clutched him with one hand and the dashboard with the other as he slammed on the brakes and skidded to a halt by a big metal gate. Wide-eyed and breathless, Sydney climbed out of the driver's door after him, and they walked quickly up to a small grouping of shade trees where the veterinarian stood.

Sydney shuddered as they approached. Large bodies of dead or dying cows were scattered all around the pasture. "What have we got, Dr. Gray?" Cole called as the other man stooped beside a thrashing animal.

"My guess? Antifreeze." The doctor looked at Cole. "And it would take a high concentration to kill this many this fast," he added.

"How many have we lost, total?" Cole asked.

"Twenty-four. Probably lose another ten or so before it's over."

"Nearly a fourth of the herd." Cole closed his eyes briefly.

"I'll stay here a bit longer," the doctor said. "But once they've swallowed a lethal dose, there's not much I can do."

Cole said that he understood, then turned and walked slowly back toward the car. "This is very bad for you," Sydney stated the obvious and he nodded. "Cole, I've been thinking about what you said last night, about how things just keep going wrong for you. Especially after this." She waved around at the dead cows. "I think it's very suspicious." Cole looked up sharply.

"I mean what are the chances of someone having witches burning calves on their property and their tires slashed at a dinner club and their cows killed by antifreeze?" she continued. "This all adds up to more than a streak of bad luck."

Cole opened the car door for her, but she didn't get inside. "I think some of my problems are related to the witch rumor," he said. "Gossip has blown it out of proportion and now the whole town is afraid of me. Some people react to fear by doing crazy things like saying that tires they have in stock won't be available until next week."

"You think the tire people lied?"

"The tires that fit the truck have always been available before. And the feed store told Lamar yesterday that they wouldn't be able to extend us any more credit. They had some flimsy excuses, but none of them were reasonable. I've always paid my bill, and they know that even if I lose the farm they can get what I owe them from the bank. I think some of the bigwigs in town have put pressure on them not to do business with me anymore."

"Because they believe you're a witch?" Sydney asked, causing Cole to smile.

"I doubt the mayor really thinks I'm involved in witchcraft. But he has to keep the voting public happy, and he's very anxious for me to sell the farm to Peyton's client. That would mean more tourists, a higher tax base, and lots of glory for him. So he may be giving the witch rumors a little more attention than he ordinarily would, hoping they will help to push me into a deal with the theme park people."

"What will you do?" Sydney was discouraged by the whole situation.

"I can buy feed from somewhere else, like the place in Columbus. But it will be inconvenient and cost me precious time. The loss of these cows won't have an immediate effect on us, but fewer cows to breed will seriously reduce the farm's future profit potential. That will look very bad when the bank reviews our finances next summer. If things keep getting worse, eventually I may have to go to another town to buy gas and groceries . . .”

"Surely the people of Eureka wouldn't go that far."

"In Salem they killed folks based on the suspicion that they were a witch."

"That was almost three hundred years ago!" Sydney exclaimed.

"In some ways times haven't changed that much. And it might be uncomfortable for my friends, too." He looked at Sydney, and his eyes were full of misery.

"I'm not scared of a bunch of busybodies," Sydney scoffed. "But the important thing is to find out who's behind all this . . ." As she spoke, inspiration struck. "Peyton!" she whispered. "Don't you see, it has to be her. You won't sell your farm so she's going to drive you out!"

Cole's expression was dubious. "She doesn't seem like a criminal."

"Nobody would ever get away with a crime if they *seemed* like criminals!" Sydney exclaimed. "It's so obvious I can't believe you didn't think of it yourself."

"I know Peyton wants me to sell, but I don't think she'd go to these extremes . . ."

"You said fear makes people do crazy things, but money is an even more powerful incentive." Sydney's mind was racing. "If I'm right and Peyton is behind all your problems, and if she's caught red-handed . . ." The thought made her smile. "Then the town will know you're innocent, and she can't try to make you sell your farm if she's in jail. And as a nice side benefit, Craig wouldn't pursue a romance with a prison inmate. So, we've got to think of a plan to expose her."

Sydney glanced at her watch. "But first I've got to get to work! Since you don't have a car, you'd better come with me now. I'll go by Grandma's to change, then we'll go to The Lure and work things out during my break."

Cole had been watching her skeptically as she outlined her suspicions, but when she made this suggestion, he swung behind the wheel and turned the Crown Victoria toward his house. "Let me take a quick shower first."

Sydney waited in the living room with Michelle and heard the old pipes squeal as he turned on the water. Michelle asked about their day and Sydney gave her the high points. The pipes whined again as Cole turned off the water and Sydney fidgeted, wishing he'd hurry.

"It was awfully nice of you to take Cole to deliver his hay today," Michelle remarked. "I've been trying to get him to stay home just one night to visit with me, but he insists he has to be with you at The Lure."

Sydney forced a phony smile. "He's so protective. What can I say?"

Cole rushed in with his damp hair combed back, wearing blue jeans and a white T-shirt. He was carrying a long-sleeved shirt in his hand and slid one arm in as he spoke to Michelle. "You want to come with us?" he offered, his muscles flexing under the T-shirt. He covered the other arm, and Sydney watched as he buttoned. Her breath was coming in little gasps, and she wondered if being around so much hay had given her asthma. "We could eat dinner, then watch Lauren sing," he continued.

Michelle declined the invitation, saying that her family was going to call at eight o'clock and she wanted to be home for that. "Well, if you change your mind, come on. I'll probably be there until late," Cole told his sister as they hurried out the door.

Cole stopped at a gas station to fill up the Crown Victoria on the way to Grandma's house, and they arrived just as Craig was dropping off the kids. "Ryan told me you were having truck problems," Craig said when they passed each other by the back door.

"Yeah, Sydney saved my life," Cole exaggerated, draping an arm around her shoulders. Craig's gaze followed the movement, then he looked back at Cole. Sydney felt warm all over and wondered if she had a fever in addition to her newly developed asthmatic problems.

"Where's Peyton?" she asked as casually as possible.

"I dropped her off at the hotel," Craig replied absently. "Well, I'd better go." He waved to no one in particular and walked down the steps.

"She's probably changing into her witch outfit as we speak," Sydney whispered to Cole on the way to the living room where everyone else was gathered.

"Look what Daddy bought me!" Sarah screeched when she saw her mother. She held up a shimmering Little Mermaid costume with a long, sweeping tail.

"How will you be able to walk in that thing?" Sydney asked crossly.

"There's a place cut out at the bottom for your feet." The child lifted the tail and demonstrated with her hands.

Trent jumped out wearing a pirate outfit. "Dad let me get the sword, a patch for my eye, and a fake scar!"

"I thought you just wanted to be a dead guy," Sydney reminded him.

"Why would I want to be a dead guy if I could be a pirate with a scar and eye patch?" he asked reasonably.

Sydney turned to Ryan who had listened to the exchange in silence. "So, what are you going to be?"

"Dad brought me some real surgical scrubs and a lab coat from the hospital, but I haven't decided if I'm going to wear them or not," he replied with caution.

Sydney was about to say that two days before he'd claimed to be too old for Halloween when Cole spoke from behind her. "I heard some kids at church say that they were going as doctors, so it must be the cool thing to do this year."

"I'll loan you some of my fake blood and you can squirt it on you like you just got through with a real big operation," Trent offered generously. Ryan smiled and examined his costume with new interest.

"Thanks a lot," Sydney muttered as she pushed Cole out of the room with her. Once they were in the hallway, she continued in a quiet tone. "Why did you have to say that?"

"What? I just wanted Ryan to know that other boys his age were dressing up."

"Well I would have preferred for him to give the doctor clothes back to Craig and tell him he didn't want them."

"Even if he does?" Cole asked and Sydney nodded. "I don't understand."

Sydney sighed. "I don't have time for a long explanation. But Craig is always doing sneaky things like taking the kids to nice restaurants and buying them expensive stuff. These costumes are just another example of how he's trying to steal their affection from me."

Cole looked over his shoulder at the boxes still stacked in the corner of the living room. "And you intended to spoil the doctor costume for Ryan just like you did the computer." He tipped his head toward the big boxes. "To spite Craig."

Sydney glanced uncomfortably at the corner and remembered Ryan's enthusiasm when he'd shown her around the computer store before his birthday. She'd been glad that he hadn't pressured her to have it set up, assuming that it meant the gift didn't mean that much to him. But in the narrow hallway with Cole Brackner standing so close she could smell his toothpaste, she had to admit that he was probably right. Ryan was denying himself the pleasure of his new computer because he thought it would upset her if he didn't.

"He can wear the stupid costume," she said finally. "I've got to get ready for work."

She took a quick shower and pulled her wet hair into a ponytail before changing into her waitress outfit. Cole was sitting on a chair in the living room, letting Trent stab him repeatedly with his rubber sword, when Sydney rushed in. "For heaven's sake Trent, put that sword away before you hurt yourself," she instructed. "Everybody give me a kiss. I'm going to be late."

When Sydney and Cole walked into The Lure, he went straight to table nine and took a seat. "Now that we're dating," he said, "I think I should sit at one of your tables."

Sydney rolled her eyes and went to work. Things were busy and she was glad Cole was at table nine. Partly because he didn't order often, but mostly because if he'd been at one of Starla's tables, she wouldn't have had a chance to even speak to him.

Henry Lee had a head cold so he blew his nose continuously. This kept the stools around him empty, which Sydney also appreciated. She made a point of speaking to Carmella every time they crossed paths and finally, when asked about the cute UPS man, the other woman smiled.

"I've been ordering things from catalogs just to give him an excuse to stop by," she admitted. "And he plans his schedule so that he can spend his lunch break at my place."

"That has got to be against company rules," Sydney remarked.

Carmella's forehead creased in confusion. "Why would UPS care where he eats lunch?"

"Because he's fraternizing with a customer."

"What does 'fraternizing' mean?" Carmella demanded, her face flushing. "And it better not be anything bad. We just sit on my porch the whole time."

"I'm sorry!" Sydney hurriedly assured her. She was trying to mend her relationship with Carmella, not make it worse. "I just know how quick you are to trust men, and I don't want you to get hurt. I guess you've checked into his marital status?"

Carmella shrugged. "He doesn't wear a wedding ring." Sydney gave her a disgusted look. "Okay, I'll ask him," Carmella promised as she pushed back into the crowd.

When it was time for her break, Sydney walked over to table nine and saw Maralee Tucker chatting with Cole. After giving Cole a fresh Sprite, Sydney sat down by the Primary teacher. "So, did you drop by to make sure I hadn't forgotten about the bread or to plan a strategy of how you're going to get me out of the car in the morning?"

The teacher smiled. "No, actually I wanted to ask if you'd mind presenting part of the lesson tomorrow. I know the kids get tired of hearing my voice, so I thought you might be willing to tell the story of the widow's mite."

Sydney doubted that the children ever got tired of hearing Sister Tucker's voice but took the piece of paper the teacher extended anyway. "You want me to read this?"

"Just tell the story in your own words," she requested and Sydney agreed with a nod.

Starla passed their table and glared at Sydney. "Starla's taking your defection from table eight pretty hard," Sydney teased. "There probably won't be any more free cheese fries." Cole agreed that his association with Sydney had already cost him dearly.

Sister Tucker looked between the two of them in confusion, and Sydney explained, "Starla waits on table eight where Cole used to sit and she has a crush on him. She was always giving him free food and better than average service. But that's all over now that Cole has switched to my table." Sister Tucker was still staring blankly and Sydney realized that it did seem ungrateful of Cole to desert the young waitress after she had been so kind to him. "Cole had to move to my table since we're dating." Sydney's tone was flippant, but the Primary teacher took her words seriously.

"I had no idea!" Sister Tucker was visibly thrilled and Sydney regretted that she had misled her. She started to clarify the situation when Starla walked behind them to take an order for table six. "I think that is so wonderful, and I'm sorry that I've intruded on your time together." Sister Tucker stood and looped her purse on her shoulder. "I'll see you both tomorrow. And thanks for your help," she added to Sydney and hurried out of The Lure.

"Now it will be all over the ward that we're dating!" Sydney groaned as the teacher left.

"Maralee isn't a gossip, but it's already all over the ward. Between Beulah and her mother and my sisters . . ."

"I get the picture." Sydney opened a package of club crackers and changed the subject. "The more I think about it, the more sure I am that Peyton is orchestrating your various problems," she told him, leaning forward and lowering her voice.

"The more I think about it, the more sure I am that she's not," Cole whispered back.

"You just don't want to believe that a beautiful woman is capable of such ruthlessness. But you've forgotten what she does for a living. She forces people to sell things."

"Forces might be too strong a word, and she does it through legal means."

"How can you be sure?" Sydney demanded. "All we know about her is what she's told us. The people who hired her in Nashville could be Mafia or international terrorists or even Iranian oil barons . . ." Cole waved for her to proceed. "She has her so-called father and secretary as accomplices, and Craig is besotted to the point that he's probably giving them all kinds of information without even realizing it. I'll bet they laugh themselves silly every night thinking about how they are fooling all of us."

"Are you serious, Sydney? You really believe that Peyton is responsible for the problems on my farm?" he asked, and she nodded. "And this isn't just another plan to get back at Craig?"

"I'll admit that having her dragged off in handcuffs before his very eyes is a pleasant thought, but I honestly think that something is fishy and she's the most likely suspect. You probably should call the police and let them question her," Sydney advised him.

Cole laughed at this suggestion. "*I* barely believe any of this, and the Eureka police would think I was just accusing Peyton to deflect suspicion from myself."

The relief waitress walked up and told Sydney that she had already covered her tables five minutes longer than she was supposed to. She said she was now covering Starla's tables and recommended that Sydney do her job before she got fired. Rolling her eyes at Cole, Sydney stood and hurried back to work.

Later the room emptied and Sydney moved over to stand by Cole. They discussed Peyton's possible culpability for a while, and when Sydney started wiping off her tables, he offered to help. "Pinkie is probably searching for an excuse to fire me anyway. If he looks out here and sees Starla's favorite customer washing my tables, I'm history."

Cole smiled. "Well, I can at least call Michelle to come get me so you won't have to drive me home."

"Don't be ridiculous," she said as she refilled the catsup bottles. "Your place is only a few minutes out of the way."

"I don't want to overstep the bounds of our friendship."

"Are you kidding? The way we've been misleading people, they're probably expecting a marriage announcement any day," Sydney said as she straightened menus. "But since I know you don't want to put me to any trouble, you can just drop me off at Grandma's, take the car home, and then pick us up for church in the morning."

Cole smiled. "Beulah will be so impressed when she finds out we arrived together."

"And in my Grandma's luxurious Crown Victoria! She'll probably think you're marrying me for my money!"

"You're getting married?" Starla gasped from behind them.

They exchanged a stunned look. "Not right away," Cole spoke first.

"We're just talking about it," Sydney added immediately and as the waitress walked off, Sydney turned back to Cole. "We may have gone too far."

"Since when has that bothered you?" he asked. "I'll be waiting by the door when you're ready to go."

*   *   *   *   *

On Sunday morning Sydney put on one of her new dresses. It was trendy enough for a divorcée, but not so short that she'd have to be tugging at it all day. She let Grandma fix her hair again and used concealer to cover the circles of fatigue under her eyes.

The bread comparison was a big hit during CTR class and the children listened politely while she nervously presented her rendition of the story of the widow's mite. She started to feel a little anxious when Primary ended, but Trent's teacher asked if she'd make salt clay for their class the next week, and the Young Men president reminded her about the brownies for the fireside. Then Cole came up and put his arm on her back, leading her into the chapel.

"Everyone thinks we're engaged," he reported quietly. "When people asked for details, I just said that we haven't set a date," he added as Bishop Middleton came by and shook their hands.

"I hear congratulations are in order." The bishop's tone expressed some doubt.

"Is that what you hear?" Sydney answered vaguely.

"Thanks," Cole accepted the good wishes.

Sydney sat spellbound throughout the Primary presentation and was sad to see it end. On the way to the Baptist Church that morning Grandma had invited Cole to eat dinner with them, and since they were all sharing the same car, Sydney didn't mind that he accepted. So after the meetings they all piled in the Crown Victoria and went to retrieve Grandma.

When Cole parked the car, Grandma said she would hang up Sarah's Sunday clothes while Sydney worked on dinner. Cole wanted to help, and since he was used to cooking for himself, he wouldn't accept simple assignments like stirring the butter beans or checking the rolls. Instead he arranged the Jell-O salad on lettuce leaves and creamed the potatoes.

"If Peyton succeeds in stealing your farm, maybe I could get you a job as a chef at The Lure," she offered with a sly smile.

He expertly sliced the eye of the round roast into thin, even pieces and placed them on a platter. "Since the manager is about to fire you, I'd probably be better off without your recommendation," he replied as her children took seats around the table.

After the meal Grandma sent everyone into the living room while she cleaned up. "I always do the dishes," Sydney whispered, following

Cole out of the kitchen. "I think she really believes that we're dating and is trying to encourage a romance."

"You're getting a day off so don't complain," he advised. "But you'd better sit here by me or she might change her mind."

Sydney settled on the couch, keeping plenty of space between them. Ryan challenged Cole to a game of chess and pulled out the old cardboard and plastic version from the closet. "It's not nice like yours," he said regretfully.

"I can beat you with plastic men as easily as I can with carved wooden ones," Cole claimed and Ryan's eyes narrowed with the determination to win.

While Ryan was considering his first move, Sarah came through modeling her Little Mermaid costume. Then Trent put in a Book of Mormon video and Sydney curled comfortably into the old couch. She dozed for a few minutes, but woke up when she heard Cole mention the new computer Craig had bought and Ryan mumbled something in response. "Well, it seems a shame for a nice computer like that to just be sitting there," Cole commented and Sydney opened her eyes to glare at him.

"Do you know how to set up a computer?" Ryan asked.

Cole looked surprised. "Me? Oh no." Ryan's face fell. "But I'll bet your dad does." Sydney sat up straight, lifting her lip into a snarl. "You should ask him." Ryan glanced toward his mother and she altered her expression quickly. "Your mom wants you to have the computer. She won't mind." Sydney gave her son the closest thing to a smile she could muster.

After beating Ryan twice and then losing in a suspiciously one-sided final game, Cole stood and said he had to get home. Again he offered to call Michelle, but Sydney said she'd drive him. The kids all wanted to go along and Ryan reminded her that he needed to feed the horses. "You don't work on Sunday," Sydney told him as they climbed into the car.

"But the horses still have to eat. I won't charge Brother Brackner for today."

Unable to fault his logic, Sydney nodded. She had hoped to drop Cole off, let Ryan feed the horses, and then get back home for a nap, but once the car stopped all the kids got out and ran into the barn. Lamar tipped his Braves hat from the door and Sydney waved back.

"Want to come with me to check on my dead cows?" Cole offered and Sydney grimaced. "Actually I'm more interested in seeing how many are still alive," he amended, holding the door open for her. She told her children not to leave the barn and put Lamar in charge. Then she got into the front seat and they rode to the pasture.

There were no more dead cows and two that had been ill were recovering. "What happened to the bodies?" Sydney looked around the empty field.

"Lamar took one to Auburn for an autopsy. The rest we sold."

Sydney made a disgusted face. "Who would want to buy poisoned cows?"

"Obviously they couldn't be used for human consumption, but the hides were good and they use other byproducts to make—"

"That's okay. I don't really want to know," Sydney interrupted.

"We lost forty-two in all."

"Can you buy more?" Sydney asked, leaning over the fence to watch the healthy cows.

"If I had the money I could. I've talked to Mr. McPherson at the bank and he's doing what he can for me. He says we'll just have to see how the directors feel about things when it's time to renew my loan."

They returned to the barn and Sydney gathered her children into the car. Then she drove to Grandma's and made brownies for the fireside. When she dropped Ryan off at church, she saw the Fords in the parking lot. They offered to bring Ryan home and Sydney reluctantly agreed.

Back at home she changed into pajamas and settled down to read a few pages of a romance novel Carmella had given her. She was in the middle of a particularly tender love scene when the phone rang. Since she never got any calls, she ignored it. A few seconds later Sarah came running down the hall. "It's for you, Mom!"

Sydney picked up the cordless receiver warily. "Hello."

"Sydney?" Cole's voice said through the phone lines. She felt herself get hot all over and held a hand to her head. Knowing it was impossible for a person to detect their own fever, she walked to the bathroom in search of a thermometer. "Sydney," he tried again. "This is Cole."

Sydney shook down the thermometer and stuck it in her mouth. "I know who it is," she said around the thin cylinder of glass.

"I hope I didn't interrupt anything." She ignored this and asked why he had called. "I think I left my scriptures in your car. Could you have someone go out and look?"

Sydney pulled the thermometer from her mouth and checked the results. No fever. Shaking her head she walked down the hall and told Trent to search the car for Cole's scriptures. He was back minutes later, breathless and holding a brown leather case by the handle. "Coleman R. Brackner," she read the name inscribed on the front. "What does the 'R' stand for?"

"Ray," he replied. "Can you bring them with you to The Lure tomorrow?"

"Sure. But how will you get around without your truck?" Sydney asked.

"I'm going to borrow Michelle's rental car and find tires for my truck if I have to drive all the way to Columbus."

"Peyton still wins. She'll have you looking for tires instead of working on your farm. And when you get back the rest of your cows might be dead," Sydney warned. "You really should turn her into the authorities."

"You must have been watching reruns of *Dragnet*. 'The Authorities' in Eureka are a few city cops, and they would laugh me out of the county if I told them your crazy theory."

"Let her kill your cows and make pacts with the devil on your property, what do I care?"

"See you tomorrow," he said and she could hear the laughter in his voice.

After they hung up she stared at the scripture case. They weren't hers, but they were just scriptures and not something personal like a journal or diary. So she didn't feel too guilty as she unzipped the case and removed them.

There were no old sacrament meeting programs folded between the pages, no handouts from previous lessons marking a reference, no hastily written talks tucked inside for future use. But Cole had turned these pages reverently, lovingly, and often. As she thumbed from one part to another, placing her fingers on the thin paper, she could almost feel his presence. With a smile she turned to 2 Nephi 31, thinking maybe she could believe the words if she read them from Cole's scriptures.

CHAPTER EIGHT

Sydney woke up on Halloween morning expecting to feel signs of impending illness. But her head was clear, her throat was not sore, and there was no congestion in her chest. In fact, after more sleep than usual, she felt wonderful. Sarah and Trent had parties at school and Ryan was supposed to bring a three-liter soft drink to his English class where they would watch the classic version of *The Legend of Sleepy Hollow* to commemorate the day. Excited, the children didn't require much prodding to get ready.

Once she had the children at school, she stopped by the Piggly Wiggly for the week's groceries. On her way back home she saw Mr. Warren walking his dog along the side of the road. She came to a stop and wished him a good morning.

He leaned forward and returned her greeting. "Been to the store I see." He waved toward the groceries in the back seat.

"Yes, sir," Sydney responded.

"Got some good specials at the Piggly Wiggly this week," he continued and she nodded. "Your grandmother says you're dating an Auburn man."

"Yes, sir, although we're really just friends." She hated to get Mr. Warren's hopes up.

"Can't believe an Auburn graduate would be involved with witch-craft and such as that."

"Cole is not a witch," Sydney assured him. "That is just a malicious rumor," Sydney promised, but Mr. Warren didn't look convinced. "Well, I'd better get these groceries put away before some-thing melts." She waved to Mr. Warren and rolled slowly into Grandma's driveway.

Sydney climbed out of the car and spoke to Miss Glida Mae, who was supervising the placement of sheet plastic over her windows. "So, when are you and that devil worshipper getting married?" the neighbor demanded. "Living next to Mormons is one thing, but Satanists . . ." Miss Glida Mae walked off shaking her head before Sydney could offer a defense.

She saw Miss Mayme watching through her front window as she took the last groceries inside and waved, but the other woman closed the curtain without so much as a smile. "What's wrong with Miss Mayme?" Sydney asked Grandma as they restocked the cupboards. "She watched me unload the car but never came out to speak. Then I waved and she acted like she didn't even see me."

Grandma sighed then turned to Sydney. "Yesterday our Sunday School class discussed Cole and the rumors about witch gatherings on his property. Afterward Mayme said as long as you're dating him, she can't be associated with you."

"How can she believe that I would date a witch?" Sydney put down a bottle of catsup and stared at her grandmother.

"Warlock," Grandma corrected, stacking canned vegetables on a shelf. "And there is so much gossip about Cole, it's hard to know what to believe."

"You think he's a witch, too?" Sydney was astounded.

"No," Grandma answered after only a brief hesitation. Then she moved closer to Sydney and lowered her voice. "But Mayme said that Faydra Simpkins said that Aletha Hall saw a mark on Cole. They thinks it's the mark of the beast."

Sydney raised an eyebrow. "Cole doesn't have any marks on him that I can see."

"Aletha said it's on his back. She saw it when he was a teenager swimming at the city pool." Grandma waited expectantly, and Sydney finally realized that she was waiting for a confirmation.

"I've never seen Cole's back, but I can guarantee you that he is not a witch."

Grandma patted Sydney's arm gently, then shuffled out of the kitchen. As she finished putting away the groceries, Sydney considered the situation. The town was turning against Cole at an alarming rate. Even Grandma had her reservations about his innocence. She wanted to call Cole, but decided he had enough to worry about already.

She had expected Ryan's soccer coach to cancel practice because of Halloween, but when she picked her son up at school he informed her that he had no such luck. "Saturday is our last game, for the league championship," he explained. "So Preston says we'll practice like usual."

Sydney took the other children home and showed them the pumpkin she had purchased at the grocery store. After homework was finished, she helped them carve it. "He's ugly," Sarah pronounced when they finished.

Sydney studied the jack-o-lantern. One eye was larger than the other, the nose was off center and the mouth was an inch lower on the right side than the left. "He's supposed to be scary."

"He looks embarrassed," Trent expressed his opinion.

"Well." Sydney briskly picked up the poor pumpkin and walked toward the front door. "It will be dark outside."

The kids begged to wear their costumes when they went to get Ryan after soccer practice, but Sydney knew the older boy would be mortified. So she compromised by letting Trent take his sword and Sarah wear her mermaid wig. They picked Ryan up at the baseball field, then drove him out to Cole's farm as the sun began to set. Cole met them at the car and admired Sarah's hair and dodged sword jabs from Trent.

"You want to go trick-or-treating with us, Brother Brackner?" Sarah invited. "Mom's going to walk us around the neighborhood."

"You're not working tonight?" Cole addressed Sydney in surprise.

"I'm going in late."

Cole gave Sarah a big smile. "Then I'll take you up on that," he said, and Sydney's eyes widened. "Bankrupt farmers have to cut corners anywhere we can," he explained. "And free candy is something I can't afford to pass up."

Ryan started his chores and the younger children ran into the barn. Sydney stood in the doorway and watched while Trent checked on Old Joe and Sarah hugged her kittens. Sydney had to threaten to cancel Halloween if they didn't get back in Grandma's car.

Michelle came out on the porch as they were leaving and said that she was flying home the next day. "I hope you enjoyed your visit," Sydney felt obligated to say.

"It's been interesting." Michelle looked between her brother and Sydney. "Not as profitable as I had hoped, but definitely interesting."

Sydney turned back to Cole and he leaned close. "You don't mind if I come over tonight, do you?" he whispered. "I'm afraid Michelle and Lauren are going to make a last-ditch effort to force me into a date with Beulah."

"Why are they so dead set on Tiffany Fancher?" Sydney wanted to know. "If you're showing interest in me isn't that good enough?"

"I figure they've got a deal worked out with Sister Fancher that if I marry Beulah, she'll insist that we sell the farm and move into town. You, on the other hand, are a woman with several children and no home. You might want to keep this place."

Sydney nodded her understanding, then glanced over his shoulder at Michelle, who was still staring. "Well, come on when you're ready. We'll need to leave the house by seven o'clock." Then, on impulse, she reached up and kissed him lightly on the lips. "That's for Michelle," she said as she felt her temperature rise again. She put a hand to her head and frowned. "Of course, if I make you sick I won't be doing you any favors."

Cole was watching her closely. "I'll risk a few germs."

"No, really, I think I'm coming down with something. I don't know what it is, but lately I've been feeling hot all of a sudden. It happened a couple of times on Saturday and then again when I was talking to you on the phone last night," she explained. "I must be getting sick, or maybe I'm allergic to you," she added with a little smile.

"Does your mouth feel dry and your breath comes in little gasps?" he asked. "Then your palms get sweaty and your heart beats fast?"

"I'm sorry, Cole." Sydney felt genuine remorse as he itemized her other symptoms. "None of the kids are sick and I didn't know I was contagious. This is the last thing you need."

He broke eye contact and stared out at the horizon. "Yes, this is certainly the last thing I need," he agreed.

"Well, go to the doctor if it gets worse." Sydney walked around the car. "As soon as Ryan gets finished feeding the animals, come on in. It's a school night so the kids need to get into bed at a reasonable hour. And I've got to get to The Lure as soon as possible," she said, and Cole nodded as she climbed in behind the wheel.

Sydney force-fed the children spaghetti, then had them all dressed by the time Ryan and Cole arrived. Grandma got out her camera and took pictures while Ryan changed into his doctor outfit. Just as they were leaving, the phone rang. Cole was bringing up the rear and answered it. After a few words he covered the receiver and spoke to Sydney. "It's Craig. He says his parents want to see the kids in their costumes and wondered if he could pick them up for a little while after they are through trick-or-treating."

Sydney shook her head vigorously. "It's not the third Saturday and it's a school night . . ."

Cole removed his hand from the receiver. "Sydney is concerned about the children being out late because of school tomorrow, so we'll just bring them by right now for a few minutes," Cole said into the phone. Sydney charged forward, but he had already broken the connection before she reached him.

"Why did you say that?" she hissed. "You had no right."

"They just want to see their grandkids dressed up for Halloween," he told her. "It doesn't seem like much to ask."

Sydney was still furious with him, but she didn't really hold Craig's parents responsible for their son's crimes, so she allowed Cole to lead her outside.

"Look, Brother Brackner's truck is fixed!" Trent announced happily as Sydney reached the driveway.

"I got it back this afternoon. How would you like to take a quick ride in my truck to test it out? We could drive it over to show your grandparents how great you all look in your costumes?" he offered and the children started climbing in before Sydney could object. She didn't say a word on the trip to the Cochran's exclusive neighborhood, but the children filled the silence. Nothing could have made her walk up to her ex-in-laws' house, and when Cole saw that she wasn't going to get out, he opened his door and followed her children up the sidewalk.

She could hear Sister Cochran's exclamations of delight and Sarah giggling in response, but she kept her eyes facing the street. Finally they returned to the truck with their bags half full of candy and big smiles on their faces. It was almost seven-thirty by the time they got back to Grandma's house, and Sydney pointed out that they'd already wasted a good bit of their trick-or-treating time.

"Gran gave us so much candy it will be okay if we miss a few houses around here." Trent was philosophical as they climbed out of the truck. They were heading down the street when Brandon Ford and several boys from Ryan's school walked up and invited him to join them. Sydney felt her heart contract, but Cole was already nodding.

"What time do you want him home?" he asked Sydney as if she was a willing participant in the plan. What she wanted was to say he couldn't go, but Ryan looked happy and the Ford boy seemed nice. So she swallowed the lump in her throat and said he had to be back at eight-thirty.

Ryan smiled his thanks, then turned to walk off with the other boys. Sydney fully intended to let Cole know what she thought about his interference with her children, but Trent and Sarah were halfway down the street and she had to run to catch up with them.

Once they got back home Sydney told Trent and Sarah they could eat five pieces of candy before she put it away. As they searched through their loot, Cole begged for Butterfingers. Trent was willing to part with a couple, but Sarah gave Cole a whole handful. He was visibly touched and gave the little girl a hug before returning all except one of the candy bars to her bag.

Sydney stowed the candy in a cabinet, then went to change clothes. Ryan came home with another bag full of candy and was regaling them with his exploits when Sydney rushed in wearing her waitress attire. She supervised teeth brushing, then told Grandma that they had to be in bed by nine o'clock. After a quick kiss for each child, she followed Cole outside.

He offered to drive even though she pointed out that he'd have to bring her home. "You've put a lot of miles on the old Crown Vic over the last few days. It would probably be a good idea to give her some rest." With a shrug, Sydney climbed into the big truck.

The Lure was busy, in spite of the holiday, and Cole had to sit at the bar for almost an hour before table nine became available. After he left, Henry Lee waved Sydney over to the end of the bar. He hadn't bothered her all night, so she assumed he wanted to order a drink. Instead he pulled out a big bag of Halloween suckers and pushed them toward her. "I got these for your kids," he said shyly.

Sydney stared at the candy for a second. "Thanks, Henry Lee, but I think you should give them to your own children," she replied, then walked over to the new customers at table three.

During her break Sydney sat at Cole's table and told him about the new rumor that he had the mark of the beast on his back. "How would anyone know what my back looks like?" he demanded, color rising in his cheeks.

"Miss Aletha Hall said she saw it when you were swimming at the city pool years ago," Sydney explained, then waited expectantly.

"What?" he asked.

"Well, do you have a mark on your back?"

"I don't know! I might have a mole or something. Do you want me to take off my shirt and let you see if I have a birthmark in the shape of a pitchfork or freckles that spell out '666'?"

"No." Sydney looked down at her hands.

Cole sighed heavily. "I'm sorry. I'm just sick of people saying crazy stuff about me. That occult specialist the Presbyterians have hired came out to the farm this afternoon. He found some rocks that he says were arranged into a common occult symbol."

"Oh, Cole!" Sydney was dismayed. "Was it really an occult symbol?"

"It was a pile of rocks!" Cole reported in exasperation. "And he claims that the area where those calves were killed is definitely a sacrifice site."

"So did he say some prayers to cast out the evil spirits?"

Cole shook his head. "That's just in the movies. In real life they give you a subpoena to appear at a hearing on Friday."

"Is it against the law to harbor witches?" Sydney whispered.

"I'm not harboring anybody. If there are witches on my farm they are trespassers. But the city is citing public nuisance, disturbing the peace, violation of obscenity laws—"

"How does witchcraft violate obscenity laws?" Sydney asked.

"Apparently they have a witness who claims that he saw witches on the farm dancing around a bonfire in the nude. It was undoubtedly just a case of wishful thinking, but it gave the Presbyterians another charge to add to the growing list."

"What can they do to you if they find you guilty?"

Cole frowned. "The court can reprimand me, fine me, or put me in jail."

"You need to get yourself a good lawyer," Sydney advised as she stood to go back to work. Then she did a double take when she looked down the counter and saw Henry Lee sipping Coke from the can. "Henry Lee, are my eyes deceiving me?" She approached him quickly. "Or are you drinking something nonalcoholic?"

He blushed and shrugged a thin shoulder. "I'm trying to cut back. I've got a new job and I don't want to lose it," he admitted.

"That's good, Henry Lee. I'm proud of you," she forced the words from her mouth and he blushed even darker. "I'm sure your wife is proud of you too," she added, lest he get the wrong idea.

As they left The Lure that night, Cole told Sydney that he intended to find out who was burning cows on his property. "How are you going to do that?" she asked.

"We'll deliver the last of the hay tomorrow, then Lamar and I can set a trap for them."

"That sounds kind of dangerous," Sydney said thoughtfully. "You're sure you don't want to call the police?"

Cole shook his head. "Not until I see for myself if it really is witches . . ."

"Or Peyton," Sydney contributed.

"Or a bunch of teenagers just messing around," Cole concluded.

"You'll take your cell phone so you can call for help if you need it?"

Cole assured her that he would. "Lamar and I can cover twice as much area together," he said, and Sydney agreed that this was true. "So I won't be able to stay at The Lure until it closes."

Sydney nodded. "I know Lauren will understand."

"Lauren?"

"I mean, I think it's great that you come every night to offer her moral support, but she's been performing long enough now to feel comfortable without you."

Cole was quiet for a few minutes. "What about you?" he said finally.

"What about me?"

"How comfortable will you be when I'm not there?" His tone was soft.

Sydney cleared her throat. "I'll admit that table nine won't be the same."

"You need to either park in front or get someone to walk you to your car," Cole warned.

"I can take care of myself."

"Well, keep in mind that if something happens to you, Craig gets the kids," he offered as a safety incentive just as he pulled up in front of Grandma's. He leaned across to push open the passenger door and paused with his face close to hers. His eyes dropped to her lips and she felt feverish again, in spite of the fact that the door was open and cool air was blowing into the truck.

"I'll remember that," she promised, moving toward him involuntarily. Then they heard a noise from Miss Glida Mae's front porch and she jerked back. "See you tomorrow." Her voice was shaky as she climbed down and hurried into the house.

The next night Cole sat at the bar for an hour, then went home to hunt witches. Sydney called him on Wednesday morning to see if he'd caught anyone. "We stayed up until dawn, but we didn't see anything except each other," Cole told her wearily. "We'll keep trying though. We're bound to run into whoever it is eventually."

"Unless you die of sleep deprivation first."

"I don't think lack of sleep kills you. It just makes you go crazy."

"Going crazy might be worse."

"Spoken like a true expert," Cole teased as they hung up.

By Thursday night there still had not been any witch sightings, but Cole did tell her that he had a lawyer who was going to accompany him to the hearing on Friday morning. "Bishop Middleton and Mr. McPherson from the bank are coming too."

"Do you want me to come?" Sydney offered as she gave him a fresh Sprite.

Cole looked up. "Why would you want to come?"

"Well, I could tell them that I've never seen you exhibit any witchlike characteristics."

"What in the world is a witchlike characteristic?" Cole asked.

"You know—a preoccupation with Latin phrases, obvious warts, and a tendency to wiggle your nose. And we just won't mention the possibility of a beast mark on your back."

"I think I'll be better off if you stay home."

"If they convict you, don't blame me," she said.

"Will you come and visit me in prison?"

Sydney shrugged. "I deal with drunks at night, I might was well visit convicted witches during the day."

When Sydney got up on Friday afternoon, Grandma told her that Cole had left a message for her to call. Grabbing the phone, she dialed his number. "So, you're not in jail," she said when he answered.

"No, the judge dismissed the charges for lack of evidence, but he gave me a stern lecture on how much this community values morality, tranquillity, and Christianity. He said if there were any more complaints, he'd be forced to reconsider."

"Well, it could have been worse."

"I guess he could have searched me for marks," Cole agreed.

"They're probably saving that for next time," Sydney predicted.

Cole didn't make it to The Lure at all that night and Sydney thought closing time would never come. When she clocked out, she almost walked to her car alone, but then remembered Cole's warning about Craig raising her children if she died. With a shudder she turned around and got the security guard to escort her outside.

On Saturday morning Ryan seemed particularly nervous as he prepared for his soccer game and Sydney finally asked if something was wrong. "Nothing's wrong, really. But today we play Dad's team for the championship. Gran and Papa will be there . . ."

"They won't care if you win or lose," Sydney assured him.

"Yeah, but when they see me play, they'll think I'm terrible," he explained desperately.

Sydney wrapped her arms around him. "Just do the best you can. Your grandparents know you're a great kid, and they don't care how well you play soccer."

When they arrived at the baseball field, Ryan ran on to join Mr. Lydell and his teammates while the rest of the family walked over to the bleachers. The Cochrans were already seated on the third row directly behind Ryan's bench. "We want to be sure Ryan knows we're pulling for him, even though Craig is coaching the other team," Sister Cochran explained as she embraced first Sarah and then Trent.

Sydney nodded, trying not to be impressed by their thoughtfulness. They made awkward conversation for a few minutes while the teams warmed up and Cole quietly took the seat beside Sydney as the officials blew the whistle for the coaches to send out their starting teams. They all watched several children run onto the field. "Why is that boy wearing a blue shirt?" Sarah asked pointing to one of Ryan's teammates.

"I don't know. Maybe he couldn't find his uniform this morning," Sydney proposed without interest. The officials reviewed the players, then had a miniconference in the middle of the field. Finally one of the men trotted over to the sidelines and motioned to Ryan's coach. The official spoke in quiet tones, but Mr. Lydell was very vocal in his objections. Apparently there was a rule against playing without a uniform and the official was telling the coach that the boy in the blue shirt had to leave the field.

Mr. Lydell was livid and insisted on talking to the director. Sydney ducked as Mr. Roosevelt walked by on his way to join the fracas. After careful consideration, the director upheld the official's ruling and the coach called them both cheaters. Mr. Lydell was finally forced to accept the decision when the director threatened to expel him from the ballpark.

Reluctantly the coach called the boy in the blue shirt over to the sidelines. Then he turned to face his other players. "Well, as you all know Terrance here is our best player. Without him we don't have a chance of beating the gray team." Several players nodded their heads in acceptance of this fact. Mr. Lydell reviewed his bench. "Cochran," the coach addressed Ryan and Sydney's heart jumped into her throat. "Come here." The boy stood and approached the coach, who draped an arm around the child's thin shoulders.

"Here's your chance. The moment you've been waiting for. Your opportunity to contribute to this team," Mr. Lydell began. Sydney smiled, thinking that this couldn't have happened at a better time. Ryan was finally going to start a game, and his grandparents and father would be able to see him. "Trade shirts with Terrance while I go change the numbers on the game roster," the coach continued, clapping Ryan on the back.

Sydney watched in horror as her son's face blanched, then turned scarlet. Fury rose inside her like lava in a volcano and she started to stand, but Cole put a restraining hand on her arm. "Let go of me," she hissed.

"There's nothing you can do to help him now," Cole told her tonelessly. "If you show up on the sidelines, it will only make his humiliation worse."

She wanted to argue, to turn and pound on Cole's chest and tell him to take back his words. Somehow she could make it better. But then she looked toward the field and saw that Ryan had already removed his jersey and was passing it to the other boy. He pulled the blue shirt over his head, then took a seat on the bench as the other boy ran onto the field.

The game began and Sydney clasped her hands together in frustration. Soon she felt Cole's hand slide down her arm and pry her fingers apart. Then he folded his hand around one of hers. At first he held firmly, as if he was afraid she might reconsider and attack the coach. But by the end of the game, she was the one holding tight, drawing what comfort she could from him.

Ryan's team won by two points, and afterward the Cochrans invited the children to lunch in celebration. "That's real nice of you, but we have plans for the rest of the day," Sydney said quickly. Brother and Sister Cochran expressed sincere regret. "I'm sorry, but the third Saturday isn't that far away. Talk to Craig and I'm sure he'll arrange some time for you then." She took Sarah's hand and turned to leave.

"Maybe . . . ," Cole started to intervene, but Sydney's murderous expression stopped him.

"Maybe you can mind your own business," Sydney told him. Cole nodded and stood back with the Cochrans as Sydney led her children to the old Crown Victoria.

Sydney barely had time to get inside Grandma's house before the doorbell rang. "Sit down at the table," she instructed her children. "I'll be back to make sandwiches in just a second." When she opened the door she found Cole Brackner standing on the front porch.

"Since when did you start using the front door like polite company?" she asked with irritation as she stepped back for him to enter.

"I just stopped by to give Ryan his paycheck. In all the excitement at the ball game, I forgot," he responded cautiously.

"You could have given Ryan his check at church tomorrow. I think you're here to talk me into letting the kids go to lunch with the Cochrans. In which case, you're wasting your time. I know that this situation isn't the Cochrans' fault, but it's not mine either. They have to live with the consequences of Craig's actions just like I do." She walked into the kitchen and opened the refrigerator to remove a bowl of chicken salad. Then she took the lid off a Tupperware bread container. "Darn!" She slammed the plastic box onto the counter.

"What?" Cole said from the doorway.

"I'm out of bread," Sydney snapped in his direction, staring at the empty bread holder.

Cole glanced across the room at the loaf of Sunbeam Round Top bread on the counter beside her. Then he walked over and picked it up. "What's wrong with this?"

"That's Grandma's. I always make my kids sandwiches with homemade bread."

"Your kids can eat one sandwich on store-bought bread," he told her, taking several slices from the plastic wrapper and holding them out.

She stared for a few seconds, then took the bread and spread it on the counter. After making sandwiches and cutting them into perfect halves, she arranged them on three plates. Then she took carrot sticks from the refrigerator and gave each child several. "I don't like carrots," Trent reminded her. "Can you cut up some cucumbers for me?"

"And I don't want chicken salad," Sarah took this opportunity to say. "Peanut butter and jelly is better."

Sydney sighed and scraped the carrots off of Trent's plate, then opened the cabinet in front of her and reached for the peanut butter, but Cole's hand caught hers. "If you don't want carrots, that's fine, but your mother isn't going to cut up any more vegetables. And for lunch today we're having chicken salad sandwiches, not peanut butter and jelly," he directed toward Sarah. Sydney expected tears and possibly even a tantrum, but instead the children picked up their plates without complaint. "Why don't you eat in the living room?" Cole suggested. "Your mother and I need to talk."

Sydney watched as they obeyed, then she turned mutinous eyes to him. "You've been pushing the limit for a while, but now you've gone too far."

"Well as long as I'm over the edge, I'm going to go all the way." He leaned forward. "That whole soccer situation—"

"I know what you're going to say." Sydney raised a hand to stop him. "Ryan doesn't like sports and I shouldn't have insisted that he play. But soccer itself wasn't the problem, it was that idiot coach." Just thinking about the man made her blood boil. "I'm going to make a formal complaint to the Parks and Recreations Board. Once I tell them about the illegal practices and his failure to play all his team members the required amount of time each game, I'm sure Mr. Lydell's career in children's soccer will be over. Then next year it will be different. What Ryan needs is a good coach who—"

"What Ryan needs is his father," Cole interrupted her. "You're right, soccer wasn't the problem. *You* are the problem," he continued heartlessly. "If you had let Ryan be on Craig's team, the whole season would have been different. Ryan would have learned a thing or two about the game, he would have made some friends and had a good time. You ruined that for him."

Sydney was too astounded to defend herself. "It won't hurt your kids to eat store-bought bread or wear clothes right out of the dryer. But if you deny them a chance to know their father and their grand-parents, if you steal Ryan's childhood by making him worry about you continuously—"

Sydney found her tongue. "How dare you!" She turned on him. "How dare you criticize the way I'm raising my children? You have no idea about the responsibilities of parenthood. You can't begin to imagine how much I love my children and how guilty I feel because I can't make Craig love me," she hurled at him. "And you don't know anything about being a father!"

"No, but I know a lot about being a son," he responded quietly. "My dad—" Sydney forced herself to meet his gaze. "My dad taught me how to work hard and treasure the land and love the Lord. He taught me how to be a man." Cole's voice shook slightly. "No one can give me my father back, but maybe I can keep you from taking Ryan's away from him. From the others too. They all need Craig. No matter how wonderful a mother you are, you can't replace their father."

Sydney was perfectly still for a few seconds, then she turned away. "Get out," she said. "And don't come back. Tell the elders quorum president to assign someone else to visit us because I'm never speaking to you again."

Cole regarded her for a moment, then walked toward the front of the house. Before the screen door slammed behind him, all the children and Grandma were in the kitchen. "Why did you scream at Brother Brackner?" Sarah wanted to know.

"Now he probably won't let me work for him anymore." Ryan was more upset by this thought than he'd been by the shirt incident at the soccer game.

"I'll let you do some jobs around here and pay you," Sydney replied dully.

"I don't want you to give me money!" Ryan cried. "I want to work for Cole. I like taking care of the horses, and they're getting used to me. Some of them will eat out of my hand," he whispered and the anguish in his voice was heartbreaking.

"Now I'll never get to see my kittens!" Sarah finally understood the implications of a war with Cole Brackner.

"And he's such a fine young man," Grandma put in her two cents. "He's been very kind and helpful to all of us."

"Yesterday you thought he was a witch!" Sydney accused her grandmother and the children stared back wide-eyed. "But all of you can go ahead and be on his side. I don't care," Sydney claimed as she brushed past them on her way up the stairs. "I'll never forgive him for the things he said to me."

Unable to sleep in spite of her exhaustion, Sydney glared at the ceiling and replayed Cole's unexpected attack over and over in her mind. Finally her eyes were burning and her chest felt tight. The thought of even seeing Cole Brackner again made her nauseated and she considered calling Pinkie and saying she was sick. But if she started giving into the pain there would be no stopping it. So a few hours later she put on her waitress clothes and drove to The Lure as usual.

Table nine was empty when she arrived and stayed that way throughout the early evening. Henry Lee was still on the wagon, slurping Coke and an occasional Dr. Pepper. When he reminded Sydney that he'd been sober for almost a week, she suggested that it would be cheaper to drink soft drinks at home.

She hated herself for looking up every time someone walked through the door, but couldn't seem to stop. By ten o'clock when she took her break, she'd accepted that Cole was not going to come. She sat at table nine alone and munched on overcooked mozzarella sticks. Finally Carmella joined her. "Where's Cole tonight?" her friend asked helping herself to one of the crunchy appetizers.

"He might be sick. We've both been experiencing cold symptoms for the past few days," Sydney replied idly, unwilling to admit that she had probably destroyed their friendship.

"Cold symptoms?"

"Hot flashes, rapid heart beat, sweaty palms, shortness of breath, dry mouth . . . ," Sydney itemized.

"Those don't sound like cold symptoms. They sound like . . . ," Carmella's voice trailed off. "Oh my gosh! You're in love with him!"

"Don't be absurd!" Sydney was shocked out of her dismal revelry.

"I've had my share of colds but I've been in love countless times and that's always how it feels. You get hot all over, your heart feels like it's going to jump right out of your chest, your lungs won't fill up with air and—"

"It's just a virus or something," Sydney interrupted irritably. "We'll both be fine in a few days." Anxious to get away from Carmella, Sydney went back to work five minutes early.

On Sunday Sydney helped the CTRs make salt clay models of Old Jerusalem and accepted the assignment to teach Trent's class the next Sunday while the teacher was out of town on business. When they got to the chapel Sydney glanced casually around the room, but didn't see Cole. She hadn't expected him to sit with her anymore, but was surprised that his animosity toward her would keep him from attending church altogether.

Sydney and her children spent a lonely, quiet afternoon. When she finally had them settled for the night and went to her room, she saw Cole's scriptures sitting on her nightstand. She considered calling him, but what could she say? "You're right, I'm a bad mother" or "You win, I'll let Craig see the kids whenever he wants to even though he threw us away like garbage." Turning onto her other side, away from the scriptures, Sydney fell into a troubled sleep.

On Monday morning Ryan asked her to deposit his check from Cole into his savings account. When he extended the piece of paper toward her, she was reluctant to touch it, but forced herself. It was even more difficult to look at the signature scrawled across the bottom. "I'm sorry that you've lost your job. I'll see if I can find another way for you to earn some money," she promised as he climbed out of the car at school.

"I don't care that much about the money. But I loved the horses and the farm and talking to Lamar and Cole," Ryan's voice was hollow.

Throughout the day Sydney was restless, bothered by a guilty conscience. And she had gotten so used to going to Cole's farm after school that when she picked up the kids, she almost turned that way without thinking. The children were quiet and, in an effort to cheer them up, she ordered pizza for dinner.

Sarah had to make a plant poster, so they worked on the kitchen table after the meal. When Sydney went into the living room to check on the boys, they had the computer out of the boxes and were trying to assemble it. Resisting the urge to stop them, she reminded the boys to finish their homework and take baths before they went to bed.

The Lure was never busy on Monday and that night was particularly slow. Sydney hated to admit it, but she missed Cole. Throughout the evening she caught herself wondering if he'd had any luck catching witches or if she'd ever see him again.

Craig and Peyton came in with Mr. Harris and Peyton's secretary just before Sydney's break. They sat at table nine as if it belonged to them, and Sydney walked by on her way to an empty spot in the corner. "I haven't seen you around for a while," Sydney spoke directly to Peyton. "I thought you might have given up on Cole's farm and headed back to Nashville."

"I've been busy with other things for the past few days," she responded pleasantly. "But I have no plans to return to Nashville. I love it here." This with a smile at Craig.

"Yeah, well wait until the summer time. The gnats are so thick you can't talk without getting a mouthful, and the mosquitoes are as big as your fist. The temperature averages about 110 degrees and the humidity is at least that high."

Peyton Harris laughed. "I didn't know humidity could be more than one hundred percent."

"That's because you've never spent a summer on Lake Eureka." Sydney glanced at Craig, but he was carefully studying the bubbles in his Sprite.

"Why don't you sit here with us?" Mr. Harris offered, but Sydney shook her head.

"That's okay. Enjoy your evening."

Sydney thought she would never live until The Lure closed, but finally the doors were locked and she had her tables spotlessly clean. As she clocked out she thought about asking the security guard to walk her to her car, but that reminded her of Cole and his attempts to run her life so she went on alone.

She regretted her decision once she was outside in the dark. The air was thick with a cold mist and the car seemed very far away. Her nerves were stretched to the limit by the time she reached the Crown Victoria and inserted the key into the driver's side door. Just as she turned the key, a hand reached out and grabbed her forearm, startling a scream from her.

"Shhhh!"

She whipped around to see Henry Lee Thornton behind her with his hand on her arm.

"I've told you not to touch me!" She angrily pulled free of his grasp.

Henry Lee pushed a wilted handful of flowers toward her. "These are for you," he said. "I didn't want to give them to you in front of the others."

Sydney stared at his gift, then lifted her eyes to his. "I don't accept flowers from married men. Take them home and give them to your wife." Without another word Sydney slipped into the car and drove off, leaving Henry Lee staring after her with the drooping flowers in his hand.

CHAPTER NINE

On Tuesday night Sydney left Grandma's house for work but had to turn around and go back in for her heavy coat. The temperature had dropped drastically since she had brought the children home from school. "You might want to run some water tonight," she told Grandma as she left for the second time. "It's cold and we don't want the pipes to freeze."

Sydney ran into Lauren Calhoun when she arrived at The Lure, and good manners required her to speak. In the course of the conversation Sydney mentioned that she hadn't seen Cole lately. "I don't know what's going on with Cole," Lauren answered as she punched her time card. "I've left several messages on his answering machine, but he hasn't returned my calls. I guess I'll ride out there tomorrow and make sure he's not dead or something!" she added with a little laugh.

Sydney forced a smile, but as she delivered food and drinks to her customers, Lauren's words kept running through her mind. What if something really was wrong with Cole? Maybe Peyton had arranged for him to be poisoned like the cows. Or kidnapped by Mafia hit men. That would explain her cheerful, relaxed attitude the night before. Carmella rushed by at nine-thirty and asked if she'd been listening to the weather.

"No, why should I?" Sydney responded absently.

"Because they are predicting snow tonight," her friend informed her.

"Too early in the year for anything much," Sydney discounted this warning.

"Well, I watched Craig's father on Channel 8 News at nine, and he said parts of Alabama already had three inches and it's still falling."

This got Sydney's attention. In the south, predictions of snow were usually unfounded, but actual frozen precipitation on the ground of the neighboring state was concrete evidence. "What else did he say?" she asked Carmella.

"The low tonight is twenty-two degrees and we could have as much as six inches of snow. Stewart County has already announced that there won't be any school tomorrow."

"No way!" Sydney was astounded.

"Cross my heart," Carmella promised as she picked up two club sandwiches and a double cheeseburger. "I told Pinkie I'll stay until ten o'clock, but then I'm out of here. I don't care if he fires me. I'm not getting stuck in a snow storm."

Sydney called Grandma during her break to check on the situation there. Ryan answered and said that schools had indeed been canceled for the next day. "Grandma made cinnamon rolls and hot chocolate. Now we're sitting in front of the fire, and she said we could stay up late since there's no school." Sydney agreed to this arrangement and asked to speak to Grandma. The elderly woman affirmed that she had the radio on, candles ready, quilts stacked on the couch, and firewood piled by the back door in case the electricity went out.

"I'll try to leave early." Sydney looked at the clock with rising anxiety.

"We haven't seen more than a few snowflakes so far, but you need to come home before the roads get bad," Grandma agreed. "And when you go by the Quick Mart, why don't you pick up a loaf of bread and some milk?"

"I just bought groceries yesterday," Sydney reminded her.

"I always feel better if I have plenty of bread and milk with bad weather coming."

Sydney agreed to stop at the Quick Mart, then went in search of Pinkie Howton. The Lure was basically deserted and Sydney noticed that even Henry Lee's bar stool was empty. She ran into Starla seconds later. "We're closing now. You're supposed to clock out and go home," the other waitress informed Sydney coolly.

"Good," Sydney replied with relief. "I don't like to be away from my kids when the weather is bad." She had to stand in line for a few minutes in order to reach the time clock, then she grabbed her purse and coat and followed her fellow employees outside. Fat, moist snowflakes were lightly dusting the ground. Sydney climbed into the car and turned the heat on high, then adjusted the volume on the radio as she pulled out of the parking lot and headed home.

The radio announcer was giving what he called a "Winter Storm Update" and kept using terms like "blizzard" and "substantial accumulation," which boosted her level of concern. She drove cautiously down the white streets, listening to the forecaster's dire predictions. As she came to a stop behind several other vehicles at a familiar intersection, her eyes were drawn to the left down the road that led to the Brackner farm. Shaking her head, she returned her attention to the light as it changed to green.

She accelerated slowly, giving the tires a chance to gain some traction. Then as clearly as if he'd been sitting beside her, she heard Cole say her name. Startled, she glanced around, but she was definitely alone. Tightening her grip on the steering wheel, she concentrated on the taillights in front of her. Then the voice came again. It wasn't loud, but there was an undercurrent of urgency and suddenly Sydney knew for a certainty that Cole was in trouble.

She applied the brakes gently and pulled into a deserted Texaco station. Shivering against the cold, she got out of the car and inserted coins into the pay phone. Grandma answered on the second ring. "Grandma, I'm at the Texaco station on Long Avenue headed home," she began. "But when I passed the North Lake Road intersection I had the feeling I should go check on Cole. I think he might need me." Grandma didn't speak for a few seconds, and Sydney waited for her to point out the foolishness of this and demand that she come home immediately.

"If Cole needs you, you should go. Drive carefully and call me when you get there," Grandma said instead. "And don't worry about the milk and bread."

As Sydney hung up the public phone, she was infused with energy. She was doing the right thing. Even Grandma thought so. She pushed open the door and hurried back to the Crown Victoria. The snow was falling in earnest now, and the windshield wipers were little help. The traffic was sparse as she turned around and headed back to North Lake Road.

By the time she reached the gravel drive that led up to the Brackner farm, the wet snow was so thick that the tires spun uselessly every few seconds. At that point she realized that once she reached Cole's house, she would not be able to leave. But for now, all her prayers concentrated on making it to Cole safely, and she abandoned the hope of being able to wait out the storm at Grandma's with her children.

Each time the car got stuck in the snow, Sydney backed up and tried again. She found that keeping the tires on the edge of the road, where the gravel was deeper, improved her forward progress. It took a full twenty minutes to make it up the road that she usually covered in two, and Sydney was exhausted by the time the farmhouse came into view.

She was relieved to see Cole's big truck parked in front of the barn. Lamar's Mazda was nowhere in sight and the house was dark. As she made a wide turn and parked beside the truck, she saw light spilling onto the snow from the open barn door. The damp snow stuck to her tennis shoes as she hurried up to the front porch.

"Cole!" she called from the top step but got no response. When she reached the door, she saw that it wasn't closed all the way, and fear gripped her. Cole wouldn't have left the front door open. Something was wrong and she was terrified at the thought of walking into the house alone.

She looked back at the Crown Victoria, which was now blanketed by an inch of snow. The tire marks she had made during her approach were nearly covered by the heavy downfall. Knowing that she had no choice, Sydney pushed the door open and stepped into the small entryway. "Cole!" she tried again without success.

As her eyes adjusted to the darkness, she listened but heard only the grandfather clock beside her and the hum of the refrigerator in the kitchen. Stepping cautiously into the living room, she turned on the crooked floor lamp. Soft light bathed the immediate area and it seemed less threatening. Apparently Cole wasn't even home, but she would be safe there until the weather improved. With a sigh of relief, she turned back to close the door and saw the blood on the floor. Five big brownish splatters were on the wood, and as her gaze turned to the stairs, she saw more.

Grasping the stair rail for support, she fought a wave of nausea. It was as if all her worst fears had been realized. She was convinced that Peyton Harris was involved in a criminal plot to run Cole off his farm, but despite her suspicions, she never dreamed that the woman from Nashville posed any real threat to Cole's safety. However, staring at the blood on the floor, Sydney accepted the possibility that someone might have been sent to hurt Cole. If that was the case, whoever it was could be upstairs now, waiting to do the same to her. She was deathly afraid, but concern for Cole drove her forward.

Staying to the far left, she was able to avoid the bloodstains. At the top of the stairs she paused and looked both directions. To the right there was a light on, so she moved toward it, following the trail of blood. The room with the light turned out to be a bathroom and it looked like a slaughterhouse. Dried blood was pooled on the floor, the sink and bathtub were streaked with it, and there were even splashes on the wall. Blood-soaked towels littered the small space. Pulling back into the hall, Sydney shook her head to keep from fainting.

Once her head was clear, she turned and walked to the next room. Through the open door she could see an office, cluttered with boxes, magazines, and computer printouts. The door across the hall was closed, and when she looked inside she found a large, neat, empty bedroom. Continuing on to the end of the hall, she walked through a third door and found Cole lying sideways on a double bed. "Cole!" she called. He seemed to be all in one piece, but he didn't respond.

She fumbled on the wall for the light switch and illuminated the small room. Then she rushed to the bed and knelt on the edge, leaning forward to shake his shoulder. Even through the thick flannel of his shirt, she could tell that he was dangerously hot. Putting the back of her hand against his forehead, she confirmed that he had a fever and his skin was very pale.

She checked his arms and chest, looking for a wound, but found nothing although both of his hands were stained with blood.

Scrambling to the other side of the bed, she tugged at the sheet tangled around him. The right pant leg was black and stiff with dried blood, and there was a hole in the fabric just above the knee. On closer examination she could see that the material was ripped all the way down to the hem.

She tried calling to him again, but he didn't answer. Reluctantly she touched the torn fabric and watched for a reaction. He didn't flinch, so she pulled back the damaged denim to reveal an eight-inch gash in his leg. The wound was held together with blood-encrusted gauze and several strips of medical tape. She tried not to shake the bed as she crawled back up to Cole's face. His lips were chapped and his breathing was shallow. He needed help quickly and certainly more than she could provide.

She found a cordless phone on the bedside table and called Grandma's number. After Sydney gave a brief explanation of the situation, the older woman advised her to call the hospital immediately. "Have them send an ambulance and then call me back," Grandma instructed.

Sydney dialed the number of Lakeside Memorial and spoke to the operator, who transferred her to the emergency room switchboard. There a man with a foreign accent informed her that the road conditions were too bad and no ambulances were being dispatched at the current time. If her situation was a true emergency, he suggested that she call 911 and see if the police or county sheriff's office could assist.

Sydney hung up on him and punched in 911. They asked for her phone number, then transferred her three times before she was connected with a police officer. He said that even their four-wheel drive vehicles could not negotiate the thick snow, and the only form of transportation that could possibly reach her was a helicopter based in Columbus. However, it was currently in use, transporting several people who had been injured in a car accident near Auburn. If her situation was life and death, then he could call once the helicopter was available.

Sydney hung up on him too, and called Grandma back. "What am I going to do?" she pleaded for advice.

"There's only one thing you can do," Grandma answered slowly. "You'll have to call Craig."

Bile rose in her throat. Call and ask Craig for help? A personal favor? It was unthinkable. Then Cole moaned softly and Sydney took a deep breath. "I'll call you when I can." She broke the connection and dialed the number for Lakeside Memorial again. This time she identified herself and asked the operator to page Dr. Cochran, then waited impatiently. Finally the operator came back on the line and said that Dr. Cochran hadn't answered and suggested that she try him at home.

Sydney hung up and stared at Cole for a few seconds. Then she dialed the familiar number and listened with dread as it rang. Craig had to say hello twice before she could force herself to speak. "Craig," she said stiffly.

"Sydney?" She could hear the instant concern in his voice.

"The kids are fine, but I need your help. I'm at Cole Brackner's house and he's hurt. I've tried the hospital and the police, but no one can get out here in this weather." Wind rattled the windows to emphasize her words.

"What's the matter with Cole?" Craig's tone was instantly businesslike.

"He has a big cut on his right leg. It starts above the knee and goes about halfway down his calf." She controlled a shudder.

"Is Cole conscious?"

"No. He made a noise a few minutes ago, but I can't wake him. And he's very hot."

"You don't have any idea what happened?" Craig asked.

"At first I thought that someone had shot him or stabbed him," she admitted slowly. "But it looks like he tried to bandage the wound, so I guess he hurt himself somehow. I haven't heard from him since Saturday after the soccer game. He didn't come to church on Sunday, and he looks like he hasn't shaved in a while—"

"Whatever it was must have happened on Saturday then," Craig interrupted. "The fever indicates infection, the unconsciousness is probably from dehydration and loss of blood. Go into the bathroom, look for a thermometer, and tell me any medications you see."

Sydney hurried into the bathroom and opened the medicine cabinet, trying to ignore the blood. "No thermometer. Only a razor, toothpaste, toothbrush, Extra-Strength Tylenol . . ."

"Take the Tylenol with you. No prescription drugs?"

"None."

"Okay, look for another bathroom. Cole said his mother was sick for a long time before she died, and I'm hoping for antibiotics and maybe some pain medication. Also keep an eye out for anything that can be used to clean the wound, like alcohol or peroxide."

Sydney walked across the hall and into the large bedroom. She opened the first door and found a closet lined with women's clothing. The second door led into a small bathroom that smelled musty from disuse. She turned on the light and looked in the medicine cabinet. "Peroxide and a thermometer," she said as she took the items off the glass shelf. Then she carefully read the labels of several prescription bottles.

"The Dilaudid is a painkiller," Craig told her. "We can use that. The others are cancer medications and won't do us any good."

Sydney checked the bottle and saw that the pills were originally prescribed for Margaret Brackner over two years before. "These pills expired in August, Craig."

"They're better than nothing," he responded. "You need to get three of those Tylenol into Cole immediately. If you can't get him to swallow them, crush the tablets and put them under his tongue. Let me know when you're finished."

Sydney put the receiver on a dresser in Cole's room, then rushed to the kitchen for a glass of water. When she got back to his room, she climbed onto the bed and cradled Cole's head in the crook of her arm as she pried his lips apart. She put one tablet as far back as she could and then held the water to his mouth. She poured some in and most of it ran out the sides, but the swallowing reflex took a little water and the pill down his throat. She repeated the procedure two more times, then laid his head back down and grabbed the phone. "Okay, he swallowed the Tylenol," she said breathlessly.

"Tell me about the condition of the wound," Craig instructed. She described the bloody gauze and tape. "We don't want to break it open, so saturate the old dressing with Peroxide before you try to remove it." Sydney did this and foam bubbled furiously. "Now find something to cut away his pant leg while the gauze soaks."

Sydney dug through Cole's drawers until she found a small pair of manicure scissors. They were dull and it took forever to saw through the resistant denim. She had difficulty reaching the material behind his leg, and was very conscious of causing him pain. Finally she pulled the mutilated section of fabric free and threw it aside.

"I'm done," she reported.

"Gently remove the old bandage, then soak a towel with peroxide and place it lightly on top of his leg." Sydney put the phone back down and went to work. At first the task made her sick, but after working for a few minutes she forgot everything except her determination to get the bandage off without breaking open the wound. Finally she was able to inform Craig that the old dressing was gone.

"That's good," Craig praised her efforts. "Now we've got to find medicine to fight the infection. You're going to have to go out to the barn. They keep medication for their animals on shelves in the office. Call me back when you're ready to read the labels to me."

Sydney pulled her coat close around her and hurried down the stairs. Her feet were damp and cold from her earlier walk through the snow. Shivering, she opened the front door and stepped out into the darkness. The snow covered any signs of injury between the house and the barn, but once she was inside the barn, she found more blood near a piece of machinery parked in a corner.

The horses started stomping in their stalls when she walked in, and she talked to them gently. She couldn't spare the time to read about each animal's diet, but she grabbed a bucket and filled it with oats, then dumped some in all the feeding troughs. She had to make several trips and was breathing hard by the time she finished.

She walked into the small office and saw large bottles of medicine lining a high shelf. Then she found an old, black rotary phone on the desk and called Craig. He answered on the first ring and she started reading labels. Some of the names were so indecipherable she had to spell them. When she reached a big brown bottle, he told her to give Cole a teaspoon every four hours.

"And you have to get some fluids in him. Try a few sips of water every thirty minutes. If he has trouble swallowing, use ice chips or some snow. Call me when you're back inside."

Sydney hurried into the house and stripped off her coat, shoes, and socks in the entryway. Then she retrieved the cordless phone from Cole's room and called Craig again. Her teeth were chattering and her damp pants clung to her legs as she walked. "Take his temperature every hour, and let me know if it goes above 104. If he doesn't respond to the Tylenol and the antibiotic, we'll have to send for the helicopter. And I'll come as soon as I can."

She realized that he was ending the call and was reluctant to let him go. She didn't want to be solely responsible for Cole's life, and it had been nice talking to Craig calmly. "I'm afraid," she admitted.

"I have complete confidence in you, Sydney," Craig encouraged. "And you can call me if you need me. I'll keep the phone nearby."

Putting the receiver down, she decided that her first step should be to find some dry clothes before she caught pneumonia. She rifled through Cole's drawers again and found a pair of sweat pants, a T-shirt, and some thick socks. Unwilling to return to the bloody bathroom, she stepped across the hall into his mother's room to change.

She hastily pulled on the borrowed clothes and went back to take Cole's temperature. It was down to 103 degrees, so she administered the antibiotic, followed by a few sips of water and some ice chips. After placing a cool compress on his head, she looked in the closet and found an extra quilt. Wrapping herself in the blanket, she collapsed in a chair beside his bed. Every muscle in her body ached from her efforts to control her shivering. Clutching the quilt, she fought sleep and watched Cole breathe.

Craig called back at midnight to check on them. He was pleased when Sydney reported that Cole's fever was down to 101 and told her to go ahead and give him a Dilaudid. "When you get some more fluids in him and the fever drops, he should come around. Then that leg is going to hurt like crazy."

After they hung up, Sydney sat back in the chair. The howling wind and creaking house made her nervous. Cole had some color in his cheeks and was moving more frequently, even though he still wasn't lucid. Sydney stared longingly at the bed. They were good friends and allegedly engaged. Surely there was no sin in lying beside a fully dressed, unconscious man to keep from freezing to death.

Quietly she walked to his mother's room and pulled the comforter off the bed. She spread her quilt over Cole to provide a barrier for propriety's sake. Then she climbed up beside him and covered them both with his mother's bedspread. Gradually her shivering subsided and she slept.

Sydney awoke later to find the room in total darkness. Realizing that the electricity was out, she held her watch toward the moonlight coming through a window. It was 3 A.M. She put the thermometer in Cole's mouth and was alarmed that his temperature was back up to 102. She quickly gave him more Tylenol, feeling guilty. In her need for warmth, she had covered him with the thick bedspread and was sure that the extra bedding had driven up his fever. She tried the cordless phone, but the lack of electricity had rendered it useless, so she had to walk down to the kitchen.

Sydney called Craig and reported the fever's return but omitted the fact that she could have been partially responsible. He said there was no cause for alarm and told her to go ahead and give him another dose of antibiotic and a painkiller. "Cover him with just one quilt until the fever breaks. I expect him to be semiconscious soon. If not, we'll have to take drastic action."

The phone rang before she reached the stairs and Sydney ran back to answer it. The policeman she had spoken to earlier said that the helicopter was now available. She explained that she was caring for Cole under the telephone supervision of a doctor and didn't need the helicopter at the moment. The policeman told her to call if her patient took a turn for the worse.

Sydney returned to Cole's room, and when she leaned over to touch his head, he startled her by reaching up and clasping her hand. His eyes flew open and he looked right at her.

"Mama?" he whispered frantically.

"I'm here," Sydney answered and he relaxed back against the pillow. Pleased with his minuscule progress, Sydney pulled the chair up closer to the bed. The room was getting colder without the furnace. She resisted sleep until finally she leaned forward onto the bed and gave in to exhaustion.

A soft noise penetrated her consciousness, and she opened her eyes to see Cole looking at her. "Sydney," he said weakly. "I thought you were a dream."

"Most men would consider waking up to find me in their room a nightmare," she replied with a crooked smile.

He reached a hand toward her. "I cut my leg."

"Yes, you did. Then you made a mess out of trying to doctor it yourself. But now I'm here to take care of you." It seemed natural to let her hand rest in his.

"You won't leave me?" His face was pale and his tone pleading.

"Of course not," she promised and squeezed his fingers. "Just try to rest." His eyes closed and he was back asleep in seconds. Sydney dozed again, then awakened as his hand clutched hers. She whispered his name, crawling up beside him. Relieved that his face felt cooler, she continued to stroke his stubble-covered cheeks long after she had established that he didn't have a fever. She leaned down and pressed a gentle kiss on his forehead, then reluctantly moved back to her chair.

Sometime later she heard the phone ringing. Clutching the quilt around her in the frigid air, she hurried downstairs and lifted the receiver. She was expecting to hear Craig's voice, but it was Lamar Hodges, Cole's foreman.

"Is everything all right there?" he demanded. "We saw on television that central Alabama and southern Georgia are covered with a foot of snow. They said power lines are down everywhere, and since the temperature won't go above freezing for a couple of days, it could be a while before it thaws."

"Where are you, Lamar?" Sydney asked instead of answering him.

"Louisville."

"Kentucky?" Sydney clarified with a sinking heart.

"My daughter had a baby on Saturday morning so I flew up here to spend a little time with her. Not much an old guy like me can do, but since her mother's gone—"

"I understand," Sydney interrupted. "Cole cut his leg on some machine in the barn."

Lamar cursed softly. "I told him to forget about that baler. We won't need it until next summer anyway. Blamed fool!" he railed. "I'll call the airport, then let you know what flight I'm coming in on." The line went dead and Sydney shivered in the kitchen until he called back a few minutes later to say that all the airports within two hundred miles were shut down.

"Even if you could get to the airport in Columbus, the roads between here and there are closed. Driving on them would be illegal and dangerous. And Cole's going to be all right so there's no point in you taking any unnecessary risks."

"I'll be there as soon as the weather lets up," Lamar promised and they ended their call.

Sydney went upstairs and lifted Cole's head to give him some water. He murmured a "thank you," then fell back asleep. She was looking out at the lightly falling snow when the phone rang again. This time it was Craig, but the line was so full of static she could barely hear him. "We're probably going to lose the phone lines," he predicted over the noise. "How's Cole?"

"He knows who I am and is talking a little."

"Keep giving him the medicine—" The phone went dead. She stared at the receiver for a few seconds, then put it down and went upstairs. When she walked into his room, she was surprised to see that Cole was awake. "The phone is dead," she reported grimly.

"And the power is out." He glanced around the dim room.

"There are several inches of snow on the ground, the roads are impassable, and you've been very sick," she itemized their additional problems.

"I'm better now." He propped his head up on one elbow and watched as she shivered in the cold air. "We probably should move downstairs near the fireplace before we freeze."

"I don't think you should try to move yet." She frowned and stepped toward the bed.

"I'm going to have to move immediately," he told her, pushing himself into a semi-sitting position. His head fell forward weakly. "But I think I'm going to need your help."

"We can stay here for a little while longer. I'll get some extra quilts—"

"I have to use the bathroom, Sydney. Now."

"Oh." She nodded with understanding as he dragged himself to the edge of the mattress. "Put as much weight on me as possible." She bent under his shoulder and wrapped her arm firmly around his waist. He stood and she braced herself against the weight.

"It doesn't hurt as much as I expected, but I'm so dizzy and weak," he told her as they hobbled into the hallway.

"I called Craig and he told me to give you cow medicine and your mother's expired painkillers. I was afraid they might kill you, but I guess they made you better."

"Well, don't give me any more of the pain medicine. I've been having the craziest dreams." He shook his head as they reached the bathroom. "I'll take it from here," he said and shut the door.

Sydney stood nervously in the hallway until he rejoined her. Then she slipped her shoulder under his arm and they made slow progress toward the stairs. "I know I probably smell terrible, but I don't think I can stand up long enough to take a shower right now," he apologized.

"All I can smell is peroxide," she assured him as they reached the top step. Sydney paused to let him catch his breath, and with effort he grasped the stair rail on one side. Holding firmly to Sydney on the other, he made his gradual descent. When they reached the living room she propped him against the wall while she pushed the couch up close to the fireplace. By the time she had him settled, he was perspiring and the wound was bleeding a little.

Sydney made several trips back upstairs to get clean towels and various medications. Cole wouldn't recline completely, but he did lean his head back against the vinyl upholstery while she arranged his leg gently on an overstuffed ottoman. Then she gave him another dose of everything except the pain pills and built a fire. She thought Cole had fallen asleep, but when she turned around he was watching her.

"Not everyone can build a good fire," he commented.

"Girls' camp," she confided. "It was the only part of Young Women I actually liked." Sydney stood and surveyed the room. There was one straight-backed chair and the ugly green couch where Cole was resting. Sydney stared at the chair as the wind blew against the windows.

"That chair is very uncomfortable." Cole studied the hard, wooden seat. "The logical thing for you to do would be to sit here by me." He lifted the edge of his quilt, tempting her.

"That chair doesn't look so bad," she lied. "Or I could sit here on the hearth." She didn't mention that the stone fireplace was uninviting and much too close to the flames.

"Come sit down, Sydney," he told her firmly.

"Aren't you hungry?" she asked as she approached him cautiously.

"I'll let you fix me something to eat in a little while, once you've warmed up." She took another step. "Tell me everything that's happened." He reached up and clasped her hand, pulling her onto the couch.

She settled herself in the far corner, careful to keep from jostling his leg or from actually coming into physical contact with him. He gave her the edge of the quilt and she tucked it around her shoulder. Then she told him about the storm and having the feeling that he needed her. She described finding him and calling Craig.

"I'm sorry," he sighed when she reached this part. "I know how you must have hated to ask him for help."

"I didn't want to call him, but he was . . . nice about it," she forced the words out. She told him about feeding the horses, and he complimented her on her good sense. "I knew Ryan would be upset if they died of starvation." Another thought occurred to her. "They won't freeze, will they?"

"I think that new barn Darrell bought is well insulated enough to keep them alive."

"I hope the kids are okay." Sydney looked out the window at the snow.

"Kids love snow. They're probably begging your grandmother to let them have a snowball fight."

Sydney turned to him with stricken eyes. "You don't really think she'll let them go outside in this awful weather?"

Cole laughed. "No, not while it's this cold."

"Lamar said temperatures won't be above freezing for several days," Sydney reported. "So I guess we're stuck here . . . ," her voice trailed off. After a few seconds, she turned to him. "Now you tell me how you got hurt."

"There's an old hay baler in the barn that hasn't worked since I got back from my mission, and I decided to see if I could fix it. I got it running, then it threw a blade and caught me in the leg. I should have called someone, but it didn't look too bad. I thought I could handle it myself. I got it bandaged up, but then all of a sudden I was so tired. And the next thing I knew I was lying on the bathroom floor."

"You fainted."

"Maybe that could be our little secret," he suggested and she smiled.

"When you didn't come to The Lure on Saturday night I thought you were just mad at me, but I should have realized something was wrong when you weren't at church on Sunday."

"On Sunday I was weak, but not really sick yet. I thought Lauren would come—"

"And I think it's just awful that she didn't." Sydney was quick to blame to Cole's sister. "After you've been coming to watch her sing at The Lure for weeks, offering her moral support and giving her rides. The least she could have done was come by to see if you were okay."

"You've just saved my life and I think, under the circumstances, I should be totally honest with you," Cole told her softly. "I came to hear Lauren sing for a while, but lately, I've been coming to see you."

"I have never met a more dedicated home teacher." Sydney struggled to keep her tone light.

He reached out a hand and cupped her chin. "Of course I wasn't just being a good home teacher." They stared into each other's eyes. "I don't know when it happened. I didn't see it coming," he admitted, his mouth descending toward hers. His kiss was soft and gentle and poignant and over too soon. "I've kissed girls before, but I've never experienced anything quite like that," he added.

"I was married for over ten years, and I've never experienced anything quite like that either," Sydney whispered and he smiled. Then he pulled her close and soon they were asleep.

A branch from a tree near the house broke off an hour later, waking them both. Sydney stoked the fire, then took Cole's temperature. "An unimpressive 100.5," she told him with satisfaction. After instructing him to keep the quilt around him, she went into the kitchen to find something for them to eat. She returned with armfuls of food and kitchen utensils and arranged them on the fireplace. Then she proceeded to fix a full breakfast.

"You must have been a great camper," Cole said from the couch as he watched her.

"Best-all-around every year," she acknowledged as she turned fluffy scrambled eggs onto plates beside crisp bacon and creamy grits. "And to show your appreciation, I expect you to eat every bite," she told him when she handed him his plate.

After they ate, Sydney cleaned up while Cole rested from the exertion of eating. She gave him another dose of medicine at three o'clock, and then he insisted he couldn't live with himself another minute unless he took a shower. Sydney protested, but he held up a hand. "I need to use the bathroom again anyway, so I might as well take care of both during one trip upstairs."

They walked slowly, taking frequent rest stops, until they reached the landing. Cole paused by the door to his room and looked inside. "I'll need clean clothes and, well, everything."

"I'll get them once I have you in the bathroom."

"I'll get my own things," he said stubbornly.

"I've seen underwear before."

"Not mine." He wouldn't budge.

"Actually I have," she said, and he gave her a startled look. "When I was digging through your drawers looking for something to put on." She waved toward her ensemble. Defeated, he allowed her to propel him into the bathroom. "I'll be right back with a towel and clean clothes."

Sydney closed the door behind her and hurried into his room. She was getting familiar with the contents of his drawers and found fresh clothing quickly. Then she returned to the bathroom and knocked. "Are you okay?" she asked and he groaned in reply. "Did you fall?"

"I'm fine." His voice was faint over the squeaking pipes as he turned on the water.

"I'm coming in," she informed him with her hand on the doorknob.

"Sydney!" he protested.

"I'm just here in case you fall." She cracked the door open and steam escaped into the cold hallway. "You have hot water?" This was a pleasant surprise.

"Gas water heater," he muttered in explanation. A few minutes later he turned off the water and asked her to hand the towel over the curtain rod. "Put my clothes by the sink, then go out into the hall and close the door, please."

"If you slip—" Sydney began to express concern.

"If I slip, even if I die, you are not to open that door again. I'd rather the coroner haul me out than you."

"You're being ridiculous," Sydney grumbled. "We've been on a pretty friendly basis for the past few hours—"

"If you have to fish me out of this bathtub, we're going to be close, personal friends," he interrupted, grabbing the towel. With a sigh, Sydney put the clothes by the sink and pulled the door shut.

Cole was trembling with cold and exhaustion by the time she got him back downstairs. Once she had him resting on the couch under several quilts, she examined the wound. It was still oozing and she tried not to worry. "I wish I'd had the strength for a shave." He rubbed a hand across the stubble on his jaw."

"I could get a razor and give it a try," Sydney suggested.

"I appreciate your offer, but I wouldn't trust anyone with mood swings like yours near me with a sharp instrument." She scowled at him as he closed his eyes. "Maybe I could take just half of one of my mom's old pain pills," he murmured and she realized that the shower must have been painful. She halved one of the tiny pills for him, then sat by the fire until he fell asleep.

Then, driven by a desperate need for a shower herself, she went upstairs and dug through Cole's drawers again. Armed with more borrowed clothing, she went into his bathroom. She saw that the bloody towels had been pushed into a corner and the sink was wiped clean. Touched that Cole had invested precious energy trying to straighten up, she climbed into the tub and stood under the hot water. It felt wonderful, but eventually started to get cool, so she got out and dressed quickly.

Sydney didn't bother to keep any distance between them when she settled back beside Cole on the couch. He opened his eyes and smiled at her. Then, side by side they watched the fire. A few minutes later he reached over as he stroked her hair. "What does your hair look like when it isn't dyed or frizzed or anything?"

"Straight and brown," she answered.

"Sounds beautiful."

"It isn't," she assured him.

"Why are you so hard on yourself, Sydney?"

"I guess I want to make sure that no one develops expectations I can't live up to."

"You're always doing something to your hair, and you diet even though you're not fat. Why?" he asked even though they both knew the answer.

"Craig didn't like me the way I was." She shrugged as the fire popped loudly. "I wanted him to regret his decision to end our marriage and, in my weaker moments, I even hoped the day might come when he would beg me to take him back—"

"Since we've been sleeping together—"

"You shouldn't use that term lightly!" Sydney objected vehemently and he laughed.

"Well, since you've seen my underwear—"

"Just in the drawer!" Sydney took exception to this remark as well.

"I want you to tell me about Craig and what went wrong."

"I never talk about that—ever." Sydney shook her head. "If I were to even try, I would probably break into a million pieces. Stubbornness is the only thing holding me together."

"What about meanness and self-denial?" he added gently.

"That too," she admitted.

"It's dark, Sydney. You can say the words, you can feel the pain, you can even cry and no one will ever know."

"You will," she whispered.

"I don't count." He laced his fingers through hers and nodded for her to proceed. "Start with something easy. How did you meet?"

Sydney closed her eyes and began. An hour later her voice was hoarse and her throat was sore, but the whole sickening story had been laid out. "That really stinks," he murmured.

"So now can you see why I hate Craig?"

"I don't think you hate Craig, and in spite of everything you've told me, I can't make myself hate him either." Cole stared into the darkness.

"I know you're not going to agree with what he did."

"I think he should have stuck with the marriage even if he was unhappy. He should have stayed active in the Church and asked for help from his bishop and maybe LDS Social Services . . ." Cole shrugged. "But if he had done all that, you wouldn't be sitting here beside me. You wouldn't have saved my life. We wouldn't have shared two of the best kisses in the history of the world." Her eyes dropped to his lips and her breath caught in her throat. "I wouldn't have fallen in love with you."

"Don't say that, Cole," she begged.

"It's true."

"I could never risk getting married again." Just the thought made her shudder.

"You'll be wasting your life if you live the rest of it alone," Cole insisted.

"I don't care."

"You didn't care before because you didn't have me." He stroked her cheek gently.

"My children . . ."

"Will be fine if we all work together."

"I don't want to talk about this any more." Sydney tore her eyes away from his and stared into the fire. She expected him to argue, but he didn't. A few minutes later she heard the sound of his heavy breathing and knew that he had fallen asleep.

CHAPTER TEN

Sydney slept fitfully in the small space relegated to her on the lumpy couch. She gave Cole his medicine every four hours and insisted he drink plenty of water, even though that resulted in two nocturnal trips to the bathroom. She was becoming accustomed to the sounds of the old house. The creaking boards, the grandfather clock, the squealing water pipes.

As pale light filtered through the windows on Thursday morning, Sydney looked around the room. Now this was a place that could use some ideas from *Home and Garden*. The stone fireplace would be the focal point, the inspiration piece. The old couch would have to go, along with the bent floor lamp. She could make new curtains, maybe out of a cheerful plaid material. Her thoughts were interrupted by voices from outside. The sound of other people was so foreign to their current circumstances that she was alarmed.

She put a hand on Cole's shoulder and gently shook him awake as a knock sounded on the door. "Help me up," he whispered and she leaned down, then assisted him slowly to the entryway.

When she opened the door she found Craig and Bishop Middleton on the porch. Peyton Harris was lurking behind them, stamping snow off her boots. "I told you they'd be fine." Craig stepped inside and the others followed. "Nice fire." He walked into the living room and stripped off his down-filled coat.

Bishop Middleton dropped his own coat on the floor by the door and put an arm under Cole's free shoulder, helping him back to the couch. Once Cole was settled, Sydney brought in two of the barstools from the kitchen. Peyton sat in the straight-backed chair, and Bishop Middleton took a barstool. Craig knelt down in front of the couch to examine Cole's leg.

"This should have had stitches." Craig frowned at the wound. "It's too late now and you're going to have an ugly scar, but I think you'll live," he pronounced. "I've brought you some human antibiotics." He pulled pharmaceutical samples from his pocket. "Sydney, if you'll get me a pair of scissors and some more of this tape and gauze, I'll fix him a decent bandage."

A little resentful at being told what to do, especially in front of Peyton, Sydney went upstairs and returned shortly with the required items. Forcing herself to be polite, she offered everyone hot chocolate. They all declined. Sydney asked Craig if he'd talked to the kids and he said they were fine. "Going stir-crazy. I've got my cell phone if you want to call them."

Sydney accepted the phone and dialed Grandma's number. She walked into the kitchen and spoke to each member of her family. As Craig had said, they were all happy to be out of school but bored, and Grandma wouldn't let them play in the snow. Sydney endorsed this decision and begged them all to be good. Afraid that she would run the battery down, she made herself hang up and returned to the living room.

As she entered she heard Craig explaining that he and Peyton had been snowed in at his house and finally borrowed horses from a neighbor in order to travel in the snow. "We made it as far as Bishop Middleton's last night and stayed there until daylight. Then Peyton and I doubled up so the bishop could come with us."

"Why was she at your house?" Sydney demanded, too shocked to be tactful.

Craig exchanged a look with the bishop, then he turned back to face Sydney. "Peyton and I got married last week." Sydney felt the blood drain from her face as he continued, "It was a spur-of-the-moment thing. We drove to Gatlinburg Thursday and came home the next day."

Home. His home. Her home. Peyton's home. "How could you have gotten married without even telling me?" her voice rose dangerously.

Craig stood and moved in front of Peyton. The protective gesture was telling. "We're divorced, Sydney," he said, his voice quiet but firm. "I don't have to tell you anything I do unless it relates to the children."

"And you don't think getting married is going to affect our children?"

"Of course it is and I was planning to tell you. I just didn't feel the need to ask you first."

"So now is she going to pack up her witch outfit and forget about trying to make Cole sell his farm?" Sydney waved toward Peyton, and Craig's face went blank.

"Witch costume?" Peyton asked.

"Oh come on," Sydney sneered. "We've been onto that for a while now."

"Sydney." Cole's tone encouraged caution, but she ignored him.

She leaned around Craig to address Peyton. "We know that you've been staging witch ceremonies on the farm to make everyone in town hate Cole. You're trying to stop people from doing business with him so he'll be forced to sell to your clients. But now I guess you'll be too busy with married life to burn calves and arrange rocks into occult symbols."

"That is too much—" Craig began, but Peyton stood and put a hand on his arm.

"What are you talking about?" The blonde was the picture of innocence.

"I'm talking about Cole's tires being cut and the feed store in Columbus not wanting to buy his hay and his water getting poisoned and his cows dying and witches burning sacrifices on his property. He may be naïve enough to think it was all one big, awful coincidence, but I know you're behind it. You're a tough businesswoman, used to getting your way. You drove into Eureka determined to make Cole sell his farm, one way or another. And as a little side bonus, you took my husband too."

"I'm not your husband," Craig tried again.

"You married me first!" Sydney turned on him, all the anguish rising to the surface. "You are the father of my children!"

"I'm sorry." He hung his head.

"You knelt across the altar from me in the temple and made eternal commitments. 'I'm sorry' doesn't fix it."

"I've made mistakes!" Craig's voice rose as well. "And goodness knows you've made me pay! How much longer will I have to suffer for my sins, Sydney? I've been working with my bishop, and I think the Lord has forgiven me. Our parents have forgiven me. Even our kids have forgiven me. When will you finally accept it and move on?"

"Never," Sydney hissed. "If you suffer every minute of every day for the rest of your life, it won't be enough."

"Even if you destroy our children in the process?"

"You are the one who destroyed our family, all of us, everything!" she hurled at him.

"That's enough!" Bishop Middleton's voice broke in. "There are several complicating issues we need to deal with here, and I don't have enough information to even attempt to offer counsel. I think this would be a good time to get some personal background. Cole, I'll need something for everyone to write on."

"There are legal pads and pens in the middle drawer of my desk upstairs."

The bishop turned to Sydney. "Will you get four of each please?"

Careful to avoid eye contact with the others, she obeyed. When she returned, the bishop took the tablets and pens from her.

"Craig and I talked last night," Bishop Middleton spoke into the angry silence. "But I need to get a broader perspective. Since I don't know some of you, I'd like everyone to write as if we'd never met. Tell me where you were born and things about your early life, then we'll move on to recent events," he instructed. "Just make yourselves comfortable and start writing."

"There's no reason for me to do this," Peyton tried to worm out of the bishop's exercise. "I don't know much about their marriage." She pointed toward Sydney, who was still glowering at Craig. "I don't know anything about witches or burning calves, and I'm not really a part of this . . ." She waved her hand at the room in general.

"Everyone here is part of this," the bishop corrected her.

"I'm not very good at expressing my feelings . . . ," Cole began.

Sydney put her legal pad on the fireplace. "If nobody else is going to do this, then I'm certainly not."

"I'll do it," Craig offered.

"You're the only one who has something to gain," she said sharply.

"I think everyone can benefit from self-examination," the bishop intervened.

"We'll all do it," Cole spoke for the group and Sydney narrowed her eyes at him. "And if I'm willing to write my life history in my weakened condition, the rest of you have no excuse."

Sydney resisted for a few seconds, but as everyone else picked up their legal pads, she scowled and grabbed hers too.

"I'm going out to see about the livestock," the bishop told them. "While I'm gone there will be no talking." Bishop Middleton directed this toward Sydney. "When I get back I expect those legal pads to be filled." He picked up his coat and put it on. Then he stuck his head back in the living room. "And don't worry about anyone seeing what you write. I'll keep anything you tell me strictly confidential." With those words he opened the front door and walked out into the snow.

Legal Pad #2

My name is Craig Cochran and I am the villain of this story although I never intended to hurt anyone. I don't really see what good this will do, but I've agreed in hopes that the bishop can help us. Sydney keeps glaring at me like she thinks I'm cooperating just to irritate her.

My parents have had a plan for my life since the day I was born. I would fill a full-time mission, marry a perfect LDS girl, graduate from BYU, and then go on to medical school. BYU sounded okay to me and I was interested in medicine, so I didn't resist. I was looking forward to college, but I turned nineteen the summer after I graduated from high school and my parents wanted me to submit my mission papers. I didn't feel ready and tried to talk them into letting me get a couple years of college in first. But that would ruin "the plan," so I left for France in July.

My mission was the most miserable two years of my life. I hated the rules and the lack of privacy and the interruption to my education. The only thing I had to look forward to were the letters Sydney wrote me. They were fun and something I could depend on.

During the last six months of my mission my parents started mentioning the name of a nice girl they wanted me to get to know when I got home. I knew this was their way of saying they had picked out a wife that would keep me traveling down the straight and narrow path. I resented the insinuation that I couldn't choose a good wife without their help and started dreading my return until I got an idea. Sydney was a great person from a wonderful LDS family. She shared my love of sports and actually had a sense of humor. If I wanted to marry Sydney instead of the other girl, my parents couldn't really object.

So I came home determined to make Sydney my wife. When we announced our plans to marry, my parents reacted with cautious enthusiasm. They wanted me settled and while Sydney was not the girl of their choice, she did meet the basic requirements. Sydney's parents were less supportive. They thought Sydney was too young and strongly encouraged us to wait a year.

During our recommend interviews, the bishop expressed concern that we were rushing into things and urged us to pray for spiritual confirmation. But we were too busy packing for our trip to Provo and making wedding plans to listen to their warnings.

During our brief courtship, Sydney and I spent our time fishing and watching baseball games and hiking in the woods. We didn't do much kissing, so I never found out until our honeymoon that I didn't feel any deep physical attraction toward her. At first I thought it was newlywed awkwardness, but as the days went by without improvement, I started to get scared.

When we got home I talked to my parents and they advised me to give it some time. I wanted to talk to the bishop, but I felt foolish since I had ignored his original counsel. So we moved to Utah and I tried to stay busy. After a year, I accepted that my feelings for Sydney were not going to change, but by then we had Ryan.

So for the next ten years I lived a lie. To survive I worked nights and weekends, avoiding situations where I would be forced to express false affection for Sydney. I stayed away from home and stopped going to church. My whole life was a sham, empty and hopeless. Then I met a nurse who worked the night shift at Lakeside. I know it was wrong to develop feelings for another woman, but I was so lonely. And when I was with Brittni, I felt alive for the first time in years.

After several soul-wrenching months I decided that things had to change. Sydney didn't deserve to live her life with a man who didn't love her. We had made a mistake, but it was wrong for both of us to be trapped in a bad marriage. I knew it would be hard on our children, but in the long run I hoped they would benefit from having parents who were happy, even if they didn't live together.

I expected Sydney to be hurt and confused, even resentful. But I also hoped that maybe she shared my longing for what a marriage could be that ours was not. I thought over time she would accept the situation and maybe even forgive me, but she hasn't . . .

Legal Pad #3

My name is Cole Brackner and I've agreed to this in hopes that Sydney will be shamed into cooperating as well. I live on a cattle farm on the edge of Eureka that my great-great-grandfather bought in the late 1800s. I worked the farm with my dad for the last year and a half of high school and the first two years of college. We were in the process of filling out my mission papers when my dad suffered his first heart attack. He was hospitalized for a while, then bedridden at home for several more weeks.

We put aside my mission plans and my father ran the farm through me. My dad wouldn't let me quit school, so I changed to night classes. His health improved for awhile, but he had another heart attack the week before I graduated from Auburn. He died of a massive stroke in the ambulance on the way to the hospital.

My two sisters were never interested in the farm, and after Dad's death they encouraged our mother to sell it. My mother knew that I loved the place and how hard I had worked to keep it going during my father's illness. She wanted for me to have an opportunity to run it, and since I had never thought of doing anything else, I was relieved by her decision. For the next five years our returns were respectable and our reserves stayed at a safe level.

Then my bishop called me in and said he thought it was time for me to go on a mission. I pointed out that I was past the age that most men go, and he said he had already talked to the stake president and Area President about my situation. He said because of my earlier circumstances, and the fact that I had no immediate prospects of getting married, they were going to make an exception and allow me to go even though I was almost 28. I told him that there was no one to run the farm, and he said the Lord would provide.

My younger sister and her husband, Darrell, were living in Memphis at that time. He was floundering in school and unsure about his major, so they moved home to take care of things for two years. I was called to serve in North Dakota and enjoyed my mission, but unlike the younger men who had no responsibilities at home, I worried continuously about the farm and my mother. She was diagnosed with pancreatic cancer a few months before I was released and was well into chemotherapy treatments by the time I got back. When I saw my mother at the Columbus airport I knew that she was going to die. But I was too grateful that the Lord had let her live long enough for me to see her again to be resentful.

I barely recognized the farm when we pulled out of the woods on the long gravel drive that leads from the main road. The old house had been covered with vinyl siding and reroofed. The wooden barn had been replaced by a sheet metal version, the tractor parked in front of it was new and the place looked deserted.

As my sister gave me a tour of the house, she scolded me for letting things get so run down. I admitted that the roof and furnace were probably necessary but questioned the need for new furniture, carpet, and a state-of-the-art kitchen. When I pointed out that my mother and I didn't cook much and never entertained at all, my sister gave me an odd look. After a few days had passed without any mention of Lauren and Darrell moving back to Memphis, I realized that they planned to stay and had made the improvements for their own benefit.

I spent the first few days visiting with my mother and consulting with her doctors. As I had suspected, the prognosis was grim and I found it hard to concentrate on mundane things like money and farm management. Finally I forced myself to ask Darrell for the financial statements and various business ledgers. He said he had things "tucked everywhere" and would have to find them. While he searched I walked around and saw numerous signs of neglect. The hayfields had been allowed to go to seed, the fences were in bad repair and the poor looking cows that milled around in our pastures were a disgrace.

Darrell gave me handfuls of unreconciled bank statements, unopened bills, and several stock ledgers that had not been updated in six months. A knot of dread started to form in my stomach as I asked about Lamar Hodges, the foreman who had worked for my grandfather since before I was born. Darrell told me he and Lamar had disagreed on several issues and he had been forced to fire the man almost a year before.

I took the paperwork up to my father's office, and after three hours and numerous phone calls, I was able to determine that Darrell and Lauren had managed to bring the farm to the verge of bankruptcy. They had used up all the cash reserves buying new equipment and renovating the house. They sold off valuable breeding stock, but when even that wasn't enough, Darrell had convinced my mother to sign two signature loans.

I called my sister and her husband in and asked for an explanation. They nervously took turns justifying their managerial decisions. Lauren said that when they had arrived the house was unlivable. When Darrell told her that there was over $200,000 in savings, she convinced him and our mother that it was only sensible to invest some of it in improvements.

Darrell didn't like the old truck my father and I had used, so he traded it in for a new one that cost $35,000. Then he let a fast-talking salesman from the John Deere dealership sell him the new tractor and hay baler. They expected to replenish the cash reserves with money from the sale of that year's calves. However, they were inexperienced and without Lamar's help, they didn't get the best price, which forced them to take out the loans.

They knew that things looked bad financially, but there was one piece of good news. A developer from Nashville had contacted them and offered almost a million dollars for the land to build a western theme park similar to Dollywood. The company would allow us to keep a couple acres of land and the newly remodeled house. So Lauren and Darrell had been thinking that I might want to look for a real job and buy a nice little place in town. Then we could sell the farm, and they could continue to live in the house with my mother.

I didn't trust myself to answer without saying something I'd regret, so I asked them to leave the office. After my mother heard all the gruesome details, she told me to take her into town for an emergency meeting with her lawyer. She instructed him to make several changes to her will and prepare a power of attorney so that I could handle all legal and financial decisions for her in the future.

Then we drove to the bank. The man who had handled our family's banking business for years had retired, so we were introduced to our new account representative. His name was Lester McPherson and he was very helpful. He said that he thought he could convince the bank's board of directors to loan me enough money to pay off the signature loans, eliminate the balances on the new equipment, and cover the minimum operating expenses for a one-year trial period.

However a loan of this magnitude could not be done on a signature basis, and the farm would have to be held as collateral. The bank board also wanted written assurance that Darrell would have nothing to do with the farm management during the trial period. I thanked Mr. McPherson for his help, then mortgaged the farm for the first time in over a hundred years.

My mother was exhausted when we got home, but she called a family meeting. She told Lauren and Darrell that she did not want to sell the farm. She thanked them for their help during the past two years and gave them the entire balance of her own personal savings account to use as a down payment on a house in town. Then she suggested that they both start looking for jobs and be prepared to move out by the end of the month.

My sister had questions. How would I care for my mother without her help? How would I manage the farm without Darrell? I told her I would hire a nurse if necessary, and Lamar had said he would come back as soon as Darrell was gone. They were not pleased with any aspect of the plan, but they finally accepted it. As the meeting ended my mother told them that the new truck was part of the mortgage and would have to stay on the farm. Later she said she knew Darrell loved that truck but shouldn't be rewarded for his misdeeds by getting to keep it.

Lauren and Darrell bought a new house, she found a job as a data entry clerk at the First National Bank of Eureka, and he was hired by a local hardware store. Lamar came back to work for me, and we put in long hours trying to restore the farm.

In the meantime, my mother's health continued to deteriorate. The Relief Society president checked on us regularly and the bishop expressed concern. My sisters halfheartedly offered to come and help me, but I told them I could handle things. In the late hours of the night I would lie on a cot beside my mother's bed and listen while she told stories about her youth and my dad. When she got tired, I talked about the future and my plans for the farm. Toward the end we didn't talk about anything. She slept and I watched her chest rise and fall with each labored breath.

The night she died she awakened suddenly, lucid for the first time in days. She turned her head and looked at me. "You're the image of your father," she whispered, then closed her eyes for the last time. I guess I'll never know if she really saw me or if my father had come for her.

At the funeral people praised me for my tender, patient care and expressed sympathy for my physical and emotional ordeal. Only I knew how precious those last weeks were and that I had selfishly cheated my sisters out of the experience.

In her will, my mother gave me control over the farm. All profits are to be divided annually with my sisters and if I ever decide to sell, the proceeds will be equally distributed. My sisters had expected the farm to be sold and already had plans for the money.

My older sister, Michelle, lives in Atlanta with her husband and five children. She explained to me the difficulty of raising so many children on her husband's income and said that she was counting on her inheritance to send her sons on missions and pay for college. I sympathized with her problems and told her that after a year or two the farm should be productive again and the annual division of profits would help out with their expenses.

"I don't want a few thousand dollars here and there. I want my $300,000 right now," she told me bluntly. When she quoted this figure I realized that Lauren had shared the news about the western theme park.

I listened with diminishing patience while Lauren added her appeals to Michelle's. Their house needed some new plumbing lines run and the used car she was driving was undependable. Darrell didn't want to spend the rest of his life selling nails and barbed wire, so he had decided to go back to school and get a business degree, but they would need money for tuition and books. I told them again that I wouldn't even consider selling and they were both furious with me by the time the after-funeral meal ended.

Lamar and I had a good year so the bank renewed my mortgage for another twelve months. It was quiet at the farm and I missed my mother, but I wasn't really lonely. Lauren, however, was convinced that man cannot live alone and started a campaign to find me a wife. I don't know whether she was genuinely interested in my happiness or if it was another "sell-the-farm-scheme." I went on a few blind dates she set up, but I was out of practice and the available women were so young they made me uncomfortable.

Then Lauren called and said she was going to sing at the amateur night at a dinner club on Lake Eureka. Darrell had to work, so she wanted me to come along for moral support. Listening to amateurs sing didn't sound like the best form of entertainment, but I wanted to improve my relationship with Lauren, so I accepted. She was very pleased and asked if I could loan her $100 to buy a new outfit for the occasion. Then she said her car wasn't running well and wanted to know if I could pick her up on Thursday night at seven o'clock.

When we got to The Lure, Lauren went back to line up with the other amateurs, and I took a seat at a table with a good view of the stage. Lauren performed well, and they offered her a regular job, which meant that all my evenings from that time forward were spent at The Lure. It was no worse than sitting around by myself at the farm, so I didn't really mind.

I got to know the waitresses pretty well, especially a less-active member of the Church named Sydney Cochran. Since then there have been rumors of witches burning sacrifices on my farm, my cows have been poisoned, my fences broken and business deals gone sour. I've been dragged into court, accused of sorcery, injured by farm equipment, and have fallen in love with the most difficult woman I've ever met. I guess you could say I was in the wrong place at the wrong time and haven't had a peaceful moment since.

Legal Pad #4

My name is Peyton Harris and I am really little more than an impartial observer. Mr. Middleton just gave me a legal pad to be polite. I'm from Nashville and have been a self-employed properties acquisition specialist for seven years. If somebody wants a piece of property, a company, a collectible, or even a fine piece of jewelry and they don't want to contact the owner directly, they pay me to handle it for them.

After I earned a finance degree from the University of Tennessee, I started looking for a job in the Nashville area and I found out quickly that the established firms wouldn't take me seriously. I had several unsuccessful interviews and finally one CEO told me that I should abandon my efforts to find employment in the cutthroat world of acquisitions and try for a modeling contract instead. He probably meant this as a compliment, but I didn't take it as one.

Once I accepted that no one was going to give me a chance, I opened my own company and operated it out of the apartment I shared with my mother. At first I got only the impossible jobs that no one else would touch or everyone else had tried. I built my reputation quickly by succeeding where others had failed, and years later, I had the privilege of handling the hostile takeover of the firm owned by the man who thought I should be a model. At our final meeting he told me he was obviously a bad judge of character. He said that in spite of my pleasant appearance I was every bit as heartless and blood-thirsty as any acquisitions specialist he had ever met. He didn't mean this as a compliment, but I took it as one.

For the first couple of years I worked terrible hours and almost lived in my car. Eventually I was able to rent a modest office and hire a secretary named Marcie Heinz. She was in her mid-forties, divorced, no children. She was also an excellent typist, organized beyond belief and had no concept of a personal life, so we got along fine. I rarely turned down a client and I never lost. During the seven years I have been in business the only deal I didn't close stalled because the client died.

For years I was able to operate well with no sleep, but lately I'm tired all the time. I used to love the challenge of difficult cases, but now I long for a few simple jobs where the people involved actually want to sell to each other. Marcie said I was lonely since my mother recently remarried and moved to Florida. My mother attributed my strange mood to the fact that I turned thirty in April. According to her, my subconscious was reminding me that I only have a few childbearing years left. I assured her that this theory was preposterous. I'd never given a thought to growing old or worried about my biological clock.

The truth was that even if I wanted a husband, I wouldn't have known where to look. I haven't been to a church in years, dating services are too humiliating, and I could never show a softer side to any of the men I work with. So I tried to stay busy.

As if I didn't have enough on my mind, out of the blue my father called a couple of months ago and said he wanted to see me. My parents separated when I was young and, except for an occasional phone call, I've not had any contact with my father since then. I didn't want to start a relationship with him at this stage of my life, so I ignored his calls.

Finally I decided to take a vacation. I hoped that a week on the beach would give me back my edge, my love of the kill, and push the nonsense about a husband into the dark corners of my mind where it belonged. I figured at worst I would get away from my father and come home with a nice tan. So I called my travel agent and bought a ticket to Hawaii.

The day before I was to leave, I got a call from one of the partners at Lieberman, Sobels, and Finn, the largest property acquisitions company in Nashville. I had applied for a job there when I graduated from college and later received a form letter thanking me for my interest and saying that they would be in touch. Seven years seemed like a long time to wait, but I canceled my vacation and went to the interview.

All the partners were there, but Mr. Finn did most of the talking. He said they had been following my career and were very impressed by my consistent success against the odds. He said they wanted me to handle an acquisition for them and hinted that if all went well, they would likely offer me an employment package including an associate partnership, an impressive six-digit salary, stock options, profit sharing, and several weeks of paid vacation each year.

It was exactly what I had been dreaming of, but I couldn't leave Marcie out in the cold. So I mentioned that I had a secretary who had worked closely with me for several years, and Mr. Finn said that if Lieberman, Sobels, and Finn offered me a job, Marcie would be part of the deal.

Then Mr. Finn explained that a client of theirs wanted to purchase a farm in southern Georgia. Three siblings had recently inherited and the only son was trying to work it himself. The land was mortgaged and producing below profitable levels. It was just a matter of time before the heirs overcame their sentimental attachment to the place and realized the only sensible thing to do was sell.

This didn't sound like a difficult negotiation and I told him so. He explained that the man was trying to prove himself. He saw selling the farm as a disservice to his ancestors and was refusing to even discuss a very generous purchase price. Mr. Finn said he was going to speak frankly and I told him I expected no less.

He admitted that they had already sent two representatives to talk to Mr. Brackner without success. First, they had tried appealing to him through simple, human greed. When this didn't work, they tried to scare him with computer models showing various kinds of financial ruin that threatened small farmers. Neither approach had been effective. They thought that a woman might be less intimidating to the young man and they had chosen me since I was a tough negotiator disguised as an attractive woman. On several occasions my appearance had been held against me, and I saw no reason not to use it to my advantage for once.

Mr. Finn described all the members of the Brackner family, and while his comments were carefully worded, I got the picture. The sisters were already sold on the deal and the Brackner brother was young, probably lonely and maybe not so bright. Mr. Finn wanted me to take advantage of his vulnerability, even pretend affection if necessary, to convince him to sell.

I could have objected on ethical grounds or told him that in spite of my appearance I had very little experience with men and no idea how to flirt. Instead I shook his hand. Then he gave me the Brackner file and told me that they wanted daily, detailed reports of my progress sent to the e-mail address clipped to the inside of the folder.

I reminded him that I had other clients that I would have to settle before I could take on a new, exclusive, responsibility. He said it was their hope that I would fly to Georgia immediately and meet Mr. Brackner. They suspected that it might take a while for me to gain his confidence, then convince him to sell the farm that had been in the family for over a hundred years. He suggested that I take a laptop computer with me to Eureka and work out of my hotel room. That way I could handle my old accounts while establishing a trusting relationship with the unfortunate cow farmer. He quickly added that the firm would pay for my plane ticket, my rental car, my food, and my lodging.

I told him that in addition to my expenses, I would charge him hourly for time actually spent on the case and he smiled. As I left, he asked me to be very specific in my e-mails and never to miss a day. He explained that little, insignificant things could help them plan their negotiating strategy. I assured him that I was meticulous about documenting all my cases and would certainly report in daily. He shook my hand again and said he had every confidence in me and looked forward to a long working relationship.

I called Marcie from my car, and by the time I got to my office, she had a neatly typed itinerary ready for my review. She had already booked me a flight into Columbus, Georgia, arranged for a rental car to be waiting, and made hotel reservations in Eureka. As I read, she informed me that several hundred dollars in traveler's checks would be delivered at any minute.

That night Marcie and I ate tuna salad plates at my desk for dinner while we worked out a plan to ambush Coleman Brackner. She said she would notify all of our clients that I was working out of town for the next several weeks on a big case for Lieberman, Sobels, and Finn. Just hearing her say the name made me feel like I had finally arrived.

The next day I boarded a plane for Columbus. During the flight, I reviewed our strategy and almost felt sorry for Mr. Brackner. Annoyed by the appearance of another emotion that never used to plague me, I pushed the unprofessional thoughts to the back of my mind. When I arrived in Columbus I picked up the rental car and drove straight to Eureka.

* * * *

It was over an hour later when the bishop reappeared. He looked half frozen and Sydney again offered him some hot chocolate, but he shook his head and moved close to the fire. "No thanks. Is everyone finished?"

Sydney looked down at the pages she had filled. Although she had been resistant to the idea originally, once she started writing the words just seemed to pour onto the paper. It was the first time she had tried to organize the painful events and analyze them in any logical way and she almost wished she could ask for more time.

"There's no hurry," the bishop assured them.

"I've written more than I should have already," Sydney muttered, walking over to place her legal pad in his hands. Everyone followed her example, then the bishop addressed the group.

"I want to thank all of you for your cooperation. I'm going to take these home and study them. Then on Sunday we'll meet at my house at three o'clock." He paused, giving everyone a chance to object, but no one did, so he turned to Sydney. "I'll stay here with Cole if you'd like to ride with Craig and Peyton back to my house," he offered generously.

The thought of accompanying the newlyweds anywhere was nauseating to Sydney. "Thanks, but I don't want to leave my car. I'll stay here until the roads are clear enough for me to drive out."

"I'll check back on you tomorrow . . . ," Craig began.

"I appreciate your help, but don't worry about me. I'm fine," Cole responded. Craig nodded, then took Peyton's arm and they followed the bishop outside. Sydney watched them through the glass of the front door until they disappeared from view.

"It's for the best, Sydney," Cole said gently.

"It doesn't seem right that he should get a second chance at happiness. He took my youth, broke my heart, ruined our family. How is it fair that after all that, he can repent and go on with a new life while mine is still in shambles?" she whispered, her warm breath clouding the cold glass.

"The Savior's Atonement is sufficient, Sydney. Even for Craig's sins. And now that Craig has remarried, he's closed the door on the past. He's set you free."

"If I have to be stuck with the stigma of divorce, he should, too."

"You have an unhealthy prejudice against divorced people," Cole said softly.

Sydney turned around. "It's other people who have the prejudice!"

"Who?"

"I don't know. Everyone."

"Well, no one ever mentions your marital status except you."

Sydney looked back at the snow. "I'm not the best person in the world," she spoke to the foggy glass. "But I'm not the worst either. So why is my life messed up?"

Cole pulled her away from the door gently. "Would you get me the set of scriptures on my nightstand?" His request reminded her that she had never returned his scriptures, and she lowered her head, ashamed.

"I'm sorry I keep forgetting to give your others back," Sydney lied. She wasn't sorry at all. She had found more comfort reading from Cole's scriptures during the past few days than she'd gained from her own in over a year.

"That's okay. I've got a spare set I use when wicked, divorced women steal mine." With a smile, Sydney climbed the stairs.

She returned a few minutes later. "These are old," she commented as she fingered the worn, leather-covered volume.

"They were my grandfather's and then my dad's. I feel close to them when I touch the pages, so sometimes I use them, even when my own are available." Sydney nodded as he took the book from her hands. "Sit here by me while I read to you about Job."

"I've heard all that before." She couldn't muster any enthusiasm for the Bible story.

"Me too, but we're going to read it anyway." Sydney settled down and listened to the comforting sound of Cole's voice as he narrated Job's misfortunes. When he finished, he closed the book and turned to her. "Job wasn't just a pretty good guy. This says that he was 'a just and perfect man.' Yet the Lord let terrible things happen to him. He lost more than his spouse, he lost everything. His home, his livelihood, his health." He paused for a second. "His children." Sydney shuddered. "Why do you think the Lord agreed to have Job tested so severely?"

"Because he had faith." Sydney thought she remembered that from Seminary.

"You think terrible adversity is a reward for faith?" Cole asked and she had to reconsider.

"I don't know. I guess not."

"The Lord knew that Job had the spiritual strength to endure great pain and suffering. Job remained faithful during his trials, and that gave the Lord the opportunity to bless him with more than he had at the beginning. You are strong, Sydney. And if you can endure your trials well, like Job, the Lord will bless you with more than you had at the beginning."

"I'm not that strong—"

"You are. You're strong enough to forgive others for their mistakes and you're strong enough to forgive yourself. Most importantly you're strong enough to accept that there are some things that are no one's fault and move on with your life."

"What life?"

"Your life with me," he said.

"Oh Cole, you just think you love me. You don't have enough experience to be sure."

"I thought of a test, to see if it's really love I feel for you or something . . . less," he told her. "I tried to picture my future without you and I couldn't." They were quiet for a few minutes while she concentrated on breathing. "What about you?" he prompted her finally.

"What do you mean?" She was cautious.

"Do you have a test for true love or do you want to borrow mine?"

"I love my children."

"I'm talking about romantic love. The kind that makes your heart beat fast and your mouth go dry and your palms sweat," he specified.

"And your face feel hot."

Cole nodded. "That's it."

"I thought I loved Craig, but I never felt that way about him. I was very proud of him and glad to be his wife . . ."

"You honestly never realized that anything was wrong with your marriage?" he asked and she shook her head. "Remember, we've agreed to be completely honest."

Sydney let out a deep sigh. "I couldn't figure out why movies and books made such a big deal out of intimacy. For us it was really nothing. I thought it was like the Bible says, just a means of getting children."

"And you never wondered if there shouldn't be more."

"No marriage is perfect and I thought it was just one of those things. Some women can't have children, others have to work outside the home to supplement their husband's income. I figured I had to accept Craig's limited ability to express affection. It never occurred to me that he couldn't stand the sight of me."

"Like you said, I don't have much experience in this area—"

"Unless we count kissing Donna Jo What's-Her-Name at youth conference when you were in the tenth grade."

"My kissing experience is more extensive than that!"

"We've been over your romantic history before, and it wasn't impressive. You think you love me, but even if I was to lose my mind completely and agree to marry you . . . ," she forced the words out. "You might end up like Craig, stuck with someone you find undesirable."

"The way I feel when we kiss?" Cole whispered and Sydney nodded. "If that's as good as it ever gets, I'll be satisfied."

"So we're going to go with the theory that anything's better than nothing?" Her voice shook slightly.

Cole smiled. "I think we'll be great together. I'll get a pair of heavy-duty earplugs . . ." Sydney punched him in the arm. "Hey! I'm wounded," he reminded her. "And I'm hungry. What's for lunch?"

"I thought we'd call out for pizza," she replied sarcastically.

"We could just sit here and kiss."

"I'll find something." Sydney rushed into the kitchen. She spent over an hour making a beef stew that a professional chef would have been proud of. Cole fell asleep during the potato peeling process and had to be awakened for his medicine and the meal.

"I would marry you just for your cooking skills and fire-building abilities," Cole said between bites of stew. "Even if I didn't love you."

"I haven't agreed to marry you, Cole." Sydney was suddenly serious. "I'm not sure I can make a big commitment like that again." Cole gave her an exasperated look. "Think of how much you love this farm. Peyton's client has offered you a fortune to sell, but you won't because it's yours and you want to keep it. Imagine how you'd feel if someone took it from you and you had to watch while other people moved into your house and—"

"I do love this farm and I'd hate to give it up. But if it came down to a choice between this place and you, I wouldn't have to think for more than a second."

"You'd sell your farm for me?" she breathed.

"I'd do most anything for you, Sydney."

She grasped for something to discourage him. "I'm not sure about having more children. You want a family of your own and that's natural. But I've had three children and my youngest is almost eight. I don't know if I want to go back through the baby stage again."

"I'll help change diapers."

"It's not just that. It wouldn't be fair to Ryan and Trent and Sarah for us to have children. Then some of the kids would be living with their father and some wouldn't."

"It won't be fair to my children that I'm not a rich doctor. But the way I look at that?" She raised an eyebrow. "Life ain't fair."

She jumped abruptly from the couch. "I'm not having children with anyone who uses bad grammar." With that remark, she marched back into the kitchen.

That night after the dishes were washed and the fire was blazing, Cole suggested that Sydney get the portable stereo from his office so they could listen to the weather report. She brought it downstairs and tuned it to a talk radio channel. Temperatures were expected to rise into the mid-forties on Friday and be into the low sixties by Saturday. "That's Georgia weather for you," Cole muttered. "Today we're snowed in, tomorrow we can get a tan."

"You don't sound happy about the forecast," Sydney mused. "The snow needs to melt so you can go to the doctor and have your leg checked."

"Why would I do that? Craig's looked at it and he said it was fine."

Sydney was appalled. "You need to have it x-rayed to be sure the bone wasn't damaged. And there could still be some infection—"

"Let's dance," Cole interrupted her.

"What?"

"If this is going to be our last night here together we should do something special." He pulled himself upright and hobbled over to the bookshelf. After digging through a box of old cassette tapes, he finally selected Garth Brooks's *Greatest Hits*. Then he stuck it in the tape player. "I want you to listen closely to the words of this song," he said as he pressed her to his chest. "It's called 'The Dance.'"

"I've heard it before."

"But this time I want you to listen," he said and they began to sway gently. At first she felt silly, dancing with Cole in his living room. Then she closed her eyes and let the haunting melody envelop her. Safe within Cole's embrace, she could almost believe that true love did exist and that lasting happiness was a possibility.

"So, what did you think?" Cole broke into her reverie and she realized that the song was over.

"It's a nice song. I've always liked it."

Cole reached over and hit the rewind button. "Wrong answer." As he replayed the song she settled back against him and felt her heart skip a beat, then fall into perfect rhythm with his. Even her breathing pattern duplicated Cole's as their feet moved with the music. She had never felt such complete oneness with any other person, and it made her realize just how lonely she had been.

She was enjoying herself too much to keep track of the number of times he played the song. Finally Cole gave into exhaustion and pulled her down beside him on the couch. "Life is like the dance," he explained. "If you went back and changed it to take out the bad, painful parts, you would also eliminate some of the good. Your children, for instance. If you hadn't married Craig, you wouldn't have them."

"If I'd married someone else—"

"You'd have someone else's children. They wouldn't look or act the same. Is there anything you wouldn't suffer to have your children just the way they are?"

"Of course not."

"Even going through a divorce and all the pain of the past year?"

"I wouldn't want to give up my children," Sydney admitted. "But why couldn't things have stayed the same? If I could learn to be content in our marriage, why couldn't Craig?"

Cole shrugged. "I miss my parents, but if they were still alive, my life would be different. I would have gone on a mission earlier and without the responsibility of the farm hanging over my head."

"You would have come home and married some nice, young, nondivorced girl."

"Probably," he agreed. "Darrell wouldn't have torn up the hay baler, I wouldn't have tried to fix it, and you wouldn't have nursed me back to health. We wouldn't be sitting here . . ."

"So you're saying all the pain we've both been through was good?"

"Not good, but maybe necessary." They were quiet for a few minutes, and Sydney thought Cole had fallen asleep. Then he spoke into the darkness. "There's no decision to make about your first marriage, Sydney. Craig made that for you and took the responsibility as well. All you have to decide is whether you have the courage to try once more."

"I'm not saying that I would even consider marrying again," Sydney hedged. "But if I did, how could it all be worked out? Craig and I were married in the temple, our children are sealed to us . . ."

"We'll talk to the bishop, he'll talk to the stake president. There's got to be a way." Sydney was grateful that he didn't say any more. He just held her hand, and they watched the fire until she fell asleep, trying to believe his words.

CHAPTER ELEVEN

Sydney woke up in the early hours of Friday morning to an unusual sound. It took her a few minutes to realize that it was the refrigerator motor. She turned on the crooked floor lamp to confirm that the power lines had been repaired. This meant that road conditions were improving, and her time alone with Cole was coming to an end.

Not sure how she felt about this, Sydney got up off the couch quietly and went upstairs. Whenever she was worried or upset, she always cleaned, so she started in Cole's room. The sheets on his bed were hopelessly stained, so she threw them into a plastic garbage bag along with the soiled medical tape and crusted gauze. She found clean sheets and stretched them across his mattress, then swept and mopped the floor. Once she had all the towels soaking in Clorox water, she tackled the bathroom.

Cole was awake and making oatmeal when she got downstairs. She accepted a bowl and they ate in companionable silence. Then she followed behind him as he climbed the stairs to catch him if he fell. He insisted on getting his own clothes from the drawers and told her not to dare stand by the bathroom door while he took his shower.

So she went downstairs and cleaned up the living room. She piled the pillows and quilts from the couch into the laundry room, then swept up the ashes in the fireplace. She was damp-mopping the hardwood floors when Cole limped down the stairs wearing jeans and a flannel shirt. He was clean-shaven and looked so dear that Sydney's heart skipped a beat.

"Getting everything in order around your new house, Sister Brackner?" he asked with a smile.

"You shouldn't call me that," she objected.

He took the mop from her hand and pulled her into his arms. "In a few months we will be married, so we both need to get used to it."

Sydney looked up at him with stricken eyes. "We've had a nice couple of days together, Cole, but I haven't made up my mind. It's a huge decision and I have to consider the children . . ."

"Your kids are crazy about me."

"I'm serious." Sydney eased out of his embrace. "And I've got to check on the laundry." She walked into the kitchen and listened to the sound of melting snow as she folded clothes and washed dishes. She heard the front door open and assumed Cole had gone out to see about his the animals. A few minutes later she saw the horses run out into the small corral beside the barn. She was stacking towels in a laundry basket when he came in and collapsed at the kitchen table.

"As far as I can tell everything is fine," he reported. Sydney paused to hand him a packet of antibiotics and a glass of water. He pushed the pills through the foil backing and popped them into his mouth. "The snow is melting quickly," he added. "You can probably make it home this afternoon." Sydney nodded. "I'll come over tomorrow and we can talk about our future."

"That's probably not a good idea," Sydney replied quickly.

"Why not."

"Well, I've been thinking . . . ," she said and Cole groaned. Sydney felt the need to defend herself. "Well I have. It's too sudden. The children have had so much upheaval in their lives already—"

"You're going to have to come up with something better than that," he dismissed this argument. "We both know that if you went home and told your kids we were getting married and they were moving out to live on the farm, they'd all be thrilled."

"We don't know each other very well."

"We know enough."

"I'm just not ready," she whispered.

"I can give you some time," he told her generously.

"You shouldn't. You'd be better off with Beulah."

"We can live apart, Sydney, but we can't ever be truly separated again," he said softly. "We're one and I think you know it too. I see it in your eyes, and I felt it last night when our hearts beat together."

Before Sydney was forced to respond, Lamar Hodges burst in through the front door. Sydney turned away from the determination in Cole's eyes and let the men discuss recent events. She took the clean towels upstairs and changed into her own, freshly laundered clothes. Then she put the ones she had borrowed into the washer with the last load of towels. Both men were standing on the front porch when she walked out.

"Don't you want to give the roads a little longer?" Cole asked, but she shook her head.

"I need to get home and check on my kids," she told him.

"Wait." Cole hobbled inside and came out a few seconds later with something in his hand. He pressed the cold plastic into her palm, and she looked down to see the Garth Brooks's *Greatest Hits* tape.

"You want me to play this at home and think about how life is like a dance and that we should be grateful for the pain?" she said, averting her gaze.

"Play it at home, but the only dance I want you to think about is the one you shared with me." He leaned closer. "And how it felt to be in my arms." He let his words sink in, then stepped back. "I'll be in touch," he promised and she nodded vaguely as she got in the Crown Victoria and started the motor.

Tears slipped out of her eyes and she swiped at them furiously as she drove along. She had made the mistake of trusting a man and her heart once before, with disastrous results. Only a fool would risk it twice, and Sydney was anything but a fool. Squaring her shoulders, she faced the mushy snow-covered road with new determination.

She was very glad to see her children and they greeted her enthusiastically. They were sad that the snow was melting, and she accompanied them into the backyard to admire what was left of a snowman they had built that morning. He was leaning dangerously to one side, and his left arm had fallen off. Sarah was trying to repair him when Miss Glida Mae called to Sydney from her back porch.

"Heard you've been snowed in with that warlock!"

Sydney looked at her children, but they didn't seem to be paying any attention to their eccentric neighbor. "He's not a warlock. Some teenagers played a prank on his property. You know how kids are."

"Oh!" Miss Glida Mae ignored Sydney's defense of Cole and stepped down into the soggy grass. "I almost forgot. Come to the fence so I can show you something," she waved, oblivious of the water that seeped into her fuzzy pink slippers. Sydney obeyed, telling the children to go back inside as she leaned over the sagging chainlink and looked at the ground in front of the old shed where Miss Glida Mae was pointing. In a sad heap lay a little bouquet of wildflowers.

Sydney's heart beat faster. "Where did you get those?"

"From my stalker, of course," Miss Glida Mae said with a smug smile. "He must have brought them to me the night before the storm although I didn't find them until today when the snow started to melt." She leaned forward and put a hand to her mouth in a conspiratorial gesture. "I think he was trying to get the courage to knock on my door."

Sydney stared at the dead flowers. "You need to be careful, Miss Glida Mae."

The old woman laughed. "Why would he bring me flowers if he meant me harm?" She turned and walked to her back porch, pink slippers flapping. "You young people have no idea about romance," she muttered as she went inside.

Sydney scrutinized the flowers and controlled a shudder. The little bouquet looked exactly like the one Henry Lee Thornton had tried to give her Monday night at The Lure. It was hard to imagine Henry Lee as Miss Glida Mae's stalker, but then he did stay drunk a lot of the time and maybe her neighbor looked considerably better through bleary eyes.

She intended to give it some more thought, but when she got back inside the children distracted her. They wanted to know about Cole and his hurt leg, so she gave them a quick description of the hay baler incident and her subsequent lifesaving efforts. Then, almost as an afterthought, she mentioned that Cole had asked her to marry him. Cole had predicted that her children would be supportive, but she was surprised by the strength of their positive reaction.

"Oh, Mom! I'd be so glad if you married Brother Brackner!" Sarah screamed.

"Then I can change Old Joe's name to Thunderbolt!" Trent was equally enthusiastic.

"After you're married, will Cole still pay me for feeding the horses?" Ryan asked.

"When is the wedding?" Grandma picked up her calendar and started flipping pages.

"I'm not sure that we're getting married. I just said he had asked me," Sydney clarified.

"You'll never find anybody with a cooler place than his," Ryan pointed out.

"Or nicer horses," Trent added.

"Or more kittens!" was Sarah's contribution.

"It might be a good idea to wait until the witch issue is settled," Grandma said quietly.

"There is no witch issue, but I'm definitely going to wait. I just didn't want the children to be surprised if anyone mentioned a possible wedding."

Sydney left her family lost in various thoughts and dialed the number for The Lure. She told Pinkie that she wouldn't be able to work that night, then went to the grocery store. Cole called after she was in bed for the evening, reading his scriptures. She was so pleased to hear his voice, then angry with herself for the reaction. "What? Did you cut your arm off or something?" she asked gruffly and he laughed.

"I've missed you too. So, why did you stay home from work tonight?" Cole asked. "Couldn't bear the thought of going to The Lure without me?"

"I couldn't bear the thought of going there at all," Sydney amended.

"Did you tell the kids that we're engaged?"

"I told them you had asked me to marry you."

"So, what did they say?"

"They were thrilled," she admitted, burrowing into the covers and putting her palm down on the open pages of his scriptures.

"You've got smart kids. I'm counting on them to help me convince you that life with me beats the eternities alone," he said.

"Well, right now getting some sleep beats talking to you about nothing," she said, then hung up the phone.

By Saturday morning all the snow had disappeared. It took Sydney most of the day to get the house clean and the laundry caught up and by dark she was exhausted. So she called Pinkie and told him that she wouldn't be able to work again that night. He said they were expecting a light crowd anyway, but that she'd better be there on Monday at 7:00 sharp.

The phone rang right after the children were all in bed, and Sydney answered it quickly. "I called The Lure and Carmella said you were out again. Did you quit?" Cole asked.

"I just took a couple of days off. Did you go to the doctor and get your leg checked?"

"Naw, it's fine, but I think it would be good if you and the kids ride to church with me tomorrow since we don't want to show any signs of premarital discord. So, I'll pick you up at 8:30."

"We can't all get into your truck!" Sydney tried to refuse.

"That's why we're going in your grandmother's car," he replied smoothly. "You can come to Sunday School with me, and then I'll introduce you to the Relief Society president."

"Are you kidding? I've got three assignments in Primary tomorrow. I don't know how Maralee Tucker and the others ever made it through a Sunday before I came back to church."

She could hear him laughing softly. "See you in the morning, Sydney. Sweet dreams." She put down the receiver, gently rubbing the words of 2 Nephi 31:20. She didn't have what she would call a perfect brightness of hope, but she did have a little glimmer. So she took a deep breath and moved on to Chapter 32.

* * * * *

When they arrived at church on Sunday morning, Sydney got numerous speculative glances, many offers of congratulations, and one gift. "What are we going to do about this?" she hissed at Cole when he sat beside her for sacrament meeting.

"What is it?" He pulled the paper loose on the end to expose a handheld mixer. "I've been needing one of these."

"We can't keep it!" Sydney was appalled.

"I don't see why not. I'm confident that I'll convince you to marry me, but if not I can get some good use out of this before our breakup becomes common knowledge."

Sydney did her best to ignore him until the meeting ended. As they walked out of the chapel afterward, they ran into Lauren and she was furious with them for not telling her that they were engaged. Sydney was about to explain the situation when Cole put a hand on her arm. She glanced over to see Sister Fancher and Tiffany a few feet to their left.

"I'm sorry, Lauren," Cole began, obviously searching for an excuse. "But now that we're engaged . . ." Inspiration struck. "All Sydney wants to do is hug and kiss! She won't even leave me alone long enough to make phone calls!"

Tiffany blushed, Sister Fancher paled, and Sydney clenched her hands into fists to keep from strangling him. Lauren's eyes got wide. "When is the wedding?"

"Soon," Cole said with a wry smile directed to Sydney.

"Wow," Lauren responded eloquently.

"We've got to go." Sydney pulled Cole toward the door.

"What did I tell you?" he said to their audience over his shoulder.

"Have you ever heard of spousal abuse?" Sydney whispered as they walked outside.

"Does this mean you're accepting my proposal?" he asked.

Rolling her eyes Sydney herded her children into the old Crown Victoria. Cole climbed behind the wheel without permission, just like the patriarch of the family, and slowly pulled out of the parking lot.

Sunday dinner was interrupted continuously by various family members calling to ask if Sydney had really agreed to marry Cole Brackner. Her oldest sister called first and Sydney fully intended to divulge the entire story, but after listening to Rebecca itemize all the rules of etiquette that had been broken by her hasty engagement, she no longer had the energy.

Cole and Ryan left during her conversation with Rachel, who was already planning to combine the forty-sixth anniversary party with a bridal shower in her honor. Cole whispered that they would feed the horses, then he'd be back to pick her up for their appointment with

Bishop Middleton. She nodded vaguely, then he leaned down and kissed her right on the lips. She was peripherally aware of the amazed expressions on her children's faces and intensely aware of her racing heart and sweating palms.

Luckily Rachel was in the middle of a discourse on the advantages of cubed cheese as opposed to slices for the party, so she didn't notice that Sydney failed to respond for several minutes. No sooner had she hung up with Rachel, than the phone rang again. It was Rebecca for the second time, wondering when she would be moving out of Grandma's house. Sydney was tempted to say that whenever she left, she would be taking Grandma's piano with her. But instead she told her sister that she had a meeting with the bishop and couldn't talk.

"Why do you need to meet with the bishop?" Rebecca wanted to know.

"Marriage counseling," Sydney responded with a sigh.

When she finally spoke to her parents, they said the phone had been busy for over an hour. Anxious to get an explanation, they had called Cole. Sydney assumed that he had told them that she was still undecided, but then her mother said she and Sydney's father wanted to give the couple a weekend in the Smoky Mountains as a wedding gift.

Sydney was irritated by the time Cole came to pick her up and her mood didn't improve when Bishop Middleton introduced his first order of business. "So, when are the two of you getting married?"

Sydney had hoped that Craig would at least be mildly shocked by this question, but he didn't react at all. Even more irritated than before, Sydney spoke before Cole could, "Craig and I were married in the temple, so I don't know how this could all be worked out . . ."

Bishop Middleton smiled. "I can't say that I have handled another situation exactly like this one, but I'll talk to the stake president and see what he says." Sydney was about to explain that this might be premature when Craig spoke.

"That would be great, if you and Cole got together," he said pleasantly.

"Yeah, that would make things nice and tidy for you, wouldn't it? If I'm married, you won't have to feel guilty anymore," Sydney's tone was sharp.

"I'll never be free of the guilt," Craig corrected her softly. "But I'd feel better if I knew you were happy."

Sydney had the decency to blush as Bishop Middleton cleared his throat and continued, "To begin with I would like to say that in my opinion, Sydney has done a wonderful job of raising three children with very little help from anyone."

"I sense a 'but' here," Sydney said cautiously.

The bishop smiled. "But they need more time with their father. I think the first step toward a healthy, shared-parenthood relationship would be for you to voluntarily improve Craig's visitation schedule." Sydney had expected this and, as much as it hurt her to admit it, she knew the children would benefit. So she nodded.

"I'm glad you are willing to cooperate and I would like to suggest that Craig take the children every Sunday after church and one night a week in addition to his third Saturday. Holidays can be arranged so that both parents and the grandparents get time with the children."

Sydney nodded again although her chest was beginning to hurt. "I would like to point out here that few divorced women find themselves negotiating with ex-husbands who want more time with their children." Sydney started to speak, but the bishop pressed on. "Craig accepts responsibility for the failure of your marriage and the divorce. But it is to his credit that he wants to remain involved in the lives of his children."

"I want you to cash my checks," Craig entered the conversation. "Even if you just keep the money in a savings account. And I want to help with their homework and school projects. Take them to soccer practices and attend PTA meetings."

"Sharing parental duties will not only strengthen the children's relationship with Craig, it will give you and Cole time alone together," the bishop stepped back in smoothly. "Motherhood is extremely important, but children do grow up. Oftentimes parents find themselves lost if they don't have a strong marriage to sustain them after their children leave home."

Sydney glanced up at Cole as she considered this and he smiled. She rolled her eyes, then returned her attention to the bishop. "I appreciate your cooperation with the legal pads. You were all very open about your feelings. I now have a much better understanding of

who you are and how your lives fit together. Craig, I encourage you
to continue working with your bishop. I'll schedule individual meetings to help Sydney and Cole deal with private issues. But the last
thing we need to discuss as a group is the problems Cole has been
having on his farm. Let's list them all and then we can try to explain
them."

Cole began with the burned calves and the witness who claimed to
have seen witches dancing around a fire. The bishop nodded as he
wrote. The list continued with alleged occult symbols made from rocks,
antifreeze in the pond near the expensive breeding stock, the feed store
in Columbus refusing to buy Cole's hay and his tires being slashed.

"What is it that makes you think Peyton is involved in these incidents?" Bishop Middleton asked Sydney after he had everything
committed to paper.

"I just think it's awfully suspicious that none of this started before
she came to Eureka," Sydney said reluctantly. Her accusations had
seemed more reasonable on Thursday right after she had found out
that Peyton and Craig were married. She had to admit that it was
hard to imagine the composed woman sitting next to Craig dressed in
a witch outfit dancing around a flaming calf. "The only logical explanation for all these things happening at once is that someone is trying
to force Cole to sell the farm, and Peyton is the obvious suspect."

"First of all, I have never had to resort to illegal means to complete
a transaction," the beautiful blonde leaned forward and addressed
Sydney directly. "Secondly, I don't really care about the deal with
Cole's farm anymore. Now that Craig and I are married, I wouldn't
take a position with Lieberman, Sobels, and Finn if they offered it to
me. So I will handle the arrangements if Cole decides to sell and will
gladly accept my commission—" this was said with a smile. "But I
won't pressure him and I certainly wouldn't stoop to sorcery."

Sydney was not convinced, but the bishop spoke before she got a
chance. "Let's set your suspicions about Peyton aside for the moment
and see if we can think of anyone else who may have had something
to gain from the sale of Cole's farm."

"According to the mayor, the whole community thinks they'll get
rich if the developers from Nashville build that theme park. So that
makes most of Eureka suspects," Cole pointed out.

"That's a very long list," the bishop murmured unhappily.

"And I guess you'd have to include my own sisters since they are so determined for me to sell," Cole added with a smile.

"We'll leave that problem for now and list any unusual events that have happened in the past few weeks, even if they seem unrelated to Cole's troubles."

"Snow in early November is unusual," Craig contributed stupidly and Sydney gave him an exasperated look.

Bishop Middleton spoke to keep Sydney from commenting. "That's good," he insisted. "Anything that seems out of the ordinary."

"If you think we're dealing with someone who has control over the weather—" Sydney began, but Cole interrupted.

"A few weeks ago someone disconnected the battery cables of Sydney's car so that it wouldn't start when she came out after work."

"Wonderful!" the bishop wrote furiously.

Sydney said she didn't see how her car problems could possibly be involved in Cole's troubles unless his witches had put a spell on the Crown Victoria, but added that she also had a leaking radiator hose. "Cole repaired it with duct tape. And speaking of duct tape, my neighbor, Miss Glida Mae Magnanney, has a stalker who stole duct tape a few weeks ago, and I think it's Henry Lee Thornton."

"Henry Lee?" Cole sat up straight in his chair. "The drunk from The Lure?" he clarified and Sydney nodded. "What do you mean by 'stalking'?"

"She says he visits her house almost every night. Once he tried to look in her dining room window, but other than taking the tape he hasn't done anything wrong. She thinks he admires her because she used to be famous."

"How do you know it's Henry Lee?" Craig asked.

"He tried to give me some flowers on Monday night. I didn't take them, of course," Sydney assured everyone. "Then yesterday morning Miss Glida Mae showed me the little bouquet in front of her shed. She said it had been covered by the snow, and she hadn't seen it until the weather warmed up."

"You're sure it was the same flowers?"

"Pretty sure," Sydney affirmed. Craig and Cole exchanged a long look. "Why?" The intensity of their expressions made her uneasy.

"If Henry Lee is stalking someone it's you—not your grand-mother's neighbor," Cole replied finally, his tone tense.

"If Henry Lee wanted to watch your grandma's house, he could do it easily from Miss Glida Mae's yard," Craig contributed.

Sydney thought about this for a few seconds. "It's true that you can see into the kitchen from that shed. The window in the laundry room is high and too small to see much . . . ," her voice trailed off.

"What?" Cole demanded.

"You can see pretty well into my room," she admitted and all the men shared another look. "The most he would have ever seen was me walking by in my nightgown."

"We'll call the police as soon as we're finished here," Bishop Middleton proposed.

"We can't do that!" Sydney surprised everyone by objecting. "It will hurt Miss Glida Mae's feelings if she finds out that I have a stalker and she doesn't."

"Sydney, don't be ridiculous. Your safety is more important than someone's feelings," Cole responded shortly.

"Miss Glida Mae is old and very vain. Something like that could have a more serious effect than you might think. And Henry Lee is not dangerous! He'd never do anything to hurt me!" Sydney was certain. "Besides, Henry Lee isn't sober long enough to poison ponds and burn calves." Reluctantly everyone agreed. "But," they all looked up at her, "sometimes I do get the feeling I'm being watched when I leave The Lure, and once I saw a car following me. I guess that could have been Henry Lee."

"Henry Lee is rarely able to drive himself home, let alone follow you," Cole said, worry lines forming between his eyes.

Sydney shrugged, acknowledging this point. Craig cleared his throat and finally spoke. "I'm the one who followed you home."

"What?" Sydney and Cole gasped in unison.

Craig spread his hands in supplication. "Since I couldn't talk you out of working there, I parked across the street and watched you come out every night. Then I drove behind you until you were safely at Grandma's house."

"The car I saw wasn't yours." She could almost feel her heart melting, and she wasn't completely pleased with the sensation.

"I borrowed cars from other people at work so you wouldn't know it was me. But once Cole started looking out for you, I stopped."

"I don't know what to say." Her throat tightened with unwelcome emotion.

"Thanks," Cole supplied for her.

Everyone else seemed to relax, but Sydney doggedly reminded them that all these events had started about the time Peyton arrived in town. The other woman acknowledged the coincidence but maintained that she was not responsible.

The bishop said he would keep the list and to call him if they thought of anything else. When Craig asked if he could go and pick the kids up for the rest of the afternoon, Sydney wanted to object, but Cole clasped her hand under the table and she nodded. Craig gave her a brilliant smile and promised to have them back early since it was a school night. After Craig and Peyton left, Bishop Middleton praised her.

"You have found yourself in extremely difficult circumstances, and I know the concessions you made today were painful. But I don't think you'll regret them."

They promised to call if they thought of any more strange events, then walked out to the Crown Victoria. While Sydney buckled her seat belt, Cole leaned over and kissed her soundly.

"You've got to quit doing that!" She composed herself, then narrowed her eyes at him. "Was that my reward for letting Craig have the children more?"

"Naw, I've just got to keep reminding you of what you're missing every day that we're not married," Cole said with a smile.

When they got to her grandmother's, Cole walked straight into the backyard and over to the corner by Miss Glida Mae's shed. "Go upstairs and stand at your bedroom window," he told Sydney without taking his eyes off the house.

"This is silly," Sydney grumbled as she went inside. When she got to her room, she gazed through the glass and saw him squinting up at her. He looked so cute in the late afternoon sun that she leaned forward without thinking, pressing her hands against the cool panes. He motioned for her to come back down, but she waved him up instead. He looked around self-consciously, then headed toward the house. A few minutes later he was standing in her doorway.

"We've really got to get married if we're going to keep spending time in each other's bedrooms," he teased and she couldn't resist a smile. His expression became more serious as he joined her by the window. "You've never seen anyone by the shed or in the alley?"

"No, but then I've never looked. And I refuse to be scared of Henry Lee Thornton."

The tension was back around Cole's eyes. "I just don't want to be responsible for putting you in danger."

"You think Henry Lee is stalking me because of you?"

"He's obsessed with you. If he thinks I'm competition, it might cause him to do something desperate." As they stared at the backyard, a head covered with butterscotch curls bobbed along the fence line and then Miss Glida Mae came into full view. "Who in the world is that?" Cole took in her flowing chiffon gown, heavy makeup, and elaborate costume jewelry.

"That is Miss Glida Mae Magnanney, and you can tell her that she doesn't have a stalker if you want to, but I'm not saying a word." They went downstairs and reached the kitchen table at the same time Miss Glida Mae did. Sydney greeted her and introduced Cole.

"I don't know much about witchcraft," she responded, peering at him closely. "I did meet a medium in Baton Rouge back in the thirties, but that was the closest I've come." Miss Glida Mae glanced up to see Cole and Sydney regarding her blankly. "A medium is someone who can communicate with the dead. People will pay a lot to talk to their dearly departed."

"Cole is not a witch and he can't speak to the dead," Sydney said tersely, although she knew explaining anything to Miss Glida Mae was hopeless.

"Will you have to go through an initiation ceremony when you marry him?" Miss Glida Mae asked Sydney. With a weary shake of her head, Sydney went to find Grandma.

"You're not leaving me alone with her," Cole whispered from directly behind her. "She might ask to see my mark," he added and she laughed. Grandma was taking a nap, but Sydney roused her and sent her down to visit with Miss Glida Mae. Cole and Sydney went out onto the front porch and sat in the swing, enjoying the warm weather.

"It's hard to believe that a few days ago the whole town was para- lyzed by snow," Sydney remarked as she saw Miss Mayme peeking out her living room windows.

"That storm almost seems like a dream," Cole agreed, sliding over and putting his arm around her. "Why is your other neighbor staring at us through her curtains?" he asked as he rubbed his lips against her temple.

Commanding herself to breathe, Sydney replied. "Miss Mayme isn't as brave as Miss Glida Mae, and she's probably never known anyone who makes a living talking to the dead."

"She's scared of me?" Cole guessed.

"Absolutely terrified. She thinks you might cast a spell on her."

"Spell casting could would come in handy when you needed to sell cows or fix tires or make someone marry you," Cole mused and Sydney gave the swing a good push with her foot.

They stayed on the porch until dark when Grandma insisted they come inside and eat fried chicken left over from lunch. Craig dropped the kids off at eight o'clock, and Cole said he needed to go home. He leaned down to kiss her good night, but she pulled back and whis- pered that he really shouldn't in front of the children. He glanced over at the kids, who were all watching him carefully.

"Okay, everybody cover your eyes so I can kiss your mother." Sydney made a noise somewhere between a groan and a laugh, and Cole pulled her into his arms.

* * * * *

Sydney was sitting on the steps of Shear Delight on Monday morning when the owner pulled up at eleven. "We're not open on Mondays," Ruby Louise Harrell said as she unlocked the front door.

"I know, but when I called your house your husband told me you were coming over to do some paperwork and he said you wouldn't turn away a woman in need," Sydney explained and Ruby Louise laughed, then told her to come on in.

Sydney left two hours later with hair close to her normal, dull brown color and cut short. What was left of her old permanent gave it just a little body, and Ruby Louise assured her the style was perfect for her. The hairdresser wouldn't even accept payment for her work. "Just tell everyone you see that I repaired the mess you had made of your hair, and I'll have more business than I can handle."

When she left Shear Delight, Sydney had every intention of going back home but found herself headed for Cole's farm instead. He was in the corral by the barn, watching the horses run around in circles. He met her at the fence and said he loved her new look. Embarrassed, she told him that men were supposed to prefer women with long, preferably blonde, hair.

Cole shook his head. "I never understood why anyone would want to deal with a tangled mess of hair everyday," he said and Sydney smiled, then reminded him that he should be resting his leg. "Craig came by to check this morning, and he says it's healing fine."

"That was nice of him," Sydney admitted.

"He's a nice guy." Cole whistled and the horses stopped running. "I was proud of you for agreeing to the bishop's suggestions yesterday. Sharing your kids is never going to be easy, but if you work together, it's got to be better for everyone." Cole whistled again and the horses gathered in the center of the corral, stomping and throwing their heads.

"Craig asked if he could have them on Monday nights for family home evening." Sydney watched the horses. "Since I get them the rest of the week, I said okay. He's going to pick them up at school, then bring Ryan out to do his farm chores." She turned to face him. "Grandma went to lunch with some of her friends, and I can't stand the thought of going home to an empty house."

"Then stay here with me," he suggested softly. "I'll make you a tuna salad sandwich and then we can go up to the cabin and fish until three o'clock."

"I'll pass on the sandwich and the fishing, but I can stay for a little while. What's happening at three o'clock?" she asked.

"A delegation from the city council is coming to search for cast-iron cauldrons, black candles, and spell books."

"You don't have to let them snoop around your property."

"I don't have to, but I hope if they look and don't find anything, they'll leave me alone." He reached out to push a strand of hair away from her eyes. "Mr. McPherson from the bank called this morning.

He said the directors are getting nervous and have insisted on a meeting tomorrow. With a fourth of our herd dead and half of our hay money listed as accounts receivable instead of cold hard cash, the projections for next year aren't looking good. After all the talk about witches, they're afraid that the property value will drop, Peyton's clients will withdraw their offer, and the bank will be left with a piece of land that's not worth the mortgage against it. He's doing what he can for me but said that they are seriously considering calling the loan in immediately."

"Can they do that?" Sydney asked.

Cole shrugged. "I guess." He walked through the barn and came out driving the four-wheeler. "Want to go for a ride?" She climbed into the passenger seat. He didn't say anything for a while and Sydney just enjoyed the view. Finally he parked on a hill overlooking the house.

"I love every rock, every blade of grass, every speck of dirt on this farm," he told her as they studied the peaceful scene below. "I can't tell you how it feels to know that I'm growing hay in the same soil, walking the same paths, breathing the same air as other generations of Brackners. My family has weathered wars and depressions and droughts and pestilence. It kills me to think that I am finally going to be the one who wasn't strong enough to hold onto it. This is my connection to the past, to my father." He turned pain-filled eyes to her. "I always thought I would have the privilege of passing it on to my children and then my grandchildren. To me it's worth so much more than a million dollars. It's invaluable."

"I'm sorry, Cole. I wish there was something I could do."

He was quiet for a while, then he spoke softly. "There is something that I think would make me feel better." She waited for him to elaborate. "A big kiss." Sydney gave him an exasperated look. "Not even a little hug to ease my pain?"

"I'll pray for you instead."

"Chicken," he accused and she demanded to know the reason. "You're afraid to kiss me because you like it too much."

"I'm not afraid of anything," she told him sharply.

"You're terrified of your feelings for me."

"If you're going to be ridiculous, you might as well take me back to my grandmother's car."

Cole leaned forward and rested his chin on the little steering wheel. "I wonder if losing the farm is my price of discipleship," he mused. "I knew when I left on my mission that it was the right thing to do, and I thought that the Lord would protect the farm while I was gone. Even when I came home and found things in such a mess, I never really worried because I didn't think the Lord would let me lose it as a result of doing the righteous thing. Now it looks like I might."

"It seems like such a high price to pay." Sydney felt her throat tighten.

"Many people have given much more. The Savior said you're not worthy to be his disciple if you don't love Him more than your parents or even your life. Losing the farm won't kill me, and I'm willing to pay that price if that's what the Savior requires of me. I have a college degree and lots of practical experience, so I can get a job. It's just hard to imagine life away from this place. It's all I've ever known." Almost against her will, she reached over and touched his hand. He laced his fingers with hers and smiled.

"So, are you working tonight?" He changed to a lighter subject. Sydney said that unless she could think of a good excuse, she would be at The Lure. "Well, save table nine for me. I'll drop by for a little while in between witch hunts." He glanced at his watch. "It's almost two-thirty," he reported without enthusiasm. "If you want to get out of here before the city council arrives, you'd better leave soon," he said then headed slowly down the hill.

Cole drove the small tractor straight into the barn, and when he cut off the motor they heard the sound of a car pulling up outside. "They can't be early!" The despair in his voice was so obvious that Sydney had to stifle a giggle. They walked out into the sunshine to find Peyton Harris Cochran standing by Craig's van. Cole and Sydney groaned in unison.

"I know I'm not a welcome sight for either of you." Peyton didn't mince words as they continued toward her. "But we need to talk."

"You've come to confess!" Sydney predicted and Peyton smiled.

"Not quite, but after our discussion yesterday I realized that a lot of suspicious things have happened since I came to Eureka. I'll admit to sending your sisters copies of each proposal the client offered . . ."

Cole's jaw tightened with irritation. "That was underhanded."

"It was perfectly legal. They are heirs, just like you are."

"You knew they wanted to sell and would pressure me."

"Of course." She waved the ethics of this aside. "I also gave copies to the board of directors at the bank—"

"That was a breach of confidence!" Cole was visibly angry now, and Sydney was enjoying the exchange.

"Actually, that was also within the law. As a lien holder, the bank had a right to know," Peyton explained. "And I gave the city council and mayor a graph showing the increases in tax revenues and municipal growth that would result if the theme park is built here."

"You didn't miss a trick." Cole's tone was frosty.

"I never do," she replied matter-of-factly. "But I did not put antifreeze in your water or set any calves on fire. I didn't even arrange for the feed store in Columbus to buy someone else's hay, although that was a good idea and not strictly illegal." She looked disappointed that she hadn't thought of it.

"But something about all this has bothered me, and this morning I realized why. When I accepted this assignment I agreed to make daily reports to my employers. This is not unusual; in fact, it's something I would do without being asked. But they specifically wanted to know details about the way the farm was run. They said this would help them formulate attractive proposals, but the coincidence between what I reported and what happened was too strong to ignore. For instance, I did tell my employers that Cole sold his extra hay for much-needed cash. And I did mention that the breeding stock was more valuable than the other cattle and essential to future earnings . . ."

"You think your employers killed my cows?" There was doubt in Cole's voice.

"It's hard to believe," Peyton admitted, leaning against the side of Craig's car. "They are a very reputable company. In fact, when they offered me this job, it was like my professional dream come true." She turned and looked toward the pasture.

"Why?" Sydney asked. "I thought you liked having your own company."

Peyton shrugged. "I was flattered. I thought I had made a name for myself and that they could no longer afford to ignore me. Now I wonder if they hired me because they didn't want their firm directly involved in this deal. Since I wasn't an actual employee, if things went wrong, they could wash their hands and leave me holding the bag."

"You should tell the police your suspicions," Sydney advised.

"I said they were a reputable firm. They are also wealthy and powerful. I can't make accusations without any evidence." Peyton waved this aside. "However, I did call and ask them to identify the client who had hired them to handle the acquisition of Cole's property. They refused to do so, and based on that, I terminated my association with them." Her eyes were earnest. "In spite of that, I encourage you to go ahead and accept their offer. If you're going to have to sell anyway, you might as well get the best price."

"You think I would sell to them knowing that they may have vandalized my farm and killed my cows?" Cole asked in amazement.

Peyton nodded. "The bottom line is money."

"Not to me," Cole disagreed.

Sydney couldn't shake the sneaking suspicion that this was just another ploy to make Cole sell. After all, they had no proof, except Peyton's word, that she was no longer representing the company in Nashville. And the fact that Craig was not present at this meeting seemed significant. "So, what will you do now that you've quit your job?" Sydney asked, watching the other woman closely.

"I've sent Marcie back to Nashville to close up our office and my apartment there. Then we'll set up an office in Eureka. It won't be a big operation, and I'll be very selective about the type of cases I take." Her expression became more serious. "I have it on good authority that the bank is going to call your loan, Cole. Legally, they have to give you ninety days, but the only way you could raise the loan balance in that length of time would be to sell everything. All your equipment, stock, your house, and probably the lakeside property as well."

"Your father's fishing cabin?" Sydney asked, confused.

"The land that borders on the lake is much more valuable than the rest," Peyton explained for him, then turned back to Cole. "But if you sell everything, just to hold on to the land, how will you pay the taxes and buy groceries? Even if you did get another bank to loan you money for more stock and equipment, you'd always be only a step ahead of bankruptcy."

Cole looked away and Peyton sighed. "I did a lot of research when I accepted this case. Small farmers face a constant uphill battle. Unless they are already wealthy, it's almost impossible for them to survive against unexpected expenses, disease, depressions in the beef market, and bad weather. Under the best of circumstances it's hard to succeed, and I think we can agree that your situation is far from ideal. The bank is nervous about property values. If my suspicions are correct, and Lieberman, Sobels and Finn, in collaboration with their mystery client, is behind your recent troubles, they won't be scared off. But they may reduce their offer and that's why I recommend that you accept immediately."

"I'll think about what you've said," Cole responded quietly.

"If you keep this farm, you will work yourself to death for the rest of your life making a modest income at best. You can't produce as much as the land is worth. Give yourself a break, Cole. Your ancestors did what they had to do, and now it's your turn. Sell the land for top dollar and give your sisters their share. You can keep the house and get a job where you'll only have to work eight hours a day, five days a week." Peyton's plea was rousing, but whatever response Cole intended to make was lost in the sounds of another car pulling up the gravel drive.

"This will probably be the city council," Cole said grimly.

"Coming to search for witch paraphernalia," Sydney added for Peyton's benefit.

As the old blue Ford came into view, Peyton sighed. "It's even worse than you thought. It's my father."

Clyde greeted everyone through a tear in the plastic that covered his driver's side window. It took several seconds for the engine to actually stop after he turned off the car, then he stepped out and stood beside Cole.

"I'm here to offer you my services, free of charge!" he announced and Peyton made a noise in her throat. "Been living in the Bugs Bunny Motel ever since Peyton and Craig got married. Didn't want to intrude on their honeymoon," he explained, making both women uncomfortable.

"But I heard Peyton talking to Marcie on the phone this morning about all the trouble Cole was having out here with witches and poisoned water and slashed tires. So I thought to myself I could save the cost of a hotel room if I brought my gear and camped out around your place every night. I just might catch whoever's playing tricks on you."

"This is ridiculous," Peyton interrupted. "If you can't afford the motel, I'll pay for it."

"It's the waste that bothers me. I have plenty of money!" Sydney saw Peyton's eyes drift over to the battered car. "I know I need to get something better to drive, but the old Ford and I have been together for twenty years. Every time I try to trade it in, I just can't make myself do it." Peyton didn't look convinced. "I made a good salary with the oil company and never had much to spend it on. And anybody who didn't make money in the stock market during the nineties would have to be an idiot," Clyde continued and Cole tried, unsuccessfully, to stifle a laugh. "What?" Peyton's father asked.

"Sydney and I are two of the idiots who didn't make any money on stocks during the nineties," Cole explained.

"Sorry! No offense intended," Clyde assured them.

"None taken," Cole answered for them both.

"I'd be glad to do something useful for a change, and I enjoy the outdoors," Clyde continued. He ran a trembling hand through his hair, and Sydney doubted that he would be any help at all to Cole. She was therefore surprised when he accepted the old man's offer.

"What about when it rains or if the weather turns cold?" Peyton grasped for an objection.

"I'll sleep in the barn."

"He's welcome in the house, for that matter," Cole invited.

"Mind if I stow my gear?" Clyde asked and Cole walked over to help him unload his car.

"I've tried everything to get rid of him," Peyton said as the women watched. "I've offered him money, I've threatened to get a restraining order, I've even thought about having him thrown in jail for vagrancy. But nothing works. He won't go away."

Clyde drove his old car around to the side of the barn out of sight, and Peyton made a hasty exit. Sydney stayed long enough to tell Cole he was crazy for inviting the enemy right onto his property. "I'm not at all convinced that Peyton and her father are the enemy," he said.

"How do you even know he is her father?" Sydney demanded. "They might just be partners in crime!"

"If so, I'd rather have him right here where I can keep an eye on him. And I'm due for a break, so maybe he's sincere and in that case, I can use the help. And as long as he's here, I don't think I'll get many visits from Peyton," Cole pointed out and Sydney had to admit that there was a certain amount of wisdom in this. Before she could comment further, the city council arrived and she left Cole to deal with them alone.

CHAPTER TWELVE

Sydney hated herself for taking extra pains with her appearance that night as she dressed for work. She pretended that she didn't care how she looked as she applied makeup and dabbed perfume behind her ears. Henry Lee was already at the bar when she arrived, sipping Coke from a can and looking miserable. "Still sober, Henry Lee?" Sydney asked as she checked her tables.

"Been almost two weeks now," he reported. His eyes drifted up to her new hairstyle but he wisely refrained from comment.

"Good for you." She considered confronting Henry Lee about the flowers but decided it would be to her advantage for him to think she didn't know. So she went to work and avoided him as much as possible. Cole came in at seven-thirty and settled comfortably at table nine. "So, is Clyde protecting the farm tonight?" she asked as she handed him a Sprite.

"With a little help from Lamar."

"Two old men. You're doomed," Sydney told him.

"I got an odd phone call from Michelle just before I left." He took a sip of his soft drink. "She was going on and on about a new house they've made an offer on. It's a five-bedroom in a better school district, and she says the owners are supposed to let them know by Friday. I asked her if they'd sold their house and she said they were about to put it on the market." Sydney stared at him, waiting for the punch line, until he asked, "Don't you think it's strange that Michelle has made an offer on a new house when she hasn't even sold her old one?"

"I don't know much about real estate," Sydney shrugged. Cole finished his Sprite, then went backstage to speak to Lauren. He returned a few minutes later carrying a set of keys.

"Lauren got here late and left her makeup in the car. She's asked me to get it."

"It's time you did something useful for a change," Sydney called after him as he rushed out. When he came back in a few minutes later, Edith Wilkerson, the police dispatcher, stopped him by the entrance. As Sydney watched them talk, Cole's face turned pale and a knot formed in the pit of her stomach. Edith left and Sydney crossed the room to meet him. "What's wrong?"

"I need to use the telephone at the bar," he said instead of answering. He didn't wait for a response, so she followed him and watched while he punched in several numbers. "Darrell? Get over here quick. Lauren is fine—for the moment anyway." With that he hung up and turned to face Sydney. "Could you find us a room for a nice little family chat?"

Almost frightened by his menacing tone, Sydney went into the back and looked around. After locating an unoccupied janitorial closet, she rushed out in search of someone to cover her tables. Carmella wasn't there yet and Sydney knew better than to ask Starla. She wasn't on a friendly enough basis to request a favor from any of the other waitresses and if she asked Pinkie, he'd probably fire her on the spot. Then she saw Henry Lee, still sitting at the bar sipping his Coke. She pulled off her apron and advanced toward him.

"Henry Lee, I need a favor," she told him bluntly. His eyes lit up with pleasure at the request, and she almost felt ashamed. "I have a pressing personal problem and need someone to cover my tables for a few minutes." The man looked startled as she held out her apron. "Here, put this on." She wrapped the apron around his thick middle.

"I don't think it's legal for me to serve alcohol if I don't work here," he said as she told him to inhale so she could tie the apron strings.

"It's not, but you're bound to know all the employees of the Alcohol Control Board, so if any of them drop in on us, tell them you're in training. I'll be back as soon as I can." She spied Cole and a very unhappy-looking Lauren approaching from the backstage area. Darrell rushed in through the main entrance at the same moment, and Sydney led them all into the janitor closet.

"What's going on?" Sydney demanded although she wasn't a member of the family and hadn't officially been invited.

"I met Edith Wilkerson when I came in from getting Lauren's makeup bag, and she offered her sympathy for the problems I was having with witches out on my property. I told her that was just a silly rumor and that there were not any witches." His eyes narrowed as he studied his sister. "She said that she heard about the witches from Lauren personally and never would have believed a word of it if it hadn't come from my sister's own mouth."

Sydney gasped and Lauren's lip trembled.

"When we were looking for the people who were causing problems for me, we really should have considered my family members," Cole said coldly. Lauren started crying, but he was unmoved. "And I thought the worst my sisters could do was make me date Beulah." His laugh was harsh. "But they didn't want to just make me uncomfortable. They wanted to ruin me completely." He turned away from Lauren and stared at the door. "I guess this explains why Michelle has been house hunting. The little plan the two of you cooked up has been successful. The bank is about to call in my loan, and I'm going to be forced to sell."

Sydney looked at Lauren, who was still weeping silently. "You started a rumor about your own brother?" She was incredulous.

"It was an accident!" Lauren wailed, finding her voice at last. "I was at Shear Delight getting my nails done, and we started talking about those burned calves that you found on the farm. The manicurist said burning a cow sounded like something witches would do." Lauren paused, looking miserable. "Darrell and I had watched a television talk show a week or so before about modern covens. I was just making conversation." She defended herself in advance.

"What did you say?" Cole demanded.

"I just said it really could be witches."

Cole looked doubtful. "That's all you said?"

"Well, I told her about the talk show and how witches took over this whole community and now the people who live there can't sell their houses."

"What else?"

"I might have mentioned how some of the more fanatical occult groups make live sacrifices . . ."

Cole sighed. "So, by the time your nails were dry, Edith Wilkerson was convinced that there were witches on the farm."

"Edith was under the hair dryer the whole time, and I didn't even know she could hear us. I guess she caught bits and pieces and got the wrong idea," Lauren admitted. "She must have spent all afternoon sharing the news with the whole town because the next morning when I got to work, everyone at the bank was talking about it."

"And you couldn't do anything to correct the situation?" Cole asked.

"I tried!" Lauren declared heatedly. "But no one would believe me. In fact, the more I insisted that there were no witches, the more they thought there were!"

"Why didn't you come and tell Cole so that he could set things straight?" Sydney asked the obvious.

Lauren looked at her feet and Darrell spoke for the first time. "I told her not to. What was done was done, and I didn't see any point in getting involved."

"Besides, you're still mad that my mother kicked you off the farm and gave me your truck," Cole guessed grimly.

"And you want Cole to have to sell the farm anyway," Sydney added.

Cole's sigh was heart wrenching. "Well, it's not going to work. I'll call Michelle tonight and tell her that I may have to sell the farm, but not to Peyton's clients. I'll sell it for just enough to cover the bank mortgage and leave the two of you nothing!"

"You can't," Lauren spoke from across the small room. "Michelle and I have made up our minds to sell to the people from Nashville, and you can't stop us."

"You and Michelle do not own the farm!"

"We own two-thirds of it. You were given the right to work it, but if it comes down to selling, Michelle and I together have more say than you do." Cole looked like he'd been kicked in the stomach, but Lauren continued. "I'm just so sick of you acting like the victim all the time!" She stepped forward, her tears drying up.

"Lauren!" Darrell held out a hand to restrain her but she shook him off.

"Why is what you want more important than what we want? The farm was our home, too! Mama and Daddy were our parents as much as they were yours. Michelle needs a bigger house and wants her kids in better schools. Her oldest son is ready to go on a mission, and that costs a lot. It's not like she wants luxuries for herself, Cole. She needs the money for her family!"

Lauren paused for a deep breath. "And we have problems of our own. Darrell only makes minimum wage and doesn't have benefits at his hardware job. We stretched our budget past the limit when we bought our new car, and now we're behind on our mortgage." She held up her hand. "I know you're going to say we should have bought a cheaper house, and I guess that's true. And maybe I should have gotten a bicycle when my car died. But it's too late now. If the bank repossesses, we'll lose our down payment and our credit will be ruined."

Sydney risked a glance at Cole, who was slumped against the dirty wall, his eyes fixed on his sister. Lauren continued more calmly. "Darrell wants to go back to school . . ."

"If he studies like he farmed, he'll flunk out in a month," Cole predicted.

Lauren drew in a shuddering breath. "I'm pregnant." Her tears returned. "And I can't keep working two jobs, but the only insurance we have is through the bank . . ."

"We thought the witch rumors would help convince you to sell and then everything would be okay," Darrell risked another comment.

"Even if the rumors made everyone in town hate Cole?" Sydney asked him.

Lauren sighed. "When we met with Peyton—"

Sydney was immediately alert. "Peyton told you to encourage the witch rumors?"

Lauren shook her head. "No, this was before there was any talk of witches. She told us that she was going to create community pressure on Cole to sell. Her plan was to appeal to the town through greed— money for better schools and that kind of thing. She was in close contact with the bank and said to try to think of anything that would help push Cole toward selling."

She risked a glance at her brother. "I'm sorry you can't be a farmer like Grandpa and Daddy, Cole. We know how much you love raising cows, but your happiness isn't more important than all of ours." Her hands dropped to her still flat abdomen. "And we did try talking to you, but you wouldn't listen."

Cole stared at a dirt-encrusted mop bucket. "When will the baby be here?"

"April."

"Was Michele involved in the Eureka witch project?" he asked dully.

Lauren winced. "No, she thought it was the dumbest thing she had ever heard, but by then it was too late."

"You realize that once we sell the land and there is a huge amusement park built on it, there is no going back. The farm will be gone forever."

"One of us will keep the house, that's part of the deal. So we'll always be able to go home for Christmas and stuff." Lauren sensed that he was weakening.

"Who would want to live next to a western theme park?" Cole asked. "You'd probably have the log ride in your backyard!"

"Maybe they'd build the country amphitheater behind your house, and you could watch all the concerts for free," Sydney added, trying to lighten the mood.

Cole took a deep breath. "I guess I won't be buying any new breeding stock, so I can give you enough money to cover your back house payments," he said slowly. "That should protect you from repossession until arrangements can be made to sell the farm."

"Oh Cole!" Lauren threw herself into his arms. "I hope you can forgive me."

He returned her embrace with a sigh. "Just don't mention witches again."

"I promise," she said, tears flowing again.

"I'm sorry, too," Darrell said slowly. "We didn't mean you any real harm—"

"I don't want to talk about it anymore," Cole cut in. "Take Lauren home. Tell the manager she's sick," he said, opening the door.

Sydney was about to suffocate in the small space and gratefully breathed in the fresh air. Cole watched them leave, but made no move to follow, so Sydney remained seated on the low sink. When the door closed automatically behind Darrell, Sydney looked at Cole in the dim light. The anger that had sustained him during the confrontation was gone, and a heavy sadness clouded his features.

"Lauren was wrong," she began, but he didn't respond. "You're such a good brother—"

"I'm selfish. I wanted to keep the farm, no matter what it cost them. And when our mother died, I didn't want to share her last days with anyone." He looked up slowly. "They offered to come, but I told them not to."

"They knew she was dying and they certainly knew where she lived. They didn't need your permission to come."

Cole ignored her attempt to exonerate him. "And it wasn't really fair that my mother gave me more control over the farm than my sisters. Michelle and Lauren have a right to their inheritance." He paused for a humorless laugh. "All this time we've been accusing Peyton, we should have looked for accomplices closer to home."

"Lauren admitted to starting the witch rumors, but she didn't poison the water or slash your tires," Sydney pointed out.

"And Peyton already told us she wasn't responsible for any of that either."

"And we're going to believe her? She even had your own family working against you!"

"Peyton may be unethical, but she's not a vandal. Like she said, it might have been her employers in Nashville. Or it could have been people from town, angry with me for harboring witches. I guess it doesn't really matter anymore."

"You have to meet with the bank tomorrow?"

"At nine o'clock."

"Will you tell them about Lauren and the witch rumors?"

He shrugged. "I haven't decided yet."

"Do you want me to come with you?" He raised an eyebrow. "I could provide moral support and a character witness, if you need one."

"I appreciate the offer, but Bishop Middleton is coming and Mr. McPherson will be there. And since everyone thinks we're engaged, they probably wouldn't consider you an impartial witness." Sydney admitted that this was true. "So, are you?"

"Coming?" She was confused.

"No, impartial."

"You're desperate," Sydney said in mock disgust. Cole continued to watch her closely. "I'm partial," she admitted finally, anxious to escape the scent of sour mop water. "I mean, I like you." He was still waiting and his solid form blocked the exit. "A lot."

"You love me," he corrected.

"Maybe," she conceded with reluctance.

He opened the door and she inhaled frantically. "I guess that's good enough for now. Who's handling your tables?" he asked as an afterthought.

"Henry Lee. He's been sober for two weeks and he's very familiar with our menu, so I figured he was qualified."

Cole leaned down and kissed her softly on the forehead. "I'll call you tomorrow," he promised, then walked out the front entrance.

Henry Lee had everything under control when she returned to the floor. "This was kind of fun. I wonder if Mr. Pinkie would let me take that waitressing class."

"Only if you can convince him that you wouldn't drink up the profits." Sydney took the apron from him but couldn't make herself put it back on. She took an order from table five and when she returned to the pick-up window, Henry Lee was still standing where she had left him. Realizing that she owed him some form of appreciation, she forced a smile. "Thanks."

Henry Lee was disproportionately pleased by the grudging word. "You know I'm glad to help you anytime, Sydney," he responded, blushing.

"I'm grateful for the offer, but I'd never risk it again. I can't believe I got away with it this time, and my luck can't hold out much longer."

Sydney took the order for table three while Henry Lee shuffled toward his stool. "What were you and Cole Brackner doing in the janitor closet?" Carmella demanded when they met by the kitchen.

Sydney leaned closer to her friend. "You know the rumors about witches out on Cole's farm?" The waitress nodded. "Well, Edith

Wilkerson, the police dispatcher, overheard Lauren say that witches burn animals and next thing you know, everybody thinks that Cole has witches."

"The little singer's a witch?" Carmella asked in confusion.

Sydney shook her head. "She just watched a television program about modern covens and told her manicurist that the burned cows on Cole's farm could have been part of an occult ceremony. But she didn't stop the rumors once they started, and Cole is understandably upset."

"I'd be mad as anything if I found out my sister was a witch," Carmella said.

Sydney knew she should put forth more effort to convince Carmella of Lauren's innocence. But the girl was getting off very easy in Sydney's opinion, and if some people in town heard a new rumor and drew the wrong conclusion, it was no worse than she deserved. So Sydney shrugged and picked up the popcorn shrimp for her customers.

That night when The Lure closed, Henry Lee was still sitting in his favorite chair and still sober. He offered to walk Sydney to her car, but she shook her head. "That's okay. I parked out front," she told him more gently than usual since it didn't seem right to yell at him so soon after he'd done her a favor.

"Well, see you tomorrow," he said with a little wave as he shuffled to the door.

Sydney fought the urge to call Cole for almost thirty minutes after she got home before she finally gave in. It was after one o'clock and she knew she'd wake him up, but he answered on the second ring and didn't sound groggy. "I just wanted to be sure that you weren't thinking of taking a bottle full of sleeping pills or slitting your wrists because of your sister's treachery."

"So far your love has sustained me."

"You're in worse shape than I thought." She hung up on him and opened his scriptures to Mosiah 3. The phone rang almost immediately.

"Will you and the kids eat dinner with me tomorrow night? Just in case I'm sinking into a deep depression by then?"

"Cook something good," she stipulated and put down the receiver again.

On Tuesday morning the kids told her that Craig had bought them a puppy. "It's a chocolate Lab, and we're trying to think of a name for it!" Trent told her with his mouth full of pancakes. "It's registered and expensive so we have to name him something good." He gave Sarah a meaningful look.

"Daddy said I can help," the little girl responded defensively, then turned to Sydney. "It's so cute, Mom. I can hardly wait for you to see him."

"Can we go by after school and give him some puppy food?" Trent wanted to know.

"Your father will have to feed him on the days you're with me," Sydney forced the words past a lump in her throat.

"Dad said he was going to call and see when a guy from the telephone company can come over and put in another line for the computer. And he has a friend who can set it up on Saturday," Ryan joined the conversation and Sydney nodded dully.

Sharing them in real life was a lot harder than just saying the words. And it was difficult to compete with a top-of-the-line computer and a new puppy. Then she remembered that they were invited to dinner at Cole's house. This announcement was met with enthusiasm, and she felt a little more popular as she dropped them off at school.

Craig called as Ryan had warned and she told him the phone man could come anytime since Grandma was always there. "You got a puppy," she said as the conversation lagged.

"I've been wanting one and now that the kids will be over here more . . . ," his voice trailed off into an awkward silence. "I can't thank you enough for the changes you've agreed to." She heard the emotion in his voice and tried not to be influenced but failed.

"Don't get too used to this good mood I'm in. I'm sure we'll have plenty of fights before the kids are grown," she warned.

Craig laughed and said he had to get back to work. Sydney stared at the phone for several minutes after they hung up until Grandma shook her from her thoughts. "Did I hear you say you were eating with Cole tonight?" she asked, squeezing Sydney's shoulders in a quick embrace.

"Yes, ma'am. Would you like to come too? He promised to fix something good."

Grandma smiled, but she said she'd prefer a quiet night at home. This reminded Sydney that Grandma had been used to a calm, orderly existence before she and the children had moved in. Grandma never complained, and in fact seemed to enjoy their company. But for the first time Sydney wondered if Grandma missed the tranquillity that she had sacrificed in their behalf.

"Maybe things will work out with Cole and me," she proposed tentatively. "Then we'll be his problems and you can have your house back."

Grandma tightened her grip on Sydney's shoulders and pulled her close. "I hope things work out between you and Cole, dear," she whispered. "But you've never been a problem and no matter what the future holds, there will always be room for you at my house."

Sydney pressed against the aged cheek that had provided comfort and security from her earliest memories and struggled to think of an appropriate response. Then she felt Grandma stroke her new, short hair, and realized that between them, words were unnecessary.

* * * * *

When she called Pinkie at The Lure and told him she'd be late that night, he was not happy. He threw out a few veiled threats and finally Sydney told him to fire her if she was more trouble than she was worth. Confident that he couldn't find anyone nearly as capable as she was, at least on short notice, she hung up.

Sydney kept expecting Cole to call and report on his trip to the bank, but by the time she left to pick up the children at school, she still had not heard from him. They went straight to the farm, where Ryan joined Lamar and immediately began his regular tasks. Trent checked on Old Joe, then watched Clyde work on his car. Sarah ran straight for her kittens.

Cole pulled Sydney behind the tractor and into his arms. She allowed him a quick kiss, then asked about his meeting at the bank.

"It went about as we expected. I have ninety days to pay the balance on the loan or they will take the farm," he told her calmly. He didn't seem as upset as he had the night before, and she was glad to see that he was coming to terms with the inevitable.

"Mr. McPherson had the latest proposal from Peyton's clients. Michelle and Lauren had already signed and he wanted me to sign too. I told him that since he had their signatures, he didn't need mine. He said logically that was true, but technically I still controlled the fate of the farm through my mother's will. My sisters can sue and force me to accept this offer, but that takes time . . ."

"You're not going to sell." Sydney was both pleased and terrified by this idea. She couldn't picture Cole living anywhere except on his farm, and she hated the thought of him being forced to sell it. But Peyton's arguments were valid, and Sydney dreaded the thought of him struggling financially all his life, especially if her future was going to be combined with his.

"I don't have a choice about that. What I told them is that I don't have to accept this particular offer." He looked toward the distant pastures. "I can't stand to think about an amusement park here. It would ruin not only this property, but the whole area. And while there is probably money to be made for the community, we have a lot to lose as well."

"So what will you do?"

"Instead of trying to figure out a way to keep from selling, for the next eighty-nine days I'll be searching for a way to sell on my own terms. I'll start by contacting local farmers, then I'll try real estate developers. If I'm lucky I might be able to keep the house and the fishing cabin."

Sydney smiled. "That would be good."

Cole stroked her cheek as Ryan walked up and said he was finished with his chores. He looked between Cole and his mother with solemn eyes. Cole suggested that they round up the other kids and go for a ride in the tractor. Sydney was doubtful about the idea, but the children convinced her.

The tractor made so much noise that conversation was impossible, so they rode in silence until Cole parked. As the children started running up the hill, Sydney called after them not to get out of her sight. They promptly disobeyed and she hurried up the hill behind them.

"Isn't this great, Mom?" Sarah asked when she found them clustered together right over the ridge of the hill, looking down on Cole's fishing cabin. The water lapped quietly at the pier and the sun was low in the sky.

"It is very beautiful," she agreed.

Trent and Sarah walked with her to the water's edge, but Ryan stayed back and waited for Cole. She glanced up a while later to see them standing on the hill, talking earnestly. Eventually they joined the rest, and Cole gave everyone a tour of the little cabin. It started to get cold when the sun dropped beneath the horizon, so they herded the children back over the hill and down to the tractor. As they turned back to the house, Sydney leaned over and shouted into Cole's ear. "What were you and Ryan talking about?"

"I think he wanted to know what my intentions were toward you!" Cole cupped a hand over her ear and hollered back.

Sydney smiled and glanced over at Ryan. He was pointing out some cows to Sarah and trying to keep her from getting too close to the window. "What did you tell him?"

Cole asked her to repeat the question, then nodded when he understood. "I told him it was my intention to make you the happiest woman in the world, if you'd let me," he said, and Sydney raised an eyebrow. "He promised to help me convince you." She shrugged and he laughed. "Your kids have always been my ace in the hole."

Conversation was too difficult so they were quiet until Cole pulled up beside the barn and parked the tractor. He sent the kids into the house to wash their hands for dinner, then turned back to Sydney. "If I take over responsibility for your happiness, Ryan can go back to being a kid," he told her with unusual seriousness.

She was considering her reply when a scream rent the evening air. Cole and Sydney both reacted immediately, but he reached the porch first. Sydney rushed up seconds later to find her children gathered around a lump of fur. It took her a few seconds to realize the lifeless corpse had once been the mother cat. Struggling with nausea, Sydney grabbed Sarah and lifted the child against her chest. Cole pulled Trent away and asked Ryan to go check on things in the barn.

The boy met Cole's eyes for a moment, then he nodded. "Whoever did this could still be here!" Sydney whispered emphatically as she watched her son walk toward possible danger.

"I don't think so. They just wanted to scare me, not risk a real confrontation." Cole had his arm around Trent's trembling shoulders.

They waited tensely until Ryan reappeared carrying four squirming balls of fur. "The kittens are okay!" he reported breathlessly. Sydney watched her son hand the kittens to Trent and Sarah, then walk over to stand beside Cole. Maybe it was her imagination, but he seemed a little taller than he had a few minutes before. They led the children carefully around the mother cat's body and into the kitchen.

"The kittens have been eating dry food for a couple of weeks, but with their mother gone they'll have to depend on it entirely." Cole took a dish out of the cabinet and poured some Kitten Chow in it. Then he set it on the floor beside Sarah. She looked up at him with tear-stained cheeks. "You and Trent watch and make sure that all of the kittens eat some of this food. Ryan, you come with me," he said grimly and they walked back outside.

Sydney tried not to think about the dead cat or her son having to help dispose of it. She wasn't sure how she felt about Ryan becoming a man or Cole helping him on his journey there. When they came back in, Cole began heating up dinner. Sydney didn't think anyone would be able to eat, but after playing with the kittens, the children seemed to forget about the gruesome experience. Sydney was starving and the beef tips served on rice with gravy were delicious. To go with the main course, Cole had homemade yeast rolls, English peas, and a squash casserole.

"You really are a good cook!" Sydney was impressed enough to take a second helping of squash.

"My mother didn't believe in helpless men." He accepted her compliment with a smile. "I also keep my whites white and my colors bright, I sew on buttons, and even wipe out the shower after each use—unless I have recently sustained a life-threatening injury," he stipulated.

"It's amazing that a male marvel like you has lasted this long without getting married."

"I think the Lord has saved me for this place in time so that I could marry you." He was no longer smiling.

Clyde and Lamar stomped in through the back door before she could reply, and Cole offered them the leftovers, which they gladly accepted. Sydney stood to make room at the counter and started washing dishes while the kids took the kittens into the living room. Cole told the men about the cat while they ate. "We were in the yearling pasture fixing a hole in the fence," Lamar explained. "Didn't hear a thing. I'm sorry, Cole."

"It wasn't your fault, but we all need to keep an eye on things for a little while." At that moment Trent rushed in and said Cole needed to be thinking of something to use as a litter box. Cole went to check on this most recent problem, and Sydney sat at the counter beside Clyde.

"I guess I owe you an apology," she said as she watched him pile his plate with beef tips and rice. "When you first came to Eureka I pretended to help you, but I really just wanted to get back at Craig. Things between you and Peyton might be better now if I hadn't interfered."

Clyde waved her words aside. "I've got too many regrets of my own to hold anybody else's mistakes against them. And the only thing that will help me with Peyton is time."

Sydney smiled at the old man. "Is it okay for you to be eating all that red meat?" she asked as he shoveled food into his mouth. He looked up blankly. "I mean, I know it's bad for a lot of medical conditions."

"You think I have a condition?"

"That first night at The Lure Craig said you didn't have long to live—"

Clyde interrupted her with a loud shout of laughter. "I said that to make Peyton feel sorry for me. And it's not exactly a lie. At my age, I can't have too long to live!" His expression grew serious. "I wasted a lot of years and I know I can't ever get them back, but I'm going to do my darndest to make the most of the time I have left."

"It's all a man can do." Lamar nodded his agreement. "My wife died when our daughter was ten. I didn't feel like I could raise a little girl on my own and sent her to live with my sister. She never really forgave me for that, felt like I didn't want her or something. She's barely spoken to me for years. But then out of the blue she called to tell me she was going to have a baby of her own and wanted me to be there. Well, I can tell you she didn't have to ask me twice. I caught the first flight out. So I guess it's never too late."

Cole came back in during this pronouncement and said he had toilet facilities set up for the kittens, and it remained to be seen if they would take advantage of them. "We step in cow pies all day, guess a little kitten poop at night won't hurt us," Clyde contributed, but Cole didn't look convinced.

Sydney checked her watch and told them it was time for her to go. The kids didn't want to leave and she certainly didn't want to go to work, but there was no way around it. "If you would just marry Brother Brackner, we could stay here all the time," Trent told her reasonably.

"And my kittens don't have a mom anymore so they really need me," Sarah added.

"Keep working on her," Cole encouraged them. As they walked out to the car, she told him he needed to call the police about his cat. "I'll report it," he promised.

Sydney watched Ryan settle his brother and sister in the back seat, then she turned back to Cole. "You treated him like a man today, and I could tell that he appreciated it," she said softly.

"He's been doing the job, he deserves the respect," Cole responded.

"I'm scared for you, Cole, out here by yourself," she admitted.

"Clyde and Lamar will be around."

"That didn't help the cat," she pointed out.

He opened the door of the old Crown Victoria and watched her climb in. "I'll stop by The Lure for a little while tonight," he told her. "After Lamar and I decide on a patrol schedule."

"Be careful, Cole."

"I will," he said gently. "Although you're a lot nicer to me when I'm hurt. Maybe it's worth another try."

With a disgusted shake of her head, Sydney started the car and drove away.

* * * * * *

The relief waitress relinquished Sydney's tables when she arrived at The Lure, and a few minutes later Carmella caught her by the bar. "You've missed more work in the past couple of weeks than in the entire year I've known you," she said, leaning against the rough-hewn half log. "When you were late tonight, I called your Grandma. She said you and Cole were engaged and that the whole family was eating dinner at his place."

"Grandma's old and she doesn't always get her stories straight," Sydney skirted the issue. What about you and the UPS man?" Sydney tried to deflect her friend's attention. "You haven't mentioned him lately."

Carmella sighed. "That's over. I asked about his marital status, like you said. He's not married now, but he's already been divorced twice. With my record, I decided I wasn't interested in those odds. But I did get a complete series of Elvis in the Army collector plates."

"How's that?"

"I kept ordering them so the UPS man would have an excuse to stop by my place. Got a pretty good price on them too, and those things go up in value." Carmella took vegetable plates to table four and then came back. "You keep watching the door. Is Cole coming tonight?"

"I am not watching the door, but he did say he'd try and stop by later," Sydney admitted.

"You're watching the door," Carmella said with a smile as she returned to her duties.

By ten-thirty Cole still had not arrived, and Sydney was fluctuating between concern and anger. "Why don't you just give into love?" Carmella asked, climbing up onto a barstool beside her. "If you were married to him, you'd be cuddled up in front of the fire at his farm instead of waiting tables and staring at the front door."

"I've thought about it a lot and I can't marry him. I'm almost four months older than he is, and it would be insane to marry another man whose name starts with the letter *C*."

"You've been thinking about it a lot, and those are the best reasons you came up with?"

"I'm scared," Sydney blurted suddenly.

Carmella reached over and patted her hand. "Of course you are. Risking your heart is a scary thing, but any woman brave enough to face the world after my awful bleach job won't run from love."

Sydney was relieved when table five waved her over and rescued her from the uncomfortable conversation. By eleven she was worried sick about Cole and had decided never to speak to him again. Then Starla rushed over and told her he was on the phone. She forgot her resolve and ran into Pinkie's office. "What's wrong?" she demanded.

"Lamar was shot earlier this evening."

"Shot? You mean like with a gun?"

"A twenty-two-caliber rifle, according to the doctor in the emergency room," Cole confirmed. "The police arrested some local vigilantes, apparently trying to get rid of the witches themselves. They ran into Lamar and one of them shot him by mistake. The bullet grazed the top of his left arm, so he's in pain but there won't be any permanent damage. I've got him back at home now." Cole sounded tired and discouraged.

"Do you want me to come out there?"

"No. The police think they got everybody, but I don't want you over here if there's any chance that gunmen are still around."

"Why does it seem like things are getting worse instead of better?" Sydney asked, sitting on the edge of Pinkie's desk. "You've told everyone that you're going to sell the farm."

"But I'm not selling it to the people who want it."

"Peyton's clients." Sydney realized with a jolt. "Cole, we still don't know for sure if Peyton quit her job. It's possible that she's still very involved in this."

"She's also very much married to your ex-husband."

"So they say!" Sydney cried as the idea occurred to her. "Craig may think they're married, but she could have set up a fake wedding! And she admitted that she hates to lose. Maybe she's using reverse psychology, making you think she doesn't care just to throw you off."

"It's hard to believe that she would go so far."

"People will do most anything for money." Sydney didn't mention Lauren's failure to stop the witch rumors, but she was sure he made the connection. "You're in danger, Cole. If Peyton is this serious about making you sell, she might not even stop at killing you."

Cole frowned. "I don't see how that would help her."

"Then your sisters would control the farm and they've already signed," Sydney reminded him quietly.

Cole considered this. "I'm meeting a man for lunch at The Pork Belly tomorrow. He's interested in the farm and I hope we can work out a deal. Then it will all be over."

"Call me when you get back to let me know how it went," Sydney requested.

"I'll call you from the truck, and if things go well, maybe you can come over for a bowl of ice cream to celebrate."

After her conversation with Cole, time crawled by. Finally Pinkie let her go home at twelve-thirty. She wanted badly to call Cole but knew he was busy with Lamar, so she didn't. Hoping that Cole might call her, Sydney started her clean-up routine. But by the time she fell asleep at three o'clock, she had accepted that she wasn't going to hear from him again that night.

On Wednesday she took the kids to school, then went by the grocery store. Throughout the course of the morning, she was tempted to call Cole several times, but frightened by the intensity of her desire just to hear his voice, she resisted. Too restless to stay inside, she went outside to go for a walk after giving Grandma strict instructions to answer the phone if it rang. Finally she came back inside, tired and hungry. Grandma made her a peanut butter and banana sandwich for lunch, and she ate while staring at the phone, willing it to ring. When it did ring, she almost knocked it off the table in her haste to pick up the receiver.

"Cole!" she said without waiting for him to speak.

"Sydney?" It was Craig's voice instead.

"Is something wrong with Cole?" Her voice sounded dull and far away to her own ears.

"I don't know." The connection was so bad she realized he had to be calling from his car. "Do you know where Cole is?"

"It sounds like your battery is about to go dead," Sydney said as she glanced at the clock. "He had a lunch meeting with a farmer who might want to buy his place, and he was supposed to let me know how it went, but I haven't heard from him yet."

"Peyton called me at the hospital while I was in surgery and left a message that she had thought of something else she needed to tell Cole. She said she was going out to his farm for a few minutes and then would meet me at The Pork Belly for lunch. I waited for almost an hour and it's not like Peyton to be late."

Sydney ignored his newly acquired knowledge of Peyton's habits and concentrated on the information he had given her. Peyton went out to Cole's this morning. She did not make her lunch appointment with Craig and Sydney had not heard from Cole. "Her secretary is on the way home from Nashville, and she hasn't heard from her either," Craig added.

Sydney's hands started to tremble. "Did you say you're at The Pork Belly?"

"I just left a few minutes ago," Craig replied.

"That's where Cole was supposed to have his meeting."

"He hasn't been there. Not for the past hour anyway." She heard the anxiety in Craig's voice. "I think something is wrong."

Sydney was very afraid he was right and that his glamorous wife was in the middle of it all. "Meet me at Cole's farm. We'll find Lamar and Clyde and see what they can tell us."

"I'm just a few minutes from your grandma's house. I'll pick you up and we'll ride out together." She didn't get an opportunity to argue because just then his battery died.

It was a warm autumn day, but Sydney grabbed a jacket in case the temperature changed. Then she asked Grandma to let the schools know that her children needed to ride the bus home. "I don't know how long I'll be gone," Sydney called over her shoulder as she ran out to the street. Craig pulled up a minute later.

"I know Cole didn't forget to call me," she told Craig as she climbed into the front seat.

"Peyton never goes anywhere without her cell phone," Craig kept his eyes on the road. "The more I think about it, the worse I feel."

"Maybe Peyton had a new offer for Cole and he decided to take it. They could be sitting at his kitchen table, ironing out the details." Sydney grasped for another possibility.

"And not answering the phone?"

They exchanged a worried glance. "Can you drive any faster?" Sydney asked, and he increased his speed.

Craig made it to the gravel drive leading up to Cole's farm in record time. He geared down for the uneven terrain and almost plowed over Clyde Harris as the old man ran from the woods into the middle of the road. Craig slammed on the brakes, Sydney hit the dashboard, and Peyton's father threw his hands up to protect his face from the spraying gravel. As soon as Craig could get the van into park, he opened his door and jumped out.

"What are you doing?" he demanded. As Sydney reached them she saw that Clyde was covered with tiny scratches and his breath was coming in huge gasps. "Where's Peyton?" Craig cried, grabbing his father-in-law's shirt.

Clyde waved behind him toward the farm. "She got here when Cole was leaving for his appointment in town." He paused to fill his lungs. "I was in the barn and peeked out when I heard her voice. I knew she'd be aggravated if she saw me, so I stayed put and just watched. Cole told her he was late and didn't have time to talk. She said she wanted to tell him something about the people trying to buy his land. He told her that wasn't important anymore because he'd already made up his mind not to sell to the folks from Nashville."

Clyde had to stop again for a few deep breaths. "Then an old truck drove up and two men got out. One was a fellow named Henry Lee. The other was a big ugly guy with a scar on his face that Henry Lee called Gus. Henry walked over by Peyton while the big man stepped up to Cole and said he represented some people who wanted to buy the farm. Cole said thanks anyway but he already had a deal in the works. Then this Gus fellow pulled out a handgun and said he thought maybe he could change Cole's mind."

"A gun?" Sydney confirmed and the old man nodded.

"It was a big, nasty-looking gun. Cole was surprised and I was so shocked I couldn't breathe. Then Henry Lee grabbed Peyton's hands and pulled them behind her." Sydney heard Craig's sharp intake of breath. "Cole looked over at them, and the big guy conked him on the back of the head with that gun. Cole dropped to his knees, kind of stunned like, then fell forward. He hit the side of his truck going down . . ."

"Is he okay?" Sydney whispered.

"I don't know. That was two pretty bad blows."

"Where did they take Peyton?" Craig shook Clyde's arm to regain his attention.

"They tied her and Cole up with duct tape. They put Peyton in the cab of the truck and threw Cole in the back. Then they went into the house for Lamar and tied him up too. I guess they didn't know I was here," Clyde continued, looking down at the ground. "I would do about anything for Peyton, and I don't want you to think I'm a

coward. But they had that gun, and there was two of them. I didn't
see how running out and getting myself killed was going to do any
good. So I waited until they drove away. Then I took off through the
woods to get help. I got kind of turned around . . ." He trailed off in
embarrassment.

"Which way did they go?" Craig asked.

"Toward the back pastures."

"Get in." Craig was already running to the van. Once everyone
was inside and the doors were closed, Craig asked how long ago all
this had taken place.

"Been a good hour," Clyde related unhappily.

Craig drove cautiously up to the house and stopped beside Cole's
truck. "Clyde, my cell phone is dead, so you need to go inside and
call the police. Tell them not to use their sirens when they come." He
turned to Sydney. "You should stay here too."

"No way." She closed the door behind the old man and put on
her seat belt. "Let's go."

They followed the dirt road for a while, then saw what looked
like fresh tire tracks pulling off into an open field. Craig turned into
the grass, and the tire marks eventually led to the base of a hill. The
tracks continued on around the left, but Craig parked and indicated
for Sydney to get out on his side. Once they were both free of the
vehicle, he closed the door quietly, then they started up the hill.

Suddenly they heard a voice and Craig reached out and pulled her
with him down to the ground. They scrambled forward on hands and
knees and dropped flat as they reached the crest. Inching up they
could see over into a small valley. Henry Lee's truck was parked beside
one of the dilapidated old houses Cole used to store hay. Sydney's
stomach churned as she spotted Cole sitting on the ground, leaning
up against the weathered wood of the building. His hands were
bound behind him and his legs were taped at the knees and ankles.
He was leaning to one side and his eyes were closed. Apparently his
captors were counting on his bindings and his injuries to keep him
from escaping, since he didn't appear to be tied to the structure itself.

Peyton was standing by the open tailgate of the truck where
Lamar's inert body was partially visible. Her hands and feet were
encircled with the tape, and Henry Lee was standing nearby with a

gun pointed in her general direction. The big man named Gus was holding some papers and talking to Henry Lee. Gus said something about not being able to wait any longer and started yelling at Cole, but didn't get a response. Finally he went to the truck and came back with a half empty bottle of water. He flung the contents into Cole's face, and Sydney was torn between outrage at the cruelty and relief that the action had caused Cole to move.

The man yelled at Cole, waving the papers. Craig inched toward Sydney until their arms were touching. "I've got to get Peyton out of there," he whispered.

Sydney considered trying to explain that his new wife might be one of the bad guys. The fact that Cole was injured while Peyton was standing almost comfortably by the truck seemed to support this theory. But she knew he would never believe her, and they couldn't spare the time to argue, so she nodded. "What are you going to do?"

"I'm going to crawl along the edge of this hill, come up behind that old house, circle the truck, and grab Peyton."

"Then they'll shoot you both."

Craig's face flushed with anger and despair. "You've got a better idea?"

"We need a weapon." Sydney said, and Craig reached into his pants and pulled out a very nonlethal-looking pocketknife. "I don't think that's going to help much."

He waved the knife desperately. "It's all I've got."

Sydney considered their options. "You could crawl around like you said except instead of going past the house, you go inside. Then reach through those spaces between the wood and cut Cole's hands free. Leave him the knife so he can cut his legs loose and go on over to Peyton. I'll cause some sort of diversion when you're ready. Then at least there will be two of you, and you'll have the element of surprise on your side."

"What kind of diversion will you create?" Craig looked skeptical.

Sydney studied the area directly around them and her eyes focused on a smooth rock about the size of a baseball. She reached over and picked it up, weighing it in her palm. "I don't think Henry Lee would really kill anyone. If I can take out the big guy, we'll be okay."

"You're going to try to hit him with that rock?" Craig whispered incredulously.

"It's about the distance from left field to home plate and I used to throw that far all the time," she reminded him.

"That was years ago!"

"The worst that will happen is I'll miss, and the rock will still distract his attention for a few seconds. The best that will happen is that I'll catch him right in the back of the head."

"How will you know when to throw it?" Craig asked.

"I'll watch Cole. When his hands are free I'll start counting. I'll give you to thirty before I throw the rock."

"I can't leave the knife with Cole," Craig told her softly. "Peyton's safety is my first priority."

Sydney nodded in resignation. "Cut his hands free at least." They heard Gus yelling again and this time he kicked Cole viciously. "Hurry," Sydney begged, giving Craig a little shove. He eased himself down a few feet, then crouched and ran toward the far side of the hill. Sydney waited anxiously, trying to hear what the man was saying. She caught a word or two, but couldn't make sense of it. Glancing at Peyton, she saw tears shining on the other woman's cheeks. Lamar was still motionless in the back of the truck. Sydney rubbed the rock, getting its feel. Then she tried to clear her mind of everything except the task at hand, as if she was in the biggest game of her life and everything depended on her.

Finally she saw Craig dart from the bushes at the edge of the hillside into the old house. She concentrated on Cole's face, trying not to see the man she loved, but watching for an indication that Craig had cut the tape that bound his hands. She wasn't sure what it would be. A slight relaxing, a tensing, a twitch, but somehow she would know. And then she saw it. A muscle in his jaw jumped, his arms flexed, and she started to count. By the time she got to twenty-five, she saw Craig stooping by the back tire of Henry Lee's truck. At thirty she stood, pulled her arm back, and fired the rock at the back of the big man's head.

Craig hesitated for just a second, then as the rock hit the man's skull with a sickening thud, he pulled Peyton to the ground. Henry Lee waved the gun around in confusion and Sydney started running headlong down the hill. She was vaguely aware of Cole forcing himself into a standing position, his movements hampered by the tape at his knees and ankles. She saw Craig roll Peyton under the truck, out of harm's way. Henry Lee watched her with a combination of dread and admiration as she barreled toward him.

She wanted nothing more than to go straight to Cole and bury her face in his neck, to feel his heart beating, and reassure herself that he really was all right. But Henry Lee had the gun and she didn't know how long the other man would be unconscious. So she did the only reasonable thing. She ran straight into Henry Lee.

They both fell to the ground on impact, but he managed to hold onto the gun. "What are you doing here?" she asked The Lure's best customer as they both sat up cautiously. She pointed at the gun. "I know you wouldn't hurt me."

Henry Lee shook his head. "But that doesn't go for him." He waved the gun at Cole.

Sydney held out a hand, drawing Henry Lee's attention back to her. "Forget about him. Think about how much you enjoy coming to The Lure. If the police find out that you're involved with criminals, they'll put you in jail and you'll never get to sit on your favorite stool again." Sydney saw Craig reach out from under the truck and hand Cole the knife.

"And I was hoping you were serious about going to waitress school. It only takes a few weeks and then we'd be working together. I could cover for you and you could cover for me . . ." She forced herself not to watch as Cole sawed carefully through the silver tape.

"You mean it?" Henry Lee breathed and Sydney would have felt guilty if it hadn't been for the gun.

"Sure! And I could show you how to balance plates on your arms and keep track of tips."

"You'd really help me?"

"Of course," she said. Cole's legs were free and he was creeping up behind Henry Lee. She grabbed his free arm with both hands. "You're scaring me to death with that gun, Henry Lee!" she cried, and he lowered it just a fraction as Cole pulled him down from behind. Sydney screamed and the gun fired, but the bullet flew harmlessly into the trees. Craig slid from under the truck to twist the gun out of Henry Lee's hand and Cole pushed him to his knees.

"Sydney, check inside his truck for some duct tape." Cole's voice sounded muffled and Sydney looked up to see that his lips were puffy. She scrambled over to Henry Lee's old truck and yanked open the passenger door. On the floorboard were several rolls of silver tape and one small roll of bright red. She brought Miss Glida Mae's Christmas tape to Cole, and he used it to bind Henry Lee and the unconscious thug.

Then Cole and Craig threw the men into the back of the truck and helped Lamar out. Cole put him in the cab of Henry Lee's truck while Craig and Peyton started around the hill toward his van, hand in hand. Sydney barely noticed. She was too busy drinking in the sight of Cole, alive and well. His lips were bloody and swollen, he had a huge lump on his forehead, and his clothes were covered with dirt and dead grass. But he was unquestionably the most beautiful sight she'd ever seen.

She scooted into the middle of the seat as he got behind the wheel and turned the truck around. The suspension system was terrible, and Cole had to drive very slowly to keep from jarring Lamar. Craig's van fell in behind them as they reached the dirt road.

"It's a good thing we didn't need the police," Sydney muttered as they parked in front of the house. "Craig dropped Clyde off at the house and told him to call them ages ago. In fact, I'm going to write a letter of complaint!" Sydney promised as they helped Lamar out and moved toward the steps. Then a voice called to them from the front porch.

"Thank goodness you're all right! I've been so worried about you!" They looked up to see a man wringing his hands on the top step.

"Who is that?" Sydney whispered to Cole.

"Mr. McPherson from the bank," he answered.

"I was just trying to decide if I should attempt to come after you myself or wait longer for the police," the banker added as they neared the house.

"What about them?" Sydney tipped her head at the men in the back of the truck.

Cole barely spared them a look. "There's a knot on the back of the bad one's head, which unfortunately I think is a sign that he'll live." He paused to help Lamar with the first step. "We'll leave them for the police to deal with, if they ever get here."

"When I arrived a few minutes ago I found Mr. Harris close to collapse," the banker said as he followed them inside. "He told me about his ordeal, and I insisted that he go upstairs and lie down. Before he fell asleep he did tell me that the police are on their way."

"They could have been here from Columbus by now," Cole grumbled as he settled Lamar on the couch.

"What should I do with this?" Craig held up the gun they had taken from Henry Lee.

"Put it on the counter in the kitchen before somebody gets shot by mistake," Cole replied.

"Where did you say my father is?" Peyton asked Mr. McPherson.

"Upstairs. I put him in the first room I came to."

"I should probably go check on him." Peyton looked at the stairs without enthusiasm.

"Oh, I don't think that's necessary!" The banker took her arm and led her into the living room. "He was sleeping soundly when I left him—"

Mr. McPherson was interrupted by the sound of the front door opening. Sydney looked up to see Peyton's secretary, Marcie Heinz, standing in the entryway. "Goodness gracious, what is going on around here?" As Marcie posed the question, her eyes searched the room until she found Peyton. After a quick visual examination, she seemed satisfied that her boss was uninjured. "One of those guys in the truck outside looks dead," she added and Sydney shuddered.

"The world will be a better place if he is," Craig responded for everyone.

"Well, we've waited long enough. I'm going to call the police again." Cole reached for the phone, but Mr. McPherson caught him by the wrist.

"I don't think that would be a very good idea," he said and Sydney watched in horror as the banker pulled a gun from the inside pocket of his suit coat. Then he calmly yanked the phone out of the wall and threw it into a corner. There was a sound from the kitchen and Sydney looked up to see Henry Lee's pudgy form filling the doorway. The gun Craig had put on the kitchen counter was back in his hand and pointed at the room in general. "It's about time," Mr. McPherson told him crossly.

"I didn't want to leave Gus alone out there." Henry Lee looked around uncertainly. "He needs to go to the hospital."

"Forget about him. He's so dumb a blow to the head couldn't affect his intelligence, and he's so ugly it could only improve his looks." Mr. McPherson smiled at his cruel wit.

"But he might die." Henry Lee wasn't ready to abandon the injured thug.

"If he does, so what? You just concentrate on holding that gun steady."

"Why are you doing this?" Craig asked, looking between Henry Lee and the banker in confusion. "What could be worth hurting people, maybe even killing them?"

"You might want to ask your lovely wife that question," Mr. McPherson said, confirming Sydney's worst suspicions. As she watched the pain and disbelief spread across Craig's face, she actually felt sorry for him.

Peyton squared her shoulders and faced Cole. "Mr. McPherson and I have been working together from the start. That's what I came to tell you this morning."

"Why?" Cole demanded. "What difference did it make to the bank if I sold the farm?"

"Lieberman, Sobels, and Finn offered to let the bank handle financing for the western park if they encouraged you to sell," Peyton admitted in a remorseful tone, and Sydney had to admire her acting abilities. "Mr. McPherson was assigned as my liaison."

"I negotiated a little side deal with Lieberman, Sobels, and Finn for myself," Mr. McPherson added. "They were glad to provide me with an incentive to go above and beyond the call of duty, so to speak." He pulled some duct tape from his briefcase. "Now we need to bind up everyone's hands in back, except for Mr. Brackner. Since he's about to sign his farm over to me, he'll need his hands taped in front. Here, honey, help me with these nice folks." Sydney watched as the duct tape sailed through the air and was surprised when Marcie, rather than Peyton, reached out to catch it. "Stand still and you might not get shot," Mr. McPherson advised pleasantly.

"Marcie?" Peyton whispered. "You know Mr. McPherson?"

The secretary laughed at this question. "We were married at one time."

Peyton looked between Marcie and the banker. "You don't have the same last name . . ."

"I took back my maiden name after the divorce, but Lester and I have remained close friends. Which is a good thing since he's been very helpful in furthering your career," the secretary continued. "Do you really think you've been successful on every case you've ever taken with just good luck and hard work?" Marcie demanded in response to Peyton's confused expression. "If Lester hadn't been able to help us out from time to time, you'd be about fifty-fifty in the win/lose category," she disclosed as she wrapped tape around Sydney's hands.

"What are you talking about?" Peyton asked, so pale that Sydney could almost believe Craig's wife was honestly appalled.

"You remember Mr. Willbanks, the pawn broker who wouldn't sell his shop in downtown Nashville to the people who wanted to build a hotel?"

Peyton nodded. "He died."

"The ornery old coot wouldn't budge." Marcie shook her head. "Lester tried to play it nice, but he finally had to call in some boys from Chicago. They're pros, made it look like a heart attack."

"Are you saying your ex-husband had Mr. Willbanks killed?" Peyton's voice was barely audible.

"He would have been your first loss," Marcie explained with a shrug. "And you were so proud of your winning record." Peyton actually staggered. "Lester helped us out a few other times as well. Just a little arm-twisting. Nothing fatal."

Peyton sat down heavily on the ugly green couch and stared at her feet while Marcie taped Cole's hands in front as Mr. McPherson had instructed. The banker spoke to Cole as Marcie worked.

"In case you're getting any ideas about resisting, let me promise you that if you cause trouble, Sydney Cochran will die." Sydney watched the blood drain from Cole's face. "Is that clear?" Cole nodded. "Some investors I've worked with before were looking for a place to build a high-class amusement park. I found your farm and thought it would be a perfect place for their new enterprise. I sold your sister and her husband on the idea, but then you came back from wherever you were and put a stop to the deal."

Marcie finished with Cole and moved on to Craig while Lester McPherson continued. "I've used Lieberman, Sobels, and Finn before with good results and thought they could handle it. But as the weeks dragged on, I got frustrated. I spent the weekend with Marcie a couple of months ago and told her my woes. I had this peach of a deal about to slip through my fingers because of one stubborn cow farmer. She was the one who came up with the idea to have Lieberman contract it out to Peyton."

Marcie picked up the story. "I enjoyed working for Peyton, but I was sick of that dumpy office we had. So Lester got his friend, Mr. Finn, to agree to hire us after this deal went through. Then Peyton went crazy and got married. Decided to give up the career I helped her build and move to this little hole-in-the-wall town!" She shook her head regretfully. "You really should have asked me how I felt about it first," Marcie said, looking at her boss.

"So you killed Cole's cows and slashed his tires," Sydney deduced.

"And disconnected Sydney's battery cable," Cole added.

Mr. McPherson nodded. "We wanted you to take an interest in Peyton," he addressed Cole. "So when Ms. Cochran started sitting at your table at The Lure, we wanted to scare her off. Gus was supposed to disable her car and rough her up a little." Gasps were heard from around the room. "No broken bones or anything. Just enough to keep her away from work for a few days, but then Mr. Brackner arrived and ruined that."

Sydney clasped her hands together to keep them from trembling. "Gus was going to try again, but we never could catch her alone," Mr. McPherson told them casually.

"Peyton is so much prettier than her." Marcie waved toward Sydney as she wrapped tape around her boss's hands. "We figured Mr. Brackner would be sure to like Peyton instead, even if Craig's ex-wife did sit at his table."

"Then we found out that every night after the booze wears off, Henry Lee sneaks out of his house and stares at Ms. Cochran's bedroom window. So we hired him to report all her movements." Sydney looked toward Henry Lee and he hung his head in shame.

"Did you kill the cat?" Sydney whispered.

Lester McPherson took up the narrative. "Gus said he couldn't take a step around the Brackner place without tripping over you or one of your kids. He was hoping if he killed the cat you might stay away."

"You shot the calves and burned them?" Sydney was sure of the answer before she posed the question.

Mr. McPherson's cheerful expression dimmed. "Gus was supposed to steal a few calves and take them off the property, but they were harder to handle than he expected." The banker shook his head in disgust. "So the imbecile shot them and then set the carcasses on fire to destroy any clues. I thought that he had ruined my entire plan. Then like a blessing from heaven, the witch rumors appeared." This with a hateful smile at Cole. "So I guess you could say that your little sister saved my life."

"Did you shoot Lamar?" Cole asked bitterly.

"Oh no!" Mr. McPherson denied. "Gus encouraged a few local boys to take the witch hunting into their own hands, but we weren't personally involved in that incident. Everything was falling into place perfectly, then Peyton told Marcie she was going to tell Mr. Brackner about her working relationship with me and I knew we had to wrap this up quickly," the banker concluded as Marcie walked over to stand by her former husband.

"Why are you admitting all this?" Sydney asked finally.

"Because they're going to kill us and don't care what we know," Cole responded dully.

"Actually, that's not true. I'm not averse to killing folks when necessary, but you can't prove anything against us. So we're going to leave you very much alive, after you've signed these papers selling the farm to me at a new, bargain price." Mr. McPherson's smile was cold. "Then I will turn around and sell the property to the theme park people for a healthy profit."

"A document signed under duress isn't legal," Craig contributed, finding his voice for the first time since his wife had declared herself a crook.

"There will never be any mention of duress," the banker said with confidence. "And just to be sure, I'll take a little insurance with me." He stepped over to the coat closet and pulled Clyde Harris out. Peyton's father was all taped up and looked barely conscious. "As long as the rest of you don't cause a fuss, Mr. Harris will remain alive and well. At the first indication that anyone has talked to the police . . ." He let his voice trail off, the consequences obvious.

"How can you possibly expect us to trust criminals?" Sydney asked derisively.

"Because you have no choice." Mr. McPherson seemed displeased by this classification. "And I have no desire to keep Clyde Harris with me forever. After the community sees that the theme park is going to be a reality, if you start making noises about not wanting to sell your land it will look like sour grapes. And if you cause too much trouble, things can get ugly fast. Children are especially vulnerable." He smiled, knowing he had hit home with all of them. "Well, as much as I have enjoyed this little chat, we've got a plane to catch." He smoothed the contract out on the coffee table in front of Cole and handed him a pen. "I'll turn the pages for you," he offered politely.

Sydney watched miserably while Cole signed away his farm. Then Mr. McPherson had Peyton and Marcie witness his signature. "What will we tell whoever finds us all taped up?" Sydney asked as Marcie retied Peyton's hands.

"I'll leave it to you to think of a reasonable excuse, preferably something that won't endanger the lives of Mr. Harris or the Cochran children." Mr. McPherson put the papers and the duct tape in a briefcase and shut it firmly. "Maybe you could blame it on the witches!" he suggested as he grabbed Clyde by the collar and dragged him toward the door.

"Henry Lee, I'm going to put Mr. Harris in the back of your truck beside Gus and cover them both with a tarp. I've got to go into town and file this contract so it will be legal. Then we'll meet at your place where I'll pay you and take the old guy off your hands." He pointed at Clyde.

Sydney knew that trying to negotiate with Mr. McPherson or Marcie would be a waste of time, but Henry Lee was a different story. She leaned forward, her gaze focused firmly on her admirer. "You can't believe a word he says, Henry Lee," she told him desperately. "He can't leave behind a witness with a reputation for staying drunk." This comment hit its mark and Henry Lee looked nervously at the banker. "And he'll never pay you," Sydney pressed her advantage.

"Of course I'm going to give you the money I promised. I know a good man when I see one, and I might need your services in the future," Mr. McPherson said soothingly.

"He'll kill you, Henry Lee," Sydney warned again.

"Tape her mouth closed." Mr. McPherson pulled the silver roll from his briefcase and handed it to Henry Lee, who tore off a piece and walked slowly toward Sydney.

"You're not a bad person, Henry Lee," she tried one last time. "Anybody who could be nice to someone as mean as me has to have some goodness deep down." The tape moved closer. "I found the flowers you brought me." He covered her mouth with the adhesive, but his hands were shaking and his eyes were filled with tears.

Sydney watched with the others as Marcie walked out onto the front porch. Mr. McPherson followed directly behind her, dragging poor Clyde. Henry Lee brought up the rear, and risked one glance back at Sydney before he closed the door.

A second later, Darrell and Lauren slipped silently in through the kitchen. Lauren unnecessarily put a finger to her lips, urging silence as she and Darrell cut everyone's hands loose with kitchen knives.

"We came to apologize again," Lauren explained softly. "When we saw all the cars and the dead-looking man taped up in that awful truck, we knew something was wrong. So we came in through the back and found you all being held at gunpoint."

Cole and Craig stood simultaneously. "We've got to stop them!" They surged forward.

"Don't go out there!" Lauren blocked the way and locked the latch. "We cut the tires on all the cars." She pushed Cole back into the living room.

Cole regarded her steadily. "All of them?"

"Every one. Even ours."

"Even the four-wheeler," Darrell added proudly.

Cole spread his hands. "So now we're trapped here with them."

"And they have guns," Sydney pointed out after she pulled the tape from her mouth.

"It was the only thing we could think of to do without getting ourselves killed," Lauren replied as someone threw their weight against the front door. She screamed when a bullet was fired at the doorknob, followed closely by Mr. McPherson charging into the room. Peyton was standing near the entryway so he grabbed her, putting the gun to her head. Craig lunged toward them but pulled up short when the banker pressed his finger against the trigger.

"Nobody move," he instructed curtly as Henry Lee walked in through the kitchen.

"You didn't lock the back door when you came in?" Cole asked his sister helplessly.

"You have left me no choice," Mr. McPherson said. "Marcie is unreasonably fond of Peyton, so I guess we'll take her with us." He turned to face Henry Lee. "Marcie's rounding up some horses for us to ride out of here. I'll take Peyton to her while you shoot everyone else. Then I'll bring the old man in." He paused to consider. "Maybe an occult-related murder-suicide is our best bet." Sydney controlled a shudder as she listened to him speak of multiple deaths as if he was discussing the weather. "Go ahead, Henry Lee." He shoved the man forward. "I'm tired of fooling with these people."

The gun trembled in his hand as Henry Lee raised it at Cole, who had moved to within a few feet of Mr. McPherson and Peyton. Sydney knew he was going to make a desperate attempt to save Craig's new wife and would probably get killed in the process. Desperate to prevent disaster, she stepped toward Henry Lee. "Please don't hurt him."

"Shoot him!" Mr. McPherson insisted. "Now!"

Henry Lee steadied the gun and aimed it at Cole's chest. "Please!" Sydney begged again.

After a moment's hesitation, Henry Lee shifted the gun slightly and pulled the trigger, shooting Mr. McPherson in the left shoulder. The banker screamed in fury, then spun around and fired at Henry Lee, who fell to the ground as Craig tackled Mr. McPherson, knocking the gun from his hand. Craig punched Mr. McPherson repeatedly in the face until Cole held out the duct tape, telling him to tie the man up first and kill him later. The rage receded in Craig's eyes and he took the tape from Cole's hand. Lauren was screaming hysterically.

Sydney scrambled over to where Henry Lee was bleeding on the new carpet, and Cole picked up Mr. McPherson's gun. "I'm going out to find Marcie and Clyde," he told them as he peeked around the splintered doorframe. "The other guy is still in the back of Henry Lee's truck." He moved cautiously toward the door. "For Pete's sake, Lauren, will you shut up?"

The screaming stopped abruptly as he walked outside. Craig finished taping up the banker then asked Lauren to use her cell phone to call the police. "Tell them we need an ambulance," Sydney said calmly, taking Henry Lee's hand in hers.

"I'm sorry, Sydney," he whispered weakly.

"Don't try to talk now. Save your strength," Sydney advised.

"He offered me a lot of money. Enough to buy a nice trailer and bikes for my kids. I knew it was wrong, but he said nobody was going to get hurt. He promised, especially about you." Sydney tried to ignore the gurgling noises coming from his chest and concentrated on his words. "It wasn't right the way Mr. McPherson was treating Gus and the old man. And I figured what you said about him not paying me was true."

He had an alarming coughing spell, and when she got him calmed back down the sucking sounds were worse. "Betty Jean is the best wife a man could have, better than I deserve for sure. But I just can't help the way I feel about you."

"I don't think you should be trying to talk." Sydney was uncomfortable with the conversation and concerned about his condition.

"I wouldn't have let Mr. McPherson hurt your kids." Henry Lee's eyes were closed and the words were slurred. "And I'm sorry I told him what time you got home and stuff. I didn't mean to steal your neighbor's duct tape," he continued his confession. "It's about the same color as the seats in my truck, and I just wanted a few strips to fix some cracks. I was going to put it back, but I was afraid it might have my fingerprints on it or something."

"She only uses it at Christmastime. I'll buy her a new roll," Sydney assured him.

He was quiet for a while, and the sporadic rise and fall of his chest was her only indication that he was still alive. Finally his fingers exerted weak pressure on hers. "You found my flowers?"

Sydney nodded, then realized that since his eyes were closed he couldn't see her. "I found them by Miss Glida Mae's shed after the snow melted. They reminded me of spring time," she told him softly.

"Nobody has ever given me flowers before." It was true. Her parents gave sensible gifts like books and savings bonds, and Craig, well . . .

"Really?" The corners of Henry Lee's mouth turned up in what was almost a smile.

"Cross my heart," Sydney promised as the wounded man's chest stopped moving. In the distance she could hear the sirens wailing, but knew they would arrive too late for Henry Lee. She was vaguely aware of Cole as he came inside and crouched beside her. "He's gone."

Cole didn't insult her by insisting otherwise. "In the end, you brought out the best in him, Sydney," he told her instead.

The police rushed in, followed closely by ambulance attendants with a gurney. They worked on Henry Lee for a few minutes, then covered him with a paper sheet and said they would put in a call to the county coroner. Lamar and Clyde gave their statements, then rode in the ambulance to the hospital. Mr. McPherson refused to say a word without his lawyer present and demanded the phone call he was entitled to.

"He sounds like somebody who's been arrested before," the policeman told Cole and Sydney as they loaded the banker and the big man with the lump on his head into the police car.

Craig and Peyton rode into town in the wrecker that came to tow his van. Darrell and Lauren left with a friend they had called to come and get them. While Cole answered questions, Sydney listened to Marcie Heinz in the kitchen, trying to convince the police that she had been coerced into cooperating with her ex-husband. When the police were finished with Marcie, they offered everyone a ride into town.

"I guess I do need to go check on the kids," Sydney said. Now that all the excitement was over, she felt drained and didn't trust her ability to control her emotions.

"I hope I can find someone who will sell me a whole new set of tires for my truck," Cole remarked quietly. "And I'll have to get a new front door."

"You didn't let Peyton leave with that contract, did you?" Sydney asked suddenly, looking around the room.

"It was in Mr. McPherson's briefcase. The police said it was evidence and so they took it with them."

"Just make sure they know it's not real. I still don't trust Peyton any further than I could throw her."

"You threw that rock pretty well. You might be able to toss Peyton farther than you think." Cole managed a wan smile.

"You can make fun of me if you want, but I'll never be convinced that Peyton wasn't more involved in this than she let on. At the very least she overlooked a lot of things that she shouldn't have."

"That's something she'll have to live with, not us." Cole stared out the broken door at Henry Lee's old truck.

Sydney walked up to stand beside him. "So, what are you going to do after you get your tires changed and your door fixed?" she asked, looking down at the policeman who was waiting patiently to take her home.

"Oh, I thought I might drive over and impress my girlfriend with my new tires."

Sydney rolled her eyes. "I'm too old to be anybody's girlfriend."

"Then how about being my wife instead? If we didn't learn anything else today, we learned that life is fragile. If we wait too long on happiness, we might miss our chance."

It was hard to look at his battered face without crying, so Sydney closed her eyes for a few seconds. Then she spoke to the cloudless sky. "How can I ever bring myself to trust a man again?" she whispered.

"I'm not asking you to trust all men," Cole told her gently. "Just me." She felt tears seeping out of her eyes and wiped at them angrily. "I've never welched on a deal in my life, Sydney. I'm not about to start now."

Sydney squared her shoulders and put her foot on the second step. "I guess I'll have to wait and see how impressive those new tires are before I make a final decision." Then, with a little smile over her shoulder, she climbed into the back of the patrol car.

* * * * *

When she got home, her children were eating homemade cookies around Grandma's kitchen table. Sarah asked how she'd gotten so much ketchup on her hands, and Sydney looked down to see that she was splattered with blood. She turned toward the bathroom, where she undressed quickly, anxious to get out of the soiled clothes. Ryan called through the bathroom door, wanting to know when she was going to take him to Cole's house to do his chores. She pretended that she didn't hear him and stepped into the hot water, trying to wash the fear and sadness away with Henry Lee's dried blood.

Cole got there in time to eat red beans and rice with the rest of the family. The children were horrified by the bruises on his face, but he assured them he was fine. After dinner, he helped the kids get started on a computer game, then insisted that Sydney come out and look at his new tires. "Why would Mom want to see your tires?" Trent asked in amazement as Cole pulled Sydney toward the front door.

"Good tires are very important to your mother," Cole replied with a grin. The tires were big and new, but it was dark and Sydney couldn't tell much more about them. She told Cole so and he expressed offense. "They have a 100,000 mile warranty, are safety tested for all weather conditions and cost almost $300 apiece."

"No way!" Sydney gasped, examining the black rubber more closely.

"If you don't believe me, you can go to the Tire Warehouse and look for the happiest salesman in the place." He reached over and pulled her into his arms. "And you can make me even happier than he is by saying you'll marry me tomorrow."

"I can't marry you tomorrow," Sydney said with certainty.

"But you will marry me!"

"You'll probably be sorry . . ."

"I'll never be sorry. How about Friday?" Cole suggested.

"We can't get married on Friday either. We'll have to talk to the bishop and see about getting a temple divorce . . ." She forced her eyes up to meet his. "It could take a while."

"I've waited this long for you." He brought her hand up to his lips. "I can wait a little longer." Sydney swallowed hard, touched by his gallantry. "I can't offer you as much as I'd hoped. I'm still going to have to sell the farm, or at least most of it, and find a real job."

"I've been working at The Lure and living in my grandmother's house. Anything will be up from there," she murmured.

"And that reminds me. I do have one requirement," he informed her, and Sydney raised an eyebrow. "You have to quit your job at The Lure."

"You've never objected to me working there before!"

"It was okay for Craig's ex-wife, but not my fiancée," he said firmly.

"Well, lucky for you I'm sick of my job there, and Pinkie will probably fire me before I get a chance to quit. Besides, for the next few months I'll be too busy redecorating your house to waste time at The Lure."

"What's wrong with my house?" Cole pulled back in surprise.

"Well, for starters that ugly green couch in the living room has got to go!"

"I have very fond memories of that couch," Cole objected.

Sydney was immediately contrite. "Spending time in the fishing cabin with your dad?" she asked gently.

"No, squished next to you during the snowstorm." He pressed soft kisses along her brow.

"Oh." Sydney melted against him. "Our situation is so messed up, it is probably going to take forever. But since you've told everyone we're getting married and I don't want them to know you're a big liar, I guess I'll marry you," she murmured into the hollow of his neck.

Cole laughed. "We can try for a Friday the thirteenth wedding day."

"That would certainly be appropriate." Sydney smiled against his soft skin. "Maybe I can wear a witch costume to the reception."

"That might be going a little bit too far," Cole decided. "Even for you."

* * * * * *

Henry Lee's funeral was on Friday. Carmella and Starla and many other people from The Lure were there. Sydney had charged a beautiful spray of wildflowers on her Visa card but knew they were worth every borrowed penny. The Presbyterians were in need of a cause now that the witch threat had been eliminated, so when they heard of Betty Jean Thornton's plight they organized a community drive. After the funeral Henry Lee's family was moved into a brand new trailer, the children were given more clothes than they could ever wear, and Betty Jean was offered a job in the high school cafeteria.

The town's weekly paper, the *Eureka Monitor*, ran a two-page story eulogizing Henry Lee and regaling readers with his role in the arrest of Mr. Lester McPherson, formerly an officer of the Eureka National Bank. Miss Glida Mae Magnanney bought numerous copies of the special edition, telling all who would listen that the local hero was her very own stalker.

On Sunday after church, Craig and Peyton came by Grandma's house to pick up the kids. Cole answered the door and the men greeted each other with a handshake. Peyton was reserved, as was proper for an exposed criminal. Craig asked if they could talk for a few minutes before they took the children for a picnic on the lake. Sydney reminded them that rain was predicted for later that afternoon as Cole led the way into the kitchen. Once everyone was settled, Craig leaned forward on his elbows and addressed them earnestly.

"Peyton and I are both very sorry for any problems you have had as a result of her involvement with Lieberman, Sobels, and Finn or Mr. McPherson at the bank," he began. "Peyton has assured me that her actions were purely professional and that she meant Cole no personal harm. And in spite of what Mr. McPherson said, she was not involved in anything illegal." Sydney raised an eyebrow and the woman had the decency to blush. "So we'd like to put that subject aside permanently."

"I'll just bet you would," Sydney murmured.

"Sydney." Cole shook his head firmly. "Craig's right. There's nothing we can do about the past, and we need to work together for the children's sake."

Craig exhaled deeply. "We have a proposal for you. Peyton and I would like to invest in the farm so you don't have to sell it. We'll give you the capital you need to buy out your sisters and pay off the bank."

Cole frowned. "Then you'd own the farm."

"Just a share in it."

"A pretty large share," Cole replied thoughtfully.

"And there'd be a theme park sitting on it in no time," Sydney whispered loud enough for Craig and Peyton to hear.

"Cole will still have control of the farm management. We can meet once or twice a year to go over the financial statements and make plans for the future," Peyton contributed to the conversation for the first time. Sydney was very uncomfortable with the idea of being involved financially with Craig and Peyton, and she noticed that the property acquisitions specialist did not completely rule out the possibility of an eventual sale. But she knew how much the farm meant to Cole, and she pressed her lips closed against all her objections.

Cole nodded and Sydney's heart sunk. "I really appreciate your offer, but I've already agreed to sell the farm to someone else."

"If you haven't signed any papers, it might not be too late," Peyton interjected quickly.

"I don't want to change my mind." Cole's tone was polite but firm.

"Can I ask who the new owner will be?" Peyton inquired and Sydney thought there was a distinct edge to her voice.

"A retired NFL football player. The guy wants to move out to the country and was looking for a good-sized place. He's a very private person, which means he wouldn't want a theme park next door, and he has more money than he can ever spend, so the monetary value of the land doesn't interest him." Sydney smiled at this comment. "He just wants a quiet place to raise his kids."

"Did he meet Lieberman, Sobels, and Finn's price?" Peyton wanted to know.

"He offered me more than fair market value for the land. They will have a new road put in and build a house a mile or so down from the existing entrance." He turned to address Sydney. "We'll keep the old house and a few acres immediately around it. So we can have some horses, kittens, and even a couple of dogs if you want."

"But no cows," she said quietly.

"No, we'll have to sell the cows. But I've got an interview next week at the veterinary school at Auburn. If I get the job, I'd work with farmers all over the southeast and get to see more than my share of cows." He gave her a sweet smile. Taking care of other people's cows wouldn't be the same and they both knew it. "The football player was nervous about his kids getting near the lake, so he didn't want the fishing cabin."

Sydney sighed. "At least you'll get to keep that."

Cole shook his head. "Like Peyton said before, that is the most valuable part of the property, and I couldn't afford to keep it and the house both. So I've sold it to Clyde."

Peyton had been staring absently for the past few minutes, but she sat up straight at this announcement. "You've sold the lakeside property to my father?" she asked. "Why?"

"He wanted it and he paid me in cash." Cole smiled at Sydney. "He says we can fish anytime, and he'll stipulate in his will that I can buy it back when he dies. So, maybe I can take our grandchildren for fishing weekends up there."

Craig pushed his chair back from the table and reached a hand out to Peyton. "Well, we'd better collect the kids and go." His wife didn't seem ready to leave but stood reluctantly.

They rounded up the children and walked out to Craig's car. It hurt a little to see the excitement in the children's faces as they waved good-bye, but before Sydney could start thinking about it too much, Cole took her hand and pulled her back inside. When they resumed their seats at the table, Sydney cleared her throat.

"There's something I ought to warn you about." Sydney struggled to control the tremor in her voice. "Craig is acting like Father of the Year now, but he was never all that involved with the kids when we were married. Once he and Peyton have children of their own, he may lose interest in mine. So you could end up shouldering a lot of the fatherhood responsibilities if you really go through with this."

"I'll take the job if Craig gives it to me, but I won't steal it."

"And there is the forty-sixth anniversary party/bridal shower next weekend. Once you've spent some time with my family, you might want to reconsider."

"Nothing could make me reconsider," Cole assured her.

"Then there is the Auburn/Alabama game on Thanksgiving weekend. My father has tickets and he's determined that we all go," she warned and Cole nodded. "Auburn is sure to get slaughtered." This didn't seem to upset him. "They insist we are going to tailgate," she added, but he just smiled. "So, everything's working out perfectly and we'll live happily ever after, like in the fairy tales!" Sydney stared at their hands.

"We both know better than that."

Sydney dragged her eyes up to his. "Trouble has followed me my whole life."

"Together we can face anything."

"I'm going to give you one last chance to back out of this," she whispered. "I'm hard to live with. I'm moody and outspoken, and a lot of times smart remarks bypass my brain and jump straight out of my mouth. If you marry me, you may be in for a lifetime of misery . . ."

"If you start saying things I don't want to hear, I know exactly how to stop you."

Sydney raised an eyebrow. "You think you know, but . . ."

Cole leaned forward and pressed his lips to hers. A few minutes later he pulled away. "Now, what were you saying?"

She blinked up at him. "I forgot."

He laughed as she moved back into his arms.

ABOUT THE AUTHOR

Betsy Brannon Green currently lives in a suburb of Birmingham, Alabama with her husband, Butch, and seven of their eight children. She is the secretary for the kindergarten campus of Hueytown Elementary School and serves as Primary chorister for the Bessemer Ward.

Although born in Salt Lake, Betsy was raised in the South. Her life and her writing have both been strongly influenced by the small town of Headland, Alabama and the people who live there. In her characters you will see reflections of the gracious gentility unique to that part of the country.

Betsy's first book, *Hearts in Hiding,* was published in May of 2001. She loves to hear from readers and can be contacted at :

betsybrannongreen@yahoo.com

or you may write her in care of:

Covenant Communications, Inc.
920 E. State Road, Suite F
American Fork, UT 84003-0416